7th SENSE

Also by John McLaren

Press Send
Black Cabo
Running Rings

7th SENSE

by

John McLaren

POCKET
BOOKS
LONDON · SYDNEY · NEW YORK · TOKYO · SINGAPORE · TORONTO

First published in Great Britain by Simon & Schuster UK Ltd, 1998
First published in paperback by Pocket Books, 1999
This edition published by Pocket Books, 2002
An imprint of Simon & Schuster UK Ltd
A Viacom company

1 3 5 7 9 10 8 6 4 2

Simon & Schuster UK Ltd
Africa House
64–78 Kingsway
London WC2B 6AH

Simon & Schuster Australia
Sydney

www.simonsays.co.uk

A CIP catalogue record for this book is available from the British Library

ISBN 0–7434–1494–2

This book is a work of fiction. Names, characters, places and incidents are either
a product of the author's imagination or are used fictitiously. Any resemblance to
actual people living or dead, events or locales is entirely coincidental.

Typeset in Palatino by Palimpsest Book Production Limited,
Polmont, Stirlingshire
Printed and bound in Great Britain by
Cox & Wyman Ltd, Reading, Berkshire

For my ever so slightly amazing parents

I owe an embarrassingly huge debt of gratitude for guidance and editorial input to Nick Webb, Martin Fletcher, and Jacquie Clare of Simon & Schuster, whom without little in this book any sense would have made. My sincere thanks also to Aruna Mathur and Glen Saville, whose cover design just caught your eye.

My good friends below helped quite massively. Special thanks go to those asterisked.

Sir Jeremy Black*
Robert Bookman*
Ning Ning Chang*
Robert Enslow*
Lorne Forsyth*

Sir Clement Freud*
Miriam Gillinson*
Cliff Higgerson*
Jacqueline Koay*
Finlay MacLeod*

Klyner Mann*
Nick Marston*
Karen & Jay Mistry*
Paul O'Neill*
Cati & Peter Patel*

Roberto Quarta*
Christopher Roberts*
Sir Colin Southgate*
Caroline Watt*
Nigel Williams*

Number Twelve. He looked away from the TV screen, down at his scribbled note, quite needlessly. *Yes!* His pulse quickened fractionally. Forty-two. That same uncontrollable reflex. YES, goddammit. Oh please, oh please, let the next little yellow ball be Sixteen. It took an eternity to bobble into place. SIXTEEN, for Chrissakes! *Thump, thump, thump.* He felt like his heart was going to explode clear out of his chest. The Nine was due next. It was the one he was surest about, and his mind was already fixed on the fifth. NINE! There it was, the little beauty. Now this was it, the moment of truth. The fifth was the cloudiest, the vaguest, the one that wouldn't come clear. He'd never been much of a believer before; suddenly he felt ripe for conversion. Oh God, if you want to send a sign, please let it be number Twenty-three. Nine weeks of trying and he'd never got more than three out of six. He was *sure* the sixth and bonus balls would fall right *if* the Twenty-three came good. The tension was *hurting*. Finally the fifth abseiled down. YEAH!!!!! . . . Oh, no, *no*, NO! The bounce had tricked his eyes. Frigging Twenty-seven. And now the sixth, too, *way* wrong. He could *not* believe it. All that expectation, that anticipation, that asphyxiating excitement. For all his nerves, he'd felt confident. It was all planned what he'd do next, it was all ready. And now . . . nothing. *Shit.* He stood up, kicked a chair out of the way, grabbed his tousled brown hair tight in both hands and let rip with a plaster-piercing scream. It wasn't enough to purge the exploding frustration. He charged over and head-butted a wall, painfully, then slumped miserably back down on the sofa. The adrenalin began to drain away, tiredness hung heavy on him, and the infinitely depressing reality started to take its grip. Yet *another* empty, lonely Sunday to endure first, and then, come Monday morning, he would have to trudge back into the goddam bank with all those obnoxious English clowns, and wait a whole *week* till he got another chance. The mid-week jackpot was too small to be helpful, and anyway Wednesday was too soon to get back the energy to go through the whole performance again.

1

'Hi, Calum. Good weekend?'

'So-so.'

'Go away?'

'With weather like this? You kidding?'

Elevator conversation the world over runs out after three floors. Then you stand in fixed-grin silence till the first to get out says 'See you later.' Calum usually ignored his fellow vertical travellers, but he couldn't be mean to the secretaries. They were the only ones who had made him feel welcome since he arrived. At the twelfth Marjorie got out and said 'See you later.' Calum pushed impatiently on the 'close' button, perfectly aware it had no effect on the capricious rhythms of the machine. It by-passed one more floor and deposited him on the fourteenth.

As he walked over to his desk, he could still sense the mystification over the clearing out he had done on Friday. No-one clears out in the City unless they've been fired or are planning to quit. The whole team thought his timing was *weird*. Today was bonus day, for Christ's sake. Surely Calum wasn't stupid enough to think a stunt like that would make Bossman up his bonus. What else could be behind it? Was it conceivable he'd got a better offer from another bank, that he truly didn't give a damn?

It was burning them up with curiosity. On Friday, like always, he'd said goodnight and sloped off home, and, like always, the rest of them – Adam, Mike, Cathy, Doug, and Borzo – had wandered over to Corney & Barrow and got in the first two bottles of house champagne. That night all they talked about was Calum.

Anti-Calum sessions were among their favourites. When he arrived a few months back, it seemed natural to give him a hard time, a bit of the good old newcomer-baiting. They saw themselves as the gang, him as the applicant. His being a foreigner spurred them on, gave them a few more hooks, but it would've been much the same if he'd been an English guy with a plummy accent. It was the newcomer's role to provide them with harmless entertainment while he figured out whether to sink or swim. If he swam, he became one of them. If he sank, he would have to go, or stick around as the butt of their in-jokes. They lost little sleep over how relentlessly they harried him, and then when Calum started to bite back, any residual sympathy was forfeit.

Throughout that Monday morning they tried to wheedle the secret out of him, the sharpness of their sideswipes increasing with their mounting frustration. For Calum himself the day dragged more miserably than ever. He hadn't yet recovered from the exhaustion of the lottery attempt and his head was throbbing violently. It was next to impossible to think about work on such a quiet day. Proprietary trading feeds on volatility and the markets were wretchedly lethargic.

On into the afternoon he gazed vacantly at the screens and doodled, doing his best to disregard the vicious barbs. It was a blessed relief when Bossman began calling them one by one into his glass box to hear their bonus. Calum watched their faces as they came out. Doug looked smug, Adam like thunder. Borzo mightily relieved, Cathy close to tears. Away from the proprietary team, it was the same story, no overall pattern of pleasure or pain. The fixed interest boys, who'd had a big year, were rather subdued, whereas the equities bunch looked less hard done by than everyone expected. The overall level was good, though, with the weakest performers getting well into six figures and the stars going past the million mark.

This was a good sign for Calum. If he had won the lottery this would have been irrelevant. Now he needed his bonus desperately, and he clung to the hope that, despite the contempt Bossman perennially showed towards him, he would still treat him fairly. In truth, he understood nothing whatsover about the fundamentals of proprietary trading, but in the few months he'd been there his secret method had generated more profits for the bank than anyone else had managed in the whole year. He should easily be worth three or four hundred thousand to them. Even half of that would be a start. He sipped his fifteenth coffee of the day. The waiting was making him nervous. Finally, past five, he got the call.

'Have a seat, Calum. Shall we get the main thing out of the way first?'

Bossman languidly fingered through his papers, delighting in keeping Calum on tenterhooks a few seconds longer. He loved bonus day, even more than days when he fired people. Firing was the real blood sport, and there could be true art in drawing it out, like a cat with a mouse, analysing the victims' shortcomings in great detail, hinting at the slenderest hope that they might be reprieved, and then suddenly slicing their heads off. Problem was, firing only worked with non-performers. The beauty about bonus day was the brief power it gave him over *all* of the bastards. Bossman had deliberately saved Calum till last as his little treat to himself. He *detested*

3

everything about this American, especially since he had been forced to hire him in the first place, and wouldn't get the credit even if the boy kept doing well. He longed for him to fail, to provide a justification for firing him. In the meantime, he would have to content himself with a little gentle tormenting. Although at twenty-nine Calum Buchanan was around the same age as the rest, there was an artlessness about him, and Bossman's laser-guided instinct divined a profound lack of confidence beneath that studied aloofness. Bossman prided himself on his skill at probing surface personality quirks to locate and exploit fundamental character weakness. It would be fascinating to see what happened when he took any grandiose expectations Calum might have and crushed them underfoot. With any luck the kid might storm right out of the bank in a petulant rage and that would be that.

'Well, let's see. It's fifteen thousand. How d'you feel about *that*?'

He found it hard not to burst out laughing at the way Calum gulped. What could he expect with a background like his? A job at some brokerage in Los Angeles they'd scarcely heard of, *plus* an unsatisfactory, unexplained gap since that job. Somehow Calum had persuaded an important old client to arm-twist the bank's Chief Executive into taking him on. Without that, Bossman doubted the lad would *ever* have found work in the City. He watched Calum try to compose himself. It would be terribly disappointing if he just slunk away without saying a word. Surely he could goad him into *some* kind of a reaction.

'I *said*, how do you feel about fifteen thousand? I want to get your gut reaction.'

'No comment.'

'What you mean, Calum? I hoped you'd be *pleased*.'

4

'I've made money for you, you know that. But if you believe fifteen's my market value, what can I say?'

'When you think about it, you don't really *have* a market value, do you, Calum? What other bank would be willing to go through the balls-aching task of getting you a work permit?'

'Oh, so *that's* it.'

'Come on, surely you realise *no* bank pays out a penny more than necessary, and in your case I simply don't *have* to. You're lucky to be getting a bonus at all. All the same, I don't want any surprises the day this hits your bank account, so can I take it this is okay with you? . . . Come on, Calum, I've had a long day, don't fuck me around.'

Calum railed at the injustice. There had been no mention of this when he was hired. He felt his blood beginning to simmer. He had been determined to stay cool, whatever the sum. Now he saw how regally he was being screwed, he couldn't stop himself getting angry.

'If I ever decide to go, I promise you'll be the very first to know.'

'Your desk. You were clearing it out on Friday. What was that all about?'

'I'm just naturally tidy.'

'I've never noticed before. Look, can I level with you?'

'Sure, I've always thought of you as a great leveller.'

Bossman's eyebrows shot up. The cheeky *bastard*. Right, he'd have him for that.

'Frankly, Calum, you're a bit of a weirdo. You make no effort to be part of your team . . .'

'How ungrateful, after they were *so* welcoming.'

'They were being *normal*. They got here first. It's *their* territory. *They* didn't choose you.'

'Nor did you.'

5

Brilliant, he'd taken the bait, he was getting mad. Now he could lead him by the nose.

'Yes, it's true. I was against it and maybe I was right. It was the Chief Executive's idea, and as he's *my* boss, I did my best to make it work. Which is more than *you've* done. You made *no* attempt whatsoever to fit in. Naturally, I have to take account of teamwork when calculating bonuses, and you've suffered accordingly, but that's not really the main thing.'

'So, what *is* the goddam main thing?'

Now he sounded *deliciously* rattled.

'I can't work out how you make your trading decisions. It's like you deal blind, without any solid basis.'

'So, fire me.'

'Nothing would give me greater pleasure, if you weren't making money. You are, though I can't fathom how. You make some good calls on tough days, but they always seem to be *hunches*. Short-term trading hunches. Great on days when the market moves suddenly, but useless the rest of the time. You do nothing long-term, nothing you can *explain*. You fritter away most of the day, hardly ever deal till the London markets are almost closed.'

'I prefer to work with New York. D'you have a problem with that?'

'Not necessarily . . .'

Now it was time to make him *squirm*.

'. . . but I do have a problem with your little games. Oh, I know, I know, don't underestimate me. You never deal without going into the conference room and staring out the windows, do you? What d'you get up to in there, eh? Need a fix to get the balls to trade, do you?'

'I like to think things over, that's all. Check out my trading instincts in peace and quiet.'

6

'I don't buy any of this feely, touchy stuff. Calum, until you explain how you make your trading decisions, you can't expect to benefit from any profits. This is a communication issue. Frankly, I've no idea if you're any good or just plain lucky . . .'

Calum stared back in resolute grim silence. Suddenly Bossman wasn't feeling so entertained. The creep didn't look as fazed by the drugs remark as he'd expected. In fact, sitting there sullenly, he was becoming a mite aggravating.

'. . . *Well*, are you going to just *sit* there? I'm trying to have a *conversation* with you.'

'Oh, is *that* what this is? I thought it was some sort of English mating dance.'

It was Bossman's turn to show a flash of temper. His face reddened slightly, his hands tightened on the pencil he was holding, and his voice hardened.

'Okay, Calum, have it your own way. I was genuinely trying to help you, but if you don't want it, you don't want it. Sometimes I wonder what the hell you're doing in London.'

'I *like* London. I don't like some of the people who live here, that's all.'

'You really are a smartarse, aren't you? Off you go, then. Don't say I didn't try . . . Oh, one last piece of advice. Bonus day the whole team gets pissed together. The lucky ones pay and the unlucky ones cry into their beer. I go myself. Why not be sociable for once, make a new start?'

'I'd like to, but I'm busy tonight.'

'Surprise, surprise. Busy with what?'

'With my own business.'

'No, tell me, Calum, I really want to know what's so *fucking* important that you have to miss the team drinks for it.'

'If you really wanna know, I'm at a night class.'

7

'Oh, yeah? Studying what?'

'Modern languages. Language, anyway.'

'Really? Which one?'

'Essex.'

'Get out of here, you supercilious American prat.'

When he calmed down, Calum relented and went along for a beer. He answered Doug's question about his bonus and took in good part the subsequent general gut-bursting hilarity. The evening was bearable until Borzo frothed up a champagne bottle and sprayed it over him. That provided a decent excuse to leave before Bossman appeared, and he walked alone disconsolately to the Tube station. The escalator was broken yet again and there was a fifteen minute wait for the next Central Line train. Great. How could Londoners bang on about it being the world's top city, with an infrastructure like that? What was the point of all those musicals, concerts, and plays if no-one could get there on time? As the minutes went by, his indignation rose and rose till it could rise no further and ran out of steam.

In truth, he despised himself for making so little of London. Resuming big city life was a wrench after six months of such extreme peace, and arriving in October, at the start of London's half-year winter, hadn't helped. Taking a job he hated made it worse. What choice did he have, though? If he didn't get hold of big money soon, he would *never* get Marianna back, and where in London could you make fast megadollars except the City? The way he'd been treated today made even that look a joke.

As the train jolted on, he reflected that he must share the blame for how things had gone at the bank. Arriving friendless in the big city, he naively expected his new colleagues to offer a nucleus of a social life, and the team's hostile response to his arrival took him by surprise. For weeks he carefully disguised his despair at being back in finance, and did his best to laugh at their crude jokes, to smile at their pathetic attempts at mimicking his accent, and to swallow the unleavened, unending diet of taunts. His anxiety to be accepted was intense and their constant rejections hurt him deeper than they knew. They wore him down, though, and, little by little, he allowed his hidden streak of feistiness to show through and began to fight fire with fire. All that did was egg them on more.

Getting any other sort of social life going hadn't been easy. Soon after he moved in, the girl in the flat above tried to be friendly and invited him to a drinks party. Her male friends were *awesomely* dreadful. It was all opera this or shooting that. The chinless wonders had the nerve to patronise him. In fact, they were very skilful at it. They also had the knack of offering a glimpse, through the veils of exquisite English understatement, of how very successful they all were. Calum wondered if he'd fare better with the women, whether being from the States would give him a competitive advantage. They weren't unduly interested. Soon after he mentioned it, they would catch sight of a long-lost Piers, Toby or Jason and be off for a heavy-duty bout of shrieking hugs and cheek-kissing. He stood in a corner nursing a glass of wine on his own, and then slipped away unnoticed.

Soon he gave up on Brits altogether and resorted to the Euros you ran across in most bars and clubs. They were open and friendly, always happy to meet up for a brunch or a drink, and exchange resentments at not being accepted in England. Calum was a good listener and would patiently hear out their schemes and complaints. However, if he ventured onto the

9

thinner ice of his divorce from Marianna and how desperately he missed her, he got glazed smiles and stifled yawns. So he gave up on them, too, and for most of that long, cold winter, his evenings and weekends revolved around movies and working out at the gym. Drab loneliness occasionally drove him to the phone, and he would call one of his parents, soon getting lost in his Mom's alcoholic haze or buried under his Dad's pre-emptive catalogue of woes.

There were times when he teetered on the brink of a breakdown and thought he must end the whole desperate project. Whenever he came close to that point, he would stare for hours at Marianna's photograph to remind himself how much worse he would feel if he abandoned hope of being reunited with her, the only exceptional thing that had ever happened in his life.

At last the shuddering, lurching, temperamental train reached Notting Hill and he went off in search of a frozen pizza. There was work to do tonight and every night that week and he had no time to waste on anything the microwave couldn't handle. Back in his cramped basement flat, he zapped the pizza incompetently and ate it half-cold, washed down with a beer. Then, wrapped up in two sweaters and a windcheater jacket, he kicked open the ill-fitting door to the tiny damp patch of concrete and carried the wooden chair outside. For the next two hours he sat, half-frozen and quite motionless, staring up at the sky as the clouds scudded by. From time to time he would hum the soft lilt of an ancient Hebridean folk tune. When finally he rose stiff and shivering, and went in to warm himself, his only thoughts were for the waxing moon and his desperate hope that next Saturday night's sky would again be clear. He undressed, brushed his teeth above the cracked old basin, and ambled into the bedroom, trying half-heartedly to remove the twists and furrows from the grubby sheets before slithering into bed. On the bedside table stood a wooden-framed photograph of an arrestingly beautiful young blonde woman on a beach. He gazed at it fondly for fully a minute before switching out the light.

*   *   *

For the rest of the week, the sniping at Calum was no worse than usual. Better, in fact. Maybe that one beer had paid a dividend. Either that, or it had helped that they had all been treated so differently. Cathy and Adam spent half their time whispering into the telephone, trying to get something going with headhunters or sussing out the landscape with friends at other banks. It wasn't going to be *that* easy for either of them. Several City houses had taken huge hits and proprietary trading wasn't flavour of the month. Anyone in the know would figure out that they weren't big performers. Granted, they would be able to get another job easily enough, provided they were willing to go foreign. Foreign meant anything except British or American. Not ownership, *management*. Nearly all the British merchant banks, and more than one American, were now owned by the Swiss, Germans or Dutch. They didn't count as foreign. Their owners' influence was limited. They couldn't very well fire five thousand Brits and Americans because they were never going to find five thousand street-wise Dutch, Swiss or Germans to replace them with. Occasionally they would respond to some disastrous loss or dire underperformance by lopping off an Anglo-Saxon head or two, but then they would go straight back into the market and pay other Anglo-Saxons even more to design the next balls-up. The *real* foreign banks were different and were staffed mainly by has-beens who, like ageing pro footballers, sliddered down a division every couple of years until they came to the very bottom of the whole league and vanished. It all depended whether Adam and Cathy felt ready for that slide yet.

By Friday normal service was resumed. Doug's cockiness had not disappeared, but his crowing was grating so much that even *he* noticed. Borzo's relief had turned to mild sullenness. Adam and Cathy must have put things in train or given up for the time being. Mike, who'd been treated averagely, in line with his own view of himself, had patiently waited for the rest of the team to rediscover their common purpose in baiting the American interloper.

'Hey, Cath, did you hear what Yankee Doodle spent his bonus on?'

'Nah, what was that, then, Mikey?'

'A bacon sandwich and a pint of bitter.'

'Bollocks, on a bonus like that, how could he afford a whole pint? Still, you got to hand it to him, his tidying-up tactics worked a treat, didn't they, Dougie?'

'There's no doubt about it, the lad's smart. Pity his desk's too tidy now to try it again. Why not help him out, Borzo?'

Borzo leapt up and emptied the contents of his overflowing rubbish bin on to Calum's desk. Mike took over the baton.

'Hey, fart-features, since you don't seem to like it here, why don't you just fuck off back to America?'

'It's kind of you to ask, Mike. Unfortunately I can't leave till I've finished the research for my Masters.'

'Oh, *Masters*, is it? What a *clever* boy! What's your thesis on, eh, Bubblegum?'

'Primates in Proprietary Trading.'

'Oh ho, fuckin' ho. Think you're funny, don't ya?'

Calum tried to end the exchange by picking the phone up. It didn't stop Adam pouring a can of Coke over his jacket. He decided to wait till later to clean it up; it was probably ruined already. Jesus, what a bunch of assholes! In other banks, proprietary trading was done by humans, some of them borderline intelligent. But *he*'d had the luck to be closeted with this neanderthal quintet! He prayed that tomorrow his method would work, that he'd win big on the lottery, and *never* have to see any of them again.

*　　*　　*

Saturday morning came, not before time. He went out for a cappuccino and flicked through the newspapers. The only thing he took in properly was the weather forecast. Mixed, but not bad. Mainly dull during the day and some chance of drizzle, with the cloud cover lifting by evening. Better than average for early March.

He put off beginning the exhausting effort, wandering in and out of junk shops in Portobello Road for half an hour. Then there was nothing for it but to head back to the flat and start his meditation. He settled down cross-legged on his bed, his eyes closed. An hour and a half passed before he had any sense of a stirring. He was dimly aware that it was taking longer than last week and had no idea whether that was a good or bad sign.

He took a brief break at one and another at four. As he settled for the last session, he was so nervous about the depth of his trance-like state that he set his alarm clock for seven o'clock. Now he could feel the energy growing within him. He had to stop thoughts of lottery numbers straying into his head prematurely. In previous weeks that had broken his concentration and confused him at the key moment.

At three minutes to seven he opened his eyes and switched off the clock. He got up from the bed and went over to the chair where he had carefully laid out a coat, wallet, pen, pound coins and house keys. Beneath the chair were his slip-on shoes, neatly parallel. He put on the coat, pocketed the other things, and stepped out of the flat and up the rickety wooden steps into the street. For all his inner calm, he felt a flutter of tension as he scanned the sky. There were plenty of clouds up there, but it looked brighter to the west. He had to pass a long line of terraced houses before he could see it.

And there it was. A big fat yellow moon. It took eight minutes more to reach the newsagent. He crossed to the opposite pavement, and closed his eyes to summon the full burst of energy. Then he opened them again and stared at the moon with massive intensity. Three, four, five minutes passed. A couple of teenagers passed him, shouting ribaldry as they went. Calum didn't hear them. Six, seven minutes. It was now twenty-six minutes past seven, desperately close to the time limit. The queue of people ten minutes before had dwindled to nothing. No-one else wanted to cut it that fine and the last was paying up now.

Still he didn't hurry. He walked calmly across the street and into the shop. A glance at his watch showed there were two minutes left. He took three cards, filled in each with identical numbers, and handed them over with the money to the Indian shopkeeper. They were stamped at 7.29. He put the receipt carefully in his wallet and left.

14

It was just the waiting now. He felt less tension and exhaustion than usual. His appetite had rebounded, so he stopped off at a pub and ordered a shepherd's pie and a beer. The last few weeks he had watched the result at home. There was a TV in this pub, though, and enough talk of the lottery going on to be sure no-one would change the channel.

His pulse registered a rise before the first ball dropped into view, but when he saw it *was* Twenty-one he calmed right down again. This time he was *sure*. All the numbers had floated before his mind's eye with stunning clarity. He felt it so strongly there was no doubting it. His heart rate hardly changed as, one by one, his fleet of ships came in.

2

Rewind: The Spring Before

'Oh, hi. Why are you still up?'

   'I was waiting for you.'

   'There was no need.'

   'Where you been, Marianna?'

   'Out.'

   'Out where?'

   'With friends. We were trying out some new places on Hollywood Boulevard.'

   'Which friends stay out till two thirty on a Monday night?'

   'Don't start on me again, Calum. If you wanna have a talk, do it when you're sober. How much vodka have you got through tonight, eh?'

   'You have one *hell* of a cheek. What got me started drinking, anyway?'

   'It's because you can't cope with life.'

   'Most of life I can cope with fine. It's the *you* bits that are a problem.'

   'So everything's my fucking fault, is it? Is it *my* fault that you can't cut it at work?'

   'I can cut it.'

   'Oh *yeah*? You call a bonus of fifty thousand *cutting* it? Have you heard what other brokers are making, like Charlie or Mike? Charlie says a chimpanzee could make good money in these markets. Sounds like you haven't made ape status yet, let alone *cut* anything.'

'I'll make money this year. Stop trying to avoid the question. Who've you been with?'

'Cal, have you ever thought of getting a life for yourself, instead of getting in the way of mine? You just can't *stand* the way I'm growing, broadening my horizons, when you're spinning your wheels, can you? This is all a jealousy thing, and you can't handle it.'

'Oh *yeah*? Whose friend got you the job in the first place? How would you have got near the movie business without my help?'

'I'd have made it some other way. Anyway, you're so hypocritical about that. Within a month of me starting there, you were wishing you hadn't done it. *Weren't you?* . . . You try to make out like you're supportive, but you're not really. You know, Calum, if you continue the way you've been going on recently, you're going to kill off whatever respect I still have for you. It's time you learnt to back off.'

'I get it. My wife hardly speaks to me, stays out till late night after night, probably in the company of other men. If I keep quiet she walks all over me, and if I say I'm not happy about it I lose her respect. Either way I lose out, right?'

'Have you noticed how often you use the word "lose" about yourself nowadays?'

'Is it so surprising when you're constantly hinting that I'm a loser? Tell me, Marianna, am I going to lose *you*, too?'

'I have to work in the morning. If you want to get heavy-duty at nearly three o'clock, you're gonna have to do it by yourself. I'm going to get some sleep . . .'

'Or have I maybe lost you already? Is there someone else?'

'That's just *typical* of you. You have *no* trust. If you had

18

any shred of self-respect you'd know better than to go round asking dumbshit things like that.'

'Is it Brett Marquardt?'

'I don't need this . . .'

'It *was* him, wasn't it? You spent tonight with that middle-aged slimeball, didn't you?'

'What makes you think you have the right to call someone like Brett a slimeball?'

'What did he buy you with, Marianna? A big shiny diamond? A mink coat? Brett's got the kind of money you *respect*, doesn't he?'

'Fuck you.'

'But tell me, did it feel revolting, touching that slack old flesh?'

'*No, it did*— I'm gonna sleep in the spare room.'

Calum's mental tape recorder could replay every one of those conversations, so seared were they in his memory, from the first niggling squabbles to the last bitter exchanges that alternated between chilly, clenched teeth civility and all-out, brutal screaming matches. This was the one he replayed most often, the first time he had discovered for sure she was having an affair. After that it was a long downhill slide, punctuated by frequent craven apologies from Calum for his outbursts, when he would hug her lovely, unyielding frame and plead vainly for a fresh start. As Marianna's interest in him evaporated, her patience disappeared and the tide of her taunts swelled. Loser, loser, loser. He would *never* get anywhere, *never* make money, *never* earn anyone's true respect. Most hurtful of all, she threw back in his face his modest prior romantic history, endlessly voicing doubts that he would ever be able to keep a woman.

He tried to ignore her constant demands for a quickie

19

Mexican divorce, still clinging to the hope that somehow he could turn everything around. It was on the twentieth of January that he made his fateful gamble, staking every cent he owned, plus plenty he didn't, on a wildly geared options bet. If the markets had run his way he would have made half a million, enough to pique her interest for a while. They didn't, and he lost his job along with his bet. For four blurred days Stolichnaya was his only companion. His resistance gone, he docilely accompanied Marianna to Guadalajara and signed the papers.

On the way down she was cool and watchful, still nervous that he might change his mind. For the return trip she didn't disguise her beaming bliss. Those were the first smiles he had seen from her for months. Calum sat numbly beside her, his heart ripped to shreds, unable to stop himself stealing sidelong glances at her astonishing, breathtaking, ravishing beauty. She pressed his hand, told him not to take it personally, and said once again that if he'd been more successful everything might have been different.

Now as he sat in the cramped aircraft seat recalling that moment, the tears welled up, like they had so many times before. Sometimes he made the supreme effort to force thoughts of her out of his mind. At other times he invited them in, preferring bitter self-flagellation to the hopeless task of getting over her. He had no wish to see his friends, who were united in the view that she'd never loved him, had only used him, that he was well rid of her. Instead he walked alone on the beach or sat for hours by the phone, *willing* it to ring and be her. After a glass too many, his fingers would creep uncontrollably to the handset: her clipped and increasingly short responses left him overwhelmed with remorse for making the call. The pain got worse and worse until it became too much to bear.

Every street, every café, every restaurant shouted memories of their time together. If he didn't do something, get away from LA, he would never escape from this black vortex. There was only one place on earth that drew him like a magnet, the place of his childhood dreams. He made up his mind, booked the flight and set off. Marianna never left his mind once, though, in the cab ride out to the airport, through the long transatlantic flight, and during the weary layovers in Heathrow and Glasgow.

At last, the exhausting journey was almost over and he could make out the first land, low grassy hummocks dipping their gnarled old toes into the cloud-hugged sea. It didn't look at all like the Lewis of his fantasies, always bathed in cool sunshine. The real one looked prodigiously damp. Rain streamed down the windows as the turboprop made its jaunty final approach, thumped down hard on the tarmac and skittered uneasily to a halt. The slim stewardess pulled the door open and was knocked half off her feet by the force of the gale.

Inside the funny little terminal there was no sign of a luggage carousel. Before he could work it out, a sodden pallet of luggage burst through a flap in the wall and the passengers lined up to reclaim their bedraggled possessions. One of the locks on Calum's suitcase had given up the unequal struggle to restrain the overflowing contents and the case gaped like a half-opened oyster, its contents drenched. Never mind, he wasn't going to let *anything* spoil the magic of arriving in this special place.

The rentcar turned up as booked. It wasn't the latest model and the bodywork was distinctly moth-eaten, but it had four wheels and an engine of sorts. Calum hardly listened to the man's explanation of the car's controls, so surprised was he by the accent. His only exposure to Scottish accents had been videos of *Braveheart* and *Highlander*, and he assumed that the further north you went the wilder the accent would become, so that by the time you got up to the islands they would sound like tumble dryers with a catarrh problem. This man's voice was soft, lilting, almost feminine. After confirming it was okay to return the car in the west of the island, Calum set gingerly off, kangarooing down the road courtesy of the unfamiliar stick shift and clutch. Keeping to the left at junctions and roundabouts was like playing some tricky computer game.

He was well aware that driving far was foolhardy in his tired-out state, and the sensible thing was to hole up in Stornoway town overnight. He decided against it. There was an hour or more of daylight left and he wanted *so* much to get there, to the village of Sgurr nan Creag, that name that had meant so much to him ever since his Grandad first mentioned it. On he pressed across the weird, barren, lunar landscape, bursting with excitement about how it would look.

The moment he got the first glimpse of the sea and the village, he braked to a halt and got out. Even in the twilight, it was dramatic: a fine range of snow-sprinkled hills sweeping down to a startlingly white beach and broad crescent bay. Though he had never seen a picture of it, he had somehow expected the scene to look comfortingly familiar. This looked alien, unknowable. He shivered. Boy was that wind biting. Better head on into the village and check out the options for somewhere to stay, preferably a cheap Bed & Breakfast. His worldly wealth was the eight hundred pounds he had in his wallet, and he couldn't afford too fast a burn-rate. Whatever the cost, he was determined to stay in the village, to let its atmosphere seep into his pores and to give him the earliest chance of tracking down the local head of the clan Buchanan.

He drove slowly around its streets. The houses were low and small, some huddled together, others widely spaced out. There was no sign of a B & B or hotel. A heavily wrapped figure was walking towards him, bent double against the fierce wind. Calum asked and got directions to the only hotel, the Shobost, a little north of the village itself.

The elderly woman who responded to the tinkle of the bell matched the hotel's dreary atmosphere. She explained unenthusiastically that breakfast was included, but other meals were by arrangement. Too tired to think of venturing further afield, he booked dinner for that evening. She produced an ancient visitors' book for him to register and checked carefully that she could decipher his handwriting. Was it his imagination, or did he detect a tiny intake of breath when she read it? Surely American tourists weren't *that* rare over here?

She shuffled ahead of him and introduced him to the modest charms of Room 4 and the bathroom at the opposite end of the draughty corridor. Hot water proved to be another subject for negotiation. After it was made abundantly clear that guests normally bathed in the morning, it was grudgingly supplied, through plumbing that vibrated and clanked in protest at mounting an additional matinee performance. At least it was warm, and Calum relaxed in the first sensation of comfort since he had bidden farewell to the rays of Californian sunshine.

He managed a slight whistle as he dressed. The bath had given him an appetite. He couldn't expect haute cuisine from the Shobost chef. Something simple would do, like a Caesar or a Chef salad. He went down to the gloomy dining room and greeted his fellow diners, a middle-aged English couple.

23

The wife offered a grimace, probably intended as a smile. The man continued eating.

Calum waited for something to happen. There was no menu; just cutlery, a water jug with glass, and salt and pepper pots, one clogged and one empty, adorning the threadbare oilcloth. After five minutes, the kitchen door swung creakily open and the doughty receptionist stomped in bearing a plate of brown soup. As she walked, the soup slopped to and fro, repeatedly breaching the defences of the inner rim, not quite escaping the plate altogether. She set it down in front of him. A discussion ensued which left both participants unimpressed, the receptionist being especially scandalised at the American's suggestion that the evening's fare might be modified at that late hour.

The three courses came and went, left largely intact. The receptionist's snorts grew louder with each removal. It was still only eight thirty. He had planned to rest up properly before beginning to make enquiries, but what the hell, why not try the hotel bar? He wasn't going to do any more binge-drinking, but a glass or two would help ease away the jet-lag. And, who knew? If this was the only bar in the village, it was pretty likely that the regulars would know which Buchanans he should try first. Come to think of it, he might walk in there and run right into a bunch of his long-lost relatives! He tingled with anticipation as he pushed the door open.

The conversation stopped as he came in. His smile of general greeting was not returned and they resumed their conversations. He sidled up to the bar where the barman was chatting in some foreign language with one of his customers. Wow, this must be Gaelic. What a thrill! Calum stood patiently while the discussion continued, taking the chance to survey the room, earnestly keeping the friendly smile on his face.

There were ten customers, all male and none younger than fifty. He turned back to the bar and tried, unsuccessfully, to catch the barman's eye. A quiet 'excuse me, sir' failed too. Only when the barman had recharged his interlocutor's glass and poured a whisky for himself did he move languidly over to where Calum stood.

'What can I do for you?'

'Hi, I'd like to get a beer.'

'What kind?'

'What d'you have? Becks? Michelob? . . . Anything you recommend.'

'Most of our regulars like the eighteen shilling.'

'That'll be fine. I didn't realise you still used the old currency here. How much is that in . . . English money?'

'We do not use the old currency, and the new currency is no more English than Scottish. It is the name of the beer. Would you like a pint or a half-pint?'

'Oh, a pint, definitely.'

The beer began to foam into the glass. Calum leant forward.

'D'you mind if I ask, are any of your customers here from the clan Buchanan?'

The barman's hand tightened a fraction on the pump handle. It took him a second or two to reply.

'I do not believe so. That will be two pounds fifteen.'

He gave up on the barman, hoping for a warmer welcome from the quartet playing darts in a slow, stately manner.

'Excuse me, is this table free? Will it disturb your game if I sit here?'

'It will not bother us.'

He sat watching for twenty minutes, applauding all their

better shots. They paid him no heed. When their second game ended, he plucked up his courage.

'That sure looks fun. Do you guys only play among yourselves, or can a stranger join in?'

'We do.'

'Oh, right . . . It *is* okay if I watch, is it?'

'Suit yourself.'

Calum politely sat through one more game, then wandered back to the bar and approached the one grizzled customer standing by it.

'Excuse me, sir, is this stool free?'

'I see no sign of anyone sitting on it, young man.'

'I was afraid it was someone's usual stool, that's all. I just got here today. Don't want to make some awful *faux pas* my first day . . . Great place this.'

'The Shobost?'

'No, I meant Sgurr nan Creag, if I'm pronouncing that halfways right.'

'And what about it appeals to you so much?'

'Everything, I guess. The beauty, the unspoilt nature. The sea, the mountains, the environment. Beats the hell out of LA, for sure.'

'LA?'

'Los Angeles. That's where I'm from. Home of Tinseltown, freeways and smog. Ever been?'

'I have never been to America. Indeed, I have only been twice to the mainland.'

'I can understand that. If I was from here, I'm sure I'd never budge.'

'And why is that?'

'Like I said, the beauty. You must feel like you live in paradise.'

'My idea of paradise is somewhat warmer. I think if you lived here longer you would find this paradise rather dull. There is not much to do here. It is too late for me now, but if I was half my age, I would leave, as most of our young people do.'

'Crazy, isn't it? Half the world is trying to downshift and come some place like this, and you guys wanna go to the big city!'

'Human nature is a perverse thing.'

'Guess so. Hey, while we're talking, there's one or two things I'd like to ask. Can I start by buying you a drink?'

'It is civil of you to ask. Please do not be offended if I prefer not to accept a drink from a stranger. Now, young man, if you will excuse me, I must go and have a word with my friends over there.'

Calum scanned the little bar but could see no other victim. His ears roamed the conversations. They all had the same pattern of throwing in the occasional word or phrase of English, but too little for him to decipher the drift of their conversations. He couldn't be sure whether Gaelic was a *real* language, one they used all the time, or whether it was an elaborate code to exclude outsiders. What would happen if he left the room and came back in suddenly, without warning? Would he catch them all talking in English?

He tried to work out why they were being so unfriendly. Back home, pretty much anybody would give you the time of day, provided you weren't a drunk or a weirdo. It must be something he was doing wrong. Was he being too brash, too *American*, accosting them in that way? Just *typical* of him to goof. Maybe he should switch to sitting on his own for a while, radiating friendliness, and leave it to the locals to make the first move. He eked out three pints of beer. The other customers roughly matched him in beers, accompanying their pints with unstinting measures of whisky. No-one addressed him and the evening wound down. Before leaving, every one of them bought and pocketed a flask of Scotch. Fraser, the man Calum had talked with, nodded as he went. The others paid him no heed. The barman returned his call of goodnight without looking up from clearing the tables.

Calum retreated to his room and sat sadly down on the bed. It wasn't meant to be like this. It was his Grandad who told him about Sgurr nan Creag, though he'd never made it there himself. He'd always sworn that if Calum ever went, the wonderful Buchanans of Sgurr would surely welcome him unquestioningly into their bosom. The vivid image his Grandad had conjured was of a place with bright hearths, happy children, and smiling grannies. A place of dancing, skirling Highland music and tales of long ago, where all was wholesome and *nothing* would ever go wrong. For Calum this meant far more than finding his roots. As his life began to fall apart, he had fantasised more and more about the Buchanans of Sgurr, building them up as kindly, forgiving folk who wouldn't care that he was so mediocre at everything. For the first time in his life he would be somewhere he *belonged*, somewhere that would put balm on his deep wounds and help him get himself back together. But if it *wasn't* like that here, what the hell would he do?

He stood up, put out the lights, forced the corroded metal window frame up and peered out towards the sea. The dense cloud cover blocked any moonlight, leaving only an inky blackness. The velvet silence was broken by the sound of distant waves breaking. In his apartment in LA, a couple of blocks back from Venice Beach, he could hear the ocean, too. This Scottish sea sounded older.

The room was getting cold. He closed the window, pulled off his clothes and got into bed. A few seconds later he switched the light on, dragged his weary limbs over to his suitcase, and pulled out the framed picture of Marianna. He set it as close as possible to the bed before sinking into heavy, dream-laden sleep.

3

He slept long and breakfasted ferociously. His spirits were much brighter. It had to be *easy* to track down Buchanans in a place this small. The monosyllabic receptionist wasn't aware of any and suggested he try the village shop. The shopkeeper couldn't help him either, and frostily asked him not to hold up the queue. The village's only public phone stood opposite the shop. He flicked through the directory. No Buchanan entry. Strange. Telephone enquiries? No listing either. Stuffing fistfuls of coins into the machine, he made a lengthy and ultimately fruitless approach to the local government office in Stornoway. No, there were no Buchanans on the electoral register for Sgurr. This was worrying. Never mind: they admitted their records only listed people who answered their questionnaires, and could be incomplete. Where to try next? There was no sign of a police station. What about the church?

'Oh, hi. Is it okay if I look around?

'Visitors to our kirk are always welcome.'

'Could I ask something, Father?'

'That is an appellation from the Roman church. Here we use the term Minister.'

'Pardon me, Minister. Out in your graveyard, there are five or six gravestones of Buchanans.'

'Yes, indeed.' The Minister's eyes narrowed. 'Will you excuse me? I am rather busy.'

'I'll only take one minute of your time. I was wondering . . . The last of the gravestones is from 1907. Is it still a common name round here? I'm a Buchanan myself, here to do a little rootwork. My ancestors were from this part of Lewis.'

'There were Buchanans here for a long time. It is an old Lewis name.'

'And now?'

'You may find some in Stornoway.'

'No, I meant here in Sgurr nan Creag. I couldn't find any in the telephone directory, but they may not be listed. Do you know any?'

'There are none among the members of my flock.'

'Do most of the villagers go to your church?'

'You will find that we prefer to call it a town, small as it is. The great majority of them attend regularly. This is a God-fearing community.'

'And how about non-combatants? Any Buchanans you know of?'

'None that springs to mind.'

'Surely they can't *all* have left or died out?'

'It has happened from time to time in these islands, what with the clearances and the poverty. People were often forced to leave. Doubtless your own forebears were driven away by some such thing. Now, if you will excuse me, young man, I must be about my pastoral duties. Good-day to you.'

Okay, what next? The little folk museum that was down near the beach? There might be something about clans or families there, something that would give him a start. If he didn't get anywhere this way, he'd come straight out with it in the bar and ask that guy. He hadn't been such a bad sort. Willing to have a conversation of sorts.

*   *   *

It was his ninth day in the area of Sgurr, and the coldest so far. Up on the hills his hi-tech jacket was defenceless. It might work fine in the Arctic, but the inventors of this much-patented, much-hyped lightweight fabric had reckoned without the Hebrides. He wouldn't let the cold stop him completing the set, though. After reluctantly accepting that no-one could recall any Buchanans, living or dead, he determined instead that he would conquer all eight of the hills that guarded the approaches to the town. Ben Mhor was his sixth, steeper and craggier than the others. Two more days and two more climbs, and he'd be gone. In spite of the bitter disappointment of finding no relatives, it *did* feel a special place to him, and he wanted to see every inch of it and lock it away in his memories.

For sure, it wasn't the people that made it so special. They were coolly civil at best, uninterested in his quest. It was the area itself that had cast a spell over him, soothing him a little, easing away some of the desperation, making him feel less panicky, slightly more grounded. There was a strange absolute quality about the place, a clarity that helped put his troubles in some kind of perspective.

His short-term future was bleaker than ever, with staying on in the hotel unaffordable, and work here apparently out of the question. He *had* asked, and regretted it as soon as he opened his mouth. What work was he fit for? The fishing? Back-breaking work and little enough to go around. Crofting? Everyone did their own digging. Where would they get the money to pay him? Anything else? Did he not know how bad the unemployment was here? Did he want to take work away from the locals?

33

With no Buchanans to help him out, there was no choice but to move on. Sad, when right now this was the only place on the globe that he wanted to be. So where would he go? Glasgow or London were probably the best bets. It shouldn't be hard to find casual work there till he found his feet. He *couldn't* bring himself to go back to LA with hardly a cent to his name, and in as dire straits as ever. How could he stand being back a few miles from Marianna, yet not *with* her? Suicide was obviously the sensible option, though his track record at it was far from reassuring, his attempt at sixteen years of age having been terminated ignominiously by a stomach pump. His Mom didn't even bother to come, and his Dad later liked to say it proved that Calum was useless at *everything*.

As he rounded the last shoulder before the peak itself, a stunning sea view opened up in front of him and, shivering as he was, he squatted on a rock to take it in. Above him, through gaps in the cloud, he picked out a golden eagle with a wing span of six, maybe seven feet circling effortlessly in the thermals. Calum was transfixed. The eagle soared higher and higher. Then, in an explosion of acceleration, it crashed downwards. Oh my God, the crazy thing was going to smash straight into the rock! At the last possible instant, after Calum had given up hope, it pulled itself out of its dive. There was a brief flickering of wings, then up and away again, with something – maybe a rabbit – in its assassin's claws. Into the cloud it went and disappeared. He found it inexpressibly moving.

He pulled himself up stiffly and clambered on upwards. By the time he reached the snow-covered peak daylight was fading, and there was only time to pause briefly before he started back down, taking a straighter, more vertiginous path than for his ascent. It was twilight by the time the slope began to flatten out. The terrain got rougher again, forcing him closer towards the sea. If the tide was out, it might be easier to head for the beach and work his way round the bay. It was close to dark now, and he was glad he carried a small pen torch in his pocket. The beach couldn't be far, judging by the sound. The waves were up in arms, making a great noisy fuss. One last hummock and he would be there.

He started in real fear when he saw the silhouette against the darkening sky. With shaking hands he pulled out his torch, and took three twists to get the narrow beam on. He shone it wildly around. For Chrissakes let it not be some dreadful monster!

It was a Celtic cross, tall and leaning slightly forward. Calum swung the beam right and left. He hadn't made out the low wall till then, though he was nearly on top of it. The little graveyard was no more than forty feet by twenty, an ancient place of rest looking out over the sea. Apart from that cross, there were seven or eight stones standing and more that time had toppled. It wasn't clear where the gate was, so he clambered straight over the wall, and picked his way over to the upright stones. They were mostly at drunken angles. Calum tried to read them in the torchlight. The first was too weathered, the next looked like MacDonald. The third name was unreadable, but the dates of 1832–1876 could be made out. Two more past deciphering, then one clear MacIntosh, an infant death in 1904. He swore as he stubbed a toe painfully on a prone gravestone. It was a MacLeod and beside it a Nicholson. On to the last one, its shape proudly, defiantly erect, like an old soldier's last salute. A strange instinct seized hold of him as he went towards it, and he lowered the beam, wanting to *feel* the stone first.

It had hard, clean edges and was almost unweathered,

obviously more recent than the rest. He aimed the torch. The words were clear and simple. Gormelia Buchanan. Born 1898. Died 1976. Mourned by her Loving Daughter, Morag.

Calum switched the torch off and fell forwards against the stone, his face pressed against it, gripping the sides of it with both hands. He didn't want to let go of it. His fingers traced the word Morag, the name on the back of the faded old photo that his grandad had inherited from his father and passed on to Calum, together with a broken watch and a Gaelic bible. Could this Morag be the child in the picture?

Getting back to the Shobost was a long and increasingly damp affair as the rain which had been threatening all day let rip. The trudge and the long soaking bath served a purpose, slowing him down. Pregnant with the discovery, he might have ploughed straight into the bar and flung it down like a gauntlet. He would have to be wiser, more careful; find out what lay behind this. The average age of the regulars made it unthinkable that none of them had known Gormelia Buchanan or her daughter. Could whisky-addling truly have swept away their collective memory of both? Surely not. All the locals were born and brought up here. There were far fewer comings and goings than in a mainland town.

And what about Morag herself? Had she moved away when her mother died or before? The gravestone gave no clue whether she was still a Buchanan or was married with some different name. Since her mother was born in 1891, the daughter would most likely have been born sometime between 1910 and the early 1920s. She would be a fair old age now, if she was alive at all. What were the chances it *was* her? Since Sgurr wasn't exactly overstocked with Buchanans today, how many Morag Buchanans could there have been back then?

He lay in the bath for half an hour thinking. It might all be innocent. They really *might* have forgotten. If so, he should not embarrass them, should simply offer a gentle nudge to help them recollect. But if that didn't work, what then? And if it wasn't so very innocent, if for some reason they were trying to obstruct him? . . . In that case he would have to be wary, cunning if necessary, might have to think up a way to outsmart them.

He went down to the bar. He had developed quite a taste for their warm beer. It was a good antidote to freezing your balls off on the hills. He knocked back two pints in ten minutes and took a whisky chaser with the second. Fraser seemed friendlier than usual and told him one or two Lewis ghost stories. What was causing this sudden surge of warmth? Was he being accepted at last, or had word of his imminent departure spread? Calum ordered a third pint and successfully persuaded Fraser to take a drink from him. This opened the floodgates. He noticed Hector, the oldest of the darts quartet, and the tallest, too, with bristly white hair and a scar under his right eye, murmur in Gaelic to the youngest, Donald, who walked over and gravely invited Calum to join them.

Their civility was extreme. It was Calum's first attempt at darts and it showed. It took time before he mastered the art of hitting the board at all, and aiming for individual numbers was beyond him. Not one word of derision was uttered, except by Calum, who maintained a constant commentary on his own incompetence. He got gentle praise for any score above ten and help in retrieving darts which bounced dangerously off the surrounding wall. His partner, Sandy, showed no sign of irritation at being shackled to a walking handicap and the bald, wiry Hamish, who had made way for him, watched with polite interest. As they played, Hector occasionally spoke. His voice had the same lilt as the others, but was deeper, more gravelly.

'So you will be leaving us soon then, is that right?'

'Yeah. Cash-flow problems, you know.'

'You came here to find your roots, is that what you were telling Fraser?'

'That's it. We Americans can't resist it . . . Great shot, Sandy.'

'So your ancestors are from Lewis, are they?'

'Yup. My great-grandfather emigrated in 1923, from this very town, in fact. Went to Canada, then on to Detroit. Not that I met him. He died in 1929.'

'So he'll have sailed on the *Metagama*, then?'

'The what?'

'The *Metagama*. It was a ship that took the emigrants. Most of the Lewis boys went on it. It was owned by the Canadian Pacific Railway Company. They were taking them to work there.'

'Do you remember it?'

'No, laddie, I was only two at the time. The *Metagama* is part of folklore here.'

'I guess that must have been it, then.'

'Your throw.'

'. . . What do we need? Double six? . . . Oh, no . . . Why am I so goddam hopeless?'

'Are you satisfied with what you've found?'

'So-so. It's been good to get a feel for things round here, but I was disappointed not to track down any relatives. No Buchanan survivors, as far as I can make out.'

'Maybe they all moved away.'

'Guess so, or died out. So none of you remember anyone

of that name? No Buchanans who died in your lifetime, or womenfolk who might've got married and changed their names?'

'Your go again . . . No, I don't believe we do.'

'Double three? . . . Well, how 'bout that! What a fluke! So, Hector, whereabouts in Sgurr do you live?'

*   *   *

He lay in bed till ten, waiting for the adrenalin buzz to slice through the stubborn hangover. There was no point in starting too soon, anyway. You couldn't go knocking on doors until a decent hour. Despite the large liquid intake, he'd remembered to scribble down where Hector and Donald lived before he went to bed. Sandy and Hamish were from the next town so they weren't a problem, and Fraser's croft was out in the middle of nowhere. He hadn't wanted to leave it to chance that the first house he tried was Hector's. He suspected Sgurr nan Creag would have a rapid bush telegraph, and if the men from the bar found out too soon that Calum was snooping round, doors would be slammed in his face or stay shut altogether.

He hated having to do it this way. For three hours in the bar he had slipped cues into the conversation, hoping that the alcohol would loosen their tongues. Every time he brought up the subject, they changed it abruptly. There was an unnaturalness about it and a tension in the looks they exchanged. He now knew for certain that something odd was going on, something they wanted to keep from him. He must take the battle to them. All was fair in love, war, and roots.

It was as cold as ever outside, but mercifully dry. He

walked once round the whole town to plan a systematic programme, making marks on his hand-drawn map as he went, noting Hector and Donald's houses with large black crosses, uncertain whether he should be feeling like a secret agent on a mission or an idiotic jerk. Reconnaissance complete, he went back out to the croft at the southern extremity of the village and marched up to the door. No answer. Try again. Still no answer. On to the next house.

'Excuse me, sir.'

'Yes?'

'I'm doing a survey on family names in Lewis and Harris. Would you be willing to help? I just need to know your surname and your wife's maiden name.'

'What is the purpose?'

'It's for the US Bureau of American History. We're comparing immigration early this century with depopulation in the places they came from. Seeing how the family numbers grew in the States and dwindled in the old countries.'

'It is no concern of mine.'

'It's only your name.'

'I will not sign anything.'

'That won't be necessary. You can just tell me.'

'I do not want my name going to some salesman. I don't need new double glazing and we already have a satellite dish.'

'Nothing like that, I promise.'

'Wait here while I have a word with my wife . . . Very well. I am a MacDonald and she was a Morrison. Now, you keep your word, mind, or I'll speak to the police about this.'

'Good morning, ma'am. Could you spare a minute to answer a couple of questions?'

'No, I can not. I am a member of the Free Church of Scotland and I want nothing to do with the Mormons.'

'I'm not from the Mormons.'

'Jehovah's Witnesses, then. What brass neck you people have, knocking on doors, preaching heathen nonsense!'

'It's nothing like that. All I need is your name for a survey.'

'Leave my house *now*.'

He noticed a brown envelope lying on the table a few feet from the door, just too far away to read.

'Hey, that's not smoke coming from your kitchen is it?'

'What? . . .'

The few seconds while she looked were enough. MacIver. Good. He'd have to do without the maiden name.

The woman came back looking furious. Calum tried not to smile.

'No? . . . Must've been my imagination. Thank you, anyway, ma'am.'

The door slammed behind him.

*   *   *

It took till four in the afternoon to work his way round all the houses except the two he purposely avoided. No answer at three of the twenty-six houses. Four people who came to their doors refused to give their names, three of them men and one woman of no more than sixty. Those who did were wary and guarded, watching out for some catch, except one old guy who offered him a whisky, then rambled interminably and completely incomprehensibly for half an hour. Calum had probably provided the bright spot of the man's whole year, and getting out of there was the hard part.

His list was bereft of Buchanans. Some secret agent he'd proved. The Shobost regulars had doubtless been told, and would be high with indignation for being doubted. His reputation in Sgurr now must square well with the view from LA. But before giving up and going back to face them, he would try the no-shows one more time. Two were occupied now, a Murray and a Mackenzie. That left only the dilapidated tin-roofed house with the low, thick walls, set back from the road, looking older than all the others. He walked up the little path and banged at the door. No reply. The thorn bushes stopped him getting close enough to peer through the tiny windows, opaque with dirt. He went back to the door and listened again. Was that something? The faintest sound. He would give it one more good knock. Nope.

What did he have to lose? It was this house or nothing. He stepped two feet back and called out, almost in a shout, 'Morag Buchanan.'

He tried the name once again. Nothing. He marched round to the back of the house, and tapped urgently on the one dark pane of glass.

'Morag Buchanan, this is Calum Buchanan. I am your brother's great-grandson.'

Still no response.

'Miss Buchanan, please open the door. I *must* talk with you. PLEASE.'

Silence, except for the whistling of the wind.

He tried a last half-hearted thump on the front door, and turned back towards the path. It was time for one last desperate roll of the dice, a very sneak trick. The nearest house, not counting the three abandoned, derelict cottages, was a hundred yards away. The door there had been opened by a tense-looking little woman, who had given her name with the greatest reluctance. He trooped there again. She reappeared, looking savagely suspicious. Before she could close the door or refuse *anything*, Calum spoke.

'So sorry to trouble you again, Mrs Matheson. The old cottage down the road, where the old woman lives. I can't read my note of her name and she's not answering now. Would you mind telling me it?'

She looked like he'd asked her to swallow poison.

'I don't recall her name.'

'I can't make it out at all. Could it be Ballantyne?'

Mrs Matheson looked mightily relieved, but Calum saw the flash of confusion before her face cleared.

'Yes, I think that is it.'

'No, hang on a minute . . . I must be going blind. It's not Ballantyne . . . it's Buchanan, isn't it?'

She went white, stared at him as if transfixed, and slammed the door in his face.

Back he went to the cottage. He knocked one more time, not expecting a response, then scribbled on a piece of paper and wrapped it around a sepia photograph of a young girl in ringlets. He pushed it under the door and stood there, waiting patiently for the ten minutes it took before the door creaked open.

4

Should he or shouldn't he? Discretion said stay away. The feisty part of his nature, which his friends thought must come from his warlike Highland ancestors, said go challenge them. Why had they deceived him? Did they hate Americans so much that it gave them pleasure to thwart him? Was this a game? Would they all laugh when he went in to the bar and congratulate him on winning? Or was there something stranger, deeper to this? Could they have some genuinely good reason for their behaviour? If so, Calum needed to find out what it was. Would they at least be more open with him now that he *knew*? Or be so enraged by his phoney survey that they would cold-shoulder him altogether? Then he might only get at the truth by pressurising them. Could he have confidence in his ability to handle a tricky situation like that skilfully? Could he hell.

He mulled it over for a few more minutes while he did a bit of laundry in the little basin, using the remains of the soap bar as detergent. Finally curiosity and thirst got the better of him.

He didn't have to wait long for a reaction of sorts. Fraser had joined the foursome round a table. When he came in they fell silent, then resumed in low Gaelic tones. Calum's cheery greeting was not returned. He ordered a pint and walked over to the table where they sat.

'I think I need to get in some practice throwing darts. Any of you boys feel like a game?'

Fraser shook his head. Hector stared right through Calum.

'No? . . . Well I guess I'll just play on my own. These darts belong to anyone here?'

No response. The Gaelic murmurs continued. He was getting so nervous now, it was hard to keep a tremor out of his voice.

'Well, if they don't belong to anyone in particular, I'll try them out.'

He threw darts, badly, for ten minutes, feeling woefully uncertain what to do next.

'I'm not what you'd call a natural. I should stick to drinking. Can I get any of you guys a whisky? Fraser? Hector? Sandy?' Fraser and Sandy shook their heads. Hector didn't bother. The other two stared fixedly in other directions. Tension and unease crackled in the air. Calum felt massively uncomfortable, but there was no turning back now. He must screw up all his courage and plough on. He ordered another pint and moved a stool within a couple of yards of their table.

'So, guess what, Fraser, I found there *is* one Buchanan in Sgurr nan Creag . . .'

The Gaelic ceased.

'. . . Yeah, old girl, must be well into her eighties. Name of Morag. Lived here all her life, apparently. Odd you guys not knowing her.'

Silence.

'I guess you five must be kinda famous round here, 'cause she's certainly heard of you.'

Hector muttered something under his breath. It didn't sound friendly, whatever it was.

'Sure is good to find I've got some living roots here, after all.'

He got so used to their silence, he was taken aback when Fraser addressed him.

'So now that you've found your roots, you will leave tomorrow a happier man, I suppose.'

'Happier? Sure thing. But my plans have changed. I won't be leaving.'

The reaction from the table was wordless, but powerful all the same.

'You will be staying on at the Shobost?'

'Here? Oh, no, I couldn't afford that. Morag has invited me to stay with her for a while.'

There was a sharp exchange at the table. Whatever was said, it seemed Fraser was voted some sort of spokesman.

'Young man, we had no wish to deceive you. What we did, we did for a reason. We did it in your own interests.'

'Oh, yeah? Tell me more, Fraser.'

'It is entirely understandable that foreigners like yourself should wish to discover their roots. We are quite used to such things.'

'Well, thanks for helping me out so much.'

'In any other case we would have been happy to offer whatever assistance we could.'

'So what's the matter with me?'

'It is not a question of you. It is a question of your . . . relative.'

'Morag?'

'Yes.' Calum sensed Fraser didn't want to say her name. 'There are certain . . . *things* you cannot be aware of.'

'*Things?* What sort of things?'

'Things that happened a very long time ago. Things from

the past that are . . . *painful*, that are best left undisturbed. We did not think it was in anyone's interests, including yours, to rake over the past. We thought it better for you to leave believing that you had no living relatives here. If you have any sense, even now, you will behave as if that is the case.'

'And just *leave*, you mean? Why should I do that? I like it here, and now that I have a place, I *can* stay on.'

'Take our advice and keep away from that woman. Nothing good can come of it.'

'What are you talking about, Fraser? Is she a wicked witch or something?'

There was an intake of breath from Hamish. Hector muttered something that sounded like a fierce oath. Fraser looked profoundly ill at ease.

'I cannot tell you, Calum, but believe me, it is better that you leave.'

'Without knowing any reason? Look, Fraser, I'm real sorry if I've caused offence by the way I found out, but if there's something I should know, I need you to level with me. Otherwise, there's no way I won't take up her offer. She's *old*, goddam it. It wouldn't surprise me if she is a bit . . . idiosyncratic. She *is* family and she *has* been kind enough to offer to put me up. I can't say I'm altogether looking forward to living in that little house, but it *is* free, which in my financial condition is pretty important. So unless you have some very good reason . . .'

'We do, Calum, but it is simply better not to rake over—'

The interruption was from Hector. He spoke so loud he almost shouted, but he did not look towards Calum and Fraser.

'Tell him. TELL HIM.'

Fraser said nothing. Calum jumped back in.

'Come on, Fraser, I agree with Hector. Tell me . . . Better still, Hector, why don't you tell me yourself?'

Hector did not give him the courtesy of a response, either in words or in eye contact. Fraser started to speak again, awkwardly, hesitantly.

'Your *relative* . . . I do not wish to go into details, but she is not a *good* woman. In fact, she is the opposite, she is *evil*. She should be left alone till the end of her days.'

'Evil like how? What's she done that's so terrible?'

'She has done bad things, but it is worse than that . . .'

'Oh, I get it, she really *is* a wicked witch, right?'

'Young man, you think you are clever to mock, but you are closer to the truth than you can possibly imagine.'

'I *am*? So what does Morag do with her powers? Doesn't look like she's turned any of you into frogs.'

Hector's eyes hardened with rage and Calum cursed himself for making such a stupid flip remark. He was about to apologise when Fraser continued, now in a less friendly voice.

'Heed our advice, or you will regret it.'

'Fraser, I don't doubt that you guys are sincere in what you believe, but isn't this all superstition? Witches don't exist. If they did, we'd have them in LA, for sure. We have every other kind of weirdo there. There *are* no magic spells, no covens, no curses. You can't seriously expect me to turn down Morag's offer unless you have something more specific . . .'

Calum waited, not daring to add another word. He had handled it all miserably badly, but surely he would get the real story now. The silence was broken by a sharp sound as Hector pushed back his chair and rose. He issued a Gaelic command to the table; they rose too. Hector strode the few paces and towered over the still sitting Calum.

'We have told you we do not wish to go over the past. We

have tried to help you. You have responded with scorn and disbelief. You should listen, and if you do not, you will live to regret it. It is your choice. Do as you please.'

With that he turned away, bought a flask of whisky, and left. Fraser and the others followed him out, leaving Calum alone in the bar, more shaken by the conversation than he would have liked to admit. He needed a stiff drink. The barman had disappeared and did not answer his calls for service. Going behind the bar and pouring himself a generous measure was a tiny act of defiance against the lot of them. The malt whisky helped relax him for his last encounter with the Shobost's lumpy bed, but it did not give him a sound or dreamless sleep.

*   *   *

'Put your things over there, by the bed. That one will be yours, my mother's old bed. It is more of a cot than a bed, I'm afraid. I'm not sure how you will fit in it with your height.'

'Don't worry, Morag, I'll be okay.'

'Now come and sit and let me look at you properly. Will you have something to drink?'

'Coffee'd be great.'

'I am afraid I do not have coffee. Only tea.'

'In that case I'll have a soda, or mineral water. Any cold drink would be fine.'

'You can have milk or tap water.'

'Tap water, I guess. Why don't I go get it myself?'

'Very well. The tap is outside, to the left of the front door.'

He filled a cracked glass and sat down again. She stared hard at him through her old, much-repaired glasses, as if

50

struggling to take him in. Calum grinned back, growing more uncomfortable as the silence lengthened, marked by the ticking of the wall clock. Sitting there, tiny on her small wooden chair, she radiated an oddly powerful presence. Beneath the deeply weather-beaten skin, the high cheekbones hinted that her features had once been fine. Her thin white hair was gathered up in an untidy bun. She wore a coarse tweed skirt, a shapeless fawn sweater, thick brown stockings so heavily darned that little of the original material survived, and incongruously hefty black lace-up boots.

The bright morning sunshine hardly penetrated into the dank room. Now that his eyes were accustomed, Calum glanced around. The walls were an even dark brown, probably stained by decades of smoke from the peat fire that smouldered away. The little living room had an uneven flagstone floor and was dominated by an ancient iron-framed loom. A sink and a stove filled one corner. Next to that, a crudely fashioned oak dresser held Morag's modest supply of earthenware, battered pans and twisted cutlery. On top of it were twenty or thirty dog-eared books, and an oversized wood-cased radio that looked like it belonged in a museum. There were no ornaments or pictures. Nor could Calum see any sign of a fridge, dishwasher, TV or phone. Off opposite ends of the living room were the two tiny bedrooms, with their floors of compacted soil. The house's odour wasn't great, overall. Calum looked back at Morag. She was still looking at him with her penetrating blue-green eyes. He was beginning to feel horribly ill at ease and felt compelled to say *something*.

'So, Morag, is this the house where you lived as kids, where my great-grandad grew up?'

'No, it is not. Did you see the three ruins at the bottom of the street? We had the middle one of those. It was a blackhouse, too, but a little bigger than this.'

'A blackhouse?'

'It is the island word for these old houses. The ones built the new way we call whitehouses. This one was thatched originally. We put on this corrugated iron roof about thirty years ago.'

'Why did you move?'

'It was in a bad state, and too big when it was just my mother and me. I never knew my father. I was much younger than Murdo, your great-grandfather, and my sister, Fiona. Our father was called up three months before I was born, in 1917. He did not die fighting, but on the way back. Most of the Lewis men made the last part of their journey home on a ship called the *Iolaire*. The captain took the wrong course in a storm, and the ship foundered not far from Stornoway. More than seventy died. They say there was never mourning like it in Lewis. My mother did not like to have it mentioned; it was Fiona who told me about it later.'

'What became of Fiona?'

'She worked on the herring, salting and packing them in barrels. It was a huge affair back then. They exported them all over the world. They were always travelling, the herring girls. In the summer it was Stornoway or over on the Scottish mainland. In winter they would go to ports in England. She met an Englishman in Yarmouth and married. She died in childbirth, the infant too. It was the same as with Murdo, we never saw her again after she went away.'

'Can you remember your brother leaving?'

'As if it was yesterday. He was only eighteen, but he was a grand man in my eyes, more like a father to me than a brother. I did love him so.'

'But didn't you all feel abandoned, him being the only man in the family and all?'

'There was no work for Murdo here and he wanted a life. He said he would make his fortune and come back a rich man, or send for us to join him in America.'

'So sad it didn't work out.'

'Life can be hard. It started well enough for him there. He wrote, telling us about the girl he married, Mary, your great-grandmother. Nineteen was all they both were. He sent pictures of them together and of your grandfather soon after he was born. Murdo wrote occasionally for the next few years till we heard from Mary that he'd died of tuberculosis. I will never forget that day. It broke my mother, too, though if only she had known, there was worse to come.'

'And Mary didn't keep in touch?'

'Oh, she did for a while. She sent one or two more photographs of the child. Then the letters stopped coming and ours to her were returned marked 'gone away'. We never knew what happened to them after that.'

'They went away to New England. She died not long after. Grandad grew up in an orphanage in Maine. He died two years ago of cancer.'

'I am very sorry to hear that. I would have liked to meet him.'

'I'm sure Grandad would have wanted that, too. He was a kind, gentle man. He kept a fishing tackle shop. I was very close to him, closer than to my own folks. He remembered his own Dad amazingly well, though he was only five when he died, especially his tales of Sgurr and Lewis. Grandad passed them on to me, too. That's why I have a thing about this place.'

'When was your father born?'

'In 1946. He has a younger sister, Marnie, who lives up in Seattle now. Dad moved to Mom's home town, San Diego.'

'And is that where your parents are still?'

'No, Mom's in Oregon, married to a retired vet, and Dad's in Palm Springs, halfway through his fourth marriage. He and Mom don't speak.'

'You said you weren't close?'

'No, we grew apart. They're both pretty taken up with their own lives. I find it hard to really *talk* with either of them now. I remember loving them a lot when I was a kid. They were always arguing with each other. Mom was a great looker, but boy did she have a tongue on her! When I was about ten, Dad decided he wanted a quieter life, and left her for a dowdier, quieter number up in LA. At first I didn't mind too much. I got to see Dad once a month, and as I was an only child, I had Mom to myself. Then she took up with another guy, Denny, a disc jockey at a local radio station. After he came on the scene, Mom kinda lost interest in me. She wasn't cruel or anything; it was like her mind was on permanent vacation. She was besotted with the guy. I *hated* him, or resented him anyway. Mom wanted him to move in and I didn't, so I gave him a hard time. I hadn't figured on him doing an end-run around me. Get rid of the kid and I'll move in tomorrow. The kid stays, and you won't see me for dust. Worked a treat, so I got packed off to live with Dad in LA. That thrilled the hell out of his new wife, as you can imagine, and Dad resented it, too.'

'What about you, Calum? Do you have a sweetheart?'

'Would you like to see her picture? Hang on a sec . . . There, what d'you think? She's called Marianna.'

'She is awfully pretty. Is she the girl you'll marry?'

'I already did. We're divorced.'

'I am sorry to hear that. Do you still love her?'

'Like crazy.'

'You poor boy.'

'I'm not poor, in *that* sense, anyway. Marianna's going through this phase where money is important to her and I simply didn't have enough. Brett, the jerk she lives with now, has *lots* of money. He's a big shot at the company where she works.'

'Did you have children?'

'I wanted them, but Marianna wasn't keen. She worries about losing her figure. Mind you, she has time on her side, she's only twenty-six. If she changes her mind, I still hope she and I have kids together. She *says* she doesn't love me any more, but maybe some day the real Marianna will come back. I need to be there for her if she does.'

'But if she likes money so much, and her new man is rich . . . is it very likely that she'll come back to you?'

'Before she walked out on me, she kept saying if I had lots of money, like five million dollars or something, it would all be different. I have two choices: either get over her, or find the five million. The way I feel now, finding the money would be one hell of a lot easier than getting over her. Who knows, though? After a few more weeks here, I may forget she ever existed.'

'I hope so, for *your* sake. Lewis isn't the easiest place in the world to make millions.'

'Morag, would you excuse me? Where's the bathroom?'

'There is a lavatory outside the back door, but I don't have a bathroom. I warm a tub of water in front of the fire once a week. I wash my clothes in it afterwards.'

He went off to the lavatory and retreated from it as soon as humanly possible.

55

'Say, Morag, I'd sure like to make myself useful while I'm here. Are there things I can do to help out?'

'There are many things you can do for me, but let us leave that for another day. The main thing you can do is talk to me. The wireless has been the only thing to keep me company since my mother died.'

'Don't you have any friends at all?'

'No.'

'Whyever not, Morag? Don't you *like* people?'

'Not very much. It is more a case of people not liking *me*.'

'You don't even keep a dog?'

'I've had many dogs over the years. Collies. The last one died last year after we were thirteen years together. I'm too old to get another one now. If I died, nobody would look after the poor thing . . . Now, Calum, it's getting on, I must go and prepare our food. While you are here, you will have porridge for breakfast, soup at noon and meat and potatoes for your tea. In the evenings I weave the tweed, listen to the wireless and drink a dram. I rise at six and am in my bed by ten. You will do the same.'

Calum nodded and thanked her. He'd wanted a touch of the simple life, and it sounded like he was going to get it. She'd said he could stay a month. He hoped he would last that long. How the hell *was* he going to sleep in that miniature bed?

5

After the first couple of weeks, Calum found he didn't *mind* being ostracised. Indeed, if the whole town hadn't all snubbed him from the moment he moved in with Morag, he wouldn't have been able to feel this great solidarity with her. There was no hypocrisy round Sgurr nan Creag. Bitchiness, narrow-mindedness, plain nastiness, yes; hypocrisy, no. Calum never ventured back to the Shobost bar, and on the rare occasions when he ran across Fraser, Hector or any of the others in the street, they ignored him totally.

This didn't deter him from getting around. He wasn't refused service in the little shop, for example. They took his money sullenly. He didn't have to go there often, as Morag had a well-established system for getting a weekly delivery. Because the shopkeeper and his wife refused to visit Morag's house, the box was delivered by the tweed man, who had to go there anyway. The tweed man paid the shop, deducting it from what he owed Morag, and took care of her utility bills the same way. He was the only person who was halfways kind to her, but then he didn't live in Sgurr, and travelled around all the local villages and crofts distributing and collecting the work.

Relations with Morag started rather uneasily. Once they had caught up on all the family matters, it was harder to find things to talk about. However much Morag said she welcomed conversation, she was unpractised at it, and didn't appear to mind or even notice long silences that Calum found hard to endure. At supper the first night, he blurted out a question about Hector and Fraser. Morag shook her head, got up to clear away the plates, and went over to start her weaving without another word. After that he learnt to hold his tongue and not to try to crowd every minute with words.

Life in the blackhouse was primitive like you wouldn't believe, but it was surprising how you got used to it. The air was so sweet that the hard boards and the tiny cot couldn't stop him from sleeping soundly. Morag's food, though basic and limited in repertoire, was undeniably nourishing, as the slight spread in his midriff testified.

Over the weeks his talks with Morag began to be less stilted and grew steadily longer and more frequent. Early on, for all her unfailing kindness and civility, there was something joyless about her, reminding Calum poignantly of a neglected child who has never been taught how to play. Now he detected a change. Her eyes were losing the worst of their desolate blankness and occasionally he would catch a tiny sparkle there. It gratified him when she began to smile and show the first faint traces of a long-buried sense of fun. The agreed month came and went, without either feeling the need to raise it or fix a new time-span.

The only part that he still felt odd about was washing. He took great care to curl up in his bunk while Morag was bathing. She didn't offer him reciprocal consideration. The first time, she warmed the water in the tin tub and sat there in front of it. When he gently enquired where she was planning on going while he bathed, she said she was fine where she was. He hung around for a while, expecting her at least to turn the other way. As she showed no sign of this, he pulled off his shirt and jeans, sure that this would prompt a rapid aversion of the eyes. Not at all. He stood shivering in his boxer shorts, staring at her purposefully. She stared back. There was nothing for it but to be direct.

'Excuse me, Morag. I wanna have a bath. Would you mind . . . ?'

'Mind what?'

'Giving me some privacy.'

'What for? Don't be daft. I'm your great great-aunt. You don't have to worry about me. Just get on with it.'

And so on it went. She outlasted him. The first time, he got in boxer shorts and all, feeling like a small schoolboy. The next time he whipped them off and she took a good look at him, butt-naked as he was.

Calum helped out with the planting of the vegetables, back-breaking work as it was, and did some minor handyman repairs about the place. There were aches and pains from muscles that no Californian gym had ever discovered. She got him up on the low roof to try to secure the iron sheets better, and couldn't contain her laughter when he slid right off, landing painfully in a bush. At nights they ate early so Morag could get on with her weaving. The radio would always be on while she wove, turned up loud enough to drown the constant clacking of the loom. Morag would sometimes pause to take a sip of whisky and add her own acute commentary on the opinions being expressed by the broadcasters, surprising Calum with how well-informed she was. She had an insatiable curiosity about new things, and made Calum tell her how the Internet worked, and all about life in America. In return she told him old stories of the isles and her early childhood, but still did not volunteer any more on why the village treated her so. It was the only thing that still made him feel uneasy. Once in a while he would recall Fraser's words of warning and . . .

wonder. Until he understood what lay behind that he would always feel slightly unresolved about Morag. He bided his time, and waited till the moment felt right one evening before daring to raise it again.

'Morag, those guys at the Shobost, Fraser and his friends. They said some *strange* things. Would you mind if I asked what that was all about?'

She stopped her weaving and looked over at Calum. He could see the pain in her eyes and cursed himself. It was too late now.

'What did they say to you?'

'Nothing much, really. Just that you weren't . . . that it wasn't a good idea for me to hang out with you.'

'What else?'

'Not a lot. One of them called you a witch.'

'Still "witch", after all these years, is it? And them the age they are . . . Very well, Calum, I will tell you the whole, long, sad tale. There are parts I have never told a living soul, not even my own mother. I want your word you will keep this to yourself as long as I live. After I'm gone, no-one will care any more. Do you promise?'

'Sure.'

'It all began when I was fifteen or so. There were other Buchanans here then, four families in Sgurr nan Creag alone. One of the families – cousins of ours – had a boy the same age as me, Iain. We were born only a week apart, and as children we spent a great deal of time together. One day in summer, we were on the banks of the burn out by Ruigh. Iain started playing the fool, splashing water over me, and I did the same to him. We had done things like that many times. This was different, though. I felt odd, almost shaky, as if some strange power was taking hold of me. I looked at Iain, and I could see from his eyes that the same thing was happening to him. Before I knew it, we were kissing. We lost balance and slid down into the water, but Iain didn't let go, and we kept on kissing with the water streaming right past us. It was as well it was only two feet deep or we'd have drowned. We were soaked of course, and shivering with cold when we came out. We said nothing; we didn't even look at each other. We couldn't go home in that state, so we had to wring our clothes out and run around in the sun until they were half dry.'

'Was that your first kiss?'

'At *fifteen*? Of *course* it was. We didn't have boyfriends and so on at that age, the way they do now. If my mother knew I'd kissed *anybody* she would have skinned me alive. And us being cousins made it feel even more sinful. I had no idea what the law was, but I was sure it was wrong.'

'So what happened next?'

'Iain and I didn't see each other for a few days. I thought about him all the time. Then one evening I was out near the burn again . . .'

'By complete chance?'

'What do *you* think?'

'Go on.'

'We kissed again, on and on, for about an hour. We were careful not to fall in this time.'

'And . . . ?'

'No *and*. We just kissed. You have no idea how pure and simple we all were back then. After that we met as often as we could. It was a terrible secret and we had to take great care. If we had been found out, it would not have been only my mother and Iain's folks up in arms. The Minister would have raised Cain too. The power of the manse is still there today, but back then, you would not believe what it was like.

The Catechist used to come round the houses every month to check whether we were studying the Bible the right way. If they had known what we were getting up to, they would have hanged, drawn and quartered the pair of us. We could not stop though, we were *that* in love with each other. We planned to wait till we were eighteen, the age of consent in Scotland, and find out if we could marry as cousins. If not, we would run away together and live somewhere far away under false names.'

'So what happened?'

'The worst thing in the world. Iain's father was a crofter, and had a family of four to feed. That wasn't easy in the Depression. You see, Iain was the oldest in his family and the others were too young to help out much, they were just mouths to feed. A cousin of theirs who had emigrated to New Zealand wrote offering them part of his own land to farm. Iain's father was at the end of his tether here, and decided to go.'

'Immediately?'

'No, thank God, we had a few months together before they went. We swore a secret pact that as soon as we were old enough we would be together again. Even so, we could not stand to be apart for so long. At that age it seemed an eternity. We had to find a way to stay close. Back in those days, letters took three months . . . Calum, my glass is dry, and I don't think I can go on without another dram. Will you get that bottle from under the sink, the one the tweed man gave me at Christmas?'

'The Bowmore? I thought you were keeping that for a special occasion.'

'This *is* a special occasion . . . Now, where was I?'

'Staying close to Iain.'

62

'Oh, yes. He and I had always had this *thing* between us. I do not mean the love. Ever since childhood, we had known what the other was thinking or feeling. I could tell if there was something wrong, without seeing him. We wondered whether this would work over thousands of miles, or whether the distance would block it out. So we tried to practise communicating with each other. We would sit together and one of us would concentrate on something, and the other would have to try to guess what it was.'

'What sort of things?'

'Oh, anything. Simple things, a fish or an apple. It was hard at first. Once, to be naughty, I concentrated on the knickers I was wearing. Iain guessed the Minister. We laughed for an hour about that one. By and by, we got better, so we tried it over a distance. We could not manage to get very far apart, but we would walk in the opposite direction for two or three miles each and try again. It made no difference. We practised so hard that after two or three months we got so we could almost talk to each other. Not complicated things, of course: what we were feeling, what we were doing.'

'So you were ready for him to go?'

'We were prepared, yes. It was an awful day all the same. They went off with the pony and cart all the way to the bus stop. I walked all the way behind them, crying my eyes out. Then the bus came and took them away to Stornoway.'

'But you and Iain were "talking" the whole way.'

'As much as we could, on the steamer to Glasgow, and then on the boat down through the Suez Canal and on by way of the Indian Ocean and the Pacific. I cannot remember all the ports they stopped at.'

'And after they got to New Zealand?'

'The farm was in the South Island, near the sea. Life there

was harder than they expected. The land had not been broken and wasn't good for much other than sheep, and they had no money to buy any. To begin with, Iain's father had to work as a labourer on his cousin's farm.'

'You got all this from Iain "talking" to you?'

'Some of it. The family wrote to my mother, too.'

'Was Iain happy?'

'He only had six weeks there. It was winter here, and a hard one at that. One night I was wakened by a terrible pain. I was shaking with fever and felt that I couldn't breathe. I called out to my mother. She lit the oil lamp – we had no electricity then – and came over to me. I must have given her a dreadful shock. There was no thermometer, but I was that hot, I must have been a hundred and five. I *knew* there was something wrong with Iain. It was as if he was *screaming* something to me, but I couldn't catch it. Then I sensed something *so* clearly. Iain was . . . saying goodbye. Sorry, Calum, even after all these years I cannot think of it without crying . . . Thank you, dear, your touch comforts me.'

'What *was* it? A sudden illness?'

'He drowned. It was the first time he had swum in the sea there. He wasn't used to the size of the waves and the power of the current. He was swept out to sea and hadn't the strength to swim back. Iain's mother wrote and told us. Before that, I didn't know how he had died, but I knew he was gone, all right. It was as if someone had turned off a light inside me.'

'My God, that's a rough thing to happen when you're only fifteen. Must have taken ages to get over that. How long did you keep on loving him?'

'About seventy years so far.'

'So, what did you *do*? Did you tell anyone?'

'Not a soul. I felt so terribly alone without him. I wondered in my childlike way whether I could still talk to him in heaven. I thought if I could aim my thoughts up to the sky hard enough, eventually they would reach him. Except the sky is an awfully big place, and I didn't know exactly where heaven was, so I thought I'd start with the moon, just for practice. Whenever there was a clear night, I would go outside and stare at it, putting all my energy into getting my thoughts that far.'

'What did your mother think about this?'

'It was before the letter about Iain came, so she made no connection with that. She knew there was something upsetting me, all the same, and she did not try to stop me. I did it every night for week after week. If I was unable to *see* the moon, I tried to imagine it through the clouds.'

'And what happened?'

'It was about eleven o'clock, one cold night in March. There was a full moon. I tried *so* hard that night, I remember. Suddenly, my eyes filled with this eerie vision. It was as if there was white all around me. I could not see anything clearly, only this white colour. I thought I was entering heaven, that any moment I would see Iain. I was in a sort of trance, and I called out loud to him. But there was no reply, nothing else, only this strange whiteness, which soon faded away. As I walked back to the house, snow flakes began falling. I got home just in time. Minutes later it started to snow more heavily and the wind whipped it up into quite a blizzard. Half an hour later, everything outside was white. It was the biggest snowfall that winter.'

'Hang on, Morag, you've lost me. What's this got to do with Iain?'

'The white, the snow. I had foreseen it. Similar things happened again after that. Whenever I tried looking at the moon to talk to Iain, I had this strange sense of what would happen.'

'But Iain didn't speak to you?'

'Never. I told my mother about this funny feeling and she asked me never to tell a soul. Folk were afraid of people who had sixth sense. Her mother, who died when I was seven, had it and people kept their distance from her. My mother said the same would happen to me if anybody knew.'

'But they found out? Is that why they call you a witch?'

'That June, one lovely long evening, there was a summer moon up in the sky though it was not yet dark. I couldn't stop myself looking at it. I saw stormy water and death. I knew the fishermen would be putting out to sea from the harbour, so I ran over there and called to them not go. They were upset to see me. There's a superstition up here that it's a bad omen to see a woman before you go out fishing. They told me to go to hell and to keep away from the harbour.'

'So they went out to sea?'

'There was a squall. Three of them were washed overboard and drowned. One of those who died was Hector MacDonald's father. Hector was eleven at the time. Feelings ran high in the town. Some thought I had caused it by going there; others said I had the sixth sense. The Minister came down to the house and told my mother I should be exorcised. When she refused to do as he said, she was asked to leave the Church. That was a dreadful thing in those days. It made us outcasts.'

'And ever since then they've ostracised you, for that one thing?'

'It's not the end of the story. I grew up into a fine-looking lassie, though I say it myself. No-one forgot the drownings, but the young men put it out of their minds. There were few young girls about and I was by far the prettiest. They didn't know that the only boy I was interested in was my own dead Iain. When I refused their advances, it made them call me names again. Then the war came. Some of the men were called up right away, but Hector and his friends were too young. Their turn came in 1942. On their last night before going away Hector and two of his cronies got horribly drunk and came upon me on the road. They said . . . dirty things. Hector said he was going to pay me back for killing his father. I fought like the devil, but I was no match. Two of them held me down while Hector MacDonald had his way. I got one hand free for a moment. He carries the mark to this day.'

'I hope the *bastards* spent a long time in the slammer.'

'When I got home, my mother ran to the Minister's house. He refused to get involved. There was no policeman in the town and the nearest police station was twelve miles off. We went there the next day, but the men were away to the army by then. The police said there were no witnesses, and there was not enough evidence to warrant bringing them back. Any investigation would have to wait until they came home from the war. They tried everything they could to get us to drop the charges, saying what a terrible scandal it would be. I refused, and my mother backed me up.'

'So, when the war was over . . . ?'

'They came back in 1944, after VE, two of them anyway. Willie Nicholson was killed at Caen. The police questioned them, and it got in the papers. They both claimed it had been horseplay, that I had led them on. The times were against me. There was a lot of euphoria with the victory, and they were war heroes returning. The police said it had all happened a long time ago, and we should let it be.'

'And that was the end of it?'

'That was the end of it. Everyone here knew they had done it, but it was me and my mother they blamed for bringing shame on the town. No-one talked to us again. They didn't deny us a living. They let us weave. But we were no longer part of the community.'

'I can't believe the *injustice* of it. Are you saying Hector got off *altogether*?'

'More or less. Since they believed I was a witch, I decided to have a go at it. When I next saw him in the street, he smirked at me. I went over to him and told him I had cursed him. Of course, it was stuff and nonsense. I wanted to frighten him, that was all. He thinks the curse worked. He had two children. One died and the other is simple. He's in his fifties now. Hector's wife has to look after him like a baby. It is all my doing, according to Hector.'

'Ever since your mother died you've been on your own?'

'Yes.'

'I can't *imagine* how lonely you must have been.'

'Not as much as you think. You get used to it, you know. The company of people can be over-rated. Most of them spend their time gossiping or complaining. This way nobody lies to me or cheats me. It will sound daft to you, but I chat away to the wind and the rain: they are my real friends. If there were younger folk in the town, I daresay it might be different. *They* would be less likely to believe nonsense about witches. But as you'll have noticed, there aren't any young ones left. They've all moved away and they won't be back. There is something unhealthy about this place, as if it's a town that wants to die.'

6

Another month passed. He loved it here. However, underneath it wasn't getting better, wasn't going away. He still hugged Marianna's picture every night before going to sleep. In the buzzing parliament of his thoughts his head cited her many misdemeanours, but his heart was unpersuaded and held the casting vote.

His resolve not to talk too much to Morag about Marianna rarely succeeded. He loved to reminisce about the early days after he met her on that trip to Albuquerque. She was twenty-four, working in a local factory. Calum was in a bar there, on vacation with his best buddy, Pete. Marianna and a friend marched right up and asked if they would buy them a drink. She was the most beautiful thing Calum had ever seen.

Pete always claimed she threw herself at Calum, the way she came to LA two weeks later and just moved in. It was true Marianna did the proposing, but what the heck, he would never have had the nerve himself. When he admitted that fear of being hurt made it hard for him to commit, she swore by all that was holy she would stay with him till the end of time. Calum had never been in love before, never really had many girls. He guessed he wasn't *that* bad looking, it was mainly this confidence problem. All the pretty ones went for guys who talked a good line, had an easy way about them, came across as natural winners. Calum's shyness and lack of prowess was a standing joke. How the tables were turned when he, of all people, got a knockout girl like Marianna! . . . As she walked down the street, guys' necks would swivel so hard they hurt themselves.

It was *so* wonderful for the first year or so. Marianna had never been to California before, and it thrilled Calum to watch her enjoyment when they went to a fancy restaurant or hotel. She persuaded him to move to a more expensive apartment, a really *nice* place, and she spent a bunch of his money doing it up as *their* love nest. She said she didn't care that the job she got at the local telephone company bored her monumentally. If all went well with Calum's work at the brokerage, they wouldn't *need* a second income for long. His confidence began to rise a little from its natural resting place at rock bottom, and he saw that life could be more than one long obstacle course. Marianna made him behave more positively, insisted on it even, pushed him to do better, made him act like he *was* somebody.

Morag listened carefully, but kept her own counsel even when he got on to the more painful parts. Marianna's withdrawn moods when he failed to make big money, the frustration of her own mind-numbing job, and the ratcheting pressure on Calum to find her something better. Calum pleaded with friends and got her work as an assistant at one of the big Hollywood agencies. She was delighted, and everything went well for a month or so. Then the glitz began to take hold of her. When she went off to parties at smart Beverly Hills homes, she came back *changed*. It wasn't enough to peek at this glossy, gilded world: she wanted some of it for herself. Calum was slow to see what would follow. Once Marianna made up her mind she wanted something, there was no deflecting her. Calum couldn't compete. His income at the brokerage generated just enough cash to rent a high-maintenance lifestyle, but far too little to buy one outright. If it hadn't been Brett Marquardt, it would have been some other hunter, willing to offer wealth, power and style in return for that amazing body and dazzling good looks.

Morag sighed sympathetically, prompting Calum to criticise his own part in the catastrophe and mount a spirited defence of Marianna. It wasn't *her* fault that she'd reacted like that to money. Her own folks didn't have any and it was hardly surprising that it knocked her off balance. In so many ways the break-up was *his* fault, not Marianna's. When things began to go wrong, instead of giving her space and the chance to experiment, his fear made him possessive and demanding. If he hadn't put so much pressure on her, bitching and interrogating her, she might still be with him today.

Morag just let him ramble on, keeping her thoughts to herself. They managed more of a dialogue when they talked about his work. There was something about Morag that helped Calum discuss things with unfiltered candour. It was the first time he had admitted, maybe even to himself, how far he had gone trying to be one of the gang at the brokerage. The way he copied the star performers' clothes, hairstyles, expressions, mannerisms, and opinions. How he sucked up to them to survive and was tolerated as the butt of their jokes, but insanely blew their goodwill when they pushed him too far and he snapped back. When Morag heard his tales of office politics, back-stabbing, and the relentless pressure to perform, she shook her old head in astonishment. It mystified her why Calum should have chosen a job he so clearly disliked and which, by his own admission, he had no aptitude for.

'I cannot understand you, Calum, dear. From what you

say, you love painting more than anything else. Why not be a full-time artist?'

'Oh, didn't I tell you? I tried it for a year before I went into broking. You don't make much of a living from it, unless you're *very* successful.'

'Why should that matter, as long as you love what you do? Some of the greatest painters lived in poverty, and only became famous after they died.'

'What's the use of posthumous fame if people don't know in advance? Morag, I don't want to be a failure *all* my life. Where I come from, if you don't do well financially, you *are* a failure.'

'It sounds a sad way to measure the worth of a person.'

'It's not only a measure, it's what it gives you. Although I was no good as a broker, it *did* give me a decent lifestyle. You know . . . a big apartment, nice car, fancy vacations and so on. If I hadn't been in that league, my friends would've written me off and a girl like Marianna would never have *looked* at me. People's opinions *do* matter, you know.'

'Calum, there's one thing you should *never* forget. When you get old, and look back on your life, you'll see how well you spent your years. It won't matter then what others think of you, and grand houses and cars will be of precious little comfort. There comes a point when you have to answer, not to others, but to *yourself*.'

'I know that you're right, Morag, but it's *different* for you, don't you see?'

'Because I'm old and have no friends?'

'No. Because you're *you*. You know who you are and what you are. My problem is I'm not *me*, yet.'

'I'm sure it will come with time . . . Now be a good lad and turn on the wireless. There's a programme on the Indonesian rain forests I want to hear.'

Calum waited patiently for the programme to end. For days now he'd tried to work up the courage to broach the subject. Tonight was the night he'd do it. He poured some more whisky into both of their cups and sat down close beside her.

'Morag, there's something I want to ask you about.'

'What's on your mind, my boy?'

'Tell me more about sixth sense.'

'What do you want to know?'

'Start with your granny. You said she had it.'

'Oh, she had the gift all right.'

'How did it show?'

'She could tell when there was going to be a death. If there was someone going to die, she would see them in a winding sheet, though they were dressed normally and appeared to be perfectly well.'

'Do folks in the islands still believe in it today?'

'The young ones maybe not, but the older ones, every last one. Did your grandad ever tell you about Coinneach, the Brahan Seer?'

'No. Who was that?'

'It was a very long time ago, in the sixteen hundreds. Coinneach came from around here. He had the gift and he met a bad end because of it. His master, the Earl of Seaforth, was away in Paris and his wife forced Coinneach to say what he was doing there. He told the truth, that he was carrying on with a Frenchwoman. Lady Seaforth was so angered that she had the Seer burnt at the stake. As he was taken to his death, he gazed at a white stone that his mother had given him, and declared that the Seaforths would all die out.'

'What was so special about this stone?'

'One night Coinneach's mother was herding cattle, down near the graveyard at Baile na Cille, ten miles from here. By the light of the moon, she saw the graves open and spirits rise and disappear into the dark. She stayed till the dawn, when the spirits returned and all the graves were filled except one. She crept down into the graveyard, and, recalling an old tale that spirits cannot cross rowan wood, she placed her staff over the hole. Soon a beautiful woman came rushing through the air from the North, wearing a band of gold in her lovely hair. "Lift your staff from my grave so I can return to the land of the dead," she begged, "I am the daughter of the King of Norway, drowned here long ago. Once a year all spirits can return to their homes, but for me it is far, and I always return late." Coinneach's mother lifted her staff and let her pass. Before the ghost disappeared into the earth, she took a stone from her breast, saying "give this to your son when he is seven years old, it will give him the gift of prophecy."'

'And did it?'

'His predictions about the Seaforths came true. The Earl's four sons all died young and before long the line was extinct.'

'Is sixth sense passed on? I mean, is it some genetic thing?'

'No-one knows for sure. It is not in every generation. It seems to run in families, though.'

'How about ours? Were there others, apart from your granny?'

'There was nothing I'm aware of on my father's side. My granny told me her own mother had the gift, too. She claimed we come from the same stock as the Brahan Seer himself, though that may be stuff and nonsense.'

'Is there any way to test whether somebody has the gift?'

'What on earth are you thinking of? You should not fill your head with things like this.'

'If it *is* genetic . . . well, we're from the same gene pool. Is it conceivable that I might have it or could develop it?'

'Why would you want that? It is a burden, not a happy thing. Look what it did to my life.'

'Morag, I don't know how to say this . . . you see, I'm desperate. When I was out walking, it occurred to me that . . . if I had the same gift you had . . . I could look a little way into the future and . . .'

'And *what*?'

'And . . . you'll hate this, won't you?'

'And do *what* with it, Calum?'

'. . . Use it to get Marianna back.'

'You mean, use it to make money? Why, you . . . Calum Buchanan, I never want to hear one word about this *ever* again.'

'Oh, Morag, I don't mean to offend you . . . It's not the money I want, it's Marianna. How the hell else can I get her back?'

'Not *one* more word . . . What you are talking about is impossible. Impossible and wrong. Now, let that be an end of it. Put the wireless back on *now*. We're missing the news.'

'. . . that interest rates are likely to rise by another half a percent within the month. Deaths in Hong Kong have risen to six and over four hundred are thought to have been detained following the crushing of protests over the human rights record of the Chinese government. In London, the Prime Minister issued a statement calling for restraint and tolerance by the Chinese authorities. Newspapers in Beijing have described foreign criticism of their actions as unwarranted interference in China's internal affairs. World

Trade Organisation officials in Geneva have denied that these events will affect the talks over China's membership of the Organisation. In Washington, a Republican senator, Larry Winston, called for further investigation of China's record on market liberalisation measures before . . .'

'Morag . . .'

'Shush, I'm listening. So should you, this is important.'

'Why on earth . . . ?'

'Are you not worried about China?'

'No. Should I be?'

'Over the last two hundred years the Chinese have been humiliated time and again. They have long memories, those folk. For them the Opium Wars or the Rape of Nanking are like yesterday. Now they have the economic and military power to go with their size, they will want to show the rest of us who's boss, you mark my words.'

'I still don't see why that concerns me, *or* you. If the Chinese decide to go marauding, they'll hardly pick Lewis as their first target.'

'I like to take an interest in the wider world, that's all. It would do you no harm, either.'

'Maybe . . . Morag, about what I asked earlier . . .'

'I said not another word.'

'I know. I wanted to say it was wrong of me. I'll never mention it again. I'm sorry.'

'That's all right. It's time we were both in bed. Sleep well, Calum lad.'

*   *   *

It is about 1,700 kilometres, and half a million miles, from

Sgurr nan Creag to Number 10, Chemin de Bellefontaine. This house gained brief notoriety a few years back when it was described as the most desirable ambassadorial residence in the entire British diplomatic service. It is fashionable to dismiss Geneva as dull; it is no more so than many a French provincial town, and if tectonic movement nudged the city a fraction west, that is exactly what it would be. The British ambassador to the United Nations is spared the need to dwell on this issue. Chemin de Bellefontaine is a couple of miles to the south-east, in the suburb of Cologny, and the breathtakingly beautiful view from his garden, embracing all of the Jura range and half of Lac Leman, is unsullied by any sight of Geneva itself.

He has to brave the town when he is driven along the lake front to the UK Mission in the Rue de Vermont and back to the residence for lunch. An elegant morsel and the briefest of siestas later, the whole journey begins again. It is rare for him to venture townwards at night. Evenings, it is true, are studded with diplomatic dinners, but most of the grander ambassadors and heads of UN agencies have the good sense to reside in the same stylish suburb.

Christopher Ransome's first decision after arrival had been to outlaw weekend work. There were so many delectable things nearby, beginning with Mont Blanc – a mere hour in his sleek convertible – and all but the rarest emergency could be handled satisfactorily by the bright eyes and bushy tails of his Counsellors and First Secretaries. Ransome had not targeted this as his last post before retirement to work round the clock. If that was what he was after, he would have pursued one of the grander embassies that his pedigree would have merited, like Rome, Tokyo, or Paris. All those came with a vast staff, an enormous, echoing residence, constant visits by Ministers, and a knighthood thrown in for good measure.

A knighthood meant little to him. He would have taken it if it had come his way, but it was certainly not worth four frantic years. This was one of the many compensations of staying single. How many wives, he pondered, would gracefully have borne a Mrs in perpetuity when a Ladyship beckoned? The Geneva die being cast, if Madam Right now came along he could at last marry safely and acquire an elegant femme to adorn his dotage. Too late. Too many evenings, week-ends and holidays had gone by in undisturbed comfort, and when he conjured up the ghastly image of some chirruping matron stormtrooping into his life, he quailed. Imagine having Levine's recording of *Rheingold* interrupted by an enquiry about soft furnishings or being compelled to foresake quality time with Trollope for an hour of well-meaning prattle!

Having completed the tedious round of introductory calls on senior UN officials and fellow-ambassadors, his life had settled into an agreeable pattern. Ministerial visits happened rarely and were usually day trips from London. The distance from the residence to the airport meant that most of the Ministers who did stay preferred a hotel and, provided the ambassadorial car was available to ferry them to their early morning flights home, our man was absolved from dancing attendance in person.

The light touch with which Christopher Ransome ran the Mission was genuinely appreciated by his staff. He did not bob up pointlessly at meetings where only experts understood the arcane proceedings, and limited his own participation to occasions, such as the monthly meetings of EU ambassadors, where his presence was incontrovertibly required. It was not that he was lazy, and in previous posts he had confronted necessity with a prodigious workrate. Nor did he have nothing to do: there were occasional magisterial telegrams to be written and regular bouts of lobbying to be done. However, he did not believe in inventing work. He hoped that Geneva would provide a modicum of professional interest at a steady, predictable tempo. He did *not* want a crisis. So the conversation that morning with his Head of Chancery, Nick Whitney, prompted the faintest of queasy feelings.

'Ambassador . . .'

'What's up, Nick?'

'You saw the telegrams from Washington and Beijing about the World Trade Organisation? Sounds like we could be in for some fun and games. If China joins, the Americans want the WTO to have a permanent inspection team monitoring their market liberalisation. This has got the Chinese all in a lather. Our embassy in Beijing is keen to distance Britain from the US initiative. The American ambassador, Art Patterson, has asked to see you today to talk about this. London wants our views on this question by close of play tomorrow.'

'Will they want our thoughts on how the other EU countries will react?'

'Yes. We need to call the other Missions and take some rapid soundings. The Americans will be lobbying *them*, too. The US can't block Chinese membership much longer, but they have some powerful pressure groups back home who are still opposing this. They can't be seen to cave in completely. It could get lively.'

'Mmmm. Nick, it sounds as if I need to start getting myself more up to speed on the workings of the WTO. I wonder if one of your bright young things could knock out a quick idiot's guide?'

'Of course. It'll be on your desk within the hour.'

* * *

'You'll get the hang of it soon enough. Be patient. Weaving is like bicycling. Once you get the knack, you never forget.'

'When did you last ride a bike, Morag?'

'Come to think of it, I don't recall that I ever did.'

'Well, I don't think I'll make a living as a weaver . . . Morag, I've been thinking. Maybe it's time for me to move on.'

'I'm sorry to hear that, Calum. What will you do, go back home?'

'To LA? No, I don't think so. I couldn't stand to be near Marianna if I wasn't *with* her. Maybe I'll try somewhere on the Continent.'

'What would you *do*? How would you live? You don't speak any languages, do you?'

'I can learn.'

'I suppose so. I'd worry for you, though. I can't help feeling that you should bide here longer. At least you have a roof over your head. Time is a great healer, you know. It'll pass, believe me.'

'Oh, yeah? That's good coming from someone who's still in love with a boy who died seventy years ago.'

'It's not the same, Calum. The *pain* went a long time ago, and don't forget, Iain never did anything to hurt me.'

'No? He may not have meant to, but if you ask me, he fucked up your life good and proper.'

'Calum Buchanan, if you use that word one more time in

this house, I'll put you over my knee and give you a good walloping.'

'I'm sorry, Morag. It's not getting any easier and I'm getting more and more depressed. Time's not on my side. If I don't get back in the loop soon, Marianna's gonna forget all about me. If only I could crack the money thing and get back in touch with her . . .'

'Don't start that again, Calum, dear, you know how it upsets you.'

'I know, but you don't know how it feels, Morag. I don't *want* to get over her, I don't want to forget her, I want her *back*. And if I can't have her back, I really might as well . . .'

'Might as well *what*? . . . Take your own life, is that what you mean? Calum, for all the way the Church treated my mother and me, I still believe in God, and that is something for God, not man, to decide. Do you think it never crossed my mind, with what I went through? But it would've been *wrong*, wrong and weak. Think of all you'd be throwing away, all those years you have in front of you.'

'That's exactly what I want to escape: years and years of unhappiness. What's the point?'

'Then don't think about yourself, think of those you would hurt. Imagine how your poor parents would feel.'

'I doubt they'd notice.'

'That's self-pitying nonsense. You must stop wallowing, it'll do you no good.'

'Yeah, you're right. Anyway, I think I'll move on, and I may as well get on with it. I think I'll set off tomorrow.'

'*Tomorrow*? With no money, no plans, and nowhere to go?'

'I'll be okay.'

'Well at least you'll take something from me. It's little

enough, but I've something put by in the tin under my bed. There is almost two thousand pounds.'

'There's no way I'm taking your life savings.'

'Don't refuse me, Calum. If you will not take it all, take half.'

'Okay, I'll take half, and I'll send it back as soon as I'm in work. Morag . . .'

'What is it?'

'Nothing.'

'You weren't going to ask *that* again, were you? I thought you promised . . .'

'I know, that's why I said it was nothing.'

'Calum, it's wrong. And it was *such* a long time ago. I don't think I could still do it if I wanted.'

'Of course. You know, I might go out for a last walk up Ben Mhor before it gets dark. I should be on my way bright and early tomorrow.'

'That's a grand idea. I'll have your meal ready when you're back.'

'See you later, then.'

'Yes . . . Calum, come back here a moment.'

'What is it, Morag?'

'There is something I want to ask. Are you so sure that having Marianna back would make you happy?'

'It's the *only* thing that could. You can't know how it felt to be loved by a woman like that. I know I'm very ordinary, but for a while she made me feel *extraordinary*. Marianna's the key to everything. If she came back to me, I'd have some purpose in life again. Without her . . . it's all meaningless.'

'So you still love her as much as ever?'

'I'll never stop.'

'If you truly feel as much as I did for Iain, I can't be too hard on you. All the same, lad, I hope you know your own mind better than I know mine. I am not at all sure I should be doing this.'

'Doing what?'

'Thinking hard . . . while you are out walking.'

'Thinking hard about *what*?'

'About a turnip or a carrot.'

'*A turnip or a carrot?*'

'That's right. I want you to concentrate like *hell* on which it is, and tell me when you get back.'

* * *

'Again. Write the four objects down one at a time.'

'I'm pooped, Morag. Let's do the rest tomorrow.'

'Now, we are going to do it *now*.'

'We've been going five hours today without a break.'

'Iain and I did more.'

'That was different. You were in love. You enjoyed doing it.'

'Well, pretend you're in love with me.'

'You're too old.'

'You could be my . . . what was that word? . . . toyboy.'

'Yuck.'

'*Yuck?*'

'Sorry, I didn't mean it like that.'

'Get on with it, you're *pathetic*. We've only been going a fortnight and you want to stop already.'

'No, I don't. I just want a break . . . Listen. That's the tweed man again. What should I tell him this time?'

83

'Say I'm still sick. Tell him to come back on Friday.'

'. . . He says it's okay, but he really needs your tweed then. You'd better do it, Morag. I don't want to get you in trouble.'

'It'll get done. This is more important. We have *months* of this ahead of us. You had better get used to it, you wimp.'

'Who're you calling wimp? You only learnt that word from *me* last week.'

7

Fast Forward

As soon as the lottery result came through, Calum Buchanan picked up his fork again. He was ravenous, and the shepherd's pie was tasty. He munched away, a benign smile on his face, daydreaming of what Marianna would say. He hoped she and Brett hadn't taken off somewhere for the weekend; he *couldn't* contain his excitement till Monday. Maybe he should suggest giving her half the money outright, so they would be truly equal from the start. Yeah, that sounded good. He fashioned one last forkful from the smeared traces on the plate, then went over and ordered a whole new helping and a second pint of beer.

*   *   *

That same Saturday evening in Geneva, Christopher Ransome thought he would *never* get to finish his dinner. It was the third time in an hour that he had been called to the phone. The brouhaha over China's membership of the World Trade Organisation had changed his life. Over the last few months he had rarely made it back to Cologny for lunch, and siestas were a distant memory. The luxurious calm he had sought had

85

vanished, replaced by pressure, deadlines, and adrenalin. He was loving every moment of it.

Throughout his career, he had avoided any involvement with commercial or economic matters. Nowadays, lip service had to be paid to helping with trade promotion and it was getting trickier for diplomats to avoid at least *one* stint at it, though most of them still viewed it like nappy changing: impossible to refuse, but to be undertaken so unenthusiastically that the invitation was not repeated.

Multilateral trade negotiations were an honourable exception and had provided diplomats with many entertainingly dyspeptic international exchanges, especially at the launch of the Uruguay Round at Punta del Este back in 1986 and during the 1994 sessions in Marrakesh, which ended the Round and established the World Trade Organisation.

This particular brand of entertainment had never come Ransome's way. The WTO was one of many Geneva-based organisations that he could bone up about on a need-to-bone basis. He was an old boning hand and had soon absorbed all he needed to know it.

It wasn't that Ransome had to participate directly in the protracted negotiations with China over joining the WTO. The external trade policy of member states is handled by the European Union Commission itself, so it was Gerhard Hirsch, the Commission's ambassador in Geneva, who dealt face to face with that formidable Minister, Tian Yi, and her entourage from Beijing. Ambassadors from European countries were only present as observers.

When it came to approving or rejecting an application to join, theoretically all members had equal votes. In practice, it was the US, the EU and Japan that held sway. Japan was a pushover for the Chinese. The Japanese might wring their hands in private over some of Chinese demands, but as China's biggest trading partner, they wouldn't say boo to the golden goose, let alone kill it. America was tougher. China remained an emotive issue in the US, and the hardliners had made the Chinese sweat every year over renewing the package of concessions known as Most Favoured Nation treatment. Beijing had not only worried about those renewals; they massively resented the humiliation of this procedure, especially as it provided a regular platform for meddling do-gooders to raise human rights issues. As China's economic might grew, and with it the scale of American investment there, renewal was bound to become almost automatic. Nevertheless, Beijing was pleased that being allowed into the WTO would sweep away that infuriating process once and for all.

Not that the Americans readily agreed to their membership; they had found one reason after another to delay it. However, once the EU supported China's application, the Americans could not oppose it for ever. So the pass was sold, and the debate moved on to the detail.

China wanted permanent exemptions from many of the key WTO rules, prompting all other member states to throw up their arms in horror of an idea that would have driven a coach and horses through the most basic obligations. The Chinese backed down, and the focus switched to transition arrangements, the terms and duration of temporary exemptions. Everyone knew how important this was. Give China too much rope and they would mount a huge assault on overseas markets, while simultaneously blocking foreigners' access to their own market long enough to let Chinese companies build impregnable domestic strongholds. This was especially worrying if those strongholds were controlled by the Chinese army. The diplomatic battle raged.

Tian Yi played her hand with great skill, and little by little the scope of concessions on steel, chemicals, aircraft, machine tools and cars increased. It looked as though financial services and intellectual property would slide down the same slippery slope. The Americans were determined not to give ground on this, and yet knew that acceptance by the Europeans would undermine their own position gravely. The potential for Britain to get caught in bitter cross-fire was all too obvious.

And so struck Christopher Ransome's hour. He had the unique qualification among European ambassadors in Geneva of being a sinologist. He had studied Chinese language and literature at Oxford, and on the strength of that, had been posted to Beijing in the seventies. For all the suave urbanity of his fellow-ambassadors in Geneva, they persisted in thinking of China as a firmly closed book and considered the Chinese as creatures from another planet. Having among their number a colleague who not only knew China, but spoke their impenetrable language was a fascinating novelty, and in reporting to their respective capitals on likely Chinese tactics they drew heavily on his opinions.

In dealings with Gerhard Hirsch, Ransome used his advantage discreetly and wisely. Naturally, he could not be seen to usurp Hirsch's authority, but that did not stop the two of them dining together with unusual frequency. Hirsch was bamboozled by the Chinese approach to negotiations and badly needed expert advice. Christopher Ransome was ideally positioned to assist, and if this fortuitously provided natural opportunities to influence Hirsch along the lines most favoured by Her Majesty's Government, then Ransome was merely doing his job.

Finally, it was all resolved with surprising speed. The UK

got most of what it wanted without getting too exposed. Lynne O'Neill, the US Trade Representative, huffed and puffed, then went along with the wider consensus, and Tian Yi showed a shrewd sense of when concessions were inevitable, undertaking to sell off the army's monopolies. A deal was struck, and to the sound of popping champagne corks China joined the WTO.

The self-congratulatory mood in Geneva and Western capitals evaporated within months when the first signs came through that China had no intention whatsoever of honouring its promises. Which was why Christopher Ransome's dinner was being interrupted.

*　　*　　*

Calum walked briskly home from the pub and immediately telephoned to get confirmation of his win. There had been seven winning tickets in all. The lottery's popularity had waned over the years and even the Saturday pot often fell below £5 million. This week was a little better at £6.2 million. Having three of the seven, he should get £2.85, or in real money just north of $4 mill. Not superwealth, but not too scummy for a £3 investment, and close enough that he need have no qualms in rounding it up to the magic five million.

Tracy, the girl from the lottery organisers, Avalon, sounded attractive. Did he want her to come over right away, or would he prefer tomorrow? No, not tonight. If he got hold of Marianna, they might want to chat and plan for hours. He arranged the visit for eleven o'clock on Sunday morning, poured himself a whisky, and raised his glass in tribute to Morag. He had missed her a whole lot since he left Lewis. She had insisted that she didn't want to know how he was making his money, and that he should not attempt to contact her until he got Marianna back or abandoned the mission. If all went well in the phone call to LA, he might try to blast through the ether and tell the old girl tonight.

'Hello, this is the Marquardt residence.'

'Hi, is Marianna there?'

'She's busy.'

'This is important, can you connect me please?'

'I'm sorry, sir. She gave specific instructions not to be disturbed.'

'What's your name?'

'Maria.'

'Maria, I'm Calum Buchanan, Marianna's . . . former husband. This is a vital family matter. Would you mind letting her know I'm holding? She'll want to take the call, for sure.'

'Okay, please hold on . . .'

'. . . Hello.'

'Marianna. *Hi!*'

'No, sir, it's Maria again. She says if you leave a number she'll call you back when it's convenient.'

'Okay, I'll give you it. It's nine forty-five p.m. here now, so it would be good if she could call in the next hour or so . . .'

The level of the whisky sank with the hours. What was keeping her? Everything should be okay now, but the wait still made him nervous. He doodled another sketch of Morag's blackhouse, then went back to drumming his fingers. He dialled again.

'Maria, is that you? Calum Buchanan again . . . No, I know. It's just I wanted to say I'm still up if Marianna wants to call . . . Oh, another hour at least. I may stay up the whole night. Tell her any time's fine . . . Thanks. Bye.'

The bottle emptied. Before Lewis, he'd never been a big whisky man, but now it was pretty much his tipple. One thing he would do in LA was build a library of every malt whisky under the sun. More finger drumming. What would be best to suggest? That he fly right back? Or that she jump on a plane to Europe? Maybe get remarried in Lewis, with Morag as a witness.

What would he have done without Morag? She'd shown her severe side when he left, mind you, with her fierce parting speech. Tell *no-one* how you came by this, and *no-one* how you do it. If you can make your fortune with it, God bless you, but *never* say how. When you have what you need to get Marianna back, do *not* try to use the gift again. I did not help you in order to make you rich and powerful, I helped you because your heart was breaking. Do not betray me, my lad. If you keep your word, I will be your fast friend to the end of my days. If you fail me, I will never speak to you again. Do you understand?

She made him repeat the promise three times before she softened. They had a last dram together though it was scarcely ten in the morning. Her face was terribly drawn. The effort of training him had taken a great toll over the months. He hoped she would now rest and recover. When he rose to go, she hugged him fraillly, deeply. He felt the shudder as she pulled back her arms and let him go. Calum expected her to stand by the open door until he was out of sight and intended to keep turning back, waving until he was out of sight. But

91

she closed the door quickly behind him and he couldn't see whether she was watching through the grimy glass. He never knew if she cried.

From the stiffness of his neck, he must have fallen asleep on the sofa at a very odd angle. Four o'clock. Eight p.m. in California. Time to try again. He sensed this Maria was on his side. With a bit of charm and persistence it would be okay. He went on at her till he got through to Marianna.

'Calum, is that you? We have guests. Please do not bully my staff again. I *cannot* possibly talk now. If there *is* some reason, you can call back on Monday or, better still, next week. I have to go now . . .'

'Marianna, I *did* it.'

'Did what?'

'Got the money. Five million dollars.'

'How did you manage that?'

'They have a lottery thing here. I won it. Now we can be together again.'

'*What?*'

'You said if I got money, it'd be different.'

'Look, Calum, I do vaguely remember saying something about five million a while back. That was long before I felt so deeply about Brett.'

'I don't get it. What are you saying?'

'I'm saying that I've changed a lot since then. It may have *appeared* that money was a big thing for me. Now I know it was only a reflection of a deeper yearning. I understand much better now what's truly important.'

'Like what?'

'Simple things that money can't buy, like walking along our beach in Maui or through the vines we're planting at the ranch in Napa. Our home here in Brentwood Park may be lovely, but Brett and I would *happily* give all this up and go live in a log cabin together. Basically, Calum, I'm saying I've moved on, I've learnt to connect.'

'Connect with *what*?'

'With my inner self, and with what I really need from a partner. What attracted me to Brett wasn't his money, it was his drive and dynamism and confidence. You may find it hard to see this, Calum, but success is such a positive, it makes people at ease with themselves. I'm happy for you that you've . . . lucked out and got some money to start over, but, knowing you, you could just as soon blow it and be back where you were before.'

'You mean a loser?'

'You said it, not me.'

'Marianna, you said time and again if I had five million clear, you'd come back to me. I sweated blood to get it and . . .'

'You sweated blood to win a *lottery*? Give me a break! Have you even been in work?'

'Yes I have, goddammit. I kept faith with you, kept my side of the bargain, and now you start saying—'

'Pardon me, Calum, but I'm getting pretty fed up with this. It wasn't a contract, it was just . . . words. If it helped give you a kick start, I don't regret it. There were other reasons our marriage didn't work out, not only money . . .'

'Like what?'

'Calum, what's the point? We've been through this a hundred times. It's in the past. It's *over*, Calum. Brett and I are very happy together. We're planning to get married and start a family.'

'Start a *family*? You always said—'

'People change. Maybe I felt that way because subconsciously I knew it was wrong with you, that it wouldn't last. Now I'm more in touch with myself, I feel I've grown enough to take on the enormous responsibility of parenthood.'

'Marianna, don't do this . . .'

'One moment . . . tell him I'll be right there . . . Calum, I have to go now. I'm being rude to our guests and unfair to Brett. I'm glad about your stroke of luck. Use the money well. In time you'll get over me and find someone else, someone more suited . . .'

'I have enough money now for us to live together in luxury for the rest of our lives . . .'

'Calum, stop going on about this. If you really wanna know, these days five million seems like loose change. If Brett's latest deal goes through, he stands to make fifty on that alone, so quit talking like you've *made* it or something.'

'Marianna, I love you with every fibre of my body. I'm not giving up on you, I'm coming to take you back.'

'Calum, remember, you tried some of that weirdo shit on me after I moved out. I called the cops then and I'll do it again. You don't know what love *means*. Get yourself together and keep out of my life.'

'. . .'

'Don't give me the silent treatment, Calum. I'm sorry to get heavy duty on you. At some level I still care about you, but I *don't* wanna hear from you again for the time being. When you're settled and *with* someone, maybe . . . but for now I want you out of my face. Okay?'

'. . .'

'I don't want to end this call this way, but if you're gonna sulk . . . Okay, I'm gonna hang up . . . *Goodbye*.'

He put the phone down and crumpled in a heap on the

floor. How could she *be* like that, after he'd slaved for a year to get what she wanted? Oh, *God*, how it hurt! As he replayed the conversation in his head, the shards of her words cut him again. It had never *occurred* to him that Marianna might *love* that disgusting old man. If she had been together with any good-looking guy, Calum would have thrown in the towel right away. But Brett Marquardt had a face like a wrinkly mutant sweet potato. Calum had been *certain* it was only Marquardt's money that kept her there, and if he matched that Marianna had no reason not to come back. Now if she and Brett had children, it might be *years* before they split up. Oh, Jesus, what was he going to do?

He went into the bedroom, picked up Marianna's photograph and held it to his chest. She didn't know what she was saying . . . she *couldn't*. Unless she really felt nothing for him, the news must have unsettled her. Would she call him back later? He could see her point about the lottery. If she thought it was pure luck, why *should* she be impressed? Lottery winners were hardly role-models. You saw them every week in the British tabloids, moving out of their council houses, buying villas in Marbella, and unloading the lot in three months. If Marianna knew what he'd really achieved . . .

He looked at his watch. Oh Christ, it was four forty. Better try for some sleep before the Avalon people came round.

8

'Well, hello, Mr Buchanan, I'm Tracy. This is Emma, from our financial advisory team. Congratulations on your win. May we come in?'

'Of course . . . It's a bit of a tip. I was up late . . . celebrating.'

'So I see.'

'Oh, throw those anywhere. Take a seat . . . Where do we begin?'

'First things first. Could we see the tickets?'

'Sure . . . there.'

'That's fine. We're happy to confirm your winnings. Two million, eight hundred and forty-four thousand pounds. You know, it's quite unusual for our clients to have multiple bets on the same numbers.'

'There's no rule against it or anything?'

'Oh, no.'

'Good.' What a dummy, thought Calum. Why didn't I do more of them?

'How many other combinations did you back this week?'

'Nothing else. I had a . . . hunch.'

'Well, lucky old you, is all I can say. Wish we got hunches like that, eh Emma? . . . Anyway, I must stop chatting and get on with business. Let me tell you what we need to do. First, I'll take down some personal details. This is strictly for our own files and won't be revealed to *anyone* without your approval. Now, as you know, it is entirely *your* choice whether to keep your success confidential or to inform the media . . . No, I thought not. After we have the personal information, we move on to the money itself. We find that many of our winners don't have a lot of experience of investing, so Emma will give you a few pointers on how to approach that. Then we'd like to have a chat about *reacting* to a big win. Many people find it very disorienting, especially if they've never had a lot of money before . . .' She couldn't quite stop her eyes surveying the squalor of the room to illustrate her point.

Calum was on the point of airily dismissing all this, assuring them of his familiarity with the huge sums he dealt in every day, but caught himself just in time and stubbed out the words. He might not need the advice, but then they might leave. He didn't feel like being alone so soon. He mumbled thanks and pretended to take notes as Emma plodded remorselessly through kindergarten explanations of equities, dividends and bonds. He spent the time wondering if he could find a way to invite the shapely Tracy for lunch without her sidekick tagging along. Ingenuity and courage failed him and the girls departed, trumpeting renewed expressions of cheery congratulations.

Sleep and the visit had shut out the stinging horror of Marianna's words. Now it all flooded back. She had not said *one* kind thing. How could he have deluded himself so completely? Was there never a chance that she would come back, or had he played it all wrong, springing it on her like that? Should he have written to her, or at least called when Brett wasn't around?

For nigh on an hour, he lay on the sofa, in a state of unrelenting self-torture, his hangover pounding furiously all the while. He *had* to pull himself out of this black mood.

Maybe a walk would help. He showered, shaved, pulled on warm clothes and caught a taxi to Hyde Park.

There was too much weather about for it to be a park kind of day. The wind tugged and jostled and rain threatened constantly. The few walkers maintained a brisk pace, heads down, hands firmly pocketed. Overhead, low clouds jogged by athletically. Calum took no notice; he was too busy working himself into another state about Marianna. Not interested in his money, was she? A couple of years ago she'd have sold her soul for a tenth of that. He knew what she had in mind when she recommended he find someone more *suited*. She meant someone less beautiful, less challenging, less glamorous, less of a woman. Someone more average, more dowdy, more plain, with lower life goals, someone who wouldn't mind being with a loser. Well, to hell with loser, he was gonna find himself a girl as gorgeous as Marianna and with talent and goodness dripping from every pore. If only this goddess would come *soon* and take away the awful, gut-wrenching pain.

He drifted over towards Speakers' Corner. The orators were duller and dafter than usual, the chill wind crimping the flow of their rhetoric. Calum gave up on it quickly and wandered on down Park Lane. It was past one now and he felt a drink calling him. He'd have one at the Dorchester if they'd serve him dressed like that, or the Metropolitan if they wouldn't.

The walk took him past one car showroom after another, prompting the first thought of the money itself. He could afford anything now. Mercedes-Benz? Too plush and middle-aged, though the new SL looked rather sharp. BMW? That's what he'd had in California. Now he wasn't so sure about the image. Borzo, Dougie and Cathy drove them: that said it all. Both Audi and Lexus were overly sensible. He walked on a

99

few blocks. The Jaguar sports was too American-looking for his taste. Porsche? Nice lines, well built, pity about the owners. On the other hand, Porsches always came with good-looking passengers as standard equipment, so he shouldn't be *too* hard on them. Lamborghini? In the metallic purple of the display car, it was more of an automotive statement than he could imagine making.

There were no more showrooms. What had he missed? Rolls-Royce? Forget it. Hey, where was Ferrari, the car that made Marianna drool when one snarled by? He smiled at how badly he'd wanted one back then and how much Lewis had influenced him. Now he'd probably prefer a Land Rover if he bought a car at all. Hang on, though. If Marianna changed her mind and flew over to England, wouldn't it be *great* to meet her at the airport in a brand new Ferrari? They could tour the Continent in it for a few weeks and then drive it up to Lewis and take Morag for a spin. Boy, would that blow her octogenarian mind! Why not order one tomorrow? He could get some other things for Marianna, like jewellery and clothes. If they did do a tour, he would take them along secretly and give her wonderful presents every day. What about things for himself? He guessed he would need to look smart for Marianna. Apart from that, there was nothing much he wanted. Ironic, really.

* * *

Sunday morning got off to a bad start in the Georgetown house of US Special Trade Representative Lynne O'Neill. Lynne had come back on Saturday night exhausted from a series of trade talks in Santiago, Lima and Buenos Aires, and had *sworn* to her long-suffering husband, Ed, that Sunday would be sacrosanct. The phone had roused them at half past seven. It was now nearly nine, Ed had stomped off on his own for a walk, and she was no nearer to getting this low-life off the line. Indeed, he was working himself up into more and more of a lather.

'If we don't see some action on this soon, we're goin' public on it ourselves. I'm not bluffin', Lynne. I've been jerked around by those Chinese long enough.'

She hated the familiar way Tyne addressed her. To have reached high office as she had and be lectured like this stuck in her craw. She put him on hold for a minute, just to piss him off.

'. . . Sorry, Bob.'

'I was sayin', Lynne, I've had *hundreds* of my people in Shanghai for *months*. I *never* trusted the Chinese. *Wait*, you said, *be patient*, it'll come good. Well now I see how good it's come.'

She held the phone away from her ear. The storm hadn't blown itself out yet.

'. . . Not only do we get no government contracts, now their precious Sunrise Corporation has copied our consumer products. Yes, *our* products. They may have a few different tweaks here and there, but for all practical purposes those are *our* programs. The performance is *identical* for most applications. Sunrise are selling them there for *half* what we charge. If we cut our prices they'll attack us for dumping and you'll damn well *support* them. Whose goddam side are you guys *on*?'

She was hating every minute of this, but for the time being she had no option but to soak it up. Relations between the US and China had taken a battering during the WTO accession talks. It had all been to no end. The Europeans, with the slight exception of the Brits, had caved in and left them high and dry. The US government had crash-landed between two stools, pleasing no-one. For years people like Bob Tyne had argued that if they didn't take a hard line with China the US would get ripped off, and he was incandescent when she and the White House backed down in Geneva. The way the Chinese had behaved since they joined had put Lynne O'Neill in one hell of a hole, and having Tyne whip up anti-China fury in the business community wouldn't help. She *had* to make the right noises and rein him back.

'Bob, the President and I understand the strength of feeling on this. We really do believe it's part of their teething troubles. It was bound to take some time for them to implement the agreements fully. As you know, there are clear transitional arrangements in place . . .'

'They're not working in intellectual property.'

'We understand that arrangements for other product sectors are consuming a *vast* proportion of their Ministry's time—'

'Bullshit. Forgive me for speaking straight . . .' Even Tyne knew this was pushing his luck with the Special Trade Representative. '. . . There is no reason why the Ministry cannot implement the measures for government software contracts *immediately*. However, there's another thing that worries us even more. At Geneva the Chinese undertook to sell off their military's main commercial assets, right?'

'Yes.'

'Well, we *all* know how significant Sunrise is, and I hear that the Chinese military *still* control it. Those new owners they transferred it to are just a front . . .'

Jesus! How the hell had Tyne picked this up? She'd only seen the CIA report on Friday herself. It looked as if it

102

was true. The nominee ownership was all a sham. If Sunrise continued to dominate the Chinese software market, their army would make *billions* from that investment alone. If Tyne let rip publicly with that accusation there was no telling how much fur would fly. She needed to buy time, fast.

'Bob, I think you should know that we're not sitting on our hands over this. In strictest confidence, I can tell you that we are looking very closely at the WTO dispute settlement procedures. They've never been used before, but they do have teeth, and if we find evidence that the Chinese are deliberately failing to implement the agreed measures, the US government will not hesitate to—'

'Can you kick them out? . . . Can you expel them from the Organisation?'

'No.'

'Great. So now they're in, they can do what the hell they like.'

'That's not true. If we protested, the WTO would convene the Disputes Panel in Geneva which would look at the rights and wrongs. If there was a clear infringement, they would adjudge in our favour and the Chinese would have to comply.'

'And if they didn't?'

'We would be free to impose suitable penalties.'

'And how fast can we get this Panel together?'

'It's unlikely we can get it before next year.'

From Tyne's intake of breath O'Neill realised this was 180 degrees the wrong tack to pacify him. When it came, his response erupted like a volcano.

'*NEXT YEAR?* . . . Do you have *any* idea what a delay like that would mean? We'd be outa the ball game for ever!'

'Hold on, Bob, I've said it's *unlikely*, I didn't say it's *impossible*. If the President and I get right behind this, we might—'

'I can tell you, Lynne, if you guys don't do *something*, and do it fast, I'm goin' public on this with all guns blazing.'

Great. Right back where they started the conversation. What an asshole the guy was, multi-billionaire or not. This was the last time she was going to take a call from him at home. And before she got him off the line, he went through his whole damn litany again.

*   *   *

Calum spent Sunday night at home with a bottle or two of wine. He yielded to the temptation to call Marianna again, and wisely hung up when a man answered. He cheered himself up by reconsidering his options for quitting the bank. Previously, he'd assumed he would leave without a word, simply never go in again. On reflection, wasn't a little teasing called for?

So it was that on Monday morning he went to the bank, pointedly late at 10.30. He strolled insouciantly in to the fourteenth floor, got a coffee from the machine and, without a sideways glance or a greeting to anyone, sat down and switched his screens on. He had it all worked out. He *wanted* them to know he'd struck gold, but didn't plan to admit it was the lottery. He scanned the screen with apparent earnestness, tapped the glass with his pencil's eraser-head, and, sighing contentedly, lolled back in his chair and put his feet up on the table.

'Gooood, up another half mill.'

'What, the Swedish?'

He managed the right tone to Cathy, distracted, as if only half aware of her presence.

'No, not the Swedish, we sold that on Friday. I'm talking personal account. I took a little punt with my bonus.'

'And you're up half a *mill*? Half a mill what? Yen?'

'Greenbacks. I didn't say I was *up* half a million, I said up *another* half million.'

Doug perked up at this. 'Your bonus was only, 'ow much was it?'

'Fifteen.'

'Yeah, that's what I thought. 'Ow much you say you're up?'

Wait for it, thought Calum, savour it, say it nice and slow, nice and quiet.

'Four and a half million.'

Borzo's head was in its usual resting place on his right hand. His elbow slid right off the desk, bringing his chin crashing down onto the hard surface.

'Bollocks.' Doug had a way with words. 'Absolute total bollocks.' His denial didn't make him look happy all the same. Mike got closer to the truth.

'What you been buying? Options on the three-fifteen at Newmarket?'

'Noooo.' Calum sucked his pencil, leant forward towards the screen and smiled another satisfied smile. The entire team jumped up simultaneously and huddled behind his chair. He changed the page on the Bloomberg screen before they could see what he had been looking at.'

'What the hell is it, Calum, mate? Tell us, for fuck's sake.'

He had them now.

'A little warrant play I figured out. Pretty heavily geared, I have to admit.'

'Are you still in it?'

'Sure am, this one's gonna run and run. I reckon I'll double up again by the end of the week. It's not as wild a punt as it sounds. Bossman told me I should communicate more. So, let me tell you, I have some *very* private information on this one.'

'Can we get in on it?' There was fire and pleading in Cathy's eyes.

'I'd like to help you guys out, but my source made me swear I'd tell no-one.'

'Fuck 'im, we won't tell anyone, will we?'

'Sorry, Adam, I gave my word.'

'You . . . *bastard*. If we got a line like that, we'd let you in, no question.'

'Sure thing, Mike. Remember all those nice things you said to me last week?'

'That didn't mean nothing. We was foolin' about, that was all. Can't you handle a joke? Come on, matey, do us a favour, we'll help you out next time.'

Solemnly, Calum shook his head. Doug returned to the charge.

'I think this is all the biggest load of ol' bollocks. He ain't made no millions, the bastard's just windin' us up.'

The scheduled phone call came in right on the button. Calum had to lay it on thick to make sure they understood.

'Thank you, Mr Williams. Now how are we getting on with that new car . . . ?'

You could have heard a pin drop.

'. . . No, it's only the 555 I'm interested in. The 375 is too slow . . . Yes, I do know about the waiting list . . . I'm happy

106

to pay that premium, *provided* it's in red . . . No, nothing else
. . . That's too late. Next week at latest. Good. You'll let me
know? Till this afternoon then. Thank you.'

Adam looked seriously impressed.

'You gettin' a F'rari?'

'That'll do to start with. I might get some other cars, too.'

Borzo had a brainwave and leapt out of his seat with
delight.

'Oi, 'ave you filled in a dealin' form? You gotta fill in a
dealin' form, it's the bank rule. If you don't tell us *right now*
now what stock you're in, I'll go straight to Bossman, I'm
tellin' ya.'

'Oh no, Borzo, don't do that, I *need* this job.'

Borzo's dander was up so high he had his irony detection
kit switched off.

'Just watch me, you Yankee turd.'

He disappeared into the glass box, had a brief conversation
and marched back, giving Calum the finger so close it almost
went up his left nostril. Bossman opened the box door and
yelled out,

'Buchanan, I want a word with you. *Now.*'

'I guess I'm for the high jump.' They were convinced. Calum
had more theatrical talent than he'd realised. Borzo smirked
triumphantly.

'Serves ya right, you selfish fucker.'

With head slightly bowed, Calum entered the box and
closed the door behind him.

'Siddown.'

He sat.

'Now let's start with what you mean, strolling in at this
time?'

'There was this interesting programme on breakfast TV . . .'

107

'What . . . ?'

'. . . Apparently sparrowhawks are making a big comeback in some urban areas where they were almost extinct.'

'Shaddup. Borzo says you've been dealing unauthorized? Is that true?'

'You know, there's something I've always wanted to ask you. Do you drag your hair sideways across your scalp to *emphasise* how bald you are?'

'Answer the fucking question . . . NOW!'

'Yeah, I had a flutter. So far I'm up, oh, I'd say about ten times your bonus.'

'Did you know that buying or selling securities without filling in a dealing form is a dismissable offence? And I'm talking *summary* dismissal!'

'*Oh, NO. Not that!*'

'Yes it is, sweetheart. So you can start by writing down the details of all the trades you've made and we'll unwind them. Any unauthorised profits you've made go to the bank, that's the rule.'

'Listen, I have something to tell you that's *very* confidential, *very* private. I can only say it if I whisper. Come closer.'

Calum crooked his index finger. Bossman looked exasperated but couldn't stop himself leaning in slightly

'*Closer*. I don't want anyone else to hear . . .'

He moved in another inch and turned his ear towards Calum.

'. . . It's this really *personal* thing, you see. It can be *our* little secret. You promise not to tell anyone?'

Bossman nodded impatiently.

'It's that . . . I want you . . . to take my job as a suppository.'

'WHAT???? Why, you little *fucking*—'

If he could have got within range, Bossman would have

hit him. Calum jumped back from the table and danced out
of the glass box, leaving Bossman vermilion-faced, punching
numbers furiously into the phone to get Security to throw him
out. Calum paused at his desk just long enough to scribble
something and stuff it in an envelope. The team stared at him
in wide-eyed silence. He smiled back warmly.

'Well, I'll be off. See you around. You guys've been real
fun to hang out with. Thanks for welcoming a foreigner in
your midst. I've changed my mind, I think I *will* leave a
little suggestion for you all. Don't open it till I'm in the
elevator, then act on it as quick as you can. He placed the
envelope carefully on his desk and walked round the circle,
solemnly shaking hands with each one. He walked over to
the lift and pressed the button. Looking back, he saw Borzo
make a move.

'No, no, Borzo, *down* boy! No peeking till I'm gone. SIT!'

Borzo did as commanded. All their eyes were glued to him
as the doors opened and with the sweetest farewell wave
he was gone. The instant the doors closed, Borzo leapt from
his chair and snatched the envelope away from several other
claws. He tore it open and yelped with rage.

His constant use of the foulest oaths left no epithets in
reserve for special occasions. Brand new words for private
body parts might have been coined at that instant, had not
Borzo's creativity deserted him, forcing him to make do with
a spitting recital of his usual brutish repertoire. The note fell
from his hands to the floor. Doug picked it up. He read out
the suggestion. It did not refer to investment policy. The three
words were unambiguous. En masse, they rose to their feet
and howled in unison with Borzo.

9

Giving up work felt great for a few hours. Then it simply meant he had more time to dwell on his unhappiness. Late on Monday afternoon he took his mind off it with a Bond Street shopping spree for Marianna, tingling with the sensation of choosing wildly extravagant things, delightedly imagining her excited reaction to each gift. He stayed in on Monday night, willing the phone to ring and be her. It stayed silent. He watched TV distractedly and went to bed soon after ten. By lunchtime on Tuesday, the handsomely wrapped pile of gifts seemed only to emphasise Marianna's absence, like a laden Christmas tree in a house without children. He felt a strong urge to get out, away from the pile.

He took in two movies that afternoon, then passed some time walking aimlessly around the West End. He mustn't let this get him down. If only he had some feminine company to help him forget the pain for a while. It didn't matter if she was no goddess; anyone kind would do. He hung hopefully around a few clubs, getting a few looks, some giggles from the gaggles, but no approaches. At midnight, back to the flat, lonely as hell.

On Wednesday a downpour imprisoned him until early evening when he set off again for the West End. After three hours desperation finally overpowered shyness and he asked the waiter in the bar at the top of the Park Lane Hilton to offer a drink to the two girls at a window table. Leaning back slightly, he watched the foray in a mirror, avoiding the embarrassment of a direct line of sight. He saw the momentary lack of comprehension, the sideways movement of the waiter's head to indicate the source of the generosity, the none too friendly flash of their eyes, and their simultaneous refusals. Oh God, now he was trapped. They were between him and the door and he couldn't face running that contemptuous gauntlet.

By and by another girl came into the room and sat at a table on her own. Nice-looking, good legs, pretty green dress. The two vixens were watching him watching her, sneers at the ready. The new girl glanced in Calum's direction and they shared a moment's eye contact. Sending drinks over didn't seem to work too well. Could he risk actually *approaching* her himself?

His nerve subsided. Better wait a few minutes. He stared out at the night panorama. When he turned back with studied casualness, the waiter was bringing her bill. Frantically, Calum waved for his. The waiter nodded acknowledgement, but stayed by the girl as she finished paying. Christ, she was signing! That meant she must be staying at the hotel. On her own, probably at a loose end. She stuffed the receipt in her handbag, stood, and with a last look in Calum's direction, made her way out. *Where* was that frigging bill? Come *on*, man, he was going to lose her. How much had they been, his two whiskies? £15? £20? The waiter was still fiddling around at the till. Through the glass doors he saw the lift open, disgorging new arrivals. She was still there, waiting to get in. He threw down £30 in ten-pound notes and rushed past the lip-curling duette, who were willing the lift doors closed as fervently as he prayed for them to stay open. They won. The green dress disappeared into the machine and the doors sliced shut, defeating his final sprint.

What a fool for not making a move sooner! He would have one last drink at the Inn on the Park and go home.

* * *

She was chatting with the barman, twiddling her twizzle stick, her shapely, slender legs coiled snake-like around the tall stool, the off-the-shoulder black dress revealing her unseasonable tan. She had got through six tonic waters and had almost given up for the night when the slim young American came in, sat at the bar, leaving one stool between them as a decency zone, and ordered a Bowmore whisky. She was very doubtful that he was the type, but you could never be sure. Could be lonely or bored, a long way from home. With a show of exaggerated interest, he examined the vast ranks of bottles arrayed behind the bar, occasionally sneaking a sideways glance at her. She was expert at exuding an air of friendliness, but this time it wasn't working. Was he *never* going to speak? Looked like she would have to help him out.

'Are you from America? I *love* America. Which part?'

'California.'

'Lucky you!'

'You've been?'

'Mmmm. Had a wonderful time. What brings you to London?'

'Business.'

'D'you always stay at the Inn on the Park?'

'Oh, I'm not *staying* here . . . I keep a place in London. How 'bout you?'

'I live here. I was supposed to be meeting a girl friend. Looks like she stood me up.'

'Same with me. I was scheduled to meet . . . one of my staff. Hungry work hanging round waiting. Say, if we've both been stood up, how'd you feel about a bite to eat? I'm sure they have a decent restaurant here.'

Her instinct told her this would go nowhere, but, olives and nuts apart, she hadn't eaten, and sardines on toast were all that awaited her back at the flat. She flashed a smile.

'What about your colleague? He'll turn up any minute, won't he?'

'To hell with him. Let's get outa here before he shows . . . excuse me, I'll take the check . . . No, together's fine.'

'I pay my own way.'

'No, I insist. There, it's done.'

'How was the filet mignon?'

'Ve-ry good. The wine was *delicious*.'

'You can't beat a Lafite.'

'So, tell me more about your business, Calum. Is it all films, or are you in TV as well?'

'Oh yeah, we do a lot of TV. Music, too.'

'How fascinating. How wonderful it must be to have a job that's *so* stimulating and pays so well.'

'I guess I've been lucky. There are downsides, like the travel.'

'If it's all these private planes and Concorde, you won't get much sympathy from me. Where's your place in London?'

'Holland Park. Sometimes I don't even bother going back there if it gets late, I just flop down in the nearest hotel. I might tonight. Hey, this won't do at all, Sophie. We've spent the whole time talking about me. Let's get back onto you. Where do *you* hang your hat?'

'Maida Vale. Well, more like Kilburn, in truth. I bet you've never been. We don't get many film moguls round our way.'

'Like it there?'

'It's okay. Well, it's not okay, *actually*. It's a tiny rented place. I'm hoping to move and buy, *if* I can get a mortgage. It's difficult if you're self-employed.'

'Banks are the same everywhere, never willing to help entrepreneurs. You said you had your own business, but you didn't say what line of business it was.'

She got out a long, elegant cigarette and held Calum's hand steady as he lit it for her, then inhaled deeply, looking straight into his eyes as the smoke fled her nostrils. This was it. If her guess was right, he would go red in the face, pay the bill and be gone with hardly a goodnight. She took her voice down an octave to super-husky.

'Well, actually, I'm in the business of entertaining men.'

He *did* go red in the face, but it was hard to tell how much it was the embarrassment and how much it was the massive coughing fit. Sophie drew deep on her cigarette and watched him with amusement. It was probably the first time he'd even *spoken* to a hooker. She sensed that through his splutterings he was completely at sea as to what to do next. Was he trying to think of a way to get out of this situation without looking deeply uncool, or was part of him tempted? If so, she needed to help him by being the first one to speak.

'I hope I didn't shock you, Calum, I thought you'd guessed. Don't get me wrong, I don't mean that you and I have to do . . . anything, though you might enjoy it if we did. Mine is a *very* special service. Any time you're tired after one of your big business deals, I could help ease away your stress. You could think of it as a kind of alternative medicine.'

Still he couldn't get a word out. She found it hard not to

smile. She hadn't believed a single word of his big-shot movie talk. In Sophie's considerable experience, men nearly always started out talking big. Looking at him now, his boasts seemed particularly ridiculous. The face was of a confused little boy caught hopelessly between wanting to run away and trying to prove he was a man of the world. It was getting late and she couldn't be bothered to coax him much longer.

'Calum, I think I'll go to the lobby while you pay the bill. If you want to indulge yourself a little, join me there and get us a room. If not, it's been a pleasure being with you. I really enjoyed dinner.'

As soon as they reached the room, Sophie disappeared into the bathroom and checked her watch. Christ, it was already half past midnight. Better get this over fast and go home to her own bed. No time for any gentle seduction routine. She slipped everything off except underwear, stockings and suspenders, and strode confidently out.

Calum had taken off his jacket and opened a half bottle of champagne from the minibar. He looked horribly nervous and was sweating buckets, big damp moons forming around the armpits of his blue shirt. As he took a glass over to her, his hand trembled uncontrollably. It looked like he was already regretting venturing out of the shallow end. If she didn't get on with it, he might take fright and then refuse to pay. Better get to the no-refund stage fast. She took one sip of champagne, put the glass firmly down, and moved both hands behind her back to her bra clip.

The mini-striptease was over in a bare twenty seconds. Calum watched with a fixed grin as Sophie threw her bra over his head and used it to pull him towards her.

'Okay, Calum, let's party.'

'Sophie, how would it be if we talked a little more first?'

That was what she was afraid of. She shoved him firmly backwards onto the king-size bed, leapt on top of him, unbuttoned his shirt at a rate of knots, and began to grab at his belt buckle.

'Okay, Mister Movie Man, let's see what you've got for me down here.'

Anything he had for her down there was a fast-wilting memory. He grabbed at his belt too, and a minor tug of war ensued.

'Come on, Calum, *relax*. How can I ease away your stress if you won't let me touch you? I promise I'll show you a good time like you've never had before.'

What she had in mind was downloading this pathetic twerp in five minutes or less. What the hell was the matter with him, grinning at her in that inane way and hanging on to his trouser belt like grim death? She tried one more time to unbuckle him. He was having none of it.

'Look, if you're not in the mood, that's okay, as long as I get paid. Is there something else you want me to do?'

'Sophie, how much does it cost for your . . . normal service?'

'Three hundred, but if you've something kinky in mind, it's extra.'

'I'll pay you double . . . if you'll let me do what I really want.'

'What's that?'

Her voice sounded wary.

'I'd like you to put out the lights, hug me for a while and . . .'

'And *what*?'

'Let me call you Marianna.'

'Whatever turns you on, loverboy.'

*   *   *

He paid Sophie and the hotel, put her in one cab and got into another. He felt ashamed and cheap. Why had he gone in for that ridiculous big talk? It was *definitely* the last time he'd proposition a stranger. Why the hell hadn't he left as soon as she told him? Would it have mattered so much if he had looked a jerk? No, it had been more than that. At that moment, *anything*, even *that*, had seemed better than going miserably back alone to his empty, cold apartment. It was only when they got into the hotel room that he realised he couldn't go through with it. Perhaps if she'd taken it more slowly, been a bit more romantic, not just *yanked* her clothes off like that, it might have been all right . . . Thank God no-one he knew had seen them together and, apart from his first name, she had no idea who he was.

The taxi pulled into his street. He was actually *glad* to be home. He went in and collapsed on the sofa. Maybe it was time to try Marianna again, to see if she was warming to the idea. After the horror and shame of the evening's encounter, it would feel comfortingly familiar and *decent* to talk with Marianna, even if she *was* in another of her moods.

'Maria? It's Calum. Calum Buchanan. How are you today? There's one thing I forgot to tell Marianna the other night. It's very important . . . Thank you.'
    '. . . Calum, this is the *last* time I take a call from you. You *spoiled* our party on Saturday. If Brett was here now he'd get mad at me for talking to you again. I promised I wouldn't. I

118

want you out of my life, Calum. We have *nothing* in common, and if you're gonna make a nuisance of yourself, as far as I can see, we don't even have a basis for any form of friendship. So *back off*!'

'Marianna, listen to me. There's one thing I didn't tell you about my lottery win . . .'

'I don't believe for *one* minute that you really won five million dollars. It's just some bullshit story you made up to try to impress me.'

'If you don't believe, call the girl at the lottery, I'll give you her number . . .'

'I have no intention whatsoever of—'

'It *is* true, but the whole point is it *wasn't* luck.'

'What crap are you talking? How can winning a lottery *not* be luck?'

'I have a . . . system.'

'So you can win a lottery any time you like?'

'If I want to.'

'Like this week? You could do it again?'

'If I had a reason. At the moment I have more than enough money for *my* needs. If I needed more, sure I could. As much as you want. *Imagine* the life we could have together, your every whim . . .'

'Calum, are you drinking again?'

'No I am *not*.'

'Well, whatever's causing you to be like this, I've had enough of this bullshit.'

'I'll *prove* it's not bullshit. I'll win it again on Saturday. I'll call you one o'clock LA time.'

'You are *so* full of shit, and now you're resorting to these . . . *pathetic* fantasies. You try calling on Saturday and see what happens. GOODBYE.'

119

* * *

Getting the right numbers took more out of Calum that Saturday than the previous week. He went straight back to the flat and crashed down on the sofa to watch the result. When it was done, he didn't move, didn't feel a flicker, just lay there fretting about the coming phone call. Would it be different, now that she'd see it was no lucky break? Last night he'd hardly slept, his thoughts oscillating endlessly between Marianna and his troubled conscience about Morag. Was it breaching faith to do it again? The first win simply hadn't worked. Surely Morag wouldn't have wanted him to stop now, while the chance was still alive. But what if Marianna turned him down despite a *second* win? What *else* could he do so he didn't lose her for ever? It made him as twitchy as a cat on a hot tin roof. Better relax for the evening, and make the call later when he was feeling more mellow. How about getting Tracy from Avalon round and try inviting her to dinner afterwards? That reminded him; he needed to call them to confirm the win, in any case. It took a while before they put him through.

'I can't believe it! It's never happened before! Astonishing! How are you *doing* this, Calum?'

'Another hunch, I guess.'

'And six tickets this time, so you get two-thirds of the total! Four point six million pounds.'

'Great. So what time are you coming over?'

'For what?'

'Don't we have to go through the process again, like last week?'

'Not really. We have all your personal details and Emma's

120

already given you the investment commentary. I don't think there's much more to add.'

'Oh . . .'

'Of course, it would be different if you were planning to go public this time. That would make a *great* story. There hasn't been much coverage of our winners recently. Unless there's a big roll-over the papers think it's old hat. This would *really* catch their eye. You being an American would add a bit of spice. But I don't suppose you're interested.'

'I could think it over.'

'Are you *serious*?'

'I'm not committing to anything. I'd need to think about it and *talk* it over, with someone who has experience.'

He knew it was wrong to lead her on, but he was desperate for company.

'Well, if you *are* willing to consider this, maybe we *should* come round tomorrow.'

'I wanna decide tonight, to get it sorted out one way or the other.'

'I'm sorry, I can't tonight. I could ask one of my colleagues, Mike.'

'Forget it. I'll stick to the confidentiality.'

'Calum, I'd *really* like to do it, but I've promised to go to a party with my boyfriend. He'll *kill* me if I pull out. *Please* let me do it tomorrow.'

'Tonight or no dice.' He knew he was being a real brat, but *his* need was greater than any boyfriend's.

'Okay, I'll be with you in half an hour.'

'Why don't we have something to eat while we talk. Let's meet at the Savoy at nine forty-five.'

'See you there in the main lobby. If you go public, Avalon will pay for dinner.'

It was a wonderful evening. The only mistake he made was telling her he'd ordered a Ferrari. So downright *stupid* to try to impress *her*, of all people. When he asked what the smile meant, she coyly admitted that she kept a secret chart of what they all bought. Since she'd started at Avalon, the tally was twenty-six Rolls-Royces, fifteen Bentleys, forty-seven Porsches, and, wait for it, fifty-four Ferraris.

After that it got better. There was a bit on the boyfriend, but she didn't slobber over it. There was nothing she said that directly encouraged him, but she was *great* company, and she behaved like she found him attractive, too. He observed with genuine respect the way she always worked the conversation back to the main agenda. He promised to sleep on it and call her in the morning. She resisted sharing a taxi, but accepted a double cheek peck as she got into her black cab.

Calum walked the whole way home. Persuasive as she was, there was no way he was going to do it. During the dinner, there had been moments when he'd flirted with the idea, but as the warm glow of the evening and the wine wore off, Morag's words kicked down the door of his consciousness and forced their way back in. Whatever happened now, the saga was over. No more lottery, and no more using this gift. *Ever.* Either it worked or it didn't. It was in Marianna's hands now. Surely she'd recognise that he'd done something special and would agree to meet to talk about it. If he couldn't persuade her, finito. He would build a new life somewhere a long way from LA or London.

As soon as he got home he made the call.

'We are sorry. The number you dialled is not currently in service. Please check the number and dial again.'

He dialled again. Same recording, He checked with the operator. No mistake. He tried directory enquiries. Not listed. The *bitch*! She'd changed their number. How could he get hold of the new one? They had no friends in common now. The few they'd once shared had sheared along the natural fault line into two mutually exclusive bands. He tried two of her girl friends. One had her answering machine on. The other was home but gave him the deep-freeze treatment. She said she didn't have it and wouldn't tell him if she did.

He went and lay on top of the bed in the dark. The burning resentment spread within him like a rapid cancer. He'd been decent. He'd done everything the right way, the way Morag wanted. He hadn't despaired, hadn't given up, and what happiness had it brought him? If he had lost Marianna for good, where did that leave him? Someone who had accomplished something mind-blowing and wouldn't get a shred of recognition for it. A lonely multi-millionaire unable to enjoy his money without the vision of an old woman's face flashing before his eyes. The win wasn't *all* Morag's work, goddammit! It may have been Morag who invented the method and trained him, but it was *his* idea to make money that way, and *his* awesome effort getting there.

What would Morag expect him to do with the money now that Marianna wasn't coming back? Give it to charity and live in poverty and obscurity the rest of his life? My God, he would enjoy taking it all out of the bank in one-dollar bills and driving it in a truck to Marianna's house, just to show her it was real. So he was still a loser, was he? How many losers made fifteen million bucks in a couple of weeks through their own efforts? Maybe he should show people a thing or two. No,

Morag, give me a break, you can't have it *all* your way, I have a say in this, too. And if I can't have Marianna, why shouldn't I have some pleasure myself? Right on! Once again, the vision of Morag's sad face, the simple blackhouse and the silhouette of Ben Mhor rose up in his mind, and, quite deliberately, he thrust them away till he drifted to sleep.

As soon as he woke he looked at the clock. It was ten past eight. Too early. He opened the curtains and went back to bed, a humourless, cold smile fleetingly on his lips. On the stroke of nine he called the home number Tracy had given him.

'Hi, Calum, I really enjoyed dinner. *So?* Are you going to do it?'

10

And so Calum got his press conference, his TV moment of fame, and his sheaf of press clippings, including one from the *LA Times*. The conference itself went pretty well, considering. They pressed him a bit on how he did it, but let it go after he repeated three times that he had a 'method' and he wasn't revealing it. They wanted to know where he was from, how old, how long he'd been in the UK. No one asked, or had any reason to know, about his time in Lewis and he certainly wasn't volunteering information on that. Was he married? No. Girlfriend? No. Where did he work? He was over here on a sabbatical. Where did he live? West London. Address? Confidential. The Avalon people had rehearsed him carefully and they knew what questions they would have to field themselves. No, there was no rule against multiple wins, and, no, they saw no need to introduce one. They didn't think it too likely, ho ho, that they would have to deal with a situation like that too often. Did the gentlemen of the press know the odds against it happening two weeks running? Mr Buchanan had something to say on this. He would *not* enter the lottery again and planned to donate ten percent of his second win to charity.

After the questions, there were *lots* more photographs. Handshakes with the Avalon Chairman, raised glasses of champagne, a jumbo-sized cheque. Whatever antics the photographers asked for he aimiably provided. Later he groaned at the pic in the *Evening Standard* of his idiotic grin and thumbs up, and his fear that similar shots would be used elsewhere – the *LA Times* included – were confirmed. What a jerk he looked! In future he would keep well away from the press. At least the articles themselves were okay. They didn't know much about him, so there was nothing negative they could write.

So much for the Tuesday dailies. Wednesday was different. Someone stuffed a *Sun* through his letterbox. He was the second lead story. The newspaper thoughtfully provided his address and a lurid description of his ejection by security guards after he was fired at the bank. Former colleagues, unnamed, described him as 'lazy', 'hopeless', 'arrogant', and 'foul-mouthed'. *Foul-mouthed?* That was rich, coming from them. They had been 'glad to see the back of him'. He was also a 'serial liar' and 'boasted non-stop'. Calum almost barfed into his cornflakes. Which of those *bastards* had called the paper? Borzo, he bet it was Borzo. He'd find a way to get his own back. He would hire some thugs to castrate him.

There was a knock at the door. It was a *Sun* reporter and photographer. The reporter was short and overweight, with clammy skin, plentiful dandruff and an absurd pencil moustache. Unctuously he explained that he'd tried phoning on Tuesday evening, and when Calum didn't answer they *had* to run it for fear their City sources would call another paper. Now he'd like to help Calum out, let him give his side of the story in his own words. Calum gave him a two word comment. Smart move. The next day he was back on their front page, complete with a photo of him being doorstepped and his quote in huge letters with the inevitable outsize asterisks.

Thursday brought some more journos and a few photographers who looked equipped for a six-month siege. It also brought the first sackful of mail. Begging mail, fan mail, hate mail. Offers, some exotic, from female hopefuls of all ages, sizes, races, and proclivities.

The doorbell went again. He ignored it, like he'd done all day. This one kept on and on. He could faintly make out the plaintive calling of his name. Let him stew.

'Mr Buchanan, Mr Buchanan . . .'

How long was it going take for *this* one to get the message? It stopped. Good. Then the silence was broken by a sharp series of bursts on a car horn. What was *with* these guys? His patience snapped. He would give this one a right screamer, and if it got him back in the papers, so frigging what? He thundered to the apartment door, tore it open and yelled out an encore of his *Sun* quote.

Oh, God, the Ferrari! On Monday, before all the press stuff blew up, he'd confirmed the order, transferred the money, and arranged for them to deliver it today. He'd bought so much else on Monday – including three Swiss watches, a whole wardrobe of clothes, and shoes galore – that it had quite slipped his mind. How *could* he have been so dumb as to forget? They would *love* this. He could see the headlines. 'Lottery Brat's Ferrari F**k Up.' He climbed up the steps and shook the guy's hand, while the snapparazis clicked away.

'Good morning, Mr Buchanan. Brian Williams. Sorry to have to use the horn. These gentlemen were pretty sure you were home, and I didn't want a wasted journey. I *did* try to confirm before I left the office, but there was no reply. I left a message on your machine.'

'My fault. I forgot to check it.'

'No problem now I've found you. Shall I show you over the car? I think this will be the first time I've delivered a car quite so *publicly*.'

Was it Calum's imagination, or was Williams's tone less than positive? Understandable, perhaps. After all the headlines, this mightn't be quite the customer image Ferrari wanted. Specially if they thought he had staged this. Oh, what the hell. It was only a car and there was no sign they thought his money wasn't good enough.

'The door and ignition locking is all done using *this*, there *is* no key. Why don't you sit in the driver's side and I'll run through the controls . . .'

They both got in and closed the doors. Throughout the explanation, large numbers of fat-lensed cameras were pressed against the car's side windows. One of the lizards slithered onto the car's aluminium bonnet for a full-frontal through the windscreen. Calum felt like some aquarium's latest exotic acquistion. Williams tried his level best to ignore them.

'. . . Seven speed gearbox, controlled with Formula One style paddles . . . there, between the spokes of the steering wheel. Right one is for up-changes, left for down. They can shift in nought-point-one-two-five seconds, faster than a racing driver. This lever here switches the change to full automatic. Air conditioning controls are all obvious. Lights and wipers work by twisting this way . . . and the horn is in the steering boss right here . . .'

'I think you've demonstrated that enough.'

'Of course. Seats are electrically adjusted using these buttons. Bonnet release catch is under . . . there. Next I'd like to show you the toolkit and how the fitted luggage fits in.'

'Mr Williams, if you don't mind, can we leave it at that? With these lowlife staring at me, I can hardly concentrate. I'm sure I'll get the hang of it.'

'As you wish. If you wouldn't mind signing . . . here. We recommend keeping it to five thousand revs for the first five hundred miles. The initial service is at one thousand. If you wish, just give me a call and we'll come and collect it. Shall I park it properly for you?'

'No, I think I'll take it out now and get away from the vermin for a while.'

'Goodbye then. Congratulations on your purchase. It is *magnificent*, a true driver's car.'

As Calum drove off, he could see in the mirror the scum collaring Williams. How much did Buchanan pay for it? Top speed? How many seconds nought to sixty?

It was the first time he had driven since Lewis. Driving on the wrong side of the road was still going to be a problem, especially in these narrow roads, squeezing past cars parked on both sides. He made it to end of the street okay, having put it in auto mode without a second's hesitation. This paddle thing might be good for showing off to girls, but London traffic wasn't ideal for playing Schumachers. The lights seem to be stuck on red. Oh, shit, that was one of *their* cars coming up behind him. He'd have to lose them.

How could you lose *anybody* in traffic moving at this speed? Oh well, they'd get bored sooner or later. *He* had a full tank of gas and most likely they didn't. Why not relax and enjoy the car?

It felt good. Even crawling along at twenty miles an hour, it felt different from any car he'd driven, incredibly precise in everything. The controls were perfectly weighted, the throttle response astonishing. He couldn't wait for a bit of space to open it up and leave those rattlesnakes in his wake. He turned into Ladbroke Grove.

The radio. How was that? Wow, what sound! Must be three hundred watts of oomph in it. Pity it was tuned to a classical station. Let's try for some rock. Kinda fiddly, these controls . . .

She'd been looking for a meter for twenty minutes. It was infuriating. Liz would give up on her if she didn't get to the café soon. She had seen one, but the cretins parked in the next bays had encroached into her airspace too much to get the big Volvo in. Round and round she circled. Hopeless! Not a space *anywhere.* For the third time she turned into Ladbroke Grove. Quick, *there*, that man might be leaving.

One second earlier and he would have seen it in time. On the fourth press of the tiny search button he found his station and looked up again. *Shee-it!*

His frantic stab on the brakes came too late. He was hurled back by the white cloud of the exploding airbag.

It was one of the journos who opened the door and asked if he was all right. Calum stumbled out. Victoria Llewelyn-Smith was standing by the squashed rear of her estate, elbows out, fists planted firmly and fiercely on her sides.

'You *stupid* PRAT!'

The photographer switched to his third camera to run off another roll. Some of the pictures turned out blurred. Convulsed with laughter, it had been hard to hold the camera steady.

* * *

Christopher Ransome was surprised that the China business

had got the Foreign Secretary worked up enough to convene a special meeting. Not that Ransome minded the extra, unscheduled trip to London courtesy of the taxpayer. There were a few new CDs he couldn't get in Geneva which he was keen to listen to. He would walk through the park afterwards and up to HMV in Oxford Street.

They were kept waiting in the ante-room for five minutes before the Private Secretary threw the door open and ushered them into the Foreign Secretary's outsize corner office, with its splendid view over St James's Park and Horse Guards. Though there were eight officials present, there was no doubt that the key players were Tom Ferguson, the Permanent Under Secretary, and Christopher Ransome. The Foreign Secretary kicked things off.

'The Americans are getting *absurdly* hot under the collar about Chinese trade. The President called the Prime Minister again last night. This man Tyne has forced Lynne O'Neill's hand into demanding that the World Trade Organisation's Disputes Panel is convened immediately. I think we can anticipate *immense* resentment from Washington if we are not seen to support them on this. Tom, how important do you think this issue is?'

'Enormously, is the answer. Before we're all too much older, the Chinese may have outstripped the US as the world's largest exporter. If they allow other countries proper access to their own market, the impact on major Western economies may not be too serious. You could think of it as a balance of terror, in trade instead of arms. However, if the Chinese use their privileges as a member of the WTO to flood world markets with their own cheap products, while simultaneously finding covert ways to stop the foreigners selling in China, giant-sized sparks will fly. By that I mean a really major world crisis.'

'Well, if it's as clear-cut as that, won't the Euros go along with the Americans?' The Foreign Secretary scratched his chin hopefully.

'Unlikely. The French and Germans will *never* support it without cast-iron evidence of Chinese misdeeds. The Germans always believe they have more to lose than to gain by taking a hard line. The French will welcome a split, hoping that their companies will benefit if the Americans fall from favour in China. That leaves the Japanese. If they support it, the Americans will get it convened, whatever the European line. The Japanese will never support a final judgement against China, but they might bow to American pressure at this stage.'

'Mmmm. That brings us on to practicalities. We know what Lynne O'Neill wants, but what are the actual *rules* on how quickly you can convene this wretched Panel, Christopher?'

'The WTO agreement does not lay down *any* timeframe. However, to convene it as fast as the US wants, without first giving China any more opportunity to remedy the fault, would obviously be provocative. On the other hand, the Americans' concerns are clearly legitimate, and this *could* be the best way to nip the problem in the bud.'

'And what happens if it is convened?'

'First the Panel issues a provisional judgement and then member states hold a meeting of the full WTO Council to accept or reject it. In view of how the Chinese have behaved since they joined, any provisional judgement must condemn them. However, the final outcome will depend solely on the votes of key member states.'

'Do the Americans have any alternatives if the final judgement goes against them? Could they impose tariffs on imports from China or penalise them unilaterally in some other way?'

'This would be a *far* more dangerous scenario. Reapplying national tariffs would be incredibly inflammatory. If the Americans added *penalties* there would be chaos, anarchy. The whole WTO structure might collapse. The Chinese would . . .'

'Would what, Christopher?'

'I won't hazard a guess, but, to borrow an expression from our American friends, you can bet your bottom dollar they'd do *something*.'

'Well, let us hope we can avoid that. Even Lynne O'Neill's approach sounds highly risky. The Prime Minister wants to discuss this with me before he speaks to the President again. I think I'll advise him to back-pedal pretty sharpish. I can't *stand* the thought of another bust-up with the Euros.'

The officials were dismissed and Ransome was free to set off towards Oxford Street. The Foreign Secretary had a reputation in his Party for having a safe pair of hands, but lacking the 'vision thing'. It wasn't enormously hard to see why.

* * *

By Friday afternoon, Calum felt his life was in tatters. He had not heard a squeak from Marianna. The whole media thing was spinning wildly out of control. Avalon were hating it, and Tracy was not rushing to return his calls. Now the horror was turning truly nightmarish. Sophie the hooker had sold her story, such as it was, to the *News of the World* and their investigative reporter called him for a comment. When he got none, he bade Calum have a nice day on Sunday.

The next call restored his spirits. Channel 5 were inviting

him on a live chat show on Saturday afternoon. *Perfect.* Tell the story on TV and spike the paper's guns. It might not reflect *that* well on him, but if he told it well it could be kinda funny. It would nail the paper's planned lie that he was a regular user of call girls. He accepted without hesitation and spent the night rehearsing. There was one great thing about live TV: they couldn't fool around editing things out.

*   *   *

He could get used to this, it was fun being a celeb. Getting made up, chatting with the other guests, feeling that he was *somebody.* He was on last and felt his nerves jangling as he sat in the green room, watching the assured performances of his fellow-guests on the closed circuit set. He was relieved when the girl came for him and chatted to him by the door till she got the signal to send him on. He could hear the presenter, Marvyn Mitchell, doing the intro.

'Have you ever thought "It could be Me?". . . Now, most of us might feel fortunate to win the lottery once, but this afternoon we're going to meet a young man from the US of A who has not only done it *twice* and won a total of over nine million pounds, but he says that luck played no part in it. Please give a warm welcome to . . . CALUM BUCHANAN.'

Calum jogged casually down the curving staircase, the way he'd seen the stars do on chat shows a thousand times.

'Calum, you've had a lot of coverage in the press this week, but you seem to have kept pretty mum about how you do it.'

'Yes, Marvyn, that's my little secret.'

'And you won't give our viewers a teeny *hint* of how it works.'

''Fraid I can't. Wouldn't help if I did, would it? *Everyone* would win the lottery and the payout would be less than a pound.' That line had been Tracy's idea when he called for advice.

'Well, I suppose you have a point there. But tell us, does your secret "method" apply only to the lottery, or would it work with other things?'

'I . . . *think* so.'

Where was this leading? He had little choice but to play along.

'Take horse racing, for example. If someone like you could predict which horse was going to win, you'd make a fortune, wouldn't you? *And* put the bookies out of business once and for all. How about it? Is that something you could do?'

Talk about a dilemma. Say yes and you get in deeper. Say no and you get into explanations about night time and moons. He needed time to think. He didn't have it.

'I . . . I . . . *guess* that . . . in principle, maybe . . . I could. I'm not into horses, so I wouldn't bother.'

'But you think you *could* do it?'

'I guess so.'

'Well, we have a little surprise for you. On the monitor over there . . . we're going over live to Kempton Park where in five minutes the third race, the two-fifteen, will start. We want you to do a little demonstration. We've kept it simple by picking a race with only seven horses. Should be easy for someone like you. Will you have a go?'

'Marvyn, I don't think it's appropriate to . . .'

He hated live television. This was *awful*. What the hell could he do? He could walk out in a huff and give up on the hooker story. Unattractive. The paper would crucify him even more. Or he could refuse to pick a horse and try to laugh it off. Then they'd all say he *was* just a boastful brat. Oh *God*!

'To try to persuade you, we're going to offer a little inducement. We know you've won lots of money for yourself, but I understand you're keen on giving to charity. If you're willing to give it a whirl, Channel Five will put a bet of *five thousand pounds* on the nose of the nag you pick, with *all* the winnings going to a charity of your choice.'

There was a great roar from the studio audience. They didn't need to be egged on by the studio hands. They were *baying* for it. Marvyn Mitchell was beside himself. His ratings were bumping along the bottom and the rest of today's show had been humdrum. This was *great* TV, a *brilliant* idea. Thank God for Liza, the researcher he was currently bedding.

'Calum, the clock is ticking. Four minutes to the off. What do you say? It's *only* for fun. No hard feelings if you lose.'

'DO IT. DO IT. DO IT.' The baying went on. They started a sort of synchronised clap. It was deafening. Oh, what the hell. At least they would be off his back and he could get on with the vital story.

'Okay, okay. I'll do it.'

A vast, primaeval roar went up from the crowd.

'Right, Calum, we don't have much time. Can you see the list of runners? . . . Tell me what it's to be.'

'Hold on, hold on, give me time.'

He tried desperately to concentrate. Without a moon, without calm meditation, it would never work. Still he tried, eyes closed, screwing himself up in a tight ball. There were only seven goddam names, the merest glimmer would do. Help me, Morag.

Nothing at all.

'Calum, you *must* tell me. We have the bookmaker on the end of the line. If you don't decide in the next . . . fifteen seconds, all bets are off.'

The roars grew louder than ever. He looked at the list for any kind of inspiration, any hunch. He was out of time. He'd have to pick one at random.

'Parson's Pulpit.'

'Thank you . . . Parson's Pulpit. Five thousand pounds to win. Are we on? . . . Good. Now let's settle back and enjoy the race.'

Calum slumped back in the chair. All eyes were on the huge monitors, and something approaching silence fell so they could listen to the commentary.

It was a three-mile steeplechase. They circled at the start, the ribbon rose and they were off. The commentator began with a calm, almost conspiratorial whisper. Parson's Pulpit made a poor start and settled in at the back as they all sailed safely over the first three fences. There was a faller at the fourth and another at the sixth, who sprawled so badly he almost tripped up Calum's choice. There was a sharp collective intake of breath from the audience. The jockey earned his pay with a skilful swerve and by the turn had made up the leeway to the rest of the pack.

The commentator's pitch began to rise, matched by a blossoming hubbub in the studio. Calum was the calmest of the lot. He was the only one who knew the truth. Parson's Pulpit had the same one chance in seven – five now – as the others. As he watched the horses accelerate into the final turn, Parson's Pulpit still last, he realised that he might have lucked out choosing a garbage horse. Picking the winner might please Channel 5 and get him out of the studio in one piece, but what about after that? If it was believed he could do *that*, the pressure would get worse. Way worse. He loved Parson's Pulpit for being so useless.

'And with three fences to go, Victoria's Dream is fighting it out with Silver Slipper. Irish Lament is making ground on the stand side. It looks like it's between these three as Happy Camper and Parson's Pulpit are losing touch with the leaders.'

A groan from the audience. Calum was busy calculating how he could work this failure into a link with the hooker débâcle.

'Over the second from home and Happy Camper has pulled up. Parson's Pulpit is making ground, but has left it too late. Irish Lament is now three lengths from the leaders. There's still *nothing* to choose between Silver Slipper and Victoria's Dream. Parson's Pulpit has gained another few lengths . . . Coming to the last and it's between those two, Silver Slipper looking slightly more comfortable . . .'

The audience was subdued, deflated. The smile on Mitchell's face looked fixed.

'. . . Over the last and . . . oh *no*, Silver Slipper has *fallen* . . . *And* he's brought down Victoria's Dream! For a moment I thought Tommy Ellery had managed to cling on . . . It's Irish Lament who will take the Mercury Chase. Or will he? . . .'

The audience had seen it before the commentator and were on their feet, yelling like wild things. Parson's Pulpit had got a turbocharger from somewhere and was flying up the hill.

Irish Lament's jockey was whipping a groove in the tiring animal's side.

'And it's Irish Lament with a hundred yards to run . . . Parson's Pulpit making a marvellous run on the inside, but he's not going to make it . . .'

The audience hadn't given up. They were in a frenzy. Calum *willed* Irish Lament to the line.

'PARSON'S PULPIT IS STILL GAINING GROUD. IRISH LAMENT IS HANGING ON GAMELY. HALF A LENGTH. NOW IT'S ONLY A HEAD . . . And at the post it's Irish Lament . . . There'll be a photograph, but I'm pretty sure Irish Lament just pipped Parson's Pulpit . . .'

There was a mighty groan from the crowd and another from the flimsy benches as 30,000 pounds of wobbly flesh thumped down simultaneously. Calum wiped his forehead in vast relief.

'Let's take a look at the action replay . . . I think we'll see, by the tiniest margin, a nose, no more, that Irish Lament has . . . no, wait, I'm not so sure. If we can freeze that . . .'

They were back on their feet. Was it the studio lights or did Calum look green? That *fucking* animal!

'. . . Yes, I was wrong. It looks like Parson's Pulpit by a *hair's breadth. Amazing!* We'll have to wait for the official photo, of course, but it looks like Parson's Pulpit and Frankie Daventry have won the Mercury Chase.'

The women were doing excited little hops, the men waving triumphant fists everywhere. Marvyn Mitchell tried to silence them long enough to ask Calum a question, but they were having none of it.

'. . . and yes, that's it, Parson's . . .'

The commentator was drowned out by the screams and yells. It took minutes for them to settle. Marvyn Mitchell looked like the cat that got the cream. He shook Calum's limp hand on and on.

'CALUM BUCHANAN, that was *amazing*! *Fantastic*! *Astonishing*! How *did* you do that? And I'm just being told, Channel Five has won . . . how much, Tina? . . . *thirty-five thousand pounds*! *Brilliant*! Ladies and gentlemen, let's hear it for Calum Buchanan.'

The clapping went on, punctuated with whistles and yelps. Calum smiled weakly. He was burning with nausea. Forget this circus. Concentrate on the hooker. He *had* to mention the hooker!

'Well, that about wraps it up for what has been *the* most amazing show . . .'

'Marvyn, can I mention something?'

'We're almost out of time, Calum. You've got ten seconds . . .'

'No, I *must* tell you. The other night I had this *hilarious* mix-up. I was in this hotel bar and . . .'

'Calum, I'm afraid I'm going to have to cut you off there, but you're welcome to come back some other time and tell us your stories. Thank you for coming on the show and . . . and next time you go out in your Ferrari, don't forget we drive on the left, eh??? . . . Next week I'm joined by jazz singer Ulma Shaw, Tottenham Hotspur striker Steve Derry, and a mystery guest from Ontario, Canada. Until then . . . Staaaay Cooool.'

Calum didn't even *think* about going home. He sneaked out the studio by a back door, and, trusting not even the Channel 5 minicab, took a tube to Piccadilly, bought some very dark sunglasses and checked into a hotel, eating room service and avoiding the TV news. He asked to see the hotel manager and offered a bounty of twenty thousand pounds if his whereabouts were kept secret for two weeks. It was comforting that the phone didn't ring and he could access his calls at home remotely. The only call he was interested in didn't come. He didn't even have his faithful companion, her picture.

11

Boredom led to naps during the day, more and more of them. He hadn't stirred from the hotel room for six days and it was driving him crazy. Sleep helped pass the time. There was no plan at first, unless you counted hiding under a duvet as a plan, but now one had crystallised. If his credit hadn't been good it would have been tougher, but his was very good. The plan was to get abroad. The fascination with him was only a British and to a lesser degree an American affair. His story might have made the press on the Continent, but they wouldn't know his face, probably wouldn't recall his name. *If* he could get away from England without being detected. Airports were the worst option. They were such public places: *hundreds* of people would recognise him and be on the phone to the papers. From what he had heard, the Eurostar train would be equally dangerous. That left ferries as a foot passenger – still risky, and he'd have to get to Dover first – or chartering a boat or a private plane. Could he trust the crew? He didn't trust anyone now. No, there was no method with *no* risk, no safe means of avoiding passport control altogether. Overall, the best option was the Channel Tunnel by car. Stay in the car for the whole transit. Only the passport officers would see his name and as he hadn't broken any law they couldn't stop him. The sunglasses should stop toll booth operators at the Tunnel recognising him. Once he was safely across, he would be hard to track.

143

His new car was too well known thanks to the papers, and would take *weeks* to fix. Renting in his own name was far too dangerous, so he would have to buy another. What, though? Might as well be something fun. A Porsche, after all? He picked a dealer from yellow pages and called using a false name. All went well at first, with all the models readily available. It was when they got on to paperwork and insurance that the going got tougher. There was nothing that made delivering a car to a hotel *impossible*, provided payment was made by bank transfer in advance, but the salesman clearly wasn't at all comfortable. Either this was a joker horsing around, wasting his time, or the guy was a drug-dealer or gangster. His suspicions were getting aroused and Calum rung off abruptly.

There was only one safe-ish way. Brian Williams at the Ferrari dealers. He had all the insurance details already and was unlikely to have mislaid them. Ferrari had featured in the papers with him already, for better or worse, and would see little advantage in drawing more attention to the association. And a Ferrari would be fun, goddammit.

So the call went in to a bemused Williams and a transaction was done. They bought back the wounded 555 at a big discount and sold Calum a 375 demonstrator in titanium silver. The bank transfer was made speedily and delivery details agreed. Williams would drive it to the West End on Saturday at midnight, and only then would Calum call his mobile and tell him exactly where to bring it. Calum's token apologies for the cloak and dagger stuff were unnecessary. Williams had followed the saga, fascinated. You could hardly avoid it, in fact. Repeated showings of the Channel 5 clip, the lurid *News of the World* splash, the mystery of where he was hiding out, a thousand theories on how his system worked;

and opinions on the rights and wrongs of it from politicians, charities, churchmen and all manner of busybodies.

The last decision Calum had to make was whether to bribe a hotel lackey to fetch his passport and the picture or risk a nocturnal visit himself. It was Friday morning and there were still thirty-six hours for him to decide. Either way, that was all he would take with him. The stores in the hotel had proved adequate for interim clothes, though the shapes and sizes were assorted. Having them delivered by room service, with the cost being put on his bill was unusual, but what did *they* care?

Part of him wanted to leave immediately, to run while he had time, but the cooler part said Saturday night would be smarter, when the dailies were off duty and it would be too late for the Sundays. Be patient, be cool.

'Meester Buchanan?'

He shot upright.

'Meester Buchanan, are you awake, sir?'

He listened again. It wasn't either of the regular two who took care of room service. His pulse began to race. He stepped over to the door, trying to look through the peep-hole. It was impossible to make out anything.

'Meester Buchanan, sir, I *do* need a word with you. It is Ernesto Perotti, the hotel manager.'

Calum relaxed, but only a fraction.

'What is it, Mr Perotti?'

'A *private* word, if you don't mind, Meester Buchanan. So sorry to bother you. Would you mind awfully . . . Thank you, Meester Buchanan.'

He secured the little chain and opened the door an inch. When he saw the second figure, he slammed it shut again. Betrayed. The *scum*. The knocking came again.

'Meester Bu-*chan*-an.'

What could he do? He was going to have to open it, wasn't he? He could hardly hold out here for months, specially with a minibar that hadn't been restocked today. Who *was* the guy the Italian rodent of a manager had brought? From the one quick glimpse he looked too grand for a journo. A television exec? A publisher, maybe? Whoever it was, he must have quite a budget if he could afford a bigger bribe than twenty thousand. Shit. He opened the door.

'Thank you, Meester Buchanan. May we come in and then I can explain?'

'I can hardly stop you. Do as you please.'

Calum glared at the manager and ignored the outstretched hand of the distinguished-looking stranger.

'Thees gentleman is from the . . . government. They inseested that . . .'

'Thank you, Mr Perotti, why don't you leave the rest of the explanations to him? I'm sure you are very busy. We needn't keep you from your duties any longer.'

'You want me to . . . ?'

'Yes.'

'Excuse me, Meester Buchanan, I hope thees doesn't affect our . . . understanding.'

The glare intensified. Then Calum's brain re-engaged. Tearing up the agreement now would *guarantee* a call to the press.

'No, our agreement still holds.'

'*Thank* you, Meester Buchanan.' He was amazed as much as pleased. 'So, excuse me, gentlemen.'

The visitor proffered his hand once more. Calum coldly gestured him towards a chair. The stranger sighed, and allowed a look of distaste and irritation to flicker across his face. He took off his overcoat, threw it on the bed, ran a hand through his splendid silver mane and sat down. He had a superior air about him, an assured loftiness that repelled Calum. He was like an older version of the English guys at that awful drinks party. Calum sensed the man was looking down his nose at him so much he might go cross-eyed. That was good: it would make it easier for Calum to refuse whatever information he wanted. During his stay in the hotel Calum had felt increasingly queasy about what Morag might think of his behaviour. He must not make things worse by revealing anything about her or the origins of his special ability. Play very dumb if need be. Most of the world already thought he was a moron; one more person sharing their view wouldn't hurt.

'Mr Buchanan, I apologise for dropping in on you un-announced . . .'

The visitor cast a disapproving eye over Calum. He was comprehensively dishevelled. A week's growth, brown hair very unbrushed, a shirt that fitted spectacularly badly, and jeans pulled on over bare feet. Looked like he could do with a spell in the army.

'My name is Charles Rivett-Carnac. I work for MI6. We checked many hotels in London and elsewhere to find you. I believe that a number of gentlemen from the media are doing the same. You have my word that we will not reveal your whereabouts to them.'

'Thanks. So, what do you want with me?'

'I have two things to discuss. The first concerns your personal welfare. You are clearly well aware of the degree of public interest in you . . .'

'I *had* noticed, thank you.'

'Of course. The pressure must be intolerable.'

'It will pass.'

'True, true, but I wouldn't hold your breath. The level of interest is . . . considerable. It may be uncomfortable for some time to come, but, as you say, it will pass.'

'So, what's your point?'

'My greater concern is not your privacy, but your personal *security*.'

'Why should that be of interest to MI6?'

'I'll come to that later. Let's first consider the threat itself. Do you realise how serious it is? You appear to possess a remarkable gift. There are many people who could benefit financially by having you assist them in making predictions. Of lottery numbers or the outcome of horse races, for example.'

'Sure, I've had lots of people asking me to do that. I won't. I'm through with all that. I'll simply say no.'

'Mr Buchanan, forgive me being blunt, but you are a little . . . *naive*. Does it not occur to you that there are people out there who may not take no for an answer?'

'Sure.' He lied. It showed. 'They'd have to get hold of me first.'

'And you think that is beyond them?'

'No . . .'

Of course this spook was right. As soon as this guy was gone, he'd call Williams and bring everything forward to tonight.

'How long can you stay in a hotel? Not for ever, surely? Are you planning to go back to the US? These people can go there, too, you know.'

'I know that. I plan on staying in this hotel for another couple of weeks. Then, I don't know. I might go to the country somewhere.'

'Like Lewis?'

'Where's that?'

'Mr Buchanan, what do you take us for? We have the records of your flights to and from Stornoway. Where did you stay while you were there?'

'You haven't found out yet? You're slipping.'

'We will.'

The mutual dislike deepened. Calum was almost amused. At least his own streak of feistiness only showed through occasionally. This guy seemed to have it switched on permanently. Who did he think he could persuade with an attitude like this? Rivett-Carnac caught hold of himself and tried for a more positive tone.

'Naturally, you have various options, with varying degrees of risk attached to them. We could offer you *absolute* security for as long as was necessary, either in the UK or in a number of locations abroad.'

'Why should you want to do that?'

'Ah, that brings me on to the second subject I wanted to discuss.'

'I thought it might.'

'Your . . . talent. We don't know whether this is a skill you have developed deliberately, or whether you are . . . how shall I put it? . . . some sort of *freak*.'

Calum glared harder than ever at him. Rivett-Carnac drawled on.

'Whatever the nature of your gift, it could be very significant for us. Let me explain. Who do you think has the edge in military technology these days?'

'The US, I guess.'

'Correct. We don't do too badly ourselves in some areas.'

'Bully for you.'

'Next question. Who will have the edge in, say, ten years' time?'

'Search me. Who, if not the good guys?'

'The answer is no-one will, not in hardware. Think of what constitutes an edge. Not warheads or anything that goes bang, we *all* have those. Missiles are basically gunpowder and electronics. Twenty years ago no-one had electronics like us, not even the Japanese, and certainly not the Soviets. Today? Think of the number of semiconductor plants in Asia. Then, how about Stealth and all that? Old hat. The detection systems improve far faster than the time it takes to develop a warplane. It's the same with warships. Military technology is being democratised, made available to any Tom, Dick, or Harry, like cars and videos. And if hardware is equal, the only edge can be in superior information.'

'Which is where you guys come in, right?'

'Wrong. Intelligence gathering will go on, of course, but that is not what I mean. I mean *technology* that gives superior information. No, I'm not talking about eavesdropping or satellite cameras. For some years our Ministry of Defence has been working on a programme to utilise the power of the human mind for military purposes. In many countries police forces now routinely use psychics to locate victims or perpetrators. Some of them have the ability to envision the layout of buildings they have never visited. You can appreciate the significance for military installations, both offensively and defensively?'

'Sure.'

'That is one major area of research. There is, however, another area which is potentially of even greater significance. Predictive intelligence. Imagine if we could harness the ability of someone with sixth sense to alert us to an enemy attack, to where and when there would be an infantry advance, a rocket attack.'

'I can see it would be a big advantage.'

'*Big?*' Rivett-Carnac hooted derisively. 'It would be *decisive*. Unfortunately, our progress in this field has been . . . disappointing. That might not matter if we were the only ones working on it. However, we are not. Among our allies, the Americans have a programme much larger than ours. The French also have a modest effort.'

'Who else?'

'The Russians.'

'I thought they were all played out.'

'Believe that and you'll believe anything. They've been working on the paranormal *far* longer than we have. The penny, or rather the rouble, dropped for them when NATO still thought it was old wives' tales. It is an area that suits the Russians rather well, since they are still somewhat *constrained* financially. This is one field where money does not guarantee success . . . There is one more major power which we think is active. China.'

'Surely the Chinese aren't a *military* threat?'

'If you mean will they attack the US or the UK, you're probably right. However, within their region, they could be very destabilising. Do you know the size of the People's Liberation Army? Are you aware how much they've upgraded their weapons over the last five years? Their neighbours in Asia are feeling increasingly uncomfortable about it and if there *were* conflict or the threat of conflict in the region, we could all get drawn into it. If I were a betting man, I would wager that World War Three will start in East Asia.'

'You may be right, and this is all very interesting, but I don't have all day. What's the connection with me?'

'I would have thought that was fairly obvious. You have demonstated a predictive ability of quite startling accuracy.

If you are willing to tell us how it works and co-operate with our programme, this would be of huge potential help.'

'You mean join a *British* programme, not an American one?'

'For the time being, we would prefer you to be *our* . . . asset.'

'Mister . . . what was your name again?'

'Rivett-Carnac.'

'Mr Rivett-Carnac, if this was my own country, I *might* stretch a point. I don't even *like* Britain that much. Since I came, nearly every person I've met has been unpleasant or unfriendly, and your scummy newspapers and TV have been the last straw.'

'Seems to me this country's been pretty good to you. Consider the money you've made here.'

'I could've made that anywhere.'

'Look, Buchanan, I've tried to appeal to your better instincts, but as I'm getting nowhere with that . . . we could make life pretty difficult for you. You might find getting a visa extension hard going.'

'Fuck you. I don't wanna stay here much longer anyway. And if you threaten me, don't be surprised if I tell some of those *nice* newspapermen about your visit. Would you please leave now?'

'I find you *amazing*, do you know that? And really rather pathetic. You possess an extraordinary skill, yet it is obvious you have given no thought at all to its wider philosophical or practical implications. You *could* be the single most important factor in the security of the Western world. And what is the only thing you think of using your skill for? Making money. Don't you feel even a *little* ashamed of yourself? . . . Apparently not, but then that's how you Americans tick, isn't it? "What's in it for me" is all you care about. Very well, let's talk in language you might understand. We *do* have a budget for this and in return for your *full* co-operation I am authorised to offer you three million US dollars. That's what's "in it for you", Mr Buchanan.'

'Mr Rivett-Carnac, I have plenty of money, and I wouldn't touch yours if I didn't. All I want is you out of this room. RIGHT NOW . . . *if* you don't mind.'

Calum went over to the door and held it open. Rivett-Carnac sighed, stood up and collected his coat. By the door he paused.

'You can turn us down if you want, but now that you've been foolish enough to tell the whole world about your talent, you will *never* get the genie back in the bottle. Sooner or later, someone will force you to use that talent and I only hope for your sake and ours it's not the wrong people. With your money and fame, you may think you've *arrived*, but I suspect your real journey is just beginning. Why don't you take my card in case you change your mind?'

He reached into his jacket pocket and pulled a card from his handsome notecase. Calum shook his head. With a parting snarl of disgust, Rivett-Carnac swept out.

Calum closed the door and skipped over to the phone. Brian Williams's number was there on the pad.

12

The spook had spooked him. No way would he trust one of the hotel people to get his stuff now. Nor could he risk alerting them by checking out. They had his credit card imprint, so they wouldn't lose out. That, plus getting the bribe to the manager, should stop them making a fuss. Worst case, what were a few more screaming headlines between friends?

He watched midnight swing round on his beautiful new white gold Blancpain. Dark glasses on, he took the elevator down to the basement level and wandered round till he found a fire door. It opened onto a blissfully deserted side street. It was chilly but dry, a reprieve after the showers that had spattered the day.

He walked briskly to the appointed spot in Mount Street outside Scotts restaurant. The faithful Williams was there, his company paid ever more for special services. They shook hands while Calum was climbing down into the passenger seat. Williams's attempts at an explanation of the car were soon cut off.

'Don't you think we've taken care of this already?'

'The two cars are different in a number of ways.'

'You drive for a while, I'll watch and learn.'

'As you please. Which way would you like me to go?'

'To near my flat in Notting Hill. I'll tell you exactly where to stop.'

*   *   *

They pulled into the street parallel to his own and parked. Williams switched off the engine.

'Okay, here are the keys. *This* is for the upper lock, and the spindly one is for the lower. Watch out for the steps down; they're treacherous when they're wet. The light switch is on the right as you go in. My passport should be either in my briefcase on the desk or somewhere on top of the desk itself. The picture is in a wooden frame on the bedside table. You can't miss it. Okay? . . . Thanks.'

It took Williams longer than expected. Calum was beginning to get concerned.

'Sorry, to take so long, the passport wasn't where you said.'

'Where was it?'

'In the fridge.'

'Oh Christ, I'd forgotten I put it there. It was my safe place in case the journos broke in. Were there any of them outside?'

'A couple. One of them took a photograph, but I don't think they recognised me immediately. I stuffed your things in my pocket so they wouldn't see them.'

'Good. Hey, thanks for helping me out, Brian . . . appreciate it. Now where can I drop you?'

'Anywhere. Which way are you heading?'

'I'll go back to the hotel. Will Marble Arch do ?'

'Perfect.'

They rode in silence. Calum concentrated on the cars in front, making sure he didn't run into the back of anybody. He didn't come near spotting the black Seven Series BMW that had kept the discreetest of distances throughout their drive from Mount Street.

He dropped Williams off, eased the car back into the traffic and headed down Park Lane.

* * *

By the end of the Limehouse Link he felt more acclimatised, and ten miles onto the M20 he was comfortable and relaxed enough to try the radio. The same set of headlights had been in his mirror, a hundred yards back, for at the last five miles or more. The Ferrari crept up to ninety again. Better back off; this wouldn't be the best time to get stopped, and the cops would *love* to give a hard time to the owner of a car like this. He slowed to seventy-five. That car should overtake him now. It probably wasn't the police, but it would be better to be sure.

It stayed back, the distance constant. Calum's nerves began to twitch. He turned the radio off. His eyes were more on the mirrors than on the road ahead. What should he do? If it was like this all the way to the Tunnel he'd be a nervous wreck. Should he stop on the hard shoulder? Was doing that an offence?

Two miles later he couldn't stand it any more. He braked, pulled over, and slowed to a crawl. To his intense relief, the headlights rolled on past. It was a big, dark BMW, maybe a fat cat businessman being driven home. Calum stepped on the gas, accelerated into the fast lane and roared past it. Wow, this car had *great* acceleration! Certain now there were no cops around, he could safely put the Ferrari through its paces. The needle swung smoothly past a hundred, and on towards a hundred and twenty. The only time Calum had gone so fast was in a plane. Jesus, this felt good . . . good but scary.

Suddenly the mirrors were full of light. Who had snuck up on him? Goddammit, it was that *same* BMW. What was that asshole driver playing at? Was this some macho crap? Did he hate being overtaken by a sports car *that* much? How was Calum supposed to *think* at this speed?

Or could it be police, after all? It didn't make any sense.

They had plenty of evidence that he was *way* over the speed limit. Why not stop him and be done with it? There they were right behind him, matching him rev for rev. Were they bored, with nothing better to do, trying to spin it out, enjoying an excuse to go fast?

His heart shot straight to his mouth as some idiot doing sixty-five pulled out into his lane, forcing him to brake hard on the still greasy surface. When the moron pulled back in, Calum put his foot down, gunning the screaming V8. It pulled away, but not decisively, and when his nerve ran out at a hundred and twenty-five the BMW began to reel him in again. That car must have plenty of cubic inches, too.

They let him run another four or five miles before putting him out of his misery. The blue and red lights came on and, cursing roundly, he retreated to the shoulder and stopped. His pursuers came to rest fifty yards behind. He looked round. There was no sign of them getting out. Were they radioing a check? He had all the paperwork with him, the receipt, the insurance cover note. Better go face the music. He opened the door and clambered out and began to walk towards them.

It was raw instinct that restrained him, screaming at him to run. He was still twenty yards from the BMW when he hesitated. They saw it and their front doors opened simultaneously. Slowly, warily, they began to come towards him. They weren't wearing hats. Should they be? He had no idea. But he knew he didn't like this. They were ten yards away now. Another second and it would be too late. He turned and raced back, jumping back in and closing the door. He jabbed at the central locking button a split second before the first of them grabbed at the delicate door handle. Start, you fucker, *start*. Jesus, Mary, Joseph, the guy had a *gun*! The engine fired, and scrabbling for grip, the Ferrari fishtailed untidily away, sending them sprawling. Calum crouched desperately down in his seat, waiting for the hail of bullets. They didn't come. He drove off as fast as his courage permitted, watching the mirror all the way.

Christ, they were catching him again. An exit was coming up. In a blur he read Leeds Castle and Landon. Anywhere would do. He had to get off the freeway, find a place he could shake them off or run to. Run to where? A police station? They *were* the police, and now they be madder than hell. Or . . . Could they be bad people pretending to be police? *Please* let it not be that. Cops might bust your ass, beat the crap out of you, but at the end of it all they'd let you go. How could any thugs have found him? No-one had followed him from the hotel.

He was almost on the exit, still in the fast lane. Leaving the manoeuvre to the very last instant, he swung violently across the lanes, right across the bows of two startled slower drivers. Then up the ramp, round a couple of roundabouts and off into the winding, twisting, wet night.

It hadn't worked. They'd made it too. There they were in the mirror, and this was *worse*. The road was twisting and narrow, the famous Ferrari roadholding no advantage in his novice hands. The surface was dreadful, bumps and ridges everywhere and scary great puddles of standing water that threw the speeding projectile off line for whole heart-stopping moments. It was hard to see anything. Light drizzle was turning to real rain, and oncoming cars were half-blinding him.

On and on he drove in the headlong rush to nowhere. He'd *have* to keep his nerve and outrun them. Just concentrate on driving this thing. The road widened a little as a bend opened out. Now was his chance. He mashed the accelerator on the apex and hurtled along the short straight. He'd gained a few vital yards. Into the next left-hander, fast, too *fast*. *Fuuuck*. The tail flew out right, almost overtaking him. He flailed at the wheel, and miraculously the car slithered round and away. Fifty yards of a lead, maybe more. He was in too deep to back off. Rain was sheeting down now. Faster, faster. He came up on tail lights doing forty and barrelled blindly past before the next corner, praying the BMW would be baulked for vital seconds.

A good hundred yards of a lead now. My God, was he *winning*? If he could pull out two or three hundred yards more, he could dart down some lane and lose them completely. A good long straight. *Gun it*. He was overflowing with adrenalin, the worst of the pure fear gone. A hundred and thirty. The BMW was falling back further. A succession of bends was helping now and their distant white lights were dancing in and out of his mirrors. They would lose sight of him soon. Wow, he was gonna do it! A few more curves, past two dawdlers and . . . what the hell was a traffic light doing *here*? Three hundred yards; two. Still red. His foot came off the gas. *Change, change!* Too late, he'd have to run the lights.

He was lucky there was nothing coming from left or right as he ploughed straight on. Unfortunately there wasn't a straight on. Only when his headlights picked up bushes where tarmac should have been, did he ram the brake pedal to the floor.

If the car hadn't spun, vitally losing speed, he was dead. If it was a wall he was a goner, too. It was the spin and the thudding, scrunching, backwards landing in the yielding bushes that saved his life.

*　　*　　*

As soon as the Ferrari distributor opened on Saturday morning, the police were on the phone.

'This is Brian Williams. How can I help you?'

'Sergeant Trafford of Maidstone police. I'm telephoning concerning a silver-coloured Ferrari 375 which we believe you may have supplied. The number plates were removed, but we found some papers from your company inside. We'd like to ask you to check the engine and chassis numbers so we can trace it.'

'We should be able to do that immediately. What are the numbers?'

Williams waited patiently to hear them, but he already *knew*. He didn't want to let Calum Buchanan down, but he had no option.

'Let me see . . . yes, it *is* one of ours, officer. Delivered it myself yesterday, as it happens.' He gave him Calum's name and address. 'Is the car badly damaged?'

'Fixing it don't look like a DIY job to me, sir.'

'And is Mr Buchanan . . . all right?'

'Don't know, sir. Gentleman appears to have left the scene without reporting the accident. No trace of him in local hospitals. Now you've given us his address, we'll get the Met to check there. He'll be in hot water, all right, if he ain't got one hell of a story.'

* * *

The front and side airbags had done their work, but Calum was pretty battered. His neck and back were badly bruised and his insides didn't feel too thrilled about the experience.

161

They'd blindfolded and gagged him, tied his hands and ankles and thrown him in the BMW's boot. The pain made him wince at every undulation or bump and the hour's drive seemed endless. He guessed it was back to London. On arrival he was manhandled roughly up a flight of stairs, along a corridor and into some room, where they untied him and threw him onto the floor. He heard a key turn. It took him ten minutes to find the nerve to take off the blindfold and gag.

The room had a skylight but no windows. A water jug plus a grubby mug, and a little pot to piss in. On the floor, a malodorous mattress with no blankets. One bare light bulb. Calum sat and waited, shivering with cold and fear. Sleep was out of the question. Oh God, what were they going to do with him? They'd taken his watch, so the skylight high above became his crude clock.

After long darkness and maybe four hours of daylight, the door opened and a short, thin, ugly man brought him a fatty bacon sandwich and a mug of tea. He said nothing and Calum asked nothing. The man left. Six hours later, same guy, same meal. This time Calum, keeping his tone nice and submissive, asked what would happen next. He got a grunt in reply.

The pattern was broken at around six in the evening, when he heard mighty footsteps approaching on the boards outside and two bulky, evil-looking men marched in, each twirling a wooden chair so effortlessly it might have been made of polystyrene. One had a huge Roman nose, eyes too far apart, and black hair with long unfashionable sideburns. The other seemed to have no hair anywhere. His absence of eyebrows made his small piggy eyes look even more menacing.

They sat saddle-style on the chairs, their elbows resting on the seat backs as they carefully examined the catch of the day

162

which knelt meekly beneath them. Calum was too scared to look at them. As he averted his eyes, he caught sight of the oddly threatening assortment of big rings both sported. He glanced back up. They were still staring curiously down at him. When Calum lowered his eyes yet again, the bald one grabbed at his hair and yanked his head sharply up.

'Fifty mill, then yer out of 'ere.'

'What?'

'Your ransom, it's fifty million.'

'I haven't *got* fifty million pounds.'

'That's a pity. Then we'll 'ave to kill you . . .'

He let go of Calum's hair, took a large handgun out of his jacket pocket and rubbed his chin with the muzzle. Calum cringed.

'. . . Unless you earn it for us.'

'What d'you mean, *earn* it?'

'You 'ave a talent that earns money quick. Not only quick, but legal-like. You could make a start with the lott'ry t'night.'

'I can't do it to order.'

'Do it anyway you want, matey. Sooner you get it, sooner yer out of 'ere.'

Think, think, try to *think*. Play for time, say yes. What do you have to lose by playing along? What *choice* do you have?

'Okay.'

'That's what we like to hear, ain't it, Dessie? Here's a pencil and paper. You put yer thinking cap on and write them numbers down. If yer right, little Ted'll cook you a nice juicy steak tonight.'

'No, no, it doesn't work like that. I can't do it here, I need to be outside.'

It was the dark one's turn to speak, his voice as rough as coarse sandpaper.

'Bollocks. No way yer leavin' this room.'

'But I *need* a clear view of the sky . . .'

'What's wrong with the skylight?'

'You don't understand . . .' There was real desperation in Calum's voice . . . 'My predictive time envelope is barely an hour. I *need* to decide at the last minute. The horse race was . . . different, 'cause that was just a few minutes ahead . . .'

'Okay, you can do the 'orses for us. Take longer, but we can be patient, eh, Sam?'

''ang on, Dessie, that'd take *far* longer. Think how many races we'd have to bet on. Lott'ry's *much* better.'

'Yeah, s'ppose you're right, Sammy. But '*e* . . .' Dessie jabbed a finger fiercely at Calum, '. . . ain't goin' nowhere. You know, Sam, I reckon the little bastard might be trying to fuck us about.'

Calum shook his head so hard he made himself dizzy. That didn't stop bald Sammy fishing a silencer out of his pocket and begin screwing it to the gun. Dessie had one last go at cajoling the captive.

'D'you want me to castrate you with a broken bottle?'

This prompted an even more energetic headshake from Calum.

'So, write down the fuckin' *numbers*.'

'Okay.'

Anything to buy time. And to avoid the encounter with that bottle.

'Good. We'll be back for the numbers soon.'

Sammy unscrewed the silencer and put the gun away. They both rose, took one more meaningful look at him and went out, banging the door hard behind them. Calum started shaking uncontrollably. He had very little time to think up some way out of this.

Was there anything he could do? The skylight was way out of reach, a good twelve feet up. What else? *Think,* for Chrissakes. In movies captives always hid, tricked the guards into coming into the room, and then hit them over the head with something. The only weapons he had to hand were the mattress, which was unpromising, and the now brimming pot. Throwing that at them *might* work, but it was more likely to make them extremely cross. It looked like he could only sit and wait. He crouched miserably in the corner. If they had *any* intention of letting him go, surely they would have disguised their names. They would shoot him in cold blood and dispose of his body like so much garbage.

Would Morag sense he was gone? How would Marianna feel when she heard? Delighted probably, to be rid of him permanently. Come to think of it, *she* would get all his goddam money. When they married she made him write a will leaving everything to her and he had never changed it. She and Brett would get to spend all *his* money. Was there nothing he could do about that? Even if he used the pencil and paper to scribble down a new will, it was unlikely that Sammy and Dessie would agree to give their names and addresses as witnesses. He put it out of his mind and went back to being terrified. If he concentrated like *crazy*, was there any way he could do it?

He put the light off and sat with his eyes closed. In this state, trying to meditate was a joke. He gave up on it and circled round the room to see if there any angle that might give a view of the moon. It was clouding over. Just *great*. He tried concentrating again. Nothing. He was only too painfully aware that time was ebbing away. Why on earth had he turned down the offer from the British spook? What a goddam *idiot*!

*   *   *

165

The door swung open and Dessie banged the light switch on.

'It's gone seven. You done it?'

Calum looked up and saw Dessie coming towards him. Before he got there, Calum picked up the pencil and scribbled furiously on the pad, picking numbers entirely at random.

'Those better be right, or you'll get what's comin' to you.'

He smacked Calum hard on the back of the head, snatched the paper from him and marched back out, switching the light off as he went.

Calum curled up foetally. He had one and a half hours before they came for him. He should he use it? Preparing his last thoughts?

*   *   *

Time ticked by, faster and faster. It would be soon now. He could almost feel their rough hands dragging him like a rag doll to the place of execution. How would he behave? Would he snivel, or squirm or beg pathetically? Should he use the pot again, so at least he wouldn't wet himself? He crawled over to it. As he unzipped his flies, something made him glance up at the skylight.

JESUS CHRIST.

He almost died of fright. A black helmet was pressed against it, the visor closed and impenetrable. Calum threw himself back in terror. He just caught a glimpse of a gloved fist as it smashed through the glass, sending a hundred fragments spearing downwards. Seconds later a rope flew down, swinging wildly to and fro. Calum looked back up. The helmet had gone.

Heavy footsteps were approaching the door. They must have *heard*. A greater terror overwhelmed the fear of the unknown and, in one blinding surge of adrenalin, he flung himself up and at the dangling rope. He was still two feet short of the skylight when the door flew open.

'*What the* . . . YOU LITTLE BLEEDIN'. . .'

Dessie led the raging charge across the room, Sammy only one step behind. Calum scrambled up the rope as if the very hounds of hell were snapping at his heels. Halfway through he let go of the rope, throwing his hands onto the skylight frame to lever himself out. He didn't even feel the sharp cuts from the glass fragments, but was only too aware of the violent tug on his right leg as Dessie jumped up and grabbed it.

Calum's arms buckled and he felt himself about to fall. Laces would have done for him. Mercifully, his loafer slipped right off. As Dessie crashed to the floor, still clutching the shoe in both hands, he saw Calum's legs disappear.

Calum stood up and looked frantically around him. The roof was flat with low parapets on either side. To left and right, identical roofs stretched as far as the eye could see, separated only by short brick divides and chimneys. The rope was tied around a chimney but before Calum could gather his wits, it was writhing under the strain of a new load. *Shit.* A second later Sammy's bald head rose up through the skylight, yelling fiercely. Calum was transfixed. Then in another torrent of oaths the head disappeared again. *What the* . . . ?

The muffled sound of Dessie's voice shouting for Ted made

Calum realise their problem. Sammy and Dessie weren't sky-light gauge. They would *never* get through that tiny square. It gave him a few more seconds to get away.

Which way though? At that instant the mysterious helmeted figure plunged back into his consciousness. Where had he gone? Calum spun desperately around looking for any sign of him.

There he was, two or three roofs further along the terrace, standing ghost-like, calmly beckoning Calum.

Calum didn't know whether to be more frightened of this figure or his captors. Another loud shout from below decided it. As soon as the spectre saw Calum run towards him, he turned and moved agilely on. Blindly Calum followed, hurdling over the first three divides, glancing back to see Ted pop out of the skylight like a jackrabbit out of a hole. For a small man, Ted's voice carried amazingly.

'Oi . . . COME BACK 'ERE.'

Ignoring the searing pain from his swollen ankles, Calum threw himself even faster over divide after divide until he was ten or fifteen houses away, Ted hot on his heels. The terrace still stretched out before them, no escape route in sight.

Twenty yards ahead the spectre stepped towards a parapet, over it, and . . . disappeared. *What the hell . . .?*

Suddenly from below came the sound of angry, yelling voices. Dessie and Sammy were out in the street and chasing along after him. *Fuck.* Calum fairly flew over the next three divides to where the mystery figure had disappeared and peered gingerly over. Just below the parapet was a ladder. The black figure was now almost down it, jumping the last few rungs onto the pavement, and stepping out of Calum's line of sight. Seconds later he reappeared astride a motorbike. Sammy and Dessie slowed as they approached him.

VROOM, VROOM, VROOM. The quiet night air was ripped apart by the frantic revving.

Little Ted was almost on Calum now, no more than one house length away, an ugly resolved look on his face. What should he do? Surrender now and he was dead. There was only one option. He threw himself over the parapet, swung his feet onto the ladder, and half-climbed, half-slithered down it. He could sense more than see the duel below as the squealing, squirming bike flashed right and left, jabbing at Sammy and Dessie, like a bull keeping picadors at bay.

As Calum reached ground level he felt Ted's feet on the upper rungs. Still the bike screamed left and right. Calum turned round. Sammy was darting this way and that, trying everything to get past the rider and clutch his prey. Dessie was tearing back to where the BMW was parked outside the house.

In a huge cloud of exhaust, the bike suddenly shot backwards at the ladder, virtually impaling Calum. Involuntarily, his legs flew apart and he was thrust onto it behind the rider. Instinctively he grabbed at the rider's sides and clung on as the bike reared stallion-like, swerved past Dessie's last diving lunge, and catapulted itself down the long empty street.

Calum turned and saw Sammy screech the BMW to a half-halt to collect the other two and set off in full-bore pursuit. Oh no, not *again*.

No, not again. It was different this time. Munich horsepower might be a match for a Ferrari: not for a Ducati. The rider swung onto a main road, leaning so low their knees almost touched the ground. The BMW took the junction too, tyres squealing furiously, but the cause was lost within minutes.

The big bike powered relentlessly ahead, slicing effortlessly in and out of traffic. Calum looked back again. The BMW was now *way* back, out of the contest already. That only seemed to make the rider go faster.

Calum's terror had been so total that it blanked out everything else. Now he had to *think*. Who the hell *was* this guy? Whoever he was, it felt like his trunk was made out of teak. This *must* be a gangland thing. He had been rescued, only to be delivered to some other bunch. What would *they* do to him?

And, Jesus, was it *freezing* on the back of this thing. It was okay for *him* in his helmet and leathers. The cold night air was tearing through Calum's thin shirt and chinos. If the ride went on much longer, he would get frostbite. He crouched down lower.

Where were they headed, anyway? His eyes were watering too much to keep them open for long. They roared on past mile after mile of nondescript, scruffy low buildings and shops, many of them boarded up. He pulled himself up an inch and managed a quick look over the rider's shoulder. Ahead high-rise towers were coming into view.

Minutes later, the Ducati's banshee wail was echoing around the deserted canyons of the City. They roared on down to the Embankment. Now Calum could see normal people, leading normal lives, walking normally down the street. He was tantalisingly close to freedom. Could he try jumping off, and if his ankles would take it, running away? This might be his only chance. He *must* take it before it was too late. Problem was, this guy didn't seem to believe in stopping for red lights or anything else. Falling at this speed would mean crushed bones for certain, and death if he fell in the path of a car. Before he had more chance to think, they hurtled right at Northumberland Avenue and on into Trafalgar Square. Lots more people there. Under Admiralty Arch, up the Mall at a lunatic speed and into Constitution Hill at eighty plus. He might have had a saviour when the ear-splitting noise caused a policeman to try waving them down, but the rider looped smoothly past him and treated Hyde Park Corner like a curve on a racing circuit.

Knightsbridge now. The bike swung sharply left, then right, and dived into a dark mews. At the far end was an open garage. The bike thundered in and braked violently to a halt. The door rolled closed after them and a light came on. Calum tried to clamber off, but his legs were too frozen to co-operate and he tumbled awkwardly backwards onto the floor. He lay there, unable to budge.

The rider seemed oblivious to his presence. Still astride the bike, back turned to Calum, he calmly stripped off the top half of his leathers, revealing a full wraparound suit of body armour. Then he pulled his helmet off. A mane of silky long black hair cascaded down. Calum gasped as the rider turned round. She had *the* most gorgeous oriental face. She smiled sweetly at him.

'Hi. May Chang, CIA. Are you okay?'

Calum managed something between a nod and a shake.

'We need some help from you. In return, we can offer you total protection, and get you out to the States this very night. What do you say?'

Calum fainted, really fainted.

171

13

Christopher Ransome was bothered. Amused, too, and possibly to the merest degree excited. He was always entertained when the Foreign Office had one of its rare internal bust-ups, and thoroughly approved of the unflagging civility and style with which they were conducted. This was shaping up to be a particularly satisfying example. Nonetheless, he was bothered. The increasingly frequent telegrams from the embassy in Beijing were thoughtful and closely argued. Expert sinologists from the Ambassador down, they were as well-qualified to comment as any group alive, and they had the Foreign Secretary convinced. It pained him that his own instincts were more aligned with the scepticism this advice was engendering at Number Ten. Ransome had no way of knowing whether the Prime Minister's trenchant views were sincerely held or flowed more from his wish to stick closely to the White House line. Evidently the temperature was still rising in the US business community and those who favoured a cautious approach were being drowned out by the increasingly shrill hawks. To the intense relief of Washington, Bob Tyne had passed up the opportunity of the *Herald Tribune* Conference to air his views, but he remained a ticking bomb, capable of exploding publicly at any time. He had temporarily transferred his energies to rounding up a posse of like-minded business vigilantes to turn the screw some more.

It was not only American businessmen who wanted action.

The Department of Trade and Industry was besieged by British companies reporting how they were being hampered in China, or protesting that the flood of cheap imports from China would put them out of business. The officials could see that this problem would only grow and do untold damage to Western economies. They, too, viewed the missives from the British embassy in Beijing with a concerned and jaundiced eye.

The Beijing embassy's attitude was unwavering. They discounted 'wild conspiracy theories' of co-ordinated plans by the Chinese authorities to evade their WTO obligations, and argued that the unwieldiness and sheer shambles of the Chinese bureaucracy made it hard to effect change so rapidly. They pointed out, in a line that brought a loud snort from the Prime Minister, that this was why the Chinese had wanted longer and fuller transitional measures, and it was only pressure from Western countries that had forced them to accept an unrealistic timetable. The embassy's bottom line was that there was nothing to be gained by forcing their hand. I *wonder*, thought Christopher Ransome, I wonder what Tommy Wu would think.

Tommy Wu was already a seasoned China watcher when Ransome was in diplomatic short pants. Born in Malaysia of Chinese parents, he had lived the life of an itinerant scholar, sometimes attached to this institute or that, occasionally publishing a slim volume or essay, always on the move, with no place really home. He kept it all going, even now in his seventies, and was currently living in Montana, working through drafts of his latest opus. They met rarely, but kept vaguely in touch, and his Montana number was unearthed after a few calls. Ransome kept it general.

'So, Tommy, what are the Chinese up to?'

'What kinda question is that, Chris? What d'ya mean, what they up to? Getting rich, mainly.'

In Ransome's youth, very few had been allowed to get away with calling him Chris. Tommy was the only one who still did.

'That it, Tommy?'

'The army's strike power is growing. *Lots* of new equipment. Same with the air force and navy. They're building three more carriers. If I were in Japanese shoes, I'd be plenty scared.'

'But what they're *saying* doesn't sound too worrying. Guaranteeing the security of South Korea, that was a slap in the face for the North, wasn't it?'

'Chris, *think* about it. They've had good trade relations with Seoul for *years* now. Why you think they went that far? They want the American military out of Korea, or cut right back. The Americans are only there to protect the South from the North. With all the nationalism in Korea, the Americans would've been slung out *years* ago if that threat wasn't there. Now it may change. The North's in a mess. No way they could attack a territory *guaranteed* by China. So, guess what, no more need for Americans. I give them five years there, *max.* And don't expect it to stop in Korea. Japan will be the next case for treatment. Now the Soviet threat's gone, what do the Japanese need US protection from? Of the hundred thousand GIs in Asia, half are based in Japan. Watch out for them getting a ticket home, too. I tell you, Chris, China won't rest till it's the undisputed military power in East Asia.'

'What can we do to stop it?'

'Nothing, it's inevitable. Fascinating, watching history unfold, don't you think?'

'Will they *use* their forces?'

'You mean march into other countries? . . . No, not for

175

the time being. Why should they do want to do that? The Chinese aren't really *interested* in any place else. They don't *need* to, as long as they can impose their will economically and any other way they choose. Take the sea. China ratified the UN Law of the Sea Treaty in 1996. That gives countries the power to declare exclusive economic zones of two hundred miles around almost any speck of land. China's in territorial disputes with *everyone* over who owns real estate. Vietnam, Japan, Brunei, the Philippines, Malaysia, both Koreas. If you draw a circle two hundred miles round every tiny island, can you *imagine* the acreage of ocean, and what the mineral rights are worth? And if China is unchallenged as a superpower, guess who's gonna win those disputes . . . They won't *need* to march in.'

'What about Taiwan?'

'That's different, there they might. Taiwan's part of China. Its independence is a running sore for them, a constant reminder of the past limits to their power.'

'What's your feeling about the trade side?'

'You know how the Chinese are, Chris. Smart people. They'll get away with whatever they can. They still need the foreign investment and technology, but only for another eight, ten years. Then they'll have pretty much what they need.'

'So how are the prospects for foreign businesses there?'

'They'll keep coming, whatever the obstacles, because they can't stand the thought of missing out on a market that vast. If I were them, I wouldn't hold my breath waiting for big profits, though.'

'Hang on, Tommy. Times have changed. The Chinese *can't* go around confiscating businesses or stopping them repatriating profits, not if they want to keep trading with the rest of the world.'

'Give them credit for being more subtle than that. They'll find their own ways to do it, but ask yourself a question. Do you seriously believe that a race of one point three billion entrepreneurs are gonna let Johnny Foreigner have a major share in *their* economy for long? They'll be clever. They'll throw the foreigners enough bones to keep them there, but eat the *meat* themselves. And by the way, whatever you guys agreed with the Chinese in Geneva, prising the juiciest steaks away from their army will be easier said than done.'

'Thanks, Tommy. Can I do anything to help your granddaughter when she's in Europe? . . .'

Ransome finished the call and went out to the terrace. He sat in his favourite chair, sipping a long gin and tonic, gazing out over the shimmering lake. He recalled Napoleon's comment, 'Let China sleep, for when it wakes it will shake the earth.' If Tommy was right, the alarm clock had already gone off.

*   *   *

'Welcome to Monument Base, Mr Buchanan. How was the flight?'

'Different. My first time on a private jet. Do they all have blacked out windows?'

'Yes, sir. Military ones, that is. Not business jets, of course. Now, let me show you your facilities. These are the best guest quarters we have, though it falls short of Hyatt standards. Bathroom's through there. Air conditioning is set to a constant sixty-eight degrees. The phone is for internal calls only. TV remote control is by the bed. We get CNN, MTV and three movie channels. Anything you need to eat or drink, just press Five and I'll be right along. Think of it as room service. I'm Private Wiltshire. I work a rota with Privates Harry Clark and Jack Delaney. We're available twenty-four hours. We've been told yours is a very special assignment and we want to make your stay as comfortable as possible, sir.'

'I need to make an international call . . . How do I do that?'

'You'll have to discuss that with Colonel Montgomery himself, sir. This is a *very* high security base. Colonel Montgomery is . . .'

'Miss Chang told me on the plane.'

'He'll be handling your case personally. He told me to say he was looking forward to meeting you. After you've freshened up and rested a while, call me and I'll take you along to see him.'

'Private Wiltshire . . . Hey, I can't go on calling you "Private". What's your name?'

'Well . . . it's Dean, but my friends call me Dino.'

'Is it okay if I do, too?'

'Sure, sir, that'd be . . . real friendly.'

'Good, and I'm not "sir", I'm Calum . . . Now that that's settled, Dino, what's local time here? I lost my watch.'

'Two twenty p.m., Mountain Standard Time. You'll find a quartz watch in the drawer by the bed and new clothes in the wardrobe over there.'

'So we're in which State? May wouldn't tell me.'

'Arizona, sir . . . pardon me, Calum.'

'Which part of Arizona? North? West?'

'That's . . .'

'Classified? . . . I thought so. I'm beginning to get the picture. Okay, Dino, I'll take a shower and a nap. Will you give me a wake-up call at four? . . . Thanks. I'm gonna be pretty interested to meet Colonel Montgomery. He sounds quite a dude.'

'All the boys here think he is. See you later.'

Calum went over to the window and looked beyond the triple mesh fences up towards the rusty brown hills. This was the first moment he'd been left completely alone with his thoughts since the rescue. Calling them thoughts was an overstatement. In the mews apartment, the CIA boys got a medic to take a quick look at his bruises and give him some pain-killers and sleeping pills. Then they rushed him straight to the General Aviation terminal at Heathrow. On the jet his attempts to keep awake long enough to think things through were soon defeated by the pills, his extreme exhaustion and maybe a reaction to all the drama. It felt like his brain wanted to block out any new information in case the overload brought his mental system down permanently. His mind was still blown, the fuses not repaired. He couldn't work out what had he got himself into now. Not that he had much choice at the time, mind you. Frankly, he'd have agreed to *anything* to get somewhere those hoods couldn't find him.

But would *these* guys now assume they had a blank cheque to use him any way they wanted? What would they do to him, and for how long? Would it be enough to explain generally how his method worked and leave it at that, or would they demand more? He must be wary and keep Morag out of this. He had seen too many conspiracy movies to have blind faith in the CIA and he would need to be on his guard. Maybe his best plan would be to put down a clear marker right from the start on what he was and wasn't willing to do, *plus* agree from the outset how long they'd need him. And trust *no-one*. What the hell *did* they want from him, though? He hoped he hadn't just flown by private jet from the frying pan to the fire. Man, was it was confusing.

*   *   *

'At last. Welcome to Monument, Calum.'

Calum wondered if Jason Montgomery *was* the monument. He filled the doorway. Six six, maybe six seven, and with shoulders that didn't know when to stop. He looked thirty-eight, maybe forty, but the granite-carved features made it hard to tell. His cropped, wiry brown hair carried no hint of grey.

The handshake was a veritable bone-crusher. Montgomery led him through to a kind of lounge and indicated two deep, luxuriously comfortable leather chairs.

'We are *very* glad that you agreed to work with us.' He gave Calum a huge, friendly smile. 'You've had an active few days, by any standards. Must feel like you've been in combat mode. I hope you managed to get some rest along the way.'

Montgomery's voice was deep and resonant, without booming. Not obviously East or West coast, unplaceable to Calum's ears. There was something reassuringly soothing about its timbre.

'Thanks, I feel okay. I got a few hours' sleep on the plane, and some more here, so not too bad.'

'You've recovered from all the . . . excitement?'

'I wouldn't want to try it again in a hurry. I'm still amazed how you guys tracked me down. May didn't give me chapter and verse.'

'She was under instructions not to say too much, but I can

give you a little more flavour. I can't take the "you guys" credit, though. It's the CIA in London who deserve that. We were kept fully informed, but they *did* it. Good job, too.'

'And "we" is?'

'Of course, I should have explained sooner. As Miss Chang told you, I am the commanding officer here at Monument. This is a Special Forces army base. I'll tell you more about what we do tomorrow. To satisfy your natural curiosity, the way the CIA watched over you was straightforward operational stuff. They figured out where you were staying and that British intelligence had made contact with you. They also knew how serious the threat to your personal security was, so they kept a close but discreet watch. It was . . . how should I put it? . . . a little naive of you to think you could call the Ferrari dealer without alerting others. Did you not realise that your room would be bugged out of existence?'

'Jesus, how dumb can you get? I didn't stop to think.'

'As a result, various people knew you were on the move. The CIA boys were instructed not to intercept you, but to monitor the situation carefully. They saw the BMW following you from Mayfair to Notting Hill . . .'

'They picked me up from *there*? . . . I didn't notice them till *much* later. But . . . hold on . . . what happened after that? The CIA can't have followed me the whole way. I *swear* there was no second car following me, at any rate once I pulled off the freeway.'

'They didn't need to. They have a clever piece of equipment. It operates like a blow-pipe, using compressed air to aim a tiny device at high speed. The device is a *very* small homing beacon. Its entire surface is magnetic, so it attaches like a limpet to any metal object it hits. It's *so* small – not more than two milimetres across – that the occupants of the

BMW wouldn't have noticed it or felt it as it hit the rear of their car. After that, the CIA had a perfect signal to follow. They reckoned those people were planning on taking you someplace; all they needed to know was where.'

'What about British intelligence? If they had me bugged, weren't they . . . ?'

'For sure, it was a busy night for everyone. They snuck up on the Ferrari when the guy from the dealer was waiting for your call in Park Lane and stuck *their* homing device right onto it. But they underestimated how imminent the threat was. They were more interested in watching where you planned to run to. As long as you stayed in Britain they would've left you alone, but the moment you headed for a port or the Channel Tunnel, which was the *obvious* place, they would've stopped you.'

'And I thought I was being smart. Seems like half of London knew what I was up to.'

'These folk have been at this game a little longer than you.'

'Yup . . . So what happened after I crashed?'

'The CIA couldn't tell you'd crashed, but when they saw the BMW start heading back for London, they were pretty sure you'd been captured. Then it was a question of figuring out who was holding you and keeping watch.'

'What good would that have done if they'd topped me right away, there in that house?'

'Why *should* they? They had captured you for a purpose. You forget one other thing. The CIA had the mother and father of fixes on that house, a whole battery of eavesdropping devices. They were listening to every word that was said. They knew they were planning to use you for the Saturday lottery, and that if you didn't deliver you were at serious risk. That's

182

why the rooftop operation was mounted shortly before the result came through.'

'Why didn't they just send the cavalry in through the front door?'

'Number one, the CIA tries to be discreet as possible, especially on foreign soil. Cavalry operations draw a lot of unwelcome attention. Also, they thought there was too big a risk you'd get hurt in any shoot-out.'

'What about when I was climbing down the ladder? The hoods could have shot me then.'

'That's why we had two marksmen hidden on roofs the other side of the street. If anyone had pulled out a gun, they would have been taken out. You were pretty safe.'

'I can't say it felt like that at the time. Still, it worked. All's well that ends well.'

'A-men to that. Now, if you don't mind . . . to work. We won't start in earnest until tomorrow, when you've had the chance of a good night's sleep, but let me tell you how we plan to organise things. First up, I need you to sign some documentation undertaking to keep secret the existence of this program, and all you do and see here. Second, I want to introduce you to the main people here you'll be interfacing with. Professor Lee is the head of our special scientific program. He's a naturalised American citizen. Grew up in Hong Kong, worked in various universities in the States for many years, and has been employed directly by the government for the last five. A world class authority on parapsychology. Then Rita Osborne, army medic with the rank of Major. Psychologist. Plays a *big* role in our operation. Finally, Lieutenant Jones. Doesn't look like a Jones. American father, Singaporean mother, but the Asian gene must've won out, at least as his appearance goes. He's our observer. He'll sit in on all your sessions. His only task is to keep a complete record, and we want you to behave as if he isn't there.'

'What about May?'

'Oh yes, May . . . She's going to be our liaison with the CIA and will stay here at Monument for the duration of your assignment. May was born in the US, soon after her folks emigrated from Taiwan. She will not participate in most of the sessions, but she will be around. If you like, she will be happy to spend some social time with you. We have a small club on the base. Fun, if you don't mind simple pleasures. Pool, juke-box, that sort of thing. It's closed for refurbishment now, but it should be open again in a few days. May can take you over there.'

'Thank you, I'd like that. Colonel Montgomery, can I ask a question?'

'Sure you can, but could I presume to anticipate it? . . . You're thinking don't we have a lot of Asians on this program? Is that it?'

'No, that wasn't it, but since you ask . . . what is the reason?'

'It wouldn't be so surprising these days, with the melting pot our great nation has become, but there is a *particular* reason in this case, which relates to one of our major objectives. I'll tell you all about it tomorrow. Now, since I guessed wrong, what *was* your question?'

'I need to make an international call. How do I do that?'

'*That* unfortunately is the *one* thing we cannot permit. We have to maintain the strictest rules about communications. However, if there's a message you would like us to get to someone . . . ?'

'No, it's not that, I need to check my answer machine in London, that's all.'

'We can do that for you. If you give Private Wiltshire the access code, he will get you a full transcript of your messages.'

'I don't think I want a full transcript. I hate to think of some of the messages. I only want to know if a certain party has called, that's all.'

'No problem. Let Wiltshire know, and he will have it checked. Now, let's leave it there for today. We find it best to serve our guests with their meals in their own quarters. How does a thick, juicy cut of American beef sound? . . . Good. Private Wiltshire will escort you back now, and I will look forward to meeting up again bright and early tomorrow. Shall we say eight a.m.? . . . *Very* good. Have a pleasant evening. On behalf of the US government, I want to thank you again for volunteering to help. It is hard to overestimate the importance of your potential contribution.'

Calum was about to put his marker down, but somehow before he could get it out, Jason Montgomery took his hand, wrung the life out of it again, and sent him on his way.

14

The next morning, after the introductions and the formality of signing the secrecy agreement, they sat around a table, with Professor Lee and Major Osborne on either side of Montgomery and Lieutenant Jones at the far end, his spiral note pad ready for action. Jones sure did look inscrutably Asian. Montgomery's mahogany voice started the proceedings.

'Calum, I want to begin by telling you what we do here at Monument, and why it is so important. As you may already have deduced, we are engaged in a program of research into harnessing paranormal and parapsychological phenomena. Let me say right away that although we use these words, it is not our belief that there is anything *ab*-normal or *super*-natural about these phenomena. They are natural forces that are little understood. You could make a comparison with radio waves. As you know, radio waves were not *invented*, they were *discovered*. They were there all the time. We think the same is true of paranormal phenomena, which is why the Pentagon gives us a huge budget to understand and apply these forces. We're not the only ones. In simple language, there's a race on and we wanna be first. If the Russians and the Chinese don't beat us there, it won't be for want of trying.'

'Yeah, I heard something about that from the British spook.'

'I'm not surprised. However, the British program is . . . very modest. They don't seem to realise that you need more

187

than string and sealing wax to make progress in this area
. . . Getting back to *our* program, we have three distinct
areas of operation: location, interdiction, and prediction. Let
me explain. Are you okay for coffee? . . . Lieutenant Jones,
would you oblige? . . . First of all, location. This means
using specially trained individuals with highly developed
psychic powers to locate key objectives or targets. It could
be rocket batteries hidden under camouflage in the desert,
or nuclear silos. It could be a missile production facility. It
could even be a person, such as a military commander or a
political leader. Many totalitarian leaders are paranoid – often
with good reason – about assassination attempts by foreign
powers or their own people. They use doubles, secret tunnels,
special transport, and keep on the move, varying their routes,
trying to be as unpredictable as possible. If the US wanted
to eliminate someone like that, a psychic could provide *vital*
information.'

Calum nodded and sipped his coffee. This was heady stuff.
He would have to redouble his efforts to keep up his guard
if this wasn't to go to his head. Not only *hearing* all these
secrets, but having these important guys briefing *him* about
it. If Marianna could see him now, this would blow her
cotton tights off! He nodded again as Montgomery moved
on to interdiction. Calum had no idea what that meant.

'. . . Now, this term is used widely in all manner of military
situations, but I'd like to tell you what it means for us.'
Montgomery leant forward, transferring his weight to his
outsize, densely forested forearms. Involuntarily, Calum did
the same with his slimline equivalents. 'You will have heard
of people who can bend spoons just by stroking them.'

'Sure.'

'There are others who can bend things without touching

them. Pure mind power. It is *that* force that we are attempting to harness, and over considerable distances. Not bending guns or missile nose cones, of course . . .' Calum was glad he hadn't spoken, since that was exactly what he was guessing. '. . . Imagine what happens to the guidance system of a missile or the computer that controls a huge radar array if someone starts fooling around with the electrons in the chips. It doesn't take much agitation to affect their calculations or send the whole system down, undetectably and safely. At no physical risk to our side, and with no chance of civilian casualties. As of today, there is no known defence against it. No bunker deep enough, no steel plate thick enough. The potential is limitless. Our experiments so far have had limited success and our operational range is still far too short, but we'll get there.'

'That's pretty amazing.'

'We think so, but don't forget, if *they* have no defence against this, neither do we. So developing counter-psychic forces may be as important . . .' Calum's nodding was getting to be a habit.

'. . . Finally, we come to prediction. That's the most self-explanatory, and of course it's where *you* come in.' Montgomery relaxed back in his seat, a mere nanosecond before Calum. 'There is ever-greater equality between the major powers in key electronic technologies. Take radar. Some years back we had a lead, but it's been eroded. If we send up a combat aircraft against theirs, it's heading for fifty-fifty whether the good guy or the bad guy will be the first to get a radar lock on. Even tangling with third world countries is getting riskier as they get hold of modern gear. So, imagine how much it would help if we *knew* where and when to expect an enemy attack, if our pilots *knew* when they were about to get locked, if our subs *knew* when they would be detected. The result would be

189

absolute superiority, *and* at a fraction of the cost of developing smarter hardware. *This* is why we need your help, Calum.'

Calum clasped his hands together, leant forward, and smiled shyly. In his whole life *no-one* had ever spoken this way, like he was valued, like he was *somebody*. He felt an unfamiliar warm glow spreading inside him.

'I've no idea if I *can* help, but I'm willing to do what I can.'

'Good man, that's what I hoped to hear. Now, in a moment I'm going to describe how your program will be organised, but before that I want to explain the *special* reason I mentioned last night.' He leant back in and lowered his voice to a conspiratorial whisper. 'This is *very* secret. Over the last few years China has on several occasions conducted naval and military exercises in the Gulf of Taiwan. Often these have had a primarily political purpose, aimed particularly at swaying younger Taiwanese. However, last year's exercises were more realistic, more like a dry run for a real invasion. Calum, how much do you follow the international political scene?'

'Not much. Recently, anyway.' Calum felt ridiculously ignorant. How he wished he'd read some books or listened more closely to Morag's radio programmes.

'Well, let me bring you up to date. There has been some growing tension between China and the US over trade. Our side wasn't wholeheartedly in favour of letting the Chinese join the World Trade Organisation. That's a sort of club that governs the rules of trade between nations. For China, getting in was hugely important. The US didn't think they'd play by the rules, but the Europeans and the Japanese kowtowed and let them join. Now it's shaping up like we were right all along and the Chinese are cruisin' for a bruisin' in Geneva.'

'Sounds like it serves them right.'

'True, but it's not as fine and dandy as that sounds. If the Chinese are penalised, they can be expected to react *furiously*. It'll be a *big* loss of face and they may want to give the finger to the States some other way. It could provide a handy excuse for something they've wanted to do for a long time: invading Taiwan. They might calculate that if the US had already stuck it to them in Geneva, we wouldn't take the chance on blocking them there, too, and risk starting a world war. Between ourselves, Calum, I reckon that assessment might not be too far off track.'

'Hmmm.' Calum nodded gravely.

'The US has never made any *formal* commitment to defend Taiwan, so we *could* just walk away. If we did, though, *we*'d lose one hell of lot of face ourselves and send a signal to the rest of Asia that the Chinese can get away with blue murder. This leaves us with a big dilemma: intervene and risk a war, or stand by and witness the collapse of American prestige and influence in the Pacific.'

'Tricky.' What a dumb thing to say. He couldn't think of anything else: dilemma was the better word, but Montgomery had got there first.

'There *is* an answer. Not sure-fire, but with a fighting chance.' Montgomery paused. Calum hoped he wasn't expected to guess, he had *no* idea. At least if it was multiple choice like a horse race, he could have a stab. He was mightily relieved when Montgomery resumed. 'Taiwan's armed forces are small, but they *are* powerful enough to give the Chinese a bloody nose and *conceivably* deter them if – but only if – they are expertly marshalled. In *precisely* the right place at *precisely* the right time. There is only one way that can reliably happen. Predictive technology. It's the one way we can give our Taiwanese friends any chance of defending themselves without the US

191

being drawn into war. That is why we have so many Asian faces around Monument at present. We are training special detachments of Taiwanese pilots in our techniques. The final thing I should say is that the risk of an assault on Taiwan is not conjecture on our part. CIA operatives in China have filed reports which corroborate that an invasion force is being readied. So now you understand why you are so important to us and why the need is so pressing.'

'So what d'you want from me? When do we make a start?'

'That's the spirit . . . The first part of the exercise comes in two parts, which will take two to three weeks. Professor Lee will work with you to try to understand *what* it is you are doing. Major Osborne's task will be to understand *who* you are, what made you that way, how much your special skills are inherited and how much learnt. This will involve discussing your personal history and personality in depth, and a whole battery of IQ, aptitude and other psychological tests. At the second stage we'll try to develop and replicate your method. This morning you'll make a start with Major Osborne and this afternoon move on for your first session with Professor Lee. If you are not too whacked, Miss Chang would like to share a drink with you this evening. The base bar won't be ready till tomorrow, so you'll have to meet her in your own quarters.'

'That's fine.' Calum liked the way Montgomery talked to him. Courteous, respectful, almost like they were equals. Did he need to put down his marker on time after all? If it was to take only two or three weeks, plus maybe another couple for the second stage, well . . . he guessed he could live with that. Why make a big issue of it now? Mention it later, if necessary.

'Good, well let's get you some fresh coffee.'

* * *

There was a tightness about Rita Osborne's expression, a tension around her lips that hinted at a controlled anger about *something* life had failed to provide for her. The professional warmth of her carefully modulated voice was startlingly contradicted by the chill of her steel-grey eyes. The way her auburn hair was combed harshly back only served to emphasise that middle age had almost claimed her.

'Okay, Calum, where shall we begin? We have quite a lot of information about you.'

'You must keep amazing files, Rita.'

'We do. In your case, we hardly needed them. The *LA Times* profile did most of the leg work for us.'

'Which profile was that?'

'You didn't know? They ran it soon after your horse-racing prediction. A front page column and all of one of the inside pages.'

'How was it?'

'Interesting for us: *you* might not have liked it so much. Most of the comments from folks who knew you weren't too flattering, and, of course, they fed off the spicy British tabloid coverage.'

'Oh.' Calum was thinking of Marianna. Would she have enjoyed seeing him dragged through the mud or hated the embarrassment of the association?

'I can let you have a copy if you'd like.'

'No, thanks. Did it quote my ex, Marianna?'

'It said she had no comment, that it was all in the past. One of her friends, Mandy something, said Marianna regarded you as a loser and was glad to see the back of you.'

'That was kind of her.' The glow had gone. Suddenly Calum felt very low. Would Marianna have let Mandy say that if there was *any* chance that she would take him back? Jones had the grace to look down at his pad and stop taking notes. Rita Osborne injected a more up-beat tone into her voice.

'Let's put all that aside. As Colonel Montgomery said, we need to understand as much as possible about your background and personality make-up. Here is a questionnaire we'd like you to fill in overnight. It may seem very probing, but we need you to answer the questions as fully and frankly as possible. You have our guarantee that the information will go no further than the Colonel, Prof Lee, and myself. As you will see, the first section primarily concerns your immediate family and wider living relations. The next section takes you from childhood right up to now. What people and events have influenced you most? Your biggest successes and setbacks, your future goals and concerns. The third is a self-assessment section. How do you rate your performance at school and college, in the jobs you have done, and in your personal relationships? How is your self-esteem? What patterns of behaviour do you have that affect relationships and personal effectiveness? Finally, there's some simple psychometric tests. If you can let me have the questionnaire back first thing tomorrow, I'll analyse it and go through it with you in the afternoon. Now let's begin with a general chat, to ease you into the process.'

*   *   *

The fried chicken had been perfect, and the Mondavi Cabernet

Shiraz delicious. Tonight May had turned up in a turquoise Chinese-style long dress and looked so amazing it was hard not to spend the whole evening staring at her. She had clearly made quite an effort. What was the game with her anyway? It was pretty unlikely that she was doing this on account of his fascinating personality or good looks. Was it part of checking him out, listening to his off-duty thoughts. Or was she an official morale-booster? Come to think of it, was she meant to be part of his R & R? Was it intended that . . . ? He wished he knew what was expected of him. He couldn't come right out and ask her, could he? But why else would they have sent her to his room? Was it to test his sexual orientation? If he didn't make a move would Montgomery think . . . ?

'And how did it go with Professor Lee?'

'Oh, it was very introductory. Wanted to show me his labs and all the gear and explain more about the rest of the predictive program. He doesn't start on the *me* stuff until tomorrow . . . Let's have a break from that, May. I want to relax a bit before I start on Rita Osborne's questionnaire. Another glass?'

'No, thanks, Calum. One more drop and my head'll be spinning. If you're *that* tired, would you like a soothing massage?'

'That sounds great.'

'You get ready then. I have some oil in my bag . . . Take your things off and lie down on your front . . . Now, how's that feel? My fingers aren't digging too hard?'

'It feels *wonderful*. How did you learn it?'

'I did a course in Taiwan last year when I was visiting my grandfather. This is a special style of Chinese massage.'

'It's special, all right . . . Mmmmm . . . How often d'you go back there?'

'Once or twice a year.'

'What's it like?'

'I love it. So green. Great food. One of the best museums in the world. And my grandfather's fantastic. I'm sure you'd like him.'

'Where are your own folks, your parents?'

'San Francisco. They have a restaurant in Chinatown. I grew up there . . . Right, that's you done. If you're a good boy, I'll do it again some time.'

'May . . .' He turned round, reached up and tried to pull her towards him.

'Uh-uh . . . *that's* not allowed. Guests have gotta keep their hands to themselves. See that up there? That's a video camera. We have rules on this base. I'd be skinned alive . . . *You've* got to fill in the questionnaire and get some beauty sleep. You have a big day with Prof Lee tomorrow. And I gotta run. Goodnight.'

15

'Good morning, good morning. As Colonel Montgomery explained, Lieutenant Jones will sit in on all our sessions together, as well as Major Osborne's. How are you feeling? Are you still suffering from jet-lag?'

'I feel fine, Professor.'

'Good, good. So, let's get on with it. Tell me, tell me. I can't wait a moment longer.'

'Tell you what?'

'How it works, how it works, of *course*.' Like an an excited child, Lee bounced this way and that in his chair, ran both hands through his thinning hair, shoved back the bridge of his slipping spectacles with a decisive jab of his index finger, and swung abruptly forward over the table. 'Out with it, out with it. In your own words. Come on, tell me, tell me.'

'It's difficult to know where to begin.'

'Begin where it began.'

'Okay. I needed to make money fast, for . . . a particular reason. I had the idea that if I could see a little ways into the future, I could make a whole bunch of cash.'

'The idea *came* to you? Just like that?'

'I was on vacation in Scotland, checking out my roots. Up there they all believe in sixth sense. I talked to one or two people who were reputed to have the gift and then kind of figured out my own system.'

Even to Calum's ears, it sounded mighty unconvincing,

197

though he'd had all night to get his story straight. Convincing or not, he was going to keep Morag well out of this.

'*Very odd.* Let's not dwell on that now, though. We must go to the heart of the matter. What *is* your system?' Lee bounced forward and back in his seat as though he had injected some rubber compound into his body.

'I guess it's some form of thought transmission. I try to project my thoughts over long distances, like telepathy back to myself.'

'I knew it, I *knew* it.' Lee executed a seated jig.

'To give me something to focus on, I had the idea of using the moon. I stared and stared at it, channelling every shred of energy to get my thoughts that far.'

'And what happened?'

'Nothing at all for ages. Then eventually I began to have this weird sensation, like there was a mist before my eyes. Nothing concrete, nothing you could make out or interpret. I kept on. Not every night. It was far too tiring for that, and the moon was only visible about one night in five up there. Little by little, the sensation became more tangible, less amorphous. If I tried hard enough, I would sense who would come walking down the road, or what my . . . landlady might say when I went in. Still pretty vague, and only a few minutes ahead. It took months of practice to stretch it further.'

'How far?'

'While I was still in Scotland, it was no more than half an hour.'

'And now?'

'It stayed that way for a long time, including the first few months I was in London. Then as an experiment, I tried meditating for hours before trying it. Suddenly the time-span went out to about an hour. That's what made the lottery possible. One hour's still about my limit, and, I tell you, it is exhausting, far more tiring than doing a shorter span.'

Lee looked disappointed. Jones's face registered nothing and his writing continued unabated.

'Have I said something wrong?'

'Not at all, not at all. It's what I would have expected . . . at this stage.' The smile returned. 'So how did the predictions work in the City?'

'I had to concentrate on very large, short-term swings, where the market could move sharply within minutes, so I went for the big announcements, like the US employment or trade figures. There was another reason for picking the American stuff. In winter at least, those announcements come through when it's already dark back in England. I would go to a conference room on the top floor of our building and stare out at the night sky. If the moon wasn't there, I'd imagine it was. Didn't work every time, but my hit rate was pretty good.'

'What about the rest of the time? Surely you had to do other trades?'

'Ah . . . that's where my *other* system kicked in. Once I could be sure that I'd be right, say, ninety percent of the time, I started trading information. I would tip off my friends in New York or wherever, who knew my hunches were usually good, and they'd pay me back when they got an inside track. That way I could leverage the whole thing up.'

'Smart, very smart. Let's move on to the nature of your predictions. Do you get a general sense of what will happen within that hour, or is it more specific?'

'It has to be *very* specific or it doesn't work. I can only predict the lottery numbers, for instance, if I exclude all other thoughts from my mind.'

'I'm not surprised . . .' Lee shoved his slipping glasses back again, clasped his hands together and looked at Calum with shining eyes. '. . . This is something I have waited for *so* long. I have done hundreds of experiments with people who have telepathic abilities, but you are the first to have a dependable, repeatable way to truly harness the potential of telepathic thought.'

'That's what you think it is? I couldn't be sure what was causing it.'

'Only fools deny the existence of telepathy or dismiss its importance. All the evidence points to it being real. Research institutes around the world spend their time doing experiments to convince the sceptics that it is real. Asking subjects in darkened rooms to guess what a randomly selected object looks like. Who cares what the sceptics think? If we depended on the sceptics, we'd still be living in mud huts. The researchers shouldn't waste their time like that: they should be concentrating on the *science* of telepathy.'

'What d'you mean, the "science" of it?'

'The physics, of course. Telepathy is a transmission like any other. Less understood, maybe, but essentially the same. A flowing river, a broadcast, a phone call. All transmissions, all with their physics.'

'I'm not sure I follow . . .'

'If a person here in Arizona sends a telepathic message to, say, New York, how long do you think it takes to get there?'

'Isn't it instantaneous?'

'*Instantaneous?* There's no such thing as instantaneous. Everything has a speed. If you switch on the light in a darkened room it takes time for it to reach your eyes. It's a very short distance and light travels rather fast, so it *seems* instantaneous, but it isn't at all. It takes a perfectly simply calculable time. So, how about telepathy? Does telepathic thought carry mass that would slow it down, or is it a form of radiation, which goes at the speed of light? Does it take more mental energy to send a signal from here to New York than to somewhere nearer, like Utah or Nevada? How *far* can signals travel? We already know that telepathic thought has no problem escaping the atmosphere. Both NASA and the Russians have done successful experiments from the ground up to crews on the shuttle or space stations.'

'How about my predictions? Do you know how they work?'

'No, but I *do* have some ideas about them. As you said, you're managing to combine in one person the roles of sender and receiver of telepathic messages. That, however, doesn't explain how the time difference happens. It can't have anything *real* to do with the moon, that would be absurd. It must just be a device that helps you concentrate. If you bounced a packet of thoughts off the moon and back, and it travelled at the speed of light, it would take only three seconds. Even if it somehow went *faster* than light, that could never produce a one hour lack of synchronicity. The planets wouldn't be much different. The return journey to Mars, for example, would last only about six minutes when its orbit is closest to earth. As I see it, there are two possibilities. The first, which I don't think at all likely, is that your thoughts are travelling a *phenomenal* distance – thousands of millions of miles – and are somehow looping back to you. If it was far enough and fast enough, it *could* happen, but it's *very* far-fetched.'

'And the other?'

'The other is harder to explain. It involves quantum mechanics and a very common experience, déjà vu. As you know, most of us have déjà vu experiences from time to time. There are those who have them far more frequently. *They* tend to have particularly vivid experiences with a clear predictive element. They know what someone is going to say or do before it happens. This is something I've spent *years* studying. The key is what causes this. No-one knows for sure, but I have my theory and that's where the quantum mechanics comes in.'

'I should warn you, I flunked every science course at school.'

'Then I'll keep to strictly layman's language. There's a natural phenomen they call "entangled pairs". This occurs, for example, when two identical atoms travel in different directions from the same point. However far they travel apart, their destinies remain tied, like Siamese twins. If one of the atoms gets excited, it will emit radiation with precisely the right frequency to excite its twin, *wherever* in the universe it is. The interesting part is that, while you'd expect a time delay until the radiation, travelling at the speed of light, reaches the twin, physicists at the European CERN Institute proved in the Eighties that the effect is actually instantaneous. The light barrier is smashed, the normal rules broken.'

'You said there was no such thing as instantaneous.'

'There is in *that* case, and this is where my theory kicks in. Of course I can't prove it, but I'm *convinced* that something similar happens with the human brain. There is some connection between the present and the future consciousness that is excited in some way and can, in flashes, travel through time. With déjà vu, people think it's either the mind having diffi-culty filing information or an old experience being repeated. My belief is that actually it's a brief flicker *forward* in time. Our minds flash forward – usually by no more than ten seconds – and back again, retaining an image of what is about to occur; so when it *does*, it feels oddly familiar. I think this is a form of telepathic thought that moves backwards and forwards instead of from one person to another. The problem is, it's *useless*. It occurs irregularly and involuntarily, and the time jump is much too short for any practical application. That's what makes your case so *fascinating*. Your intensive training and the huge mental energy you release trying to project your thoughts such a big distance have enabled you to trigger this forward jump almost at will, and over an appreciable time span. You possess a unique combination of telepathy and sixth sense. This can only be called a *seventh sense*. You must have been born with an extraordinary natural gift to be able to do it.'

'I can't think where I got it from.'

'Nor can the spoon benders. The main thing is it *does* seem to work. Together we will try to understand it better and to see how far we can push it. Hopefully you can help us pass it on to others so we can benefit more widely. There was one other thing I meant to ask. If you always need to see the night sky to make a prediction, how come you managed that horse race on live TV? That was *very* impressive.'

'Ah . . . I need to tell you about that one.'

* * *

'Okay, Rita, tell me the worst. How badly screwed up am I?'

'Oh, I wouldn't say you're screwed up at all, Calum. A few little wrinkles here and there, that's all. Let me tell you how the analysis worked out. You are intelligent and articulate, but you have very low self-esteem; this is at the root of your problems. It's what caused your lack of success as an artist and in broking, and, more than likely, it's at the heart of

203

your problems with women. Something inside you refuses to believe things will work out. In work situations that makes you give up too easily; in relationships, conversely, it makes you desperate, putting unbearable pressure both on you and your partner. Does that ring true?'

'Perhaps.'

'Something from your childhood has set up a pattern that is very destructive, rather like abused kids abuse their own children. You trust no-one and are not trustworthy yourself. You think it is okay to let people down, because you feel let down yourself.'

'Not consciously.'

'Of course not. Skipping on to the main conclusions, I believe breaking out of the negative cycle you're in is absolutely possible, and the remedy is very clear.'

'It *is*?'

'If you could make a big success of one thing, one *really* important thing, it would give you the boost you need to begin believing in yourself. You need to work with people who you are confident won't abandon you. And you in return must resolve to give your everything to those people and never contemplate giving up or letting *them* down. When you see how far mutual trust and respect can take you, you'll find you can move mountains. The dividends for your future, both in career and personal life, will be vast.'

'I guess it *is* a confidence thing, basically.'

'No question. Forgive me putting it this way, Calum, but while we certainly lucked out getting hold of you, it may be that we weren't the only ones. I doubt anyone could tailor-make a better chance for you to achieve a breakthrough than this opportunity that's fallen right into your lap here at Monument.'

* * *

It was nearly midnight. Tian Yi stretched, got up off her chair, and wandered over to the window. The view from her sixth floor office in Chang 'an Avenue stretched to Tiananmen Square and beyond. Tian was one of those fortunate women who are more attractive in middle age than in youth. In her twenties she had been pretty rather than beautiful; now her fine features and cool elegance turned many a head. However, this meant very little to her. She was married only to her job. She had a teenage daughter, but her husband had filed for divorce years before, unable to cope with her hours or her success. At forty-eight she was not only the youngest Minister in the Chinese government, but also one of the most respected.

She stood at the window and fretted about what the future might hold for her. Her work in getting China into the WTO had pushed her closer to Party Secretary Liao. As the leading moderniser on the all-powerful Standing Committee of the Politburo, he was a genuine believer in the merits of free trade and the main proponent of membership. When it became clear that the Chinese application might founder on the rocks of the army's ownership of valuable monopolies like Sunrise, it was Liao who had mounted a dramatically successful lobbying operation in Beijing to press for the sale of the army's assets.

Liao's aggressive approach was aided by the diminished state of the ailing President Zhang, who succumbed to his repeated private blandishments and declared his support early. Without that decisive vote, the Standing Committee would have been as deadlocked as ever, between Liao and the other two modernisers and Premier Chen and his two fellow hardliners.

Chen and his allies saw the world very differently from Liao. They were much less convinced of the benefits of WTO membership, especially if that meant major concessions. The differences between Chen and Liao were of long standing. Chen did not share Liao's regret over Tiananmen, and thought it had served a useful twin purpose in cowing their populace and convincing the West that interference in Chinese affairs was futile. He noted that the foreigners huffed and puffed about human rights for a while, but after the shortest, barely decent period of mourning, they cast off their weeds and came back, gaily clad, to woo the Chinese shilling. Chen's conclusion was that nothing of importance should be surrendered. If the foreigners developed unrealistic expectations from their investments in China, that should not trouble the Chinese overmuch. Had the British always been scrupulously honest when they had imposed unfair treaties on his ancestors?

This time the hardliners had not prevailed. The battle was not over, though. Ever since China had joined the WTO, Chen and his friends had mounted a cunning rearguard operation to obstruct the implemention of the promised market liberalisation measures, and had concocted a secret scheme to permit the army to hang on to Sunrise. Tian Yi knew that when the foreigners tumbled to what was going on, there would be trouble. And when the inevitable showdown between Liao and Chen finally came, many careers – hers included – would be made or destroyed. As she surveyed Beijing by night, she prayed that in siding with Liao she had backed the right horse.

*   *   *

'So, Calum, you've made it through your first month with us. How did you feel about *this* week's work?'

'I feel I'm making some progress, Rita. Maybe a bit slower than I'd like, but I think I'm getting there. A lot of it is about building up stamina. Although the prediction sessions are as exhausting as ever, my recovery time is getting shorter.'

'Is your commitment to the project as strong as you always say it is?'

'Sure. Why do you say that?'

'I just wondered. Call it feminine intuition if you like. I sense you're still holding something back. Prof Lee thinks so too, by the way. We can't work out exactly what it is. Could it be how you got your skill in the first place? Have you been completely frank with us about that?'

'Of course I have.'

It was hard not to blush. He could feel the roots of his hair go prickly with embarrassment. He was sure she could see the lie. There was nothing for it but to brazen it out.

'Because, Calum, you've got to remember that if for any reason, whatever it may be, you're not coming totally clean, *you'll* be the one who suffers in the end. You'll never climb out of that dreadful cycle if you don't learn to have complete trust. This will be the latest in your long string of failures, don't you see that? I'm different from the other team members; they care mainly about the *project*. I see this more in *human* terms. I want to see you leave Monument as a stronger, more fulfilled person, not as someone marked out as a loser till the end of his days. For me, Calum, it's *you* who counts.'

'Thanks, Rita.'

'Do you feel you get enough support from the rest of the team? We all know how arduous the process is.'

'They're all great. Jason is a big help with his morning

pep-talks. What I like is how positive and supportive he is even when things aren't going so well. The Prof is fine, too, and the weekly sessions with you help, of course.'

He was lying. She was the one team member he didn't warm to. Well-intentioned as her lectures were, she sometimes made him feel more of a loser than ever. He always felt pressurised by her. Sure, he musn't miss this chance, he *knew* that. Did she have to remind him quite *so* often?

'You haven't mentioned May. How d'you feel about her?'

'May's okay.'

He felt himself blushing. He didn't want to get on to this. Marianna still obsessed him, but occasionally when he was daydreaming, May's face would float into his mind. The last thing he wanted was to discuss this with Osborne. He squirmed every time she made him go over his past relationships, and concluded that in future the less he told her the better.

'Do you find her attractive?'

'May's good-looking.'

'That's not what I asked. How do *you* feel about her? Does it make a difference that it's for *her* people, the Taiwanese, that we're doing this?'

'All I want to think about is getting my job done.'

'It's okay for you to find her attractive, you know. As long as you don't get *too* carried away. I don't think Colonel Montgomery would like that.'

What was *that* supposed to mean? Was it unprofessional, or did Jason have the hots for her himself? He nearly blurted out the question. Better keep well off that territory. Why did Rita care so much, anyway? Why was she pursing her lips that way?

'And Marianna? Still as keen on her as ever?'

Here we go again. He couldn't refuse to answer. Just keep it short.

'I try to put her out of my mind as much as I can. I realise that until I get some self-confidence by *achieving* something, she won't look at me.'

It was short, but honest.

'Okay, Calum, I guess that's it till next week. I'd better let you run along and get to work on those Taiwanese pilots.'

Calum was so glad to get away from Rita he didn't mind the session with the pilots as much as usual. It was the dreariest part of the now well-established routine, mainly because they made so little progress. After that, May would give him a short lecture on the history of Taiwan or a description of the topography of the island. Then lunch and an afternoon rest before moving on to the meat of the work with Lee. Mental exercises and meditation every day, and predictions now nightly, if he felt up to it. It was a tiring, monotonous regimen which sometimes made him feel like a performing monkey or a freak, as that British guy had called him. The pressure was relieved only by drinks in the bar with May and a massage afterwards.

'Mine's a Bud, same for you, Calum? . . . How was today?'

'No change. Feel like a game of pool, May? What say we challenge Dino and Harry to a rematch?'

'In a while. Shall I put something on the juke-box?'

'Anything that's not Country and Western . . . Oh not that, I *hate* Elvis.'

'Too late. You can choose next.'

'Can I ask you a personal question, May?'

'Depends what it is.'

'How often have you been in love?'

'Never.'

'Come *on*.'

'I mean it. I've had lovers, but I've never been *in* love.'

'Why?'

'I don't know. Perhaps I prefer to keep my distance.'

'Is there a man in your life right now?'

'What's all this to you?'

'I'm just curious. Is there?'

'Where would I find time for a boyfriend?'

'What if it was someone at Monument? Like Jason.'

'*Jason?* What makes you think that? No, Calum, there's no-one in my life. Speaking of Jason, I hear he talked to you about timing.'

'Yup. The Pentagon think that August's the biggest risk. If the Chinese are rebuffed in Geneva, that's when they'll go for it.'

'Can you be ready by then? I mean take your time-span up to two or three hours, like they want? Sounds to me like it's too soon.'

'What I keep hoping is for a sudden breakthrough, like happened in London. If I keep making the effort I'm making, it may come.'

'You mustn't let this all put too much pressure on you.'

'I can handle it. At least I hope I can.'

'I know how many times I've told you already, but I really want you to know how much *I* appreciate what you're doing for my people. Seriously, I don't know how to thank you.'

'I can think of a way.'

'I bet you can, you . . . octopus. If you try that *one* more time, then *no* more massages.'

'Speaking of massage, let's forget pool and run off to my room now.'

*   *   *

Great massage as it was, it hadn't made him as drowsy as usual. When she was done, he kept hold of her long enough for a brushed kiss on an escaping cheek, then she wriggled away as usual. If the camera hadn't been there, would he have chanced his arm some more? He couldn't work out whether she wanted it or not. When they were alone together, she gave him *the* most amazing smiles, and her intoxicating laughs seemed to hint at real pleasure in his company. The touch of her hands on his back, his thighs, his forehead was so tender it was hard to believe that she was unattracted to him. Oh, how he longed for those hands to explore slightly more of him! As she kneaded his thighs, he would slide down a fraction to give a sweet hint. But her hands simply adjusted, stopping always an aching few inches short of true bliss.

He tried to get sleepy by starting on another paperback, but the first few pages didn't grab him and he slung it on top of the pile to go back to the library. Security on the base was so ludicrously tight, they wouldn't let him go there to browse. He had to pick from a list, like room service. The service was amazing, to be fair. Put in a request, and one of the crew-cut privates would bring it whizzing round in a flash. Calum figured he was the only guy on the base who read *anything*. Nothing he wanted was ever out on loan and all the books looked unread. Bunch of Philistines.

All the movies on TV were old. He had wearied of MTV

211

and CNN bored him senseless. He switched the set and the lights off and went over to the window. His room was near to the perimeter of the base and he often looked up to the range of hills Dino said were called the Navajos. Above their silhouette, the stars twinkled brilliantly in the clear desert air. He wished he could see more of them, go for a nice long drive in the desert night. All he got to see of the night sky was from the viewing platform, with its telescopes and electronic gear. It was great to be at the centre of things, to be *somebody*, but he had begun to feel a mite claustrophobic. It would pass. Hell, he wouldn't trade this experience for *anything*. It might even redeem him in Morag's eyes. He'd resolutely protected her secret in the face of unrelenting pressure. If Morag knew what he was doing here at Monument, she might not be *proud* of him, but she might sniff in that way of hers and grudgingly say that good could come of him yet.

Sleep wouldn't come. The light went back on and he pulled some paper and a few pencils from the bedside drawer. He amused himself making a list of all the wild vacations he might take when he finally did his stuff and got out of here. Crossing the Sahara; sailing up the Amazon; climbing Mount Kilimanjaro. He ran out of ideas and began doodling. A caricature of Prof Lee wearing glasses three times the size of his head. Rita complete with fangs, horns and a tail. The Statue of Liberty with Jason's face. Then one of May doing the karate she had told him about. He'd never drawn an oriental face before, never found an Oriental attractive before, come to think about it. The few brief liaisons he'd had before Marianna were all with blondes, too. Was it being cooped up that was giving him this thing about May? Would she lose her allure next to a bevy of blonde Californian babes? He tried again to catch those eyes and those amazing high cheekbones. It wouldn't come. He closed his eyes and thought instead about her willowy, slender body. Ohhhh. He must get her out of his mind. Otherwise, he would *never* get to sleep.

16

Bob Tyne was a past master at keeping the pressure up. Convening the WTO Panel rapidly was a move in the right direction, but no more than that. Unless the judgement went the right way and was implemented properly, his business in China would still be damaged irreversibly. He had invested the most part of a billion, if you counted all the support work back in Sunnyvale, and he was not going to see that go down the tubes. Nor was he going to miss out on the biggest business opportunity he had ever seen. It was less a case of maintaining the pressure on Lynne O'Neill and more of ratcheting it up. He had got as far as he could in one to ones with her, and the time was ripe to introduce the heads of the US's leading Internet, entertainment, and software companies. Tyne could barely resist a grin. He could see Lynne was *hating* this. That meant he'd made the right call.

'Bob, I think I've had enough examples now . . .'

'Sorry, Lynne, but these guys have flown to Washington expressly to meet you. You haven't yet heard what the Chinese are doing to our movie and music industries. Darren, could you give the Special Representative a brief comment?'

'I'd be happy to. In a nutshell, we're being ripped off right, left and centre. Our CDs and our movies on DVD are being copied wholesale. We estimate that eighty-five percent of all material being sold in China is bootleg.'

'Gentlemen, we have made representations in the strongest

215

terms to the Chinese government on this, asking for rapid and effective enforcement of their own laws.'

'With the greatest possible respect, your representations so far have had no effect at all. The Chinese have got it down to a fine art. They delay moving against companies, claiming the need to gather evidence. That buys them a few months. When they are finally planning to act, someone tips off the company, so they can sell their assets and close the company down. By the time they are investigated there is no equipment to confiscate and no money to pay any fines. They pay stooges to be company directors, so if there's a prosecution, the guy who takes the rap has nothing to do with the company. It goes without saying that by then the perpetrators have set up a new company, bought the equipment and started again somewhere else.'

'Is there nothing you can do electronically to stop them copying?'

'The answer is no. These are smart people. Beating our implanted devices is child's play for them.'

'I see. Bob, I'm running out of time, can we get back to what your group wants?'

'Sure, Lynne. We're all *convinced* that what we have here is a country that is totally unwilling or unable to fulfil its internationally agreed obligations. If something doesn't happen, and happen soon, US intellectual property businesses – and probably plenty of other businesses beside – will have lost out on the biggest opportunity *ever*. And the blame will be laid fair and square at the feet of our government.'

'I hear you, Bob, but we're already doing everything we reasonably can. We had to move mountains to get the WTO Panel convened at that speed. To get them to issue a provisional judgement by August is fast-tracking it with a capital F. That's less than ten weeks.'

'You did just dandy, Lynne, and we appreciate that . . .' God, how she detested the patronising, nerdy, dandruff-ridden little creep! '. . . but in my view, and I think it is a view shared by all the gentlemen here, the time may have come to stop limiting ourselves to the *reasonable*. After all, the Chinese don't seem to be too worried about being reasonable.'

'Just what precisely are you suggesting, Bob?' She was beginning to lose her rag with the loathsome little snake.

'If you can take effective action through normal WTO channels, all well and good. If they do *something* to get the Chinese back in line, great. By that I mean *proper* enforcement, *proper* transparency in awarding contracts and franchises, and *proper*, monitored disposal of army-controlled businesses. If we get that, fantastic. But if the Panel judgement goes against us, or the Chinese still don't implement properly, we all believe the US government ought to take unilateral action. It's the only thing the Chinese will understand.'

O'Neill did her best to keep cool. She adopted her loftiest tone.

'Bob, you know one heck of a lot about the world of hi-tech, but international treaty obligations are not your forte. The US is a member of the WTO. We *can't* ride roughshod over the whole thing.'

It was Tyne's turn to get pissed off.

'So what *are* you gonna do, Lynne? Let them get away with it? Allow the Chinese forces to amass so much wealth they can outspend the Pentagon without a penny from their government? Is that what you want?'

He'd gone too far now. Not only that. It was *infuriating* that he'd hit on the very point that was bothering the CIA and the Pentagon. She could not bring herself to shake hands with him as they left, particularly as his parting shot was a threat to call

217

the President if she didn't undertake to report their concerns to him 'without delay'. The barefaced cheek of the man!

*　　*　　*

For so very long Calum had resisted Rita's increasingly direct enquiries and Prof Lee's more subtle attempts to winkle it out of him. It was only when he reached his lowest ebb that he gave way and betrayed Morag. Had they all planned it that way? If everything had been going better, he might have had the strength to withstand all of them, even Montgomery. Unfortunately, it wasn't.

The sessions with the Taiwanese pilots had been especially disappointing. They were all hand-picked for their high psychic aptitude. It was easy enough for Calum to pass on the *theory* through an interpreter, but translating that into practice was different. Attempts to do moon gazing sessions led nowhere, with teacher, pupils, and observers all showing clear signs of frustration. He was sick at heart that by concealing how he and Morag had trained together, he was holding back on a vital part of the method and blocking any real chance of progress.

Worst of all from the team's point of view was that Calum was making no progress himself. It had started *so* well. Using the simplest of gauges, with random coloured lights coming on at specific time intervals, Lee measured Calum's range and clocked him reliably at an hour and a quarter within two weeks. Optimism abounded. May was thrilled and it showed in her body language. Osborne beamed and Colonel Montgomery gave him heartwarming pats on the back. One night he even dropped by the bar himself, sat between Calum and May and told him how proud he was to be working with a 'true pro'. It was the proudest moment of Calum's life.

Now it had all turned different. His time-span had stopped expanding and nothing Lee did could wean Calum off the night sky and the moon. It was clear that this ruled out all daylight applications and was a serious limitation. The team were as friendly and supportive as ever, but the smiles were fixed, faces were rubbed wearily in exasperation, and May's mood changed. One night at the bar she hinted that he wasn't trying hard enough. That was pretty rich, seeing as he was *exhausting* himself with the effort. She begged him to try harder for her, for her people, for her grandad. Tired as he was, he resolved to throw more into it the next night.

That next night, try as he might, it wouldn't go beyond the eighty minutes he had reached weeks before. When May came to escort him to the bar he saw the question in her eyes. Lee answered for him with a tired shake of his head. It was over the beer that she told him that Montgomery wanted a serious word in the morning. It kept Calum awake half the night, worrying what the Colonel would say, dreading the disappointment in that man's eyes.

*   *   *

'Sure, it *has* been a bit slower than we had hoped, you don't need me to tell you that, but I know you're doing your best. In the end I guess it'll come down to whether your best is good enough.'

Calum hoped desperately that it would be.

'We're all in this together, Calum. I'm taking some big-time heat from the Pentagon myself. I'm telling them to lay off, that I'm confident that together we are gonna work this one out.'

'I'll do *anything* I can, Colonel. I *have* been trying as hard as I can. I'll just have to pull out a few more stops.'

'Attaboy . . . Calum, there's one other thing the Pentagon are pressurising me on. I wonder if it's something you would feel able to help me out on? It'd sure get me out of a fix.'

'Of course. What is it?'

'We have to send them weekly reports of how we're doing and they read them pretty closely. There's one thing they keep coming back on. They say our reports are too vague on how you learnt your skill. We've told them it was up in Scotland on that island . . . what was it called?'

'Lewis.'

'Yeah, Lewis. They believe that you must have gotten the idea of the moon stuff from one of the locals up there and, whatever we tell them, we can't shake them off this. They think that our team, or maybe *you*, are holding out on them.'

'Why is it so important?'

'They have two reasons. The first is they fear that if you hold back on something . . . trivial, like this, how much else could you be withholding? It gets in the way of true trust. The second is more important. If there are other person or persons out there with this gift, we need to know it. What if they fell into the hands of gangsters or our enemies? Think what happened to you. Someone might already have jumped to the same conclusion as the Pentagon and be stalking whoever taught you. We need to make sure that doesn't happen.'

'How can you do that?'

'"Passive protection", we call it. The person concerned

would never need to know. The CIA boys would keep a discreet watch from a distance. As you know from your own experience in London, those guys don't miss many tricks.'

'Colonel, I'd truly like to help. This is a very hard one for me. I don't want to let you down. You see, there is a . . . person who helped me, but I *swore* I would never . . .'

'Never what, Calum? Put that person in danger? You wouldn't be much of a friend if, knowing what you know, you didn't do whatever you could.'

'I hadn't thought of it that way.'

'So what's it to be, Calum? Will you help me out, be my buddy, or am I gonna have to signal the Pentagon that I can't persuade you to co-operate?'

'You give me your word she . . . I mean the person . . . won't be contacted, will never know?'

'We'll seal it with a handshake.'

'Gee . . . I'm still not sure. Okay, it's an old relative of mine, Morag Buchanan. She's in her eighties.'

'And where in Lewis does she live?'

'A little village called Sgurr nan Creag on the west of the island.'

'Is it small enough that she could be tracked down easily?'

'You're not gonna . . . ?'

'No, of course not. We can't protect if we can't find her, can we?'

'It's small enough. They won't have a problem.'

If *I* could find her, it'll be cinch for the CIA, thought Calum.

'And that's it? Only Morag Buchanan? No-one else?'

'No-one else.'

'Good. Look, I sure appreciate you getting those guys off my back. Now, another thing. Tomorrow night there's no moon. We know that it doesn't work for you in the day, but Prof Lee reckons the moon could've become a kind of distraction to your efforts to go further. Perhaps concentrating that famous energy of yours on the planets or stars might make the difference. We think you should take all of today and most of tomorrow off to recharge your batteries. Have a good long session in the bar tonight to relax some. Have more than one beer, have a few. Play some pool or throw darts. Have a good time, and tomorrow go for it. How's that sound?'

'Good. Very good.'

*　*　*

The two big men checked into their rooms at the Shobost. The old woman who brought their tea was thoroughly unhelpful and the telephone company had no record, so they'd have to ask around. That would be tomorrow, but there was no harm in seeing whether the locals in the bar knew where the old hag lived. Move carefully, though, like they'd been instructed. The people in the bar might be friends or neighbours, might warn her if they suspected.

From the moment the two came in and ordered their drinks, Fraser wondered. He muttered in Gaelic and Hector and Sandy nodded in agreement. It was odd to see two men in suits together at the height of the tourist season. There were few enough commercial travellers up that way, and the ones who came were always alone, usually from Glasgow. Mostly they were familiar faces. These two stood silently at the bar, nursing their pints, surveying the room.

222

Whatever errand they were on, Fraser's instincts were that they didn't bring good news. They didn't have the smell of police, or the stuffed ferret look of taxmen. Could they be working for the English landlords that owned wide tracts of the island? Not pompous enough, the bald one or the other with the big nose and those daft sideburns. What else could they be? It was Hector who guessed first. All that stuff and nonsense in the papers about the young American, then the fuss about him going missing. He'd turned out a bad one, just as they'd expected. Could they be connected with that? Private detectives trying to track him down? Lawyers bringing an inheritance for the old witch if the lad had died? Or newspapermen? Fine thing it would be if they interviewed her, got a kiss-and-tell story out of *her*. There was no way of knowing what mischief the old bitch might conjure out of a chance like that. Hector and Fraser finished their chat just before the men wandered over to their table. Up close you could feel their formidable physical presence.

'Hello. Mind if we join you? Can we buy you a drink?'

'We're fine, thank you.' There was a slight tremor in Sandy's voice.

They sat down anyway.

'We're looking for an old woman, lives locally. Name of Morag Buchanan.'

Fraser was silently elected spokesman.

'A fine woman, a *very* fine woman indeed.'

'Glad to hear it. What's her address?'

'A sad affair, was it not, Hector?'

'Very sad, Fraser.'

'What was so sad?'

Sammy looked confused. Fraser looked right back into the man's strange little eyes.

'The fire, the terrible fire.'

'*She* was in a fire? Was she burnt?'

'Aye, she was that. To a cinder, and in her own bed. Our local fire unit couldn't get their pump to work. We did what we could with buckets of water – a veritable human chain, no less – but the flames beat us back. A dreadful night it was. Now, I trust you have not had a wasted journey. You're not *related*, or anything?'

Dessie did his best to sound solemn.

'No . . . acquaintances, distant acquaintances. Is there a grave we can see, to . . . pay our respects?'

'There is not. Morag Buchanan, God rest her soul, was not a believer. She always said she wanted no truck with churches in life *or* death. She told us that when she went, she wanted her ashes scattered over the slopes of Ben Mhor. By the time the brigade got here the house was a charred ruin. It was hard to tell poor Morag from the rest of the ashes, so we scooped everything up in pails and spread it over the hillside. As she would have wished, Morag is up there for all eternity, with the ashes of her clothes, books and furniture for company.'

'So, can we take a look at her house?' Sammy's eyes bored into Fraser's skull.

'Of course you can. It was months ago now and the grass has grown over it. The roof fell in, you see, and there was nothing to keep the elements out. It looks for all the world as if it's been derelict for twenty years. You can hardly see any difference from the two next to it, and they haven't been lived in for what, Hector, twenty-five years?'

'Twenty-five to the day. All three look the same now. It's a harsh climate here, and if there's no roof, things deteriorate *terribly* quickly. If you want to take a look, Morag's was the middle one. If you take the first right off the main road and walk three hundred yards, you can't miss it. It's just past the old blackhouse with the tin roof.'

'We'll do that, you can be sure.'

Dessie cracked his finger knuckles and addressed Hector very directly.

'You know, people in out-of-the-way places like this sometimes give visitors from London the old run-around. We wouldn't like it if someone did that to us, know what I mean?'

Sandy quailed and almost gave the game away. Hector stepped right back in.

'And, let me tell *you*, I do not care for someone who comes to *my* town and suggests that I am a liar.'

'We weren't saying that.'

'I am relieved to hear it.'

For all their toughness, something in Hector's manner cowed both of them. They retreated to the bar, finished their drink and went back up to their rooms. The next morning they poked around the grass-covered ruins. By the time they knocked at a few doors and asked at the store, everyone remembered the terrible fire with wondrous clarity.

* * *

Calum rather enjoyed the day. It gladdened and amused him, the thought of those CIA guys watching over Morag like guardian angels, without her ever knowing that it was really *his* doing. Jason had given him a real lift, made him believe in himself again, just as he was starting to fear he'd fail at this, *too*. He *would* crack the two-hour barrier and do it without using the moon. It was all a question of will-power. Relax. He needed to be at his best. Such a pity he couldn't go for a walk or do *anything* on his own. He had a few hours to kill yet so filled in the time by having another go at sketching May. This one was very good. It really caught her. He'd take it over to the bar later on and show her it to her.

Apart from the evening when Montgomery came over for a beer, it was the most enjoyable night he'd had in the bar. All the Taiwanese were in, throwing darts incompetently, having fun and making whoopee. Four of the Americans asked him to join their pool tourney. Calum was happy right where he was, up on the stool with May next to him, her eyes smiling brighter than ever. When she went to the powder room, he slipped the sketch on top of the bar, so it would surprise her when she came back. She *loved* it, and asked to keep it. Calum insisted on hanging on to it, saying his need was greater than hers. She gave in gracefully, like she was glad he wanted it. They had one more beer, and another, and joined in with the other guys singing along to the stupid juke-box songs. He surprised himself by how many of the words he knew. When a slow number came on, he pulled May down off the stool and danced a smoochy dance. It was as if their bodies were made for each other, they fitted together so well.

When the last strains of the song faded away he whispered in her ear, yelled goodnight to the guys, and, her hand in his, pushed the door open and ran down the steps and along the path. She could hardly keep up, almost tripping, laughing all the way. It might stop at a massage again, but tonight's might be something special. Suddenly Calum skidded to a halt.

'SHIT!'

'What?

'The picture, I forgot the frigging picture. I'm goin' back for it.'

'Don't bother, Calum, they'll keep it for us. I'll call from your room.'

'No way, I want it tonight. You stay here.'

'I'll go *with* you.'

'Beat you there.'

Before she had gathered her wits, he sprinted ten, twenty yards ahead. She ran, but couldn't catch him.

'Calum, *Calum*. CALUM, WAIT!'

He paid her no heed and raced up the stairs, calling back 'hah, beat you' triumphantly, as he flung the door open.

And froze.

What the . . . *hell* . . . was going on? The *weirdest* thing. The music still blared from the juke-box, but everything had *stopped*. No darts, no pool. No-one on the stools, no singing, no larking around. They were cleaning up. Not only Tom, the barman. *All* of them. Calum shuddered. May made it up the stairs and knocked him flying as she barged in the door after him. Two of the guys rushed to pick him up. The Taiwanese guys started back at the darts. A corporal reached for a pool cue. Someone called for a beer. Dino spoke first.

'Hey, Calum, you okay? That looked a nasty fall. Glad you came back. Ain't much of a party without the star of the show and his girl . . .'

He grinned at May. She managed a shy smile and brushed the dust off Calum's back.

'. . . Yessir, most of us were gonna curl up with MTV or a *Playboy*, but now that you're back . . .'

'I'm not staying, Dino. I forgot something. Left a paper on the bar over there.'

227

'Tom, you see a paper Calum left over there? . . . *Great.*
Now, you sure you won't join us for a night-cap? What you
say, Miss Chang?'

'I'll have one if Calum's in the mood.'

'No thanks, not for me. Big day ahead of me, gotta get
some sleep.'

'Okay, then, but you all take care, y'hear. G'night.'

'Goodnight.'

May slipped her hand in Calum's and they walked slowly,
not talking.

'You're quiet. Something on your mind, cowboy?'

'No . . . nothing. Suddenly feel a bit tired, that's all.'

'That was a bad fall. I'm so *sorry* I banged you in the back.
It must *hurt.* I'll give it a very special rub.'

'That'd be nice, May. Make it a short one, though. I *am* a
bit bushed.'

For the first time her hands threatened to stray northwards
from his thighs, but Calum yawned loudly and thanked her.
She didn't try to wriggle away from a goodnight kiss. She
got one, but on her forehead. She bade him sleep well and
slipped out. Calum turned out the light, leaving the curtains
open and lay, fully clothed, on the bed in the faint glow from
the perimeter lights, thinking.

On and on, till past three.

At half past four he woke suddenly, pouring with sweat,
the nightmare of Morag's accusing face still violently fresh in
his mind.

17

He woke for his big day feeling nervous. As ever, it started with the Colonel.

'G'morning, Calum. Feeling rested?'

'Sure am, Colonel. I'm up for it tonight, no question.'

'That's good to hear. Anything else I can do to help?'

'There *is*. Last night I gave a lot of thought to why things haven't been going so good.'

'And?'

'When I started doing all this . . . stuff in Lewis, I used to go way out of the village, sometimes even up to the slopes of the mountains. It helped me concentrate, get extraneous thoughts and influences out of my mind. Later on, I got so as I could do it nearer to people and buildings, as long as I could see the moon. Anyway, what I got to thinking was, if I want to break through to a new level, I may need to do the same again. Although the sky's clear as crystal from the Prof's observatory, all the people, the gear, having the base all around . . . I think it's been getting in the way of my concentration.'

'What are you suggesting, Calum?'

'With the moonless sky tonight, and the way I'm feeling about it, I'm *sure* I can get there this time. Two hours, maybe more. But I don't think I can do that *here*. Not the first time. So I thought if I was to go up into the Navajo hills, and stay out there for the night . . .'

'Calum, we can't let you shoot off like that. You could

get lost, anything could happen. There are a lot of snakes in those hills. It's too dangerous. And who would monitor the experiment?'

'Oh, I wasn't thinking of going alone. The Prof could come too. I'm sure he could rig up his gear to a jeep battery.'

'The Prof would be no safer than you. We can't risk either of you. I'd have to send a whole platoon to protect you . . . The answer *has* to be no. It's too risky. We'll all have to do the best we can from Monument.'

'Colonel, I *will* give it my best shot wherever I do it, but I have to tell you that I don't think it's gonna work from here. I'm *so* keen to do this. For the US, the Taiwanese people, and you. With the sky as it is tonight, it's *such* a chance.'

'I need to think about this.'

'Shall I . . . ?'

'No, you wait here. I have to make some urgent calls anyway. I'll be back in ten. Lieutenant, could you come with me? I want you to help me track down a phone number.'

It took less than five minutes for Montgomery to reappear.

'Okay, Calum, I've turned it over in my mind and I'm gonna back your hunch. We'll send you out in a couple of jeeps with Prof Lee and four men.'

'That's great, Colonel, but don't crowd me out. Up on a hilltop, four soldiers and one Professor will feel like Grand Central Station. I don't need *that* much protecting.'

'I suppose we *could* keep it to the two of you and three soldiers. I don't want to make it less than that, though. You'll need two jeeps, come what may, for the Prof's gear and whatever you need by way of provisions and blankets.'

'That's better, but I tell you what. Keep it to two soldiers and send May along instead. She's become a kinda good luck charm for me. Gives me good karma. Her being around helps a lot. She can look after herself, being black belt karate, and all.'

Was it Calum's imagination or did Montgomery's lip curl fractionally? Was it *such* an outrageous request?

'That we can't do. I'm sorry, but that's final.'

Lieutenant Jones moved uneasily in his chair. Calum and Montgomery looked at each other. Jones coughed nervously. It surprised Calum when Montgomery's eyes flicked over to the end of the table.

'Let me give it a little more thought, Calum. Assume it's no go, but if I change my mind, I'll call you in your room. In any case, the expedition is cleared. I'll brief Prof Lee. You should speak to Private Wiltshire about what else you need.'

*   *   *

'Pierre Alain, I always sigh with relief when we finish those tedious formal sessions and can escape to the garden for our private chats. I swear that we only go through all that tedium to make our officials feel important. Why don't we announce that in future France's President and Germany's Chancellor will take all decisions personally, and our officials and other Ministers will play no part? I'm sure it would be hugely popular with our electorates.'

'It would be *delightful*, Hartmut. However, I'm not sure I want to work that hard. Tell me, how is Inge?'

'Complaining. She doesn't want me to stand for re-election again. Says Germany doesn't deserve me.'

231

'What will you do?'

'You must remember, she *is* my wife. I will listen very carefully to what she has to say.'

'And stand?'

'Of course.'

'I am glad to hear it. I am getting too old to have to deal with someone new. You and I make a good team. Europe may not *deserve* us, but they *do* need us at the helm.'

'I will stand but I may not win. The opinion polls are not kind.'

'You still have plenty of time. Eight months, no? . . . If your coalition holds together and your cabinet colleagues keep their nerve. I cannot believe that the German people would choose a moment like this to lurch the wrong way.'

'Let us hope not. The Elysée garden is looking lovelier than ever. I think you are the first French President to have green fingers. Pierre Alain, is there anything else you want to discuss before we rejoin the worker ants?'

'One thing, perhaps. The French media is a disaster. They continue to suggest that the special relationship between our countries is eroding.'

'We both know that is nonsense. Why don't we add a sentence to the communiqué reasserting the importance we attach to it?'

'That would only fan the flames, I fear. Unfortunately, we both know there is something in the charge. The fight between our defence ministers was . . . unseemly.'

'Yes. Fassbender is an idiot. I have spoken to him.'

'Jallon is no better. However, it is not only that. The perception has grown that you have moved closer to the English, that in many economic areas your views are more aligned with theirs than ours. They say, my dear Hartmut, that you have fallen under the spell of the young British Prime Minister.'

'You must not tease me so, Pierre Alain. What is it that you have in mind?'

'It looks as if this China business could be something of a test, a *public* test of how things stand. If it comes to a stand-off with the Chinese, we know how the Americans will react, and the English will, as usual, run after them like poodles. The Anglo-Saxons show no . . . *finesse* in their dealings with China. They do not understand the oriental mind.'

'You have always prided yourself on your knowledge of that.'

'Not without reason, I hope. Look at Hong Kong, the ridiculous efforts the British made to preserve freedoms. How foolish they look now that the Chinese have cracked down. This WTO business will be the same. We *have* to do business with the Chinese. What alternative is there? If we treat them like criminals it will be worse in the end. Not only that, Hartmut. If the Germans were to support a hard-line position, it would confirm the perception that you are in thrall to our British colleague. Forgive me for speaking frankly, Hartmut, but it would make you look *weak*. It would do your electoral prospects no good at all, and it would be another bodyblow to the Franco-German entente.'

'You are sure you can oppose a hard line? You are not under pressure from your industries? I am constantly lobbied by our big concerns. They are very unhappy about their experience in China. Many feel obstructed or cheated. And in our domestic market, the companies fear being swamped with cheap Chinese goods.'

'Oh, naturally we get some mutterings, too. Businessmen are *always* complaining. It is inconsequential. You and I must

233

take the long view. When I was there last month I talked all this through with Premier Chen.'

'Not with President Zhang? Your prestige is slipping, Pierre Alain.'

'You *do* like your little jests, don't you, Hartmut? Naturally, I had a formal meeting and a banquet with Zhang. His mind is still alert and he still holds the reins, but he is too unwell for serious talks. He did not look to me like he would last long. Anyway, Chen, whom our embassy expects to succeed him, warned of *huge* problems if we push the Chinese too hard. They have all but given up on the Americans, and have no time for our British friends. They are looking to *us*, the two leading European statesmen, to give a lead in mature political judgement. If the Anglo-Saxons choose to take a hawkish line, *they* will be the ones to suffer in the long run, and *our* countries will benefit. The Chinese have memories like elephants. Can I look for your support on this?'

'I'm sure you can, Pierre Alain, but first I must look into it more. I do not have the same level of expertise in dealing with the Chinese as you do. I'm sure that with a little persuasion I can get our people to share your view.'

'Good. Now, I suppose we should go back in. As always, I enjoyed our little talk.'

'Our talks make my officials nervous.'

'Mine too. That increases my enjoyment.'

* * *

It was three hours before Montgomery called to say May could go too. He said he was now positive about it, but his voice was strangely edgy. Dino reacted with polite amusement to Calum's request for large quantities of sandwiches, candy bars, fruit, water and soft drinks. Blankets, torches, and so on were to be packed, too. The jeeps had global positioning systems and radios fitted, so getting irretrievably lost looked unlikely. The soldiers were to be armed too with officers' pistols as well as their rifles.

The afternoon rolled by and the time came. May and the Prof changed from civilian clothes into rugged army fatigues and Calum did the same. They chugged off, May driving one of the jeeps with Calum beside her and Harry Clark in the back. Dino and Lee followed in the other with most of the gear.

Without telling Calum, they had picked a hilltop close by the base, four miles at most up a winding, bumpy path. When they got there the soldiers bounded out of the jeeps to set up base camp. Calum walked to and fro, shook his head emphatically and pointed to the next little summit, a further five miles away. That too proved unacceptable. Lee was puzzled but acquiescent. May didn't object. Dino radioed in, and they drove back down to the valley floor and for a good ten miles along the rock-strewn, jarring excuse for a track. They breathed a collective sigh of relief when Calum spied a suitable hill and, on reaching the top, declared himself satisfied. There was still an hour of light to settle down and wait. Squatting in a little circle, they chatted and traded jokes. They all behaved a little differently away from the stern influence of Monument, like they were on a school outing, and the atmosphere was warm, mellow, lighthearted. Calum got them all to join in a game of rock-throwing, betting money and losing two hundred bucks to Harry and Dino. Even Lee took twenty-five off him. None of them had any cash with them, so it was all IOUs, but they knew enough of Calum's bank balance in England to hope they might get it some day.

'Thirty minutes more, then I'll start. How about one last bet, Dino? A thousand bucks to your ten says I can out-shoot you.'

'I didn't know you were a sharpshooter, Calum.'

'I've never picked up a gun in my life. Still, I bet I can. See that little outcrop up there? . . . No, the far one. That's it. I bet you can't hit it.'

'With my assault rifle?'

'No, with your pistol. One bullet.'

'The Beretta's a great gun. Low recoil, triple safety, double trigger action. But it's only accurate to forty or fifty yards. That crag's gotta be seventy.'

'A thousand dollars to you if you hit it, ten to me if you miss. Have a go? . . . Go *on*.'

'I dunno . . . We're not supposed to fool around with our weapons.'

'You disappoint me, Dino. I thought you had balls. I guess I was right, though, you can't shoot.'

'Sure I can. Tell him, Harry.'

'The man's hot, Calum, the man's hot.'

'Hearsay's no good to me. You don't think you can do it, do you? That's okay, you can't be good at everything. Don't let it get to you.'

'Prof Lee, you're in charge. Would it be all right if I . . . ?'

'I'm not sure, Private. I suppose out here no-one will know. Will you have a problem with the gunnery sergeant if you come back one bullet light?'

'Nah, that's cool. We can say we saw a snake or some-thing.'

'Go on, then. *One* shot.'

He flicked the safety catch off and took careful aim. It missed narrowly and ricocheted off the rocks behind. The sound echoed musically around the hills.

'*Shoot.* One goddam foot out. This gun's tracking to the right. If I had a second bullet, I'd hit it for sure.'

'Ten thousand says you won't.'

'Ten *thousand*? Prof, can I have one more go?'

'I said *one* bullet, Private, and one it is.'

'Oh, go on, sir. Just *one* more. Ten thousand bucks are at stake here. We still have time.'

The truth was they were all warming to the game. A big sum of money on the turn of a card is *fascinating*, and Lee was not immune.

'Okay, okay. Don't tell anybody I let you.'

'Gee, thanks Prof. I owe you one.'

He trained the pistol very carefully, hesitated, and dropped it back to his side. A deep breath, arms back up to the horizontal, legs apart, one eye closed. Before the sound of the shot rang out, a tiny puff flew up from the exploding crag.

'Yippee.'

'Not bad, Dino. You get your ten thousand. Took you two shots, though. I would've done it in one.'

'No way.'

'A hundred grand says you're wrong.'

'*What?*'

'You heard me.'

'The crag's gone. Blown away.'

'The stub's still there.'

'You can hardly see it in this light. You'd *never* hit that with a handgun.'

'If you're right, you four can share the money. Twenty-five grand each. Hell, I'll double it, fifty apiece.'

'You gotta be kiddin'.'

'I'm for real, if the Prof'll let me try.'

Both soldiers pleaded in unison.

'Prof . . .'

Lee knew this was breaking lots of rules, but what a moment! He was *entranced*. Surely there was no harm having a little fun. The game seemed to be relaxing Calum before the strain of the night ahead. He would feel quite a spoilsport if he stopped the guys getting a chance of a payout like that.

'I *guess* it'd be okay. This time it's one bullet only and no backchat. Okay, Calum?'

'Sure, Prof. Hey, are we havin' fun or what? . . . Dino, you'd better show me how to hold this thing. Like that? . . . And I just squeeze? . . . Hey you guys are putting me off . . . Go together over there out of my line of sight. No, siddown, so you don't catch my eye . . . That's better.'

The excitement was gripping for all of them. They huddled tightly together on the ground behind him, all dry mouths and tense grins. The gun was lighter than Calum expected, not more than a couple of pounds. He made like Dino, extending his arms, dropping and extending them again, getting the feel of the gun, trying to stop his pulse racing. Three, four, five times he trained it, then, in one languid, almost graceful movement, he circled round till the gun was pointing straight at the huddle. They all gasped. Harry Clark got the words out first.

'Hey, don't do that, someone could get hurt. *Lower that gun, man . . .*'

'Put your hands above your head, all of you.'

It was Dino's turn next.

238

'Calum, quit horsing around. This isn't funny.'

'Put your hands on your heads. NOW.'

They did.

'And shut up. Clark, throw your pistol over here . . . *slowly.*'

'Fuck you.' Clark's dander was up.

May did her best to overcome her fear and sound soothing. 'Do what he says, Harry. Calum will explain himself in a minute, won't you, Calum?'

Clark did as he was told. Calum picked the gun up and put it in his pocket.

'Stay still.'

He walked over to where the soldiers' rifles had been carefully set down, collected both, and slung one of them into the jeep carrying the provisions, carrying the other towards the second jeep. Dino made a half-move but thought better of it. Clark was angry, fit to be tied, muttering under his breath. May was whispering, urging them to stay calm. This might be a tasteless practical joke. Dino was horrified, bamboozled. Lee guessed Calum was flipping under pressure. If so, he should handle him gently, do nothing abrupt.

Each of the four caught a sharp intake of breath when Calum brought the rifle butt down on the second jeep's radio and GPS units, shattering both. Then he pulled up the hood and called out,

'May, give me your knife, please . . . No, throw it over.'

She had a knife in a sheath at her waist. He picked it up from where it landed, ducked under the hood and swiftly cut through the leads. For good measure, he pocketed the keys. Then he transferred the stores and the blankets to the other jeep, leaving behind only three bottles of water.

'Okay, guys, boots off, please. You can keep yours on, May.'

Lee's voice was panicky now, less from fear than from the dawning realisation that his whole program might be destroyed.

'Calum, why are you *doing* this? I don't know what's the matter with you, but you're acting *crazy*. Think of what we've accomplished together. Surely you don't want to wreck all that?'

'Shut up, Prof. Get your boots off, *now*.'

Lee started untying his laces. Clark didn't move. Wiltshire copied him. Whatever was going on, the time had come to make a stand. Calum sensed the planned resistance just in time and stepped neatly behind them, putting his gun to Lee's head. Five seconds later they would have rushed him and taken their chances on his nerve and his aim.

'Take them off. NOW!'

They unlaced them. Only when they were off and thrown well away, did he take the gun away from Lee's profusely sweating head. He added the boots to the one laden jeep.

'Thanks, fellahs. You guys have a long walk in front of you and I don't want you rushing it. May, get in the jeep.'

'Calum, I *can't*. I don't know what this is all about, but you'll get us all in deep shit. The boys, Prof Lee, me. Before you do anything rash, can we have a word in private? Whatever this is about, I'm sure we can sort it out.'

'May, we're gonna sort this out my way, and that means if you don't get your cute little ass in that jeep right now, I'll blow it right off the top of your pretty legs . . . That's *better* . . . No, you're gonna drive . . . You guys keep your hands on your heads till we're outa sight. If you don't, I'll use you for target practice.'

Clark swore a foul, impotent oath, but didn't move. May started the jeep and moved roughly off.

240

'Hey, easy does it. We're not in a hurry.'

Calum kept glancing back. Clark rose and gave him the finger, yelling some more. In the twilight it looked like he was trying to run after the jeep, but the jagged terrain prohibited fast steps in stockinged feet.

'Drive down to the bottom and turn left. Keep quiet.'

She did as directed. Calum held the gun, pointing in her general direction. It was too risky to try anything. She waited till she'd made the turn, taking them further from Monument, before she started up again.

'Calum, *tell* me what's going on. This is madness. The MPs'll be after us, they'll catch us and you'll go to gaol. D'you have any *idea* how many federal offences you've committed? *Trust me,* Calum. It's not too late, we can just go back and pick up the others.'

'Just keep driving.'

'Is this something to do with last night? If so . . . boy, is this some overreaction.'

'Shut *up.*'

He was pretty sure what her game was. She knew he'd be trying to concentrate, trying to get a glimpse of what would happen in the next hour. So she was trying to disrupt that concentration any way she could. She was wasting her breath. He would give it a try, but in this nervous state, without meditation or a moon, there was no chance. Getting no response, she gave it a rest for a while. Not for long, though.

'So where are you planning on taking me, huh? What's the big masterplan? Why am I being taken along, anyway?'

There was a new feistiness in her voice. He decided there was no harm in answering.

'I'll tell you what and why. What happened in that bar last

241

night had no explanation that I can see. There was something *very* strange going on there. I've no idea what it is, but I plan to find out. When we hit the first town or gas station, I'm gonna make some phone calls to try to check exactly what authority you guys at Monument have. I'm also going to try and get a message to one defenceless old lady who may be in grave danger. If they catch me first, okay, I'll take my chances. But I tell you, until I get a convincing explanation, there's no way I'm doing any more of that work for any of you . . . And as to why I took you, I figured that it was *just* possible that you might level with me. Otherwise, if I have to tell some Sheriff that I've escaped from a top secret military installation, at least you are living proof that I'm not a raving lunatic. How about it, May? Will you tell me what's going on? Stop the jeep and *tell me*.'

She braked gently to a halt and switched the engine off. The lights were still on, but it suddenly felt spooky in the silent desert.

'Anything, Calum, I'll tell you anything you want, but I tell you, this is one huge big misunderstanding. If you blow the program now, everything will be ruined and the people of Taiwan will be sacrificed. Is that what you want?'

Tears began to roll down her face and she sobbed, gently at first, then convulsively. It was hard for her to get the words out through the sobs.

'Please let's go back, Calum. *Please*. Let me radio and say what's happened. It'll be okay. Really, I promise. Let me.'

Calum sighed in resignation. He took the radio handset from its cradle, looked at it for a second, and brought it down violently on the dash. It was wrecked.

'Drive.'

They drove along the track for over two hours, saying

nothing more to each other. At last they emerged onto a metalled road. Calum's spirits lightened. They *must* come to a town, a store, or a gas station sooner or later. The GPS was useless to him, since Calum had only the vaguest notion of the geography of Arizona, and no idea of the longitude and latitude co-ordinates of *anywhere*. May tried one more time with words, and made an unsuccessful lunge for his pistol. They relapsed into uneasy silence. Ten, twenty, thirty miles. Jesus, this really was the back of beyond. The road surface was a disgrace, pock-marked everywhere with great divots. The State of Arizona must have *some* budget squeeze!

Finally, relief was in sight. Way ahead he could see a sign. A small sign, not illuminated. It didn't matter, as long as it gave the distance to the nearest town.

'Stop at the sign.'

A hundred yards, eighty, fifty, still he couldn't read it. He leant over for the lever and put the jeep's lights on full beam. May accelerated and drove right on past it.

'Stop and back up. NOW.'

He put the pistol to her temple.

She did so, saying nothing, and reversed a hundred yards till they were right in front of the sign. It was old and battered. The jeep's beam was too low and it was unreadable in the weak outer corona of light. Keeping one wary eye on May, he reached in the back for a torch, turned the switch on and swung it round and up. It was hard to make out anything through the sign's rust and dents. May looked away to the side, into the blackness of the desert.

Calum's mouth gaped open and he blinked uncomprehendingly at the sign, his brain desperately trying to resist what his eyes were telling it. There was nothing there he

could read. As the meaning began to sink in, he closed
his eyes and in slow motion his head slid down into his
hands.

'Oh . . . my . . . God!'

18

It took minutes for his spinning head to clear enough to speak. When he finally got the words out, his voice trembled with fury.

'*Now* will you start talking?'

'I have nothing to say.'

All trace of softness was gone from her voice.

'Okay, up to you. Drive on. Get your speed up. If you slow or brake, I will shoot you without a second's hesitation.'

The gun went to within an inch of the side of her head.

She drove too fast for the road. The jeep bucked over the potholes like a dinghy in a squall. Somehow it stayed on the road. They would have seen the lights of any oncoming traffic ten miles off, but none came.

He *had* to put out of his mind the horror of the discovery and focus on the immediate future. What the *hell* was he going to do? Now that he *knew*, he was dead meat if they caught him. It was one a.m. There was no way to know when the alarm would be raised. Without boots, the three guys would be stuck till rescuers came, but there may have been plans to radio in. Back at Monument they might know already that something had gone wrong. Should he hide as soon as possible, or try to put more distance between him and the base, regardless of which direction that took him? The bigger the area they had to comb, the harder it would be to find their quarry. That must be right. He *had* to take the risk of staying on the road for another hour or more.

Alongside the fear and confusion, he felt the rage at May building inside him. He had liked her, trusted her, been willing to make a big effort for her goddam people, and what had he got in return? A conniving, scheming, deceitful Grade A bitch. What should he do with her? Obviously she wouldn't lift a finger to help him, and she was *bound* to try some stunt. If she did, would he have the balls to pull the trigger? It might be kill or be killed. Should he ditch her right away? Not near the road where she could raise the alarm, but back in the low hills that flanked the road? Take her boots, like the other guys, and leave her to fend for herself? But what would he do then on his own? He *needed* to know more. If *only* he could somehow force her to talk.

They drove on till nearly three, Calum's adrenalin pumping and his thoughts racing the whole way. The risk was growing all the time. He gruffly ordered May to pull off the road and head for the hills. It was good that the surface was stony and the little sand on top was drifting with the warm desert wind. Any tracks they made would soon be invisible. They drove for mile after mile over the bumpy rocks, up the steepening slopes, until the road was far behind them. He gestured to stop the car and turn the lights out. By torchlight it felt scary, like they had found themselves on some strange, darkened planet. He shone it on her. She turned her head away.

'Look away as much as you want, you can *hear* all right. Do you feel like talking now, scum?'

'No.'

'Sure?'

'Yes.'

'Right, start taking your boots off.'

246

'You're not going to leave me here? They'll never find me. Take me nearer the road, or let me keep my boots. There are snakes everywhere round here.'

'Talk.'

'No.'

'Okay, boots off.'

He waved the pistol under her chin. There was something in his voice that made her avoid brinkmanship. He sounded like he was near the edge, might really shoot her, and she wanted to survive this nightmare if she could. She unlaced the boots and threw them over her shoulder into the back of the jeep. Damn, thought Calum. Seems like the crazy woman prefers to stay in this nothingness than say a word. What the hell else could he try? It sounded like she wasn't big a snake fan. Could he find one and wave it in her face?

'Don't you *like* snakes, May? I think they're kinda cute.'

She stayed silent but could not disguise the shudder. If she was so scared of snakes, how vulnerable would she feel up here not only with no boots but without her clothes? He was out of other ideas.

'Take your fatigues off.'

'*What?* . . . You pervert, you lay one hand on me and I'll . . .'

'Scream? Don't think it'll do you much good up here, but don't worry, I've got other things on my mind than groping filth. Get them off.'

'NO.'

'You can keep your tee shirt and underwear on. Just as long as the snakes have plenty of acreage to aim for.'

'I don't *have* a tee shirt on.'

'Tough luck. Do it *now*.' He sensed he had her on the run and must press home the advantage.

247

Sulkily, slowly, she began to unzip her front. Calum swung the beam from side to side, then right round behind the jeep. He fired. May almost jumped out of her skin.

'Damn. Missed the sonofabitch. Jesus, those snakes move quick.'

She started hyperventilating. *Good.* He turned the engine on to twist the knife some more.

'I gotta get goin'. Get the rest of those clothes off *now* and put them in the back.'

'Calum don't do this to me, I *beg* you. *Please.*'

'NOW.'

'Okay, okay, I'll talk. Just don't leave me here.'

He shone the torch closely in her face. Tears were pouring down and this time her nose was also dripping unstylishly. Calum suspected girls' noses only dribble when the tears aren't phoney. He switched the engine off, the torch, too.

'So *talk*. Starting with where we are.'

'China.'

'That much I worked out from the squiggles on the road sign. If I don't get more detail fast, you'll be back to strip-tease.'

'North-west. Xinjiang Region, near the border with Gansu Province.'

'Good, that's cleared that up, then.'

'If you find it easier, welcome to the Silk Road, and the edge of the Gobi desert.'

'Quit trying to be a smart-ass, or I'll blow your brains out. How far's the nearest coastline?'

'Fifteen hundred miles.'

'And the next town?'

'Dunhuang. About two hundred to the East.'

'And to get out of China overland?'

'Mongolia and Kazakhstan are to the North, Pakistan to the West.'

'Any of them close?'

He felt rather than saw her shake her head.

'No? . . . Really ace. Well, let's forget the geography lesson for a while. So Monument is actually . . . ?'

'Chinese Airforce Base number two-six-four.'

'Mm-hm. *I* get it. So, you are part of the Chinese military and I have been helping you . . . do *what*, exactly? Not to *defend* Taiwan, that's for sure . . . Get ready to *attack* it, maybe? Is that it?'

Her silence provided the answer.

'Fucking marvellous! So all that sentimental crap about your old grandfather was . . .'

'Crap.'

'Goodee. Fell for that, didn't I? And Montgomery? Kinda big for a Chinese, isn't he? Funny-shaped eyes, too.'

He had a long career in the US military. His last assignment was as chief of a US paranormal program there. He was accused of sexual harrassment and discharged dishonourably.'

'So he sold out to the Chinese? My superhero, Jason?'

'He didn't sell out. The US didn't want him. We did. What's wrong with that?'

'Nothing, apart from the little matter of treason.'

'What treason? No-one's planning to attack the US, and Taiwan is part of China.'

'In that case, I'm sure if you ask nicely, they'll be glad to hand it right back.'

'It's a renegade province.'

'Spare me the politics. Let's leave it there for now, I don't think my brain can handle any more surprises for a while. I need to hide and do some thinking. Are you coming with me? It's the only way you get to keep those Paris fashions on.'

'Yes.'

They drove around the hills for another half hour, half wrecking the suspension and once getting all but stuck in a gully. The crazy angles of the terrain made the headlights useless much of the time, beaming too sharply downwards or pouting pointlessly up at the star-crusted sky. He tried and rejected half a dozen crannies and clearings. No-one would see them from the road, but from the air they'd pick it up immediately. Then they stumbled on an area with a softer type of rock, blown and battered over the aeons, moulded into wild swirling patterns, strange indentations and, wonder of wonders, shallow caves. He found one that would *just* take the jeep in the tightest fit. They had to scramble down over the backboard to get out. She did his bidding in carrying the blankets, supplies and torches to its neighbouring little dugout. The pistol never left his hand.

They each ate a sandwich and drank some water. He asked no more questions and she kept her watchful, nervous silence. He knew he could not risk sleep. Her distrust of him was equal, and though he forced her to lie down under a blanket she managed no more than wisps of sleep. Calum sat by the mouth of the little cave, looking out. He couldn't get any concentration going, and had a disconcerting feeling that his predictive powers were deserting him just when he needed them most.

The adrenalin subsided a little. Typical, wasn't it, just typical of him. He'd used up every ounce of courage he possessed trying to get to a phone. And now *this*. Good old Calum Buchanan. He'd picked the worst place in the whole world to be a hero. If he went back to that camp, they'd kill him for sure. He had nowhere to escape to, and they had food and drink for a week at most, on the most iron rations. Frigging marvellous. He sat with his head in his hands, feeling the sorriest he had ever felt.

He sat there some more. No, surely he couldn't. However you looked at it, it was one hell of a long shot. No, definitely not. But then, what other options were there? With a backward glance at the compacted, blanketed bundle that was May, he switched on the torch, took the few steps to the other cave and clambered awkwardly over the backboard of the jeep. How did the GPS work? If only he'd been a sailor. Turning it on was the easy bit. He fiddled and cursed for ages before he pressed the right buttons. It came up on the green display. 91 degrees 49 minutes, by 41, 36. He had nothing to write with and kept reciting it rhythmically like some mathematical password as he went back into their own cave. May twisted round to see him. She'd thought he'd left her, but was too scared to react in case he suddenly came back and shot her.

Calum took up his station at the mouth of the cave again, and switched the torch off. The numbers were firmly in his head now. He closed his eyes and began deep beathing exercises. Then he furrowed his brow in intense concentration and stayed that way for hours on end.

* * *

The discussion on Radio 4 on the future of the Anglican Church was winding up. It had been heated and lively, and the clerics and theologians had scrapped with enjoyable cattiness. Another night and the jumper for next winter would be done. She knitted using the same old fawn wool as usual. Fashions didn't change in Morag's world.

It came at first like a tiny electrical shock that made her twitch, followed by a sensation like the faint throbbing of a distant engine. It did not hurt, but was unwelcome and uncomfortable. She wanted to ignore it and recruited a huge cupful of whisky to aid her in this. It infuriated her that it would not leave her, despite her grim resolution that it should. Whatever he was trying to say, she was damned if she would pay heed to it.

The whisky failed and so did bed. Sleep was impossible, so strong was the ache now. It browbeat her, ground her down as the meaning became clearer. Her surrender to it came between four and five. Damn the boy. She was beginning to sense more clearly the terror he was experiencing, and she could no more disregard his distress than a mother could ignore a crying infant. Her mind made up, she lay in the darkness and began to plan. She had no idea at all how airports worked or what terrors flying held. Too bad, she'd have to find out. She slept for one hour, washed in icy water, dressed, reached under the bed for the crumpled old banknotes in the cocoa tin, and set off for the walk in the chilly morning air to the bus stop.

A friendly girl at the BA desk patiently helped Morag work it all out, pointedly ignoring the sounds of exasperation from the swelling queue. Morag got the last available seat. She talked to no-one on that flight or the next one from Glasgow, but the cabbie from Heathrow won her over with his cockney charm and she rewarded him with a gentle, long-lasting smile. He found it peculiar that she travelled without luggage or even a handbag. In weather like this, she must be sweltering in that old woollen coat. He hoped she was all there, that she wouldn't get lost and confused in the big city, and felt a pang of concern when she clambered out at the wrought iron gates of Downing Street.

'Sergeant, I would like a word with the Prime Minister.'

'That's what they all say . . . Move along now, dearie.'

'I told you I want to see him, officer. Tell him it is very important.'

'Madam, we have a job to do. Now be a good old dear and move on.'

'Then I'll have a word with your superiors. Take me to a police station.'

'Why should we do that, eh? Run along, you're starting to get irritating, love.'

'Look . . . I've dropped some litter.'

'Pick it up, you daft old bag.'

'No. Arrest me . . . Go on, what are you waiting for?'

'What would you do with them, Dave? . . . I swear, they get loonier every year . . . *Go away!* . . . I don't care if you drop a whole barrel-load of litter, we are *not* arresting you. Now go away and bother someone else.'

'Don't be so hard on her, Sarge, she's 'armless.'

'No she's not, she's bleeding aggravating. GO AWAY!'

Morag's enquiries revealed that the nearest hardware shop was not far away, in a small lane leading off Great Peter Street. The Pakistani proprietor took time to understand her unusual request. He had never before had a customer who wanted paint, but didn't care what colour it was. All she wanted was a large can with a carrying handle, and he had to open it for her. Oh well, it takes all sorts, he supposed.

* * *

Sergeant Whaley saw her ambling back again along Whitehall and quite deliberately turned his back as she approached.

'Oh Christ, Dave, she's back. I've 'ad enough of loonies today. Only thing for it is to ignore them.'

'Pardon me, officer.'

He kept his back firmly turned.

'If I ignore her long enough, she'll stop bothering me.'

'You sure, Sarge? The back of your uniform appears to be dripping with something.'

The young constable Dave was chuckling gently. The paint was a shade the trade had little call for. The khaki did not go very well with the blue of his uniform.

'You *crazy . . . Right*, you old baggage, you are bleedin' well under *arrest*.'

Six days out of seven it would've passed them by, and they would have sent her packing with a warning. At Cannon Row police station there was a bright spark of a constable who overheard the old woman vehemently haranguing his colleague and it sparked something in his memory. A few months back the papers had been full of reported sightings at home or abroad of the infamous Calum Buchanan. The fuss had died down again fairly quickly. Missing persons were common enough. It was the unusual police circular about him that the young constable recalled. He looked it up on the station's files and persuaded the duty inspector to place the call. The speed with which the two young secret service guys got round to the station was impressive, even allowing for the proximity at Vauxhall of the SIS headquarters. The constable was disappointed when they insisted on interviewing her on their own.

*　　*　　*

'Miss Buchanan, this is very . . . unusual. You are sure it is him?'

'If I were not, I would hardly have traipsed all the way to London. I have better things to do with my time.'

'When were you last in contact – by that I mean conventional contact – with Calum?'

'Not since he left Lewis last autumn.'

'He didn't phone, even after his successes?'

'I am not on the telephone.'

'He didn't write.'

'No. I heard about him on the wireless, of course. I disapproved of his conduct.'

'I'm not surprised. Miss Buchanan, do you know anything about Calum's *special* skills?'

'Yes, I do. He acquired them while he stayed with me in Lewis.'

'We may need you to tell us everything you know about how he learnt them. It is a matter of national importance both for us and the Americans.'

'National importance or not, I am sorry to say I will not tell you.'

'Let's leave that point for the moment. Do you know whether those skills are real? Can Calum see into the future?'

'I believe he can, a little way.'

'And these co-ordinates, you are sure of them? . . . It is a very remote area of China . . .'

She grimaced in a way that did not encourage them to doubt the accuracy of her word.

'. . . Okay, well apart from him being in China, is there any more you can tell us?'

'It is a little vague. He is being pursued. He has done something terrible he needs to communicate to the authorities, but I do not know what it is. It *is* important, though, whatever it is, and he is desperate to be rescued.'

'Would you mind staying here for a little while, Miss Buchanan? We will be right back.'

'I have all the time in the world, but do not forget that my troublesome great-grandnephew may not.'

'Sorry to keep you so long. Miss Buchanan, do you have a passport?'

'What need would I have of a passport? It is the first time I have ever left the island.'

'Don't worry about it. We have to ask you to go on a journey.'

'Not to China, I hope. I'm not sure I would enjoy it.'

'Not to China. A place called Langley, in the United States of America. We have booked you on the six p.m. Concorde. One of our young men will escort you through the airport. At the other end you will be met by a Mr Rose from the British embassy and some Americans from their Central Intelligence Agency.'

'I suppose for Calum I should be willing to give up my usual social whirl for a few days. I was only on an aeroplane for the first time today. I did not expect to be getting on the Concorde. Is Langley a pretty place?'

'I think you'll find it interesting. Now, I don't want to rush you, but if you are not to miss that plane . . .'

* * *

Christopher Ransome took most things in his stride. Very few things apart from Wagner would set that quartz-regulated pulse racing. His secretary informing him that 10 Downing Street was on the line was an exception, and provoked a rise in heart-rate equal to listening to the immolation scene from *Götterdämmerung*. The truly impressive thing was that, even then, his secretary could not detect the faintest change in his voice.

'Good morning, Mr Ransome.'

'Good morning, Prime Minister.'

'I wondered if we might have an absolutely off-the-record conversation?'

Of course this was thoroughly irregular, but was he really supposed to say so?

'Of course.'

'This China matter. We are getting to a point of no return. As you know, I am visiting Washington tomorrow. The President is pressing me for a clear commitment to support them. The DTI agrees with their line. They see the Chinese as posing an immense threat to order in international trade. On the other hand, the Foreign Secretary and our embassies in Beijing, Paris and Berlin are all convinced that taking a hard line will leave us in an exposed position, that in the end the Americans will be forced to give way, and we will fall between every stool in sight.'

'Mmmm.' A pretty concise summary, thought Ransome, rather relieved that *he* didn't have to take decisions like this every day.

'I have read your reports closely. You are the one in the front line on this, and if I understand correctly, you also know something of China. I want to put two questions to you. First, if I *do* back the American hard line, do you think we have any chance of prevailing?'

'Only if we can split the Europeans.'

'Okay, second question. The Foreign Secretary believes that this isn't worth the candle. What I want to know is do *you* think I am right to take a stand against the Chinese? . . . I *do* realise I am putting you in a difficult position.'

'Prime Minister, I'm not sure I should venture . . .'

'Mr Ransome, make I make a suggestion? If you privately *agree* with the line I propose to take, just stay silent for a second.'

'. . .'

'Thank you, Mr Ransome, I found that very helpful. I wish you good-day.'

'Good-day, Prime Minister.'

Ransome's secretary waited till the call was over before bringing in his coffee. Her eyes were sparkling and she dallied in his room long enough to give him a natural opportunity to confide in her.

'Rachel, I suppose we need to decide who to invite for the Red Cross lunch.'

She nodded, sighed, and went to fetch her pad.

* * *

He knew they'd be searching on the ground as well as from the air. From time to time he heard the distant drone of diesel engines, but there was no line of sight from the cave to the road, and it was *far* too risky to go out to a vantage point to check whether it was *them* or any normal traffic. The first helicopters had clattered by in the early morning and others came at regular intervals throughout the day. One came so close Calum thought they must hear his heart thumping. While it was hovering, he had the gun pointed at May's head, daring her to move.

How long would it take them to comb every hillside, gully and cave? He'd put a fair distance between them and the camp. Assuming their tracks had disappeared, it could take quite a while. Would they play a waiting game? They knew how much food and water they had. Even if they guessed Calum had killed May, those supplies couldn't last one person more than ten or twelve days. Why not wait for him to show? But what was the point in Calum speculating about it? He couldn't take a chance on being spotted leaving the cave, and where could he run to, anyway?

May's willingness to answer questions had dried up after they reached the comparative safety of the cave, and even talk of snakes no longer convinced her. When she spoke at all it was only to issue fulsome promises of good treatment if Calum surrendered, interspersed with threats of the dire consequences if he did not. When she got no reaction to either, they fell silent and simply waited.

The cave was too shallow to keep out the heat from the intense, blanching sun. Needing to conserve water, they drank little and their mouths were parched. They sat a few yards apart, using their blankets as cushions on top of the rock floor. He watched her watching him. She might try a move any second if he dropped his guard. He mustn't forget her karate. He should stay a safe distance away and always keep the gun in hand. The day wore on and darkness fell. For the second night, Calum sat upright, knowing that sleep would be fatal.

The next day passed in silence, too. Calum used it to practise

259

meditating without closing his eyes. It was almost six in the afternoon and the suffocating heat was beginning to ease a little. He found himself staring out of the cave mouth, sleep almost overwhelming him, forgetting the danger from May. He turned round suddenly. She hadn't moved. Was that a tear she was wiping away? What ruse was *this*? His hand tightened on the gun. When he asked, she wouldn't say why she was crying, but her tone of voice was different, the hard, aggressive edge gone. She sounded weary, resigned.

In a deliberately unharsh voice, he asked her for some simple honesty. She looked back, sighed, and surprised him by asking what he wanted to know. It *seemed* she had finally realised that he wasn't going back, that there was no more point in silence or trying to maintain any vestiges of the sham. Calmly, unhurriedly, she admitted everything. How the young American soldiers, once part of Montgomery's team in the States and outraged at his dismissal, had quit the army and joined him as mercenaries in this richly rewarded escapade. How they'd converted the phoney bar for Calum's arrival, having the idea too late to get it ready in time. The simple way they taped TV and piped it through to him later so the broadcast times tallied. How they'd hired the London gangsters to frighten him and help stage the rescue.

'Is May your real name?'

'Yes.'

'And are you Montgomery's woman?'

She paused before replying.

'Osborne's his woman, has been for years. Now he's bored with her and wants me. He tries to touch me when no-one's about. He says he gets me, gift-wrapped, if this mission succeeds.'

'*What?* . . . They agreed to *that*?'

'Nobody else has told me and I haven't asked. It might be true. The way Rita looks at me, she must know it or sense it.'

'And if you're thrown in as dessert, you will *accept* it?'

'If I am *ordered* to do something, I am not given a choice. It is all irrelevant now. I have failed. The prediction program will be too damaged to help with the invasion.'

'It was hardly *your* fault. It was Montgomery's decision to let me out of the base.'

'Oh no, it wasn't. The person you know as Lieutenant Jones took that decision. He is Colonel Bo, the military head of the programme. Montgomery opposed it to the end. Bo instructed Lee and me to take great care. We let him down. This will damage Bo's career, too, though the real blame lies with Lee and me.'

'Oh, yeah, I forgot about Lee. Who is he? A character actor from Hollywood?'

'He's the nearest there is to real. He *is* from Hong Kong, but he's worked for us fifteen years. He's our top expert on military applications of the paranormal.'

'What will they do to you both?'

'They *need* Lee. The whole paranormal program depends on him. My case is different and my failure is greater. They will think that by being taken by you, I was given an extra chance to persuade you to go back *before* you discovered the truth. As it is now, if you are recaptured, I may escape with a reduction to menial work. If you die, so they lose you as an asset, I may be imprisoned. If you escape to the West, they will probably execute me.'

'Nice system you have over here. Real user-friendly and supportive. Must give all of you a good warm glow, being backed up to the hilt like that.'

'Calum, it is my country. I have failed in an important task. You may think it harsh, but it is not some *game* they are playing. The unity of our country is at stake. You think America is so forgiving to failures?'

'Jesus, I don't know everything our people get up to, but I sure as hell hope we do better then *that*. At least we have respect for the individual.'

'Like for the young blacks in your urban ghettoes? You think they get a fair deal? . . . Forgive me, Calum, but I don't think this is the smartest time to be debating these things. Tell me, are we going to sit here till the food and water run out, or what? Do you *have* any plan?'

'I'm pretty certain if I go back to the base, sooner or later they'll kill me. From what you're saying, if I manage to escape something dire will happen to you, too. Either way, one of us is dead. You may have tricked the shit out of me, but I don't want you killed or in some gulag on my account. If I was to find a way to be rescued, would you come with me?'

May shook her head gently. For the first time since they left Monument – or Base whatever number it was – her faced relaxed. It was probably the first time he had seen an unmanufactured smile from her. Geez, she could be pretty.

'You're sweet, Calum, you're sweet. You're also hallucinating. There isn't going to *be* a rescue.'

'Just say there was, hypothetically. Would you come?'

'Let's worry about it when we get there.'

They fell silent again, and watched the sky begin to darken once more. He could hardly keep his eyes open. He still didn't trust May one inch, but no determination to stay on guard would work this time. What might she try? The gun wouldn't help her much. Surely she wouldn't have the authority to plug him. She could maybe run off and raise the alarm, but that was quite a journey on foot. All he had to do was stop her using the jeep. Turning away so she couldn't see, he slipped the keys down into his underwear. Let her try getting at those without waking him.

His eyes closed and he dropped right off. When he woke it was pitch dark and . . . what the hell was this? . . . May had sort of snuggled up to him.

'Hey, what's this, enemy?'

'It gets cold at night and I felt a bit lonely.'

'Is that all? You weren't planning on seducing me tonight, by any chance?'

'Dream on.'

'Good. You had me worried. If my new system's working, that doesn't happen till tomorrow night.'

'What new system? *What* doesn't happen?'

'You seducing me.'

'Crap.'

'I mean it. You underestimate me. I knew something was odd long before that bar stuff. I've got my range past twenty-four hours now. I was keeping quiet about it, that's all.'

'Bull-*shit*. You think I'm dumb enough to fall for that?'

'Let's wait and see, shall we? Nothing either of us can do about it. Not till tomorrow, anyway.'

'You're not *serious*, are you? You say I . . . *tomorrow* . . . seduce . . . *you*?'

'That's it.'

'Baloney.'

'As you like.'

'I do *not* believe you're saying this. You're fooling around, you have to be . . . come on . . . No? . . . so, out of curiosity, how do I . . . what do I? . . . I can't believe I'm dumb enough to be asking this.'

263

'You take your things off and . . . no, hold on, I don't wanna spoil it for you.'

'Spoil it for *me*? How about for *you*?'

'Whatever. Let's leave it there. I need some more sleep. G'night.'

'No, you bastard, I won't be able to sleep now. This makes me feel ridiculous, like we've already done it. You sound so goddam smug about it.'

'Why not? It's a sure thing after all, but not till tomorrow, so goodnight.'

'And that's it? I get no say in it?'

'You get plenty of say this time tomorrow.'

'So it's all predetermined? . . . I have no control at all? . . . I can't say no?'

'You can, but you won't.'

'And what if – strictly hypothetically – I seduced you right now? Wouldn't that wreck your neat little forecast?'

'Of course, but you *can't*.'

'I can't, eh?'

'No, go to sleep . . . *Hey*, what you think you're doin', May? Get off me.'

'These are coming *right* off you now, Calum . . . And these. Oh, so that's where you keep the keys, is it? I'll remember that.'

'Leave me alone. This'll never do . . . the timing's all wrong. No, I *order* you to keep your clothes on.'

'Hey, you're not *quivering*, are you? You, the man of the world.'

'It's the cold.'

'Liar.'

'May, you are *not* to do that. No . . . I said *noo* . . . *oooooh*.'

'How does *that* feel?'

'No comment. Uuuuuuuh.'

'So what price your prediction, now?'

'I can't think what went wrong . . . Wow, these are *nice*.'

'Not too small?'

'Perfect . . . Mmmm.'

'Stay still. I'm going to turn around slightly . . . Okay?'

'Wonderful.'

'And how's it feel if I do . . . this?'

'I didn't know you were black belt at this, too. Oooooh. No, stop, STOP! Get me a pencil. I *need* a pencil.'

'A *pencil*? For *what*?'

'To take notes . . . Oooooooooh.'

'Quit trying to be funny and *concentrate*.'

'That's what I'm trying to avoid. The more I concentrate, the shorter this will last.'

'Don't worry. Relax and enjoy it. I'll just . . .'

'Oh no, not that, not *that* . . . May, the cowboy can't stay on the bronco much longer.'

'Then fall, cowboy.'

'Oooooooh . . . uuuuuuh . . . aaaaaaaaaaaaaah . . .'

They lay still for a few minutes. Gently he pulled her back to him.

'May, that was truly *amazing*! I mean, genuinely *intergalactic* . . .'

There was no answer.

'. . . Less intergalactic for you, I guess. I mean, I don't suppose it can have been very . . .'

She kissed his cheek.

'Don't worry your pretty little head about it. It felt . . . nice.'

'*Nice?* . . . The cave didn't move?'

'Ssssssh. Go to sleep.'

'Know what I'm thinking, May?'

'What?'

'In America we think we know what sex is. We aren't even *close*.'

He felt himself beginning to drift off. He was vaguely aware that the jeep keys were lying somewhere around the cave floor, but for all he cared, May could grab them and run right off. Whatever tricks she was up to, after what he had just experienced, she deserved a get-out-of-gaol-free card for *any* game she wanted to play.

'Calum?'

'. . . Mmmm?' He didn't want to spoil the delicious drift down.

'Where does that leave your system, the twenty-four hours prediction? If it's real, it could be very . . .'

'May, I don't know how to put this . . .'

'What? Oh *no*, you didn't . . . ?'

'Hey, after the way you tricked me, *you* can't complain.'

'So, that was completely . . . you . . . *scumbucket*.'

Her fists rained down on him, but not powerfully. He didn't try to stop her. When she was spent, she laid her head gently back down onto his chest.

19

They say that in most recent years there have been more tall cranes in use in Beijing and Shanghai than in the whole of Western Europe. True or not, Beijing's appetite for new building remains insatiable, a multitude of cranes across the city standing to attention like some giant imperial army. In the sprawling centre, up go new hotels, new office tower blocks, new restaurants, new shopping centres. In the outer suburbs factories are built or rebuilt at an even faster pace. The city's bleakly noble old skyline has been all but rubbed out by the new concrete forests. Soon the final fall of the bicycle to the onslaught of the car will bring still more noise, heat, dirt, pollution and chaos to the city's headlong dash towards cosmopolitan, mobile phone-infested modernity.

It is largely down to the Communist Party that Beijing still retains a few quiet spots, exquisitely manicured gardens enveloping handsome villas with lovely old courtyards. These places stay peaceful because mere mortals cannot enter. Perhaps the prettiest of all is Diao Yu Tai, meaning Fishing Platform, a delectable oasis where the most senior party officials entertain sumptuously, graciously and with enormous style. It is the custom of the chef there to offer only the rarest delicacies, so that nothing is put in front of the guests which could possibly be commonplace. Sometimes there are many guests, sometimes, as on that evening, only one.

That guest, Gao Xin Min, and his host, Premier Chen,

made a contrasting pair: Gao tall, of military bearing and frank, open countenance, and Chen short, fat, with a face so expressionless it was unreadable even by his closest aides. However, these two had much in common beside a love of fine food. They were born within days of each other in 1938, both sons of founders of the Party. Their paths had been different but with enough overlap to keep them close; close enough to stay friends and help each other. Like all countries, China has its official structures, but personal friendships and alliances cut across those structures far more than in any Western country. These friendships endure longer than the structures which change and evolve at an ever more dizzy pace. Chen knew in his heart that without his friend's support at key junctures, he might never have become Premier. It was therefore only natural that he should have reciprocated by lobbying strenuously and successfully for Gao to be appointed Supreme Commander of the Armed Forces.

That warm July evening they enjoyed each other's company as much as ever. This time, however, they trimmed back the idle chat to a minimum. Chen was soon to leave Beijing to join the other Politburo Standing Committee members at the summer resort of Beidaihe. They both knew that the stage was set for the events they had so carefully planned. Chen spoke.

'The army commanders . . . they are still with you?'

'I have full confidence. They know that without this, their grip will be seriously weakened.'

'And the younger officers?'

'Like puppies wanting to play, keen for a great adventure. They forget that bullets can fly in more than one direction.'

'With your plan our casualties should be . . . acceptable?'

'Yes, but we must have the authority to strike hard. Massive rocket attacks on all installations. Airdrop of sixty thousand troops, followed by full-scale seaborne invasion. Total application of superior strength. It is the only way.'

'And the sabotage operation?'

'If it works, it will reduce bloodshed and quell resistance. However, if it is detected, it might be fatal. I do not believe it is worth the risk. I would rather lose another fifty thousand dead than compromise the whole operation. We *must* act decisively.'

'I am with you, old friend, but there are others who may think differently. The sabotage operation and the "uprising" in Taipei have long been part of the agreed plan. It will be hard to persuade them.'

'You are the politician, not I. *You* must persuade the Standing Committee to give me a free hand. I will deliver their dream to them *if* they give me the proper tools.'

'I will try.'

'How *is* President Zhang's condition?'

'The cancer progresses. He will remain in hospital a little longer and then go directly to Beidaihe. I visited him again yesterday. His energy is sapped, his will to govern almost gone. I think it unlikely he will see out the year.'

'Will he name a successor?'

'If so, he will never choose me. His instincts are more with the modernisers. Liao, knave that he is, has persuaded him that the army must now *really* surrender its birthright and sell its assets. Nevertheless, Zhang fully realises that if the Party lost the unswerving support of the army, the whole Communist structure might crumble. That is why, when *you* send your last-minute plea to reverse the Sunrise decision, and *I* inform him that, with the French in our pocket, the result at the WTO is not in doubt, he *has* to support us.'

'You are *sure* Liao knows nothing of your understanding with the French President?'

'I have told no-one but you. It leaves only the problem of timing. If Liao was alerted and able to speak to Zhang he *might* talk him round, and that we cannot risk. We must wait until the very last moment, when Liao is in the air on his way back from Seoul, and force Tian Yi in Geneva to act on her new instructions before he can stop her.'

'And then?'

'The Americans will be furious. However, without European support, they will not get final WTO judgement against us, and the French President has *guaranteed* he will deliver the German Chancellor. That stitches up Europe completely. There are therefore two possible outcomes. One is that the Americans back down with the rest. Then we will *know* that they will never stand up to us and, if we maintain the merest veneer of civility, we can act with impunity. For decency's sake, we would delay the strike on Taiwan for a few months, not more. The other possibility is that the US government is so wild with rage that they impose unilateral penalties on us. That would be *provocative*, and our signal to strike. The Americans will be criticised everywhere at home and abroad for their insensitivity and bungling. They will have to stand quietly aside while we take the island . . . Oh, of course they will issue protests and make a fuss at the UN. The great battles of history were not decided by rhetoric. Our fathers did not defeat Chiang Kai-shek's Nationalists with pieces of paper.'

'With either result, for Party Secretary Liao this would be . . .'

'Humiliation. A total collapse of his power base.'

'And Zhang would disown him as a possible successor and choose you instead.'

'He would have no choice. If he did not, he would be ousted immediately.'

'So the waiting is almost over?'

'Almost. I can virtually *touch* it. Let us drink to the memory of our fathers.'

They raised their glasses, filled to the brim with the fashionable blend of Great Wall red wine and Seven-Up. Gao smiled generously. Chen responded with a thin, cool smirk.

*   *   *

Marianna did not like being kept waiting, even for five minutes, even in a such a comfortable chair in the luxuriously panelled reception area. Especially by a lawyer *she* was paying, or would pay, anyway. Repeatedly she sighed ostentatiously to make the receptionist uncomfortable. At last, Larry Abraham came out and ushered her into his office.

'Marianna, I do believe you're looking lovelier than ever, if that's possible.'

It wasn't flattery. Money suited her. The chic-est hairdresser in LA, and more spent on clothes in the last year than the national debt of some third world countries. Today's was a fabulous jasmine silk number. *God*, she was a magnificent specimen.

'Thank you, Larry.'

She rewarded him with a smile.

'So, Marianna, has Brett agreed?'

'He says he's too busy to think about it.'

'I still think you're being unrealistic. Brett was badly stung by his first wife, and the last one accepted a pretty restrictive pre-nuptial. I'd be *amazed* if he went ahead without one, especially as his net worth has risen so much.'

'Why should he care if he means it when he makes that vow? He's fifty-two, for Chrissakes, isn't it time he settled down properly?'

'I'm older than him, Marianna, and there are days when I feel frisky myself. If I were you, I'd back off and try for a generous agreement. But obviously it's *your* call.'

'He'll agree in the end. I'm giving him a dose of the refrigerator treatment so he gets the message. Anyway, that isn't why I'm here. What do you know about English law, Larry?'

'A big fat nothing. Why?'

'My ex, Calum. You remember all that stuff in the papers about the money he won?'

'Who could forget?'

Marianna uncrossed her divine legs, offering the briefest glimpse of soft high thigh. Larry Abraham pulled out a handkerchief to wipe away the beads of perspiration. Brett Marquardt was one fortunate sonofabitch.

'He's been missing for over three months now. Must be dead, for sure. Years ago, soon after we got wed, Calum made a will leaving everything to me. Does us getting divorced automatically cancel that or anything?'

'Not unless he subsequently changed it.'

'I'd say that's unlikely.'

'And you have a copy of this will?'

'Yeah. I need to find out how to get him pronounced dead so I get the money.'

'In that case, I don't think it's necessarily anything to do with English law, even if his main assets are over there. The courts here in California could approve a ruling.'

'Great! So what do we do?'

'Hold your horses, Marianna. They won't even consider that for a long time yet. A minimum of five years.'

'*Damn.* And there's nothing we can do to speed it up? We just have to *wait*?'

'That's right. If you take my advice, you'll concentrate on the Brett in the hand, or almost in the hand.'

'Don't worry, Larry, he'll be okay. I know what I'm doing.'

*   *   *

'How's the cheeseburger, Morag? . . . It *is* all right if we call you Morag, isn't it?'

'If that is what you consider appropriate. The cheeseburger is . . . interesting.'

'Call me Jack.'

'Thank you, Mr Balletto.'

'It's really your first burger, *ever*? I can't cope with that thought. I'm forty-two years old and by now I must've eaten millions of the damn things. That's what makes me so fat.'

'I believe you are the fattest person I have ever met. It becomes you very well.'

Balletto's colleagues were sniggering fit to bust.

'Well, what can I say after a compliment like that? . . . How about a Coke? . . . You pull it open like . . . let me . . . no, round here we drink it straight from the can.'

'How civilised. Do you take your baked beans the same way?'

'No . . . hey, Morag, I *do* believe you are teasing me. For some reason, folks always take the . . . mickey outa me, but usually it takes a day or two before they start. You've only been here what . . . half an hour and you've started *already*. What can that mean?'

'It probably means that I like you.'

'Morag, you leave me speechless . . . it's many a long year since anyone had me blushing. I'd better get on with some work or you'll make me swollen-headed.'

'And I think I've decided to call you Jack, after all.'

'Well, *thank* you.'

'Don't mention it . . . That is what you Americans say, isn't it?'

'Perfect. You're picking our jive real quick. You want us to get you a cup for that Coke?'

'No, I'm sure I should try to learn your customs, however primitive they may seem . . . It tastes a little like cough medicine.'

'You don't like it? . . . What else can we get you? Mineral water? Fruit juice?'

'Whisky. It helps me think. If we have a lot of work to do, which can be the only explanation for you bringing me all this way, I may need a whole bottle.'

'Good, we'll have one rushed round right away, and also kit you out with a coupla changes of clothes. Now, let me explain who everybody here is. I'm the head of East Asia for the CIA, and Tom and Radek work for me. Major Gillespie over there, Paul to his very few friends, is from the Pentagon . . . Excuse me asking, Morag, but you know what the Pentagon is?'

'I do indeed. It is a five-sided object.'

'Ye-s, but it is also what over here we call . . . *Morag*! Last time I ask you a dumb question, I can tell you. Finally, on the left, Orson Wells. Real name is Peter, if I remember right, but no-one calls him that. Orson's a boffin from our special psychic research training program. We all wanna thank you very much for coming here to Langley. As Calum is a US national, we have agreed with British Intelligence that from now on *we* will handle all aspects of this operation . . . Now as you know, we need to make haste, so let us go right to the heart of the matter. Morag, how does this communication with you and Calum work? Is it like a free telephone call?'

'I have never made a telephone call. However, what Calum and I do is much less clear and much harder work than conversing.'

'How do you do it?'

'When I am trying to receive a message from him, I try to clear my mind as much as possible, try to make it blank. If he is saying something to me, a vague sense of it eventually comes to me. It is very hard to describe. It is not in the form of words, it is as if someone has planted a thought or a sensation in my own mind. It can be hard to interpret at times.'

'I'm sure. And if you want to *send* a message, how does that work?'

'In that case, I concentrate on that thought as hard as I can. If it works, it will enter his mind in the same way.'

'What have you tried to say to Calum since he . . . contacted you?'

'That I am trying to help, that is all.'

'Good. And have you received anything more?'

'He repeats that he needs help, to be rescued. It is important that you get him out of China so he can tell you what he has done.'

'That's it? . . . so far, I mean.'

'That is it, apart from the numbers. He repeats those often. It is not much, I am afraid. I am out of practice.'

'No, no, Morag, that's a great start. Now, Orson here has prepared a special room for you to relax in, meditate, send, receive . . . whatever. It has a bed and some other furniture. It is totally soundproofed, so you won't be disturbed. I'm gonna give you a list of questions that we'd like you to *try* to get answers to. Don't worry if they don't all work. Orson'll be just outside the door at all times and whenever you have anything to report, this team will convene to hear you and formulate some more questions. Is that okay?'

'Yes, Jack.'

'Okay, here we go. Is he hurt? Is he alone? How long can he hold out? That's the first group. Then we need to know *something* about the work he's been doing for the Chinese. We've no idea why he did it or what's changed now, but we have to know *what* it is. We realise that this will be hard to communicate, but it's vital that we try. In view of Calum's unique talents, it's pretty darned obvious that he's been working on something predictive. We don't think it's the Beijing lottery. Almost certainly something strategic, something with a military application. *Anything* you can find out about that would be invaluable. Is he training their people or doing something for them directly? Is there some *particular* objective or target? When are they planning to use it? . . . There we go. It's a long list, I'm afraid. Orson will take you there right away, and . . . no, I won't forget to send over the whisky. Would you like an ice bucket? . . . oh, oh, another silly question, I guess. Thanks again, Morag, we sure appreciate you having a go . . . I'll be right here at my desk, anything you need.'

'Thank you, Jack, have a nice day.'

She set off with Wells, chuckling away to herself in a delightfully girlish way.

* * *

'What does May mean?'

'Could, might, perhaps.'

'Uhhh? . . . Oh quit foolin' around. What's it really mean?'

'Beautiful.'

'That figures. Your folks were good at predictions, too. Are they still together?'

'Yes.'

'Where are they? Beijing?'

'Rome.'

'As in Rome, Italy?'

'Uh-huh. My dad works for the AnQianBu. It's like the CIA. He's in the embassy there.'

'Is that their first time abroad?'

'No, no. They've been abroad most of the last twenty years. Paris, Washington, London, Tokyo.'

'Were you with them too?'

'Sure I was. Not Tokyo, the others. You don't get English this good in a classroom, you know.'

'No, of course. So, the spying game, it's like a family business for you?'

'Seems so.'

'Do your brothers and sisters get up to the same tricks?'

'I don't have any.'

'Oh, I forgot, you Chinese are limited to one child each, aren't you?'

'That's not the reason. I *had* a brother. He died.'

'I'm sorry. What did he die of?'

'A bullet. He was a student at Tiananmen Square.'

'He was *executed*?'

'Not officially. The way the soldiers fired at them was a form of mass execution, though.'

'I remember it on TV. How could those soldiers *do* that to their own people?'

'They had to ship in soldiers loyal to Deng Xiaoping. They were mainly peasants' sons who had no idea what it was all about. The Beijing garrison refused to do the dirty work.'

'Good for the Beijing garrison.'

'Not so good. Ninety-two of the soldiers who refused were shot.'

'*Jesus Christ* . . . May, I just *do* not get it. These people kill their own students, their own soldiers, kill *your* brother . . . and you still *work* for them?'

'My brother disobeyed my father. He should *never* have—'

'Are you so hard and unfeeling that that's all you care about? That he disobeyed your father? Your brother does something maybe foolhardy, but incredibly brave, gets killed and you don't care?'

'I didn't say I didn't care. I *loved* my brother.'

'But you don't blame the government?'

'I didn't say that, either.'

'But you *do* choose to work for them.'

'I did *not* choose to work for them, I was assigned. I had no choice whatsoever in the matter. This isn't California, Calum.'

'If I understand right . . .'

'You understand *nothing*. My father was disgraced and demoted because of my brother. He and my mother have never got over his death either, but they have to *live*. Do you think a Chinese spy can just quit and go take another job? Get *real*. And d'you know what would've happened to them if, after that, I had refused?'

'I'm sorry, May. I didn't realise . . .'

'It doesn't matter. Let's drop it. Calum, you have to level with me. I can see from the way you're meditating for hours on end that you're trying to do *something*. Won't you tell me what it is? Our supplies won't last much longer. If I'm about to starve, I think I should know what's on your mind.'

'I'm not sure I should . . .'

'What? . . . If you're willing to sleep with me, I think you should be willing to *trust* me. We may have started out on opposite sides, but we seem to be pretty much in this together now. Can't we leave sides out of this and try to work out what to do? Starving to death doesn't strike me as a masterplan.'

'Okay, I'll do it, I'm gonna trust you. If you let me down . . .'

'Shut up and get on with it.'

'The woman who taught me how to do my stuff . . . Morag. I'm trying to reach her through telepathy to get a message to . . . whoever, to send help.'

'Oh my *God*.'

'What?'

'Your teacher, Morag Buchanan . . . after you told Montgomery, we . . .'

'*What?* Oh no, you *didn't* . . . You *fuckin'* barbaric . . .'

'No, no, no. I honestly don't know whether the plan was to kill or capture her. We didn't need to. She died in a fire a few months back.'

'Hold on, this can't be true, unless I'm imagining . . . Did they actually see her *grave*?'

'No, there wasn't one. Our guys were told about it by the locals. Apparently they scattered her ashes.'

'That's . . . hilarious.'

'*Hilarious?* Your only hope's dead and it's *hilarious*?'

'She's not dead. I *know* she's not. Your guys got had. I bet

279

my old friend Fraser had a hand in it. Morag's alive and well, and she's on the move.'

'Calum, I don't know who's right and who's wrong, but if this woman *is* alive, who will *listen* to her? She's just a strange old lady, isn't she?'

'She's *very* strange, but I'm pretty sure someone's listening, all the same.'

*　　*　　*

Morag settled in to her quarters. She examined the complicated-looking shower mechanism doubtfully and opted instead for the bath. She hadn't wanted to show it to these Americans, but she was dog-tired and wracked with the arthritic pain she had never disclosed to a living soul. She gulped down a glass of whisky and slept for five hours. It was four a.m and light was already coming in through cracks in the drapes. Morag closed them tighter and lay there, the darkness hiding the grim resolution of her expression.

For hours there was nothing. Was he asleep? Had he stopped trying? On and on she waited, waving away the occasional enquiry from Orson, disregarding the sandwiches he set beside her, taking only an occasional sip of whisky.

It began to come to her, borne like a faint whisper on the wind, hard to catch. She could be sure of nothing at first, had to try many times to get any sense at all. She persevered until late afternoon, then went to the door to tell the patient Orson that it was time for a meeting. Orson phoned it through, summoned the group – hard-edged sceptics for all their welcoming smiles

– and escorted Morag along the long corridors back to the conference room. There was a quiet dignity in her bearing that made them all stand up when she came in. Radek dashed over to pull back a seat for her.

'Okay, Jack, I have a little more information for you.'

'Great work, Morag. Shoot.'

'He can hold out for a few more days. He is not hurt. He is not alone, he has a girl with him. They tried to make him teach others, but it hasn't worked. The target of the work is Taiwan. The Chinese plan to attack it, he thinks soon . . . That's all.'

'*All?* That's pretty amazing, wouldn't you say, fellahs?'

They gave her a friendly round of applause. Morag permitted herself the luxury of a shy smile.

'Morag, we need to know more about this girl. Does she know he's in touch with you, is she from the base, is she part of their program? Can you do that?'

'He will be asleep now, and I need some rest myself. When he wakes, I will start again.'

'Great. In the meantime, we'll talk to our superiors about what guidance we can give him next.'

Morag allowed herself to be taken to the canteen by Orson. She had too little energy to respond much to his attempts at chat. The journey, the jet-lag, the unfamiliarity of everything, and most of all the concentration had drained her of all but the last fragments of her will-power. For Calum's sake she *had* to keep going and hide her frailty. If they thought she couldn't take it, they might give up on her and stop trying to use her to communicate with him. They would send her home, and she would not be able to try to save her boy.

*   *   *

The days dragged more for May because she had nothing to occupy her mind. Sometimes to keep her spirits up Calum would stop his mental endeavours and chat or sing songs with her. The rest of the time he concentrated or deliberately put his brain in neutral to rest. Once when his mind was wandering, it struck him that since his escape he had not thought once of Marianna, and even now when he did, it felt . . . different from before. He didn't have the usual churning sensation in his gut, or the wish to strangle Brett Marquardt. He consciously kept his mind on Marianna for a while, waiting for those familiar emotions to flood back. They didn't. He shrugged it off as something to do with the heat and went back to meditating. Two hours later he got up and went over to sit beside May.

'I'm excited. I sense something's stirring.'

'What are they saying, Calum?'

'Wait till I get a real answer. Let's keep our fingers crossed that they can get here before the searchers find us. I don't see how they can rescue us without being picked up by the Chinese. They have those Stealth planes, of course, so maybe they have helicopters like that, too. Or d'you think they will touch down someplace else and come for us overland? . . . Come to think of it, how the hell will we be able to signal where we are without bringing the whole goddam Chinese army running this way? . . . It's beyond me. I guess *they*'ll have a plan, though. Can't be the first time they've done something like this.'

'Won't Morag tell you what to do?'

'I sure hope so. Just have to wait and see, I guess. Hey, May, a while back I was wondering . . . remember you saying you prefer not being in love? Why is that?'

'I can't risk mixed loyalties.'

'You mean with your work?'

282

'No, with my parents. Ever since my brother's death, I have felt responsible for them, and my superiors have made clear that my performance may determine their fate. I must put them first in all things. If I loved a man that would change.'

'Love doesn't have to be *that* serious.'

'For me, it would be.'

'So what happens to your parents if we escape together?'

'Calum, I don't really believe that anyone *is* coming to rescue you, but if I am wrong and they do come, I *cannot* go with you. If I did, my parents would be punished terribly. I will not try to stop you going, and you must not let your rescuers force *me* to go too. After you leave, I will drive back to the base and face my punishment. My parents may still be treated badly, but my returning will save them from worse.'

'What if I could get the US to rescue them too, and grant them asylum, or whatever?'

'Impossible. Bo will have alerted Beijing as soon as the alarm was raised, and our Ambassador in Rome will have banned them from leaving the embassy compound. They will be guarded twenty-four hours a day.'

'Look, compared with rescuing *us* from the heart of China, springing your folks from Rome should be a cakewalk for our boys. I'm not giving up on you yet.'

May smiled and kissed Calum tenderly on his temple.

* * *

It was getting clearer now, scything through her consciousness, sometimes so powerfully it would wrench her from her fitful sleep. At other moments it left her in peace, to rest and try to recover a little. The throbbing from the arthritis had receded a touch, but now she had some pains in her chest. She didn't dare ask for any medicine. At least her appetite had returned, which was some sort of good sign. The sandwiches and pickles tasted good and she had another go at the Coca-Cola from the little fridge. Hmmm, maybe it didn't taste *quite* so horrible as before.

Even when Calum wasn't in contact, she worried about him constantly, which wore her out more. So to distract herself for a while she got Orson to explain how the television worked, and played for half an hour with the little grey plastic box that changed the programmes so handily. Then she sensed it coming again, and at once switched the set and the lights off and went back to work. Little by little she reeled it in.

'She *is* from the base. She *was* working for them, but has changed sides now. She knows about the contact.'

'Okay, Morag. You've done a great job. Now we come to the difficult part. We have a message we need you to send to Calum that's gonna be a big disappointment to him. I know he's expecting a rescue, but unfortunately I'm not Felix Leiter and we're not in the James Bond business. We can't stroll into the Chinese interior and scoop them up; we'd never get near them. The Chinese would pick up our helicopters on the radar and force them down or shoot them out of the sky. That would also cause one hell of an international incident. I did ask, Morag, but the answer was a very firm *no*. I'm sorry to disappoint you, too, truly I am. It's not a realistic option.'

Morag felt duped, and very cross with Jack. She struggled not to let it show until she found out what plans he had now.

'So what can Calum do, Jack?'

'In any case, he has to give himself up, unless he wants to starve to death. There's no way he could escape from there. What we want to ask of him is more than just surrendering. Morag, we need Calum to go back and start working with them again.'

'I do not understand, Jack.'

'He would only be pretending to work with them, of course. In reality he would be working for us, informing us, through you, of their plans. Trying to warn us when and how they might attack Taiwan. D'you think he might be willing to try that?'

'I do not know. It is a great deal to ask. If I judge from how he has behaved in the past, I would have to say no. He knows that if he goes back they may torture him or kill him. The Calum I knew would choose suicide rather than facing something like that. Mind you, I was rather surprised that he had the courage to escape in the first place. Perhaps something has begun to change in the boy.'

'Let's hope so. However, there is another instruction we must give him which may be even more painful. The girl, do you sense that he is close to her?'

'I believe he is.'

'If they both go back and she tells them that he was in contact, everything will be wrecked. They wouldn't use him again, and they would kill him immediately.'

'She might not tell.'

'And they might torture it out of her. It's a risk we cannot take. I wish I could see some other way. Sadly, my superiors are very insistent on this. Calum must silence her.'

'And that means kill her?'

'It does.'

'He will take that very hard. He is trying his very best not to

285

let people down again. You are forcing him to choose between two forms of betrayal. Taking a human life is a terrible thing, whatever the reason. I'm not at all sure he will do it. In his position *I* would not.'

'Morag, he *must.*'

Morag looked back at Jack Balletto. There was nothing to be gained from arguing the toss. Whether or not Jack had strung her along, it was probably true that he didn't have the authority to order a rescue attempt. Though they were sending the poor boy right back into the lion's den, Calum's only hope of survival still lay in following what these people said. She tried not to show her biting worry that Calum would feel betrayed by *her*, and that might make him give up altogether.

20

They had kept the President well briefed. Now he wanted all of them at the Oval Office for an assessment. For someone getting a daily buffeting in the press, on TV, and in all manner of opinion polls, he looked ludicrously well. There can have been few Heads of State so unbowed by the pressure of the most difficult years. His height had always helped. His movie-star looks – as good close up as from a distance – resolutely refused to sag or fade, and his hair was of the high-tensile variety that drives trichologists to drink. The exercise of supreme authority and the burden of the nation's responsibility had merely added new lustre to the shine from those blue eyes. They said it was the way he could sleep, any place, any time. And keeping his beauty timeless for another four years would need no plastic surgeon's scalpel, but the rarer, more exotic, infinitely more expensive drug of a second term of office.

'Jim, give me the Pentagon's assessment.'

'It's simple, Mr President, the island is indefensible. If the Chinese make an all-out attack, they can't be stopped. We have done what we can with arms supply. The Taiwanese have just taken delivery of a further twelve F-15s and thirty mobile missile launchers. That should help their defences survive the first wave of missile and bomb attacks. They may even give the paratroop transports a nasty surprise. However, eventually they will be overwhelmed. Once the Chinese are really committed to this thing, they won't be able to pull back. The loss of face and prestige would be so great, it would put the whole Party and military apparatus under unbearable strain. They would have no option but to prevail, whatever the price.'

'Is there anything we can do?'

'In our view, once hostilities start, there is nothing we can do without getting directly involved, and we all know where that might lead.'

'Yeah, I don't think rockets landing in California would help my re-election chances any.'

They all knew it was wise to laugh. They competed for who could keep smiling the longest.

'Having carriers close by would have no deterrent effect if they knew we wouldn't use them. It would make us look weak, standing idly by. The Chinese would love it. We should keep all surface warships out of the region.'

'So if they want it, they take it? Johnny, does the CIA think they will go for it?'

'We think the chances are increasing, Mr President. For years the Chinese have tried to generate a consensus in Taiwan in favour of unification by infiltrating key institutions there and giving lucrative deals to top Taiwanese companies. However, the old Taiwanese leaders are stubborn and Beijing is getting impatient. They may not believe that time is on their side. Today, for all their flashy new clothes and stock market speculation, the Chinese people still do what the Party tells them. What spooks their military is that this could change, like happened here over Vietnam. Give them another ten years of prosperity, foreign travel, and guess what? The next generation might find mass-slaughter of ethnic Chinese less okay. Bottom line is the army fears if they don't act soon they may never be able to.'

'Any more intelligence on the military build-up?'

'May I suggest you look at the map in your briefing pack, sir? . . . There is a lot of naval activity going on at their base in the Straits of Taiwan on the small island of Xian Men. They have moved six Han class subs there, plus a whole bunch of surface craft. Way above normal levels of activity. We also think they have moved large numbers of air transports to their airbases here at Shantou and here, to the South of Fuzhou. There is one other piece of information. It's pretty wacky, not anything we can attach much credibility to. It seems that a young civilian, an American, has been helping the Chinese with a paranormal military program. He's still in China, but has tried to inform us that the purpose of this program is an imminent attack on Taiwan.'

'Who is this guy? Does he work for you?'

'No, we think he may have been recruited by the Chinese and changed his mind, or even forcibly abducted by them. He does appear to have real paranormal powers.'

'So what did he do? *Telephone* the CIA from China?'

'No, sir. He's in touch with us . . . telepathically, through the medium of an elderly female relative.'

'Johnny, have you guys *flipped*? What kinda New Age bullshit is this?'

'As I said, Mr President, we are not ascribing any serious decision-making importance to it.'

'Better keep it that way, or I'll close down Langley and get a bunch of tarot readers instead. Save the taxpayer a whole lot of money . . . Now, back to more serious stuff. Lynne, how's Geneva coming?'

'Slowly. The WTO Director General, Signor Fratelli, is still freaking out, but the Panel has now convened. After immense pressure on the Secretariat, they have agreed to produce a provisional judgement within two weeks, by August sixth to be precise. This is a big variation from the normal procedure, but it has been accepted. The French were against it and are still protesting. Your call to Prime Minister Nakamoto proved vital. As Nakamoto told you, they will never vote against the Chinese on the judgement itself, but for us right now it's the timing that matters more. It means that negotiations in Geneva with the Chinese can start in earnest from August seventh. Our plan is to have Ambassador Patterson play our opening hand, then I will fly out a week later for talks with their Minister Tian.'

'Is Tyne happy?'

'Happy's hardly the word. His group say they'll give us till the end of August before going public on it.'

'How d'you expect the Chinese delegation to play it?'

'They must know that the breaches of their undertakings are so flagrant that the provisional judgement is bound to go against them. Everything will depend on their lobbying power and how far they're willing to push their brinkmanship. With all the pressure we're applying, they *should* see the need to make real concessions.'

'How are the Europeans lining up?'

'The Brits are still with us, the French definitely opposed. We suspect de Murville did some deal with the Chinese, so it looks like it will turn on the Germans. You may have to put in a few calls to the Chancellor.'

'Okay . . . that it for now? I'd better not keep the Mexican waiting any longer.'

*   *   *

'Calum, I can't stand this any more. You haven't said a word for *hours*. You just sit there staring into space. For God's sake, *tell* me what's happened. Whatever it is, I'd rather know. Anything's better than this. What the hell's *happening*? Is it your rescue? Are they not coming?'

'No.'

'You poor darling. Oh God, I'm so *terribly* sorry for you. How could they build up your hopes and then let you down like that? Hey, don't cry. Here, let me comfort you.'

'Oh May, oh May . . .'

'I know. You must feel so *crushed* . . . Calum, I know how hard this is, but if you're not to be rescued, you *have* to think about what we do next. We're nearly out of water and look how little we have left to eat. We *can't* simply rot here. Can't you try to escape by yourself? If we saw a truck we could hold it up and steal it. Urumqi's four hundred miles away, but it's big. If we disguise you somehow, you might find somewhere to hide out there. I could come at least part of the way with you and claim that you forced me at gunpoint. The odds will be hugely against you succeeding, but surely anything's better than *this* . . .'

'I'm goin' back . . . to the base.'

'*What?*'

'You heard me.'

'Why that, so suddenly?'

'I have no choice.'

'Well, you surprise me, but if that's what you think is best . . . What's the plan? Will you try to persuade them that you had a brainstorm or something? I suppose they *might* believe you. Don't worry about me. Whatever they do, I'm a survivor, I'll make it through . . . Calum, come on, don't cry any more. You *really* gave it your best shot. It was incredibly brave and

291

resourceful of you to escape from the base, to try to warn your people . . . You know, if you *have* decided that we're definitely going back, let's set off right away, while there's still some daylight.'

'May . . .'

'Why don't you check if the jeep starts okay and I'll bring the last of the water?'

'May . . .'

'What?'

'You're not going back. They've ordered me to go back alone.'

'Who has? Your *voices*?'

'Yes.'

'So, what happens to me? . . . What's that strange look for? . . . Hey, you don't mean . . . ? No, you *can't* be serious . . . You've been told to kill me, is *that* it? Jesus, I *don't* believe this . . . *Say it*. Is that what you're going to do to me?'

'Yes.'

'Great. So, how are you gonna do it, eh? Shoot me, strangle me, starve me? Which is it to be, you *asshole*?'

'I've no idea.'

'Not very *precise*, are they, your precious voices? I *cannot* believe that you're even *saying* this shit. We could both go back to the base and try to make it through somehow, but because some *fucking* voices tell you different, you're gonna kill me in cold blood. You're *mad*, Calum, these are probably hallucinations. Think of the strain you've been under, think how little you've had to eat or drink. The desert does funny things to people. Think how'll you feel if you get home one day and find you weren't in contact with *anybody* . . . Who *is* your ridiculous contact anyway? Some crazy old woman.

What makes her think she has the right to hand down death sentences over her own personal mindnet?'

'It's not Morag who's saying this. She's just passing it on.'

'From her nerve centre in the Hebrides, right?'

'She's not in the Hebrides now, she's in America.'

'How the hell d'you know that? . . . This is *such* . . . BULL-SHIT . . . So you're going to do it, are you? You really *are* going to kill me?'

'I have no choice. For once in my life I can't put my personal preferences first. Thousands of people's lives could depend on this.'

'I understand. I hope you rot in *hell* for this. If you're gonna do it, do it *now*. I mean it . . .'

'D'you wanna last meal or anything? You can have the last candy bar.'

'You *amaze* me. No, I do NOT. Shoot me *now*. My *God* how I *despise* you! . . . What are you waiting for?'

'Don't you want to write something to your folks . . . ?'

'*No*, you moron . . . NOW!'

'Okay . . . I'm *so* sorry, May . . . this is the last thing I ever . . .'

'I don't wanna hear another word from you. Pull the fucking trigger or I'll kick that gun out of your pathetic hand.'

'Okay . . . Hey, stay back . . . Back off or I'll shoot.'

'*Shoot?* That's what you're gonna do anyway, you *stupid* prick.'

'I said back up . . .'

Her left foot flashed up, knocking the gun clean out of his hand. As it skittered across the cave floor, they both made wild, headlong dives for it, grazing their knees and elbows. Calum's longer reach got him there first, but before he could bring it round, she was on him like a wildcat, slamming one fist into his solar plexus, and jabbing a palm hard up into his face, forcing his nose back painfully, drawing noises from him like a hog being slaughtered.

'*Gggggggg . . . Aaaaccccchhhhhhh . . . Eeeeeeeeeooooooow.*'

She was screaming in his face.

'*Drop the friggin' gun, you slimeball . . .*'

Calum clubbed the Beretta hard against the back of her head, while trying desperately with his other hand to prise her fingers from his face. The heel of her palm slipped into his open mouth and he sunk his teeth viciously into it. May yelped with pain, and pulled her hand back far enough for him to get the gun between them. They were both on the ground, panting furiously, May sucking her wound.

Calum laughed triumphantly.

'*Hah*, thought you could beat me, huh?'

Her words came through deep sucks of air.

'You are so full of *shit*. So what will you do? Boast back home how you beat up a woman, armed only with a gun? . . . You make me *sick*. I've had enough of this. Get it over with NOW!'

Oh *Christ*, he'd forgotten about killing her. He hesitated again.

'*You sonofabitch, don't fuck me around any more . . .*'

Calum spoke quietly, almost tenderly.

'I can't, May, I can't do it . . .' He chucked the gun carelessly to one side. 'May . . .'

Still on the ground, he stretched out his arms to embrace her. She wrestled herself fiercely away and scrambled exhaustedly over to where the gun had landed. Her face contorted with anger and hate, she rose slowly to her feet. It was mainly the rage that made her hands tremble as she advanced on him, the gun pointing right between his eyes. He lay there, his arms still outstretched, ignoring the weapon.

'May, May . . .'

'Kneel, scum, it's *your* turn.'

He half-rose, arms outstretched towards her. She kicked him back down very hard.

'KNEEL!'

He did not react. She grabbed at his hair and yanked it violently, forcing his head back and upwards. His voice sounded calmly resigned.

'Okay, May, I'll kneel for you.'

She let go of his hair. With a deep sigh, he pulled himself slowly up into a kneeling position. May's panting was gone. Now she was hyperventilating with seething fury.

'Okay, you scumbag, *my* voices have told me to kill you, so that's what I'm gonna do. Wanna last meal? Write to your precious ex-wife?'

'No, thanks.'

'Then beg for your life.'

'Is there any point?'

'No, I'd just wanna hear you beg. *Beg.* NOW!'

She kicked him hard on the thigh.

'BEG!'

'No, May, I'm not gonna beg. You can do it, I'm ready.'

'Don't think you can bluff me. I'm gonna do this, whatever you say.'

'So what are you waiting for? After everything I've gone through, it'll be a blessed release.'

'Right then, you little shit.'

She put the gun to the side of his head, pressing it hard against his skull. He closed his eyes in a tight, flinching clench. She held it there for a few more seconds, then in an explosion of rage yelled,

'Oh *SHIT! Shit, shit, shit!* . . . I'm just as pathetic as you . . .'

She flung the gun violently down.

BANNGG!!!!!!!! The bullet ricocheted wildly round the cave, missing them both by inches. The noise deafened and stunned them for a second. It took Calum even longer to be sure he was still alive and in one piece. May had collapsed, head down on the floor, and was directing a torrent of oaths at herself, banging her fists on the rock floor.

Suddenly Calum didn't want to be dead any more. He crawled over beside May and put his arms round her shoulders. Her fists stopped their thumping, but she seemed oblivious to his touch. He stroked the back of her head. Still no motion from her, only a gentle sobbing.

'There, darling May, it's okay. It's over now.'

He took hold of her shoulders and turned her over. She neither helped nor resisted, like a dead weight, her eyes closed. Her lips did not move when he kissed her. This was getting nowhere, so he did the next best thing and unzipped her fatigues. Still no response. He took off his own. She opened her eyes but did not respond. When she did, it was with a ferocity, passion and abandon that would have required a whole new volume in any notebook of Calum's. When they looked in each other's eyes afterwards, they knew that something powerful and strange had occurred between them. Neither chose or dared to put a name to it.

For one hour Calum and May talked earnestly and purposefully. Then they backed the jeep out, threw away the guns, and in silence drove carefully over the boulder-strewn terrain back to the road. A patrol picked them up before they had gone a further mile.

As the soldiers came over, he whispered to her.

'Will you betray me?'

296

'I betrayed you for months.'

'No, now. Can I believe in you?'

'Stop believing in words. Wait and *see*.'

* * *

'So what does he say, Morag? Has he done it? Has he taken her out?'

'He says he has.'

Morag was a fan of Jack, but as she saw it, it was her job to transmit faithfully what Calum communicated, not to add her own opinions on its veracity. It was her boy she was doing this for, not American prestige or the peace of the world.

'And he is back at the base?'

'Yes.'

'Are they willing to work with him?'

'He is not sure. They are very suspicious. He thinks they have not decided.'

'Well, no news is better than bad news. He should do everything he can to try to convince them. Do you think his predictive powers will be blocked by his experiences?'

'I cannot be sure. I think he will only get the strength to do it again if he believes fervently that what he is doing is right.'

'Does he think that?'

'I do not know. At this moment, I don't think he knows himself. He will have to rest. He has been through a terrible ordeal. We will have to hope that he does not crack under the strain.'

'*A-men* to that . . . Speaking of ordeals, it's been an *age* since we've had anything to eat except potato chips and peanuts. I know this great place that does *the* most delicious blackened chicken. How does that sound, Morag?'

'It depends how they blacken it. However, you should always be willing to give something a chance. That reminds me, Jack. I have a confession to make. I tried Coca-Cola again. It helps with my concentration nearly as much as whisky. I have developed something of a taste for it.'

'I know. Orson had to apply to the Senate Appropriations Committee for an increase in our budget, you've been getting through so much.'

21

'And you believe him?'

'I am not sure, Montgomery. It is important that Major Osborne continues to observe him very closely.'

'What about a lie detector or a truth drug?'

'Unfortunately, it is not so simple. If it is true that he had some form of breakdown triggered by the unfortunate incident in the bar, but caused primarily by the immense strain, it is *conceivable* that what he says is true. His state of mental health may still be very delicate. If we are to get his wholehearted co-operation, we need to give the impression that we have forgiven him and *believe* him. He has had a lot to come to terms with. Our deception of him was comprehensive. We need to regain some, preferably all, of his trust, to *motivate* him to work for us. For the task ahead of him, only the most total commitment will suffice. We need to let him rest, to recover, while feeling that he is not under undue pressure. Any such tests – if *obviously* conducted – could only set back his recovery.'

'Colonel Bo, pardon me for speaking plainly, but I think this could be a trap. We know that Buchanan has advanced telepathic powers. The old woman who taught him may be dead, but he might have made contact with others.'

'It is indeed possible, although, according to Lee, unlikely. And only if Chang's confidence in the totality of her conquest is misplaced, or if *she* is lying. As you know, we have interrogated her rigorously, depriving her of sleep to weaken her resolve. She has remained absolutely adamant that while he was hiding there he gave no indication of being in contact with anyone. Frankly, all he appears to have done is to run and hide like a naughty schoolchild until he ran out of candy bars. His behaviour fits more easily with an inadequate, confused personality, than with some international conspiracy theory.'

'Personally, Colonel, I find it hard to buy into this love stuff. Until his escape, all Rita heard from him was how he would love his ex for eternity. And now we're told he's fallen just as completely for May Chang. Can we really believe that?'

'I incline to Osborne's view that what we have here is a *type*. If he falls for a woman, he falls completely, and will do *anything* for her. Don't forget, we don't know what his ex-wife looked like, but I doubt she is more attractive than Chang.'

Montgomery was managing to stick fingers in the dyke of his temper, but the waters were rising dangerously.

'Colonel Bo, how can you be so sure that May hasn't fallen for *him*? A shared experience like that can create a strange bond.'

'*Really*, Montgomery, I expect more sense from you than that. I know this is vexing for you in view of our *arrangement* about Chang. We stuck to our side of the bargain. While Buchanan was here, Chang was instructed to be close, but not *physical*. For reasons entirely beyond our control, the situation changed dramatically and Chang had to improvise. Buchanan is a little boy lost. Do you think he could excite more than *pity* in a woman like Chang? I am certain that only a real *man* could seriously interest her.'

Montgomery silently acknowledged the compliment, and his fury receded a touch.

'There is one more thing. Buchanan is now insisting that Chang should spend as much time with him as possible, including staying overnight in his quarters.'

'NO. *That* I cannot accept.'

The dyke was swept away by the flood. He could stay sitting no longer and stomped furiously around the room like a penned grizzly. He turned back to Bo.

'NO WAY, *never.*' The thought of this *nothing*, Buchanan, doing *that* to his prize every night was more than flesh and blood could stand. It bugged him that it was Bo saying this, the Bo who'd ignored all his warnings and sent May out there with Buchanan in the first place. He wasn't even in a position to relieve his frustration by *saying* so. Bo waited patiently for the flood to abate a fraction.

'I have already agreed to it. Buchanan insists that her presence will be vital in relaxing him enough to work. Whether or not this is true, she is probably the only person here he trusts to any degree and she may help speed his recovery. It will give us additional opportunities to monitor his state of mind through their conversations. Several new cameras and microphones have been installed.'

'Colonel Bo, I have to come back to this. How can you be absolutely *certain* he hasn't persuaded May to change sides? . . . If there were *any* possibility of that, we would potentially be aiding and abetting a catastrophe.'

'Colonel, I appreciate your concern, but we really have no alternative. Buchanan's contribution is indispensable, *you* know that.'

'Frankly, I'm amazed Beijing is letting you use him again, after the escape. If I were in their shoes, I'd regard any mission that Buchanan participates in as seriously compromised.'

'Doubtless Beijing would agree with you, *if* they knew.'

'What?'

'I have not informed them. Everyone on the base was told the escape was an exercise, that Buchanan and Chang were practising evading the enemy, seeing how long they could hold out. That is why I chose to isolate Lee, you and your Americans after he fled. Of *course* Beijing would have cancelled his part in this. Then, without Buchanan, we would *all* have been excluded from the historic venture. You and I would have failed completely. Oh, yes, I would be the first to suffer, relieved of my post and humiliated. But think of the consequences for you, too. No ten million dollars, no luxury villa, no May Chang. Montgomery, we have no choice but to take some risks. However, in case your concerns about Chang have *any* substance, we have not advised her of the enhanced security arrangements in his quarters. If they so much as *whisper* to each other, or communicate by writing one *word* down on paper, in the light or in the dark, we will have them.'

'And . . . ?'

'We will kill them both. We will not feel the need to burden our busy judiciary with their cases.'

'We should kill *him* anyway, even if we *do* use him on Taiwan.'

'Why not? What further use would we have for him?'

'I will go along with this if you grant me *one* request. I want to be the one who executes him.'

'I don't think my superiors will have a problem with that. In the meantime, you must make an effort to rebuild a relationship with him. You may not get hero worship from him now, but you must persuade him that your motives were respectable, and draw any poison he may be harbouring against you. Such negatives may get in the way of his concentration. On

302

second thoughts, seeing you again so soon might cause too strong a reaction. It may be necessary first to restore a sense of routine, of business as usual with Lee. Perhaps you should see him only a short while before we use him operationally.'

*   *   *

Tian Yi was glad that this time she would be staying at the Hotel des Bergues instead of with the Chinese ambassador in Geneva. She preferred her privacy and liked the view over the lake, the bustle on the Pont du Mont Blanc, and the City's famous tall, windblown fountain.

Liao and she had worked it all out meticulously, and they thought they had just enough ammunition to clinch it. Their early concessions were carefully planned and strategically aimed. On cars and pharmaceuticals for the Germans. On textiles for ASEAN. On port customs processing for the Japanese. A little here, a little there. Nothing for the Brits, to punish them for their insolent criticisms of Hong Kong. Overall, though, a positive tone and an approach fluid enough to stop the danger of deadlock. That was when temperatures could rise dangerously.

The Americans' temperatures *would* rise, of course: that was a necessary part of the drama. If they were to be bought off with a single bauble, then that bauble must be gift-wrapped sublimely. They must be persuaded that only through intense pressure and outstanding negotiating skills had they wrested it from the Chinese. That would delight them and they would return triumphantly home, never counting the cost. The Chinese would have achieved a wholesale revamping of the

WTO entry terms and would be hailed as good international citizens into the bargain!

The timing of delivering the bauble was critical. Make the concession too soon, and the Americans, scenting blood, would bay for more. Leave it too late and the European mood could turn against them. Tian Yi had to execute it *pefectly*.

Whatever else happened, they must avoid the WTO confirming the Panel's provisional judgement against them. Unilateral penalties by the US would be painful and should be avoided if possible. However, they would be over soon. It was not in the Americans' nature to defy for long criticism from the international community. Concerted WTO action was quite another matter. Then China, not America, would be the renegade. A final WTO judgement would be non-negotiable, and China would be forced to pay heavy and humiliating penalties until it was implemented in full.

* * *

'Wow, take a look at Morag, guys! What a makeover and what a great new hairstyle. How about those sexy new glasses. It's nothing short of a transformation!'

'Thank you for arranging it, Jack, and for the extra clothes, too.'

'Happy to be of service. There was a reason we needed you to get some more things. We're all going on vacation together, a kind of vacation anyway. Morag, things may come to a head soon and we need to be closer to the action. There are some trade talks getting started in Switzerland that involve the Chinese. If those go well we may see no movement, but if they go badly the Chinese may use it as an excuse to move against Taiwan. If they *do* plan to use Calum, everything could switch to real time. We need to be there, or in the vicinity anyway. Of course, it won't affect the speed of your contact, *that's* not the reason. The problem we have here is that your sleep patterns and Calum's are right out of synch. We need you to be in the same time zone. Also, if Calum's trying to send information about attacks on Taiwan, we need to get you up to speed with the geography of the place, so you can understand what's on his mind. So tomorrow we all decamp to the Pacific, to Okinawa. From there the Air Force will arrange an intensive overfly of Taiwan. After that, depending on circumstances, we'll stay at our base on Okinawa or go on board a nuclear sub. Before you go to Asia, we thought you might appreciate a little background on Taiwan. Radek, fire away.'

'Right now, Jack? I thought we might do it tomorrow. I haven't quite had time to . . .'

'Let's get on with it, Radek.'

'Okay, Morag, here goes. I'm not much of an expert on it myself, so if I goof you can blame it on my CIA briefing pack . . . Now Taiwan may be better known to someone of your . . . generation as Formosa, from the word for "beautiful" in Spanish . . .'

'Or Portuguese?'

'Something like that, Morag. Anyway, it is a hundred and sixty miles long and about fifty-five wide, with a population of twenty-two million. Historically, it has always been part of China.'

'If the seventeenth century counts as "always".'

'It doesn't say anything about that here. Oh, pardon me, I didn't read this properly. Yeah, that's it . . . in the seventeenth century, some Dutch guy called Koxinga captured it and—'

'I don't mean to nit-pick, Radek, but I think you'll find Koxinga took it *from* the Dutch. He was fighting for the last Ming emperor against the Manchu.'

'Um, right. And . . . hold on a sec . . . here it is . . . in 1683, the Manchu defeated Koxinga's descendants. Ever since then, I guess it's been Chinese, at least until Chiang Kai-shek's Nationalist Party occupied it in 1948.'

'Haven't you forgotten the Japanese?'

'Have I ? Oh *yes*, so I have. The Japanese held it from 1895 till the end of World War Two. Since the 1950s the Taiwanese GDP – that means Gross Development Product, Morag, it's a kind of measure of how good a country's doing . . .'

'Radek . . .'

'. . . has grown at an average rate of . . .'

'*Radek.*'

'Yes, Jack?'

'Why don't you quit while you're ahead?'

'Sorry, Jack, I ran out of time to mug up on it.'

'That's okay, Radek, we'd never have noticed. Morag seems to have more of a grasp than *any* of us. How come you know all this stuff, Morag?'

'From the wireless. That and being old. I remember the Chinese civil war like it was yesterday.'

* * *

Lee had lost most of his bounce. He hadn't forgiven Calum for that night on the mountain. It had dampened some of his natural enthusiasm. His other mannerisms were unchanged:

the fingers through the hair and the jab to shove his spectacles back in place, but his tone was a lot more sober than before. During the first two weeks back at the base, they met only briefly. Bo had ordered that Calum should rest and recuperate, as well as undergoing comprehensive psychological testing by Rita. It was only now that they had risked trying out what had happened to his powers. Calum was as nervous about it as they were and needed to use every ounce of his will-power to get there.

'We are relieved, Calum, your faculties seem to be intact. Your range has receded a little, back to seventy minutes. That timespan can still have a useful operational application, however.'

'Will you need me to start training the Taiwanese . . . excuse me, the Chinese, again, Prof? I think I'll find it hard enough just doing my own work with you. As you know, it was the pressure that made me flip in the first place.'

'I think we can spare you that. It is unlikely that those people could make sufficient progress to be useful operationally in the near future. Later on, perhaps, later on. In the meantime, we have much to do together. I want to get you back to eighty minutes as soon as possible. If we achieve that, we can be satisfied for the present. However, we will learn from our mistakes and limit the sessions to twice a week. You now seem to have recovered from the immediate physical effects of your ordeal, but we need you to be in tip top condition, mentally *and* physically. We will continue the special high-protein diet and assign a special trainer from the base gym to help you get back in shape.'

* * *

There were those who thought it a delightful paradox that the leading moderniser, Liao, should stick with the old way of taking his personal train to Beidaihe, and the hawkish arch-conservative, Chen, should prefer to fly. Of course, Premier Chen did not dare criticise President Zhang for *his* preference for using his own train. All his mockery was reserved for Liao, whom he accused, though never to his face, of absurdity and self-importance in adhering to the outdated pomp of the train ceremony. The truth was simpler, though knowing it would scarcely have stilled Chen's tongue. Party Secretary Liao liked to take his train because he liked trains.

He liked Beidaihe, too, both the place and the rigmarole. He loved its setting in the sweeping bay, and its gentle, unchanging atmosphere. It was not as ravaged by the bull-dozer as most places in China, and the whole town had a comforting familiarity. He loved the sumptuous villa pro-vided for him, with its lovely pine-filled gardens and the famous private beach for the Politburo, prosaically dubbed Bathing Area Number Five. Best of all in Liao's mind was the process itself. The many whispered conversations with lesser Politburo members in villa, clubs, and restaurants as plots were hatched and scotched, and faction vied with faction in delightful miniature civil wars, like the stately jousts of mediaeval Europe. The wonderful, endless banquets at the President's villa and the tense, often rancorous meetings in his conference room which usually preceded them. It was a pity that this year Zhang's illness had shortened the time they would spend there. Normally they would already be there by early July. The President's hospitalisation in Beijing meant that as a mark of respect they were all obliged to wait until well into August, when Zhang was finally fit to travel.

Liao had spent many some important summers in Beidaihe,

308

with decisions taken which had shaped and reshaped China, but as his train jolted out of Beijing station, he knew that this was to be the most momentous of all. A mere three months from now, and possibly less, he would be either annointed as Zhang's successor or cast into the outer darkness, a broken unperson. There could be no compromise with Chen. The acrimony was too intense, the rivalry too sharp. If he won, he would be as harsh with Chen. There was no other way.

Liao believed he could articulate the hardliners' views as well as they could themselves. They thought nothing must jeopardise the Party's grip on the State. Otherwise the Long March, the years of struggle and sacrifice, the whole Communist revolution, would have been for nought. They did not suggest that economic change was harmful in itself; prosperity distracted the people from political thought, which was good. And China *did* need foreign know-how and export markets for its goods, so the foreigners had to be allowed a share of the nuggets that were being mined in the extraordinary Chinese gold rush. But it must be a *controlled* share; reviewable and, if necessary, withdrawable. There must be no silicon opium, no electronic glass beads. No foreign power must be permitted *any* measure of control over the Chinese market or industrial base.

Above all, they insisted that the armed forces' position must be preserved. They were scandalised by the demands from abroad for the army's monopolies to be broken and their vast estates sold. The wealth these assets generated not only meant that the forces were well fed and well armed; it offered a honey pot that the army officers could dip their personal paws in, and ensured that there was no discontent in the senior ranks.

Sleepless for all the soothing rhythm of the wheels on the track, Liao could not fathom why the army had agreed to give up Sunrise with no more than a token struggle, or why Chen himself had not marshalled stronger opposition to the sale. This concession to the Americans should ensure a stunningly successful deal in Geneva, virtually assuring Liao of the Presidency after Zhang and ruling out Chen's absurd thoughts of taking Taiwan by force. So what *was* Chen's strategy? Liao profoundly wished that he could cancel his long-planned day trip to Seoul. Being away from events in Beidaihe, even for a few hours, would be unsettling.

* * *

They could stand it no longer. For night after night in the Shobost bar, week after week, it had hung over them like a black cloud. Word had spread fast of her note to the tweed man saying she would be away for a day or two. Now over a month had gone by. Where could the old bitch be? The bus driver said she had gone to the airport, and from the time of that bus, that would be the Glasgow flight. Surely she had no-one to stay with there or anywhere else on the mainland. She had no friends or relatives at all, unless you counted that fool boy.

But how appalling it would be if she had somehow got wind of the visit of those two men and found a way to contact them. At the time Hector and Fraser had been pleased as punch for heading that one off. Now the danger might be back. If they *were* from a newspaper or the television, the witch could be stirring up real trouble. How could they find out what she was up to?

It was Hector who decided that they had to do it and

brought along his old torch. Hated as she was, they were not confident their actions would meet with universal approval, so they resolved to tell no-one, not even their closest cronies. To get a little Dutch courage, the pair downed a few more whiskies than usual and set off into the black night. They had no clear idea what they were even looking for. All the same, they were pretty sure they would find *some* clue in there, a letter or whatever.

Fraser led the way up her little path. Hector shouldered the door three or four times, hoping that the old hinges would yield. They didn't budge. There was nothing for it but to smash a pane, and get one of the grubby little windows open. Hector picked up a stone, and leaning carefully over the top of the low thorn bush, did the needful. He ordered the smaller Fraser to go in first. Fraser hesitated. The cool night air had made off with some of his drunken bravado and he was becoming less convinced that breaking and entering was such a very good idea. Not only that; now he was there, he had a *very* odd feeling about going into that house. Hector waved aside his objections and helped him get over the bush and through the window.

In the dark, damp interior Fraser felt terrified. In a panting falsetto voice, he squealed for the torch. They couldn't take the risk of putting the light on. From outside, Hector was hissing at him to get the door open. Dammit. It was the kind you couldn't open without a key, even from inside. Cursing as he came, Hector had no choice but to force his bulkier frame through the window as well.

By the light of the ancient torch, they looked everywhere in the living room, finding nothing useful at all. Fraser was now covered in goose-bumps, and, clinging to Hector's side, kept urging him to let them leave this foul-smelling evil den.

In his harsh Gaelic tones, Hector told him to shut up. What was there to be afraid of when the witch wasn't there? He was beginning to think that if Fraser went on like that, he would make *him* scared too. There was definitely something strangely musty and clammy about the air in there. His own hands were beginning to shake; the hairs on the back of his neck were rising, and the torchlight was weakening from its full white to a wan yellow. They had better get on with it. Hector marched over to the door to Morag's bedroom. As he took hold of the doorhandle, Fraser hissed at him,

'Hector . . .'

'What *is* it, man?'

'You don't think the witch could have come back without anyone noticing, and be . . . *dead* in there?'

The torch chose that moment to fade and go out altogether. They hadn't noticed earlier the wind whistling eerily in the chimney, sounding for all the world like a lamenting soul. The tin roof was creaking hideously. Suddenly neither of them felt like being the last to leave that dark place, and they scurried over to the window, jostling for position. The more powerful Hector thrust Fraser roughly aside and managed to get his head and shoulders into the aperture first. Fraser, beside himself with terror, impatiently shoved Hector's retreating backside and legs, sending him head first into the thorn bushes and earning himself some particularly juicy Gaelic epithets. An instant later, Fraser fairly flung himself through the window frame, unconcerned that he would land right on top of his unhappy friend. They scrambled painfully to their feet and ran down the path as fast as their old legs would carry them.

Their panic receded a touch when they got a hundred yards or so up the street and they slowed to a dignified walk. Their most urgent need was for a restorative. The Shobost would be closed now. Luckily the flasks each had stuffed in his pocket had not fallen out, so they sat down by the side of the road and started on them with gusto. As they drained the last drops, a horrible thought occurred to Fraser.

'Hector, you don't suppose . . . she might curse us for going in there?'

Hector's head lolled in Fraser's general direction. In the dark he was finding it unaccountably hard to focus on his friend's face.

'Don't be daft, man. How would the witch herself know we'd done it?'

'Of course. Unless . . .'

'Unless what?'

'Unless she somehow . . . *knew*.'

'She's cursed *me* already, so I have nothing to fear.'

'Unless . . .'

'Unless *what*, you drunken fool?'

'Unless she has the power to turn folk into animals or something.'

'Stuff and nonsense.'

Fraser fell silent, much to Hector's relief. His head was spinning and he was glad to close his eyes. It was many a long year since he'd consumed so much whisky in one night. At least he wasn't as drunk as Fraser, spouting childish rubbish like that. Turn folk into animals indeed!

* * *

They were roused by the dawn at around four o'clock. For all their splitting headaches, both were secretly glad to be parted from their dreams, and to catch sight of each other in familiar, if unusually dishevelled, form.

* * *

Mid August was far from the best time to admire the view from Christopher Ransome's terrace. The muggy haze tended to obscure the mountains and mosquitos could be a pest, so Ransome permitted Gerhard Hirsch only one glass of perfectly chilled Pommery before gently shepherding him in to dinner.

'So tell me, Gerhard, how was last week's news greeted in Brussels?'

'Without surprise. The Commission had always assumed that the provisional judgement would go against the Chinese. Some of my colleagues are wondering whether Tian Yi has come to Geneva to negotiate, or merely to stage a walkout from the Council meeting in protest at the Panel's provisional findings.'

'I think that is unlikely.'

'Tell me, Christopher, at the Council meeting, do you think you will be able to catch it if the Chinese whisper to each other? It would give us a rather wonderful advantage.'

'Unfortunately not. Our Chinese friends are clever and keep excellent files. They know that I served in the Beijing embassy and speak their language. If they whisper at all, it is with their hands cupped so that a bat couldn't hear them. Most of the time they write notes to each other. So, sadly, I cannot help you cheat at cards, Gerhard. You will have to play your hand, or rather our collective hand, on its merits . . . Another drop of this rather disappointing Pomerol?'

'Thank you . . . I think it's perfectly fine. How do you read it so far, Christopher?'

'Stately gavottes, diverting minuets. Both sides manoeuvring, so the other's concessions come first. The Americans are fortunate to have Art Patterson here. Few ambassadors play the game so adroitly.'

'Do you really think so? If the Americans continue to take such a hard line, I worry how long we can appear to support them. My current instructions from Brussels, as you know, put clear limits on that.'

'Mmmm. I suppose much will depend on how Lynne O'Neill behaves when *she* arrives tomorrow. Will she be a good cop after Art's bad cop, or has he been preparing them for the real vitriol? What's your guess, Gerhard?'

'I do not think that Lynne O'Neill is one of nature's good cops. With the pressures on her, I doubt she can afford to be.'

'I fear you are right. In which case, we can expect some especially spectacular fireworks. Tell me, my friend, what news of the French? They still work the corridors energetically. Do you think they have your compatriots in their pocket?'

'They are certainly applying immense pressure on Berlin. I dined last night with Gunter Hoch. He has had calls from the Chancellor himself. The French are determined to make this a test case of Franco-German relations. Perhaps I should not say this, Christopher, but it is my impression that they also wish to use it to prove that on major policy matters, the EU's policy is decided by them and not the British.'

'Mmmm. *Plus ça change*, Gerhard, *plus c'est la même France.*'

22

'Hi, Calum, long time, no see.'

'Yup. I don't know what I should call you now. You'll have to forgive me if I drop the Colonel bit.'

'Jason's fine, if that's okay with you. How's everything?'

'You hear from Lee, don't you?'

'Sure. I meant how are *you* feeling about it all?'

'Oh, not bad, I guess. It's all a bit different from before. No more Rita telling me what a loser I am and you making it all right again. Your manipulation worked pretty good.'

'Calum, I know how you feel, and I sympathise with it. You *must* understand, though, that that stuff was *essential* to get the best out of you. Standard military procedure. Discover what will motivate a man and give him lots of it. We knew how tough the program would be, that it would take a superhuman effort for you to blast your way past the strain and the exhaustion. We needed something to keep you going. Just saying please and thank you was never going to be enough.'

'I can see your point of view.' Calum marvelled at the man. The voice was as reassuring as ever, almost good enough to convince him all over again. Montgomery filled the short pause with a warm smile and continued.

'May will have told you the circumstances under which I left

317

the US military. That was the blackest day of my life. I devoted myself one thousand percent to the army, had an unblemished record, and the respect of my men and my fellow officers. And one evil bitch of a lieutenant comes along, tells a whole pack of lies, and on her word alone – with no corroboration – I was drummed out. At the court martial, the prosecution lawyer was a young smart-ass. He deliberately tripped me up again and again, not to get at the facts or see justice done, but to look smart himself and make out I was a liar. It worked. I give you my *word* as an officer that there was no truth in it at all. Oh sure, I had a little fun with the gal, but let me tell you, she loved every moment of it. It was only much later, when she was turned by a promotions board I sat on, that she filed those complaints. D'you think good men would follow me here if they thought I was like that?'

'Maybe not. So why did you have to come here? Couldn't you just get a normal job?'

'Calum, I'm forty-two, been a soldier since I was eighteen. What kind of job d'you think I'm qualified for? After a career as satisfying and fulfilling as mine, d'you think I would enjoy working in a hardware store?'

Calum thought he had a point. 'No, I can see you wanted to stay a fighting man. Isn't there's *somewhere* in the world, in Africa or wherever, where you could've fought on the good guys' side?'

'The *good* guys? Helping one tribe annihilate another? Can you name *one* conflict, anywhere in the globe, where an American mercenary could fight and be proud of his role?'

Damn, why was he always so bad at general knowledge questions? There were probably *hundreds* of suitable battles going on. It wasn't something he kept current on.

'I have to admit, I can't think of any.'

318

'Exactly. And the Chinese may not be on our side, but they're hardly the enemy. They *were* allies in World War Two.'

They *were*? 'I do know *some* history, Jason. I also know that the US spent fifty odd years fighting communism.'

'For sure, and we *won*. Communism doesn't exist anymore. The Chinese may pay lip service to it, but take a look at any magazine article about China. Stock market's booming, the whole nation's investing, they're more consumer-orientated that *we* are. One point three billion people, and all of them natural entrepreneurs. Can you honestly say that sounds like communism in action?'

There he goes again, thought Calum, that *amazingly* persuasive voice. Better try another tack.

'I don't think attacking some peaceful islanders sounds like democracy in action.'

'Calum, how would you feel if after the Civil War, a few defeated Southerners had occupied the Florida Keys, armed themselves to the teeth, and set up as a rival government, swearing one day to take control of the whole country? Would you oppose a move by our government to reassert national sovereignty, using minimum force? *You* know from the briefings we gave you that there's no way Taiwan can resist an all-out attack. That was no lie. If the Chinese didn't care about loss of life, they'd have no need to use your skills. They could bomb the hell out of the place and then march in through the ashes. It's precisely because they *want* to avoid loss of life that they go to these lengths.'

'So why did you need to deceive me? Why couldn't you level with me?'

'You'd turned down the British. Are you saying you'd have volunteered to sign up with the Chinese?'

'I guess not.'

'Calum, I *know* how hard it's been, and how *used* you feel, especially by me, perhaps. Believe it or not, I *hated* having to do that. I wanted to come clean with you, but they wouldn't let me take that chance. Now that it's all in the open, it would give me such pleasure if you and I could be friends again, and put trust in each other. What d'you say, can we shake hands on it?'

Calum looked him in the eye for fully ten seconds, and then smiled.

'Sure, Jason, I'd like that.'

'Attaboy. Put it there.'

They stood up, shook hands and held each other's gaze with a look of warm, mutual sincerity. With a last wave, Montgomery left Calum's room and walked back to his office. Calum sat back down on the bed. Both men reflected on a distasteful job well done, and how much they despised the other.

*   *   *

Morag was getting pretty good at giving the thumbs up. The helicopter was awfully noisy and she found that this was easier than shouting into the funny little microphone that sprouted like an overgrown potato eye from the lower side of her helmet.

'Okay, Miss Buchanan, that's the last of the main military installations. Now we're going to the southern part of the island to show you possible landing sites there. If you take a look at that map, we will start on the west side at Tainan, overfly the city of Kaosiung and on to Tung-chiang, Fang-Liao, and Chu-K'eng. There's some bays down there they could use. Then we want you to take a look at the south-east. It may be counter-intuitive that they would go the long way round, but they might get sneaky. Specially if they send in a bunch of saboteurs before the main landing. For obvious reasons, that area's less well defended. We'll swing back up from the most southerly point and show you Ta-Wu, Ta-Ma-Li, T'aitung, Shanyuan beach and on up to Hsing-ch'ang. Don't worry about memorising the names. We'll have a big map on the sub that you can study tomorrow and get used to the pronunciation. Just try to get a feel for the place. Okay, we're approaching Tainan now. Okay?'

Thumbs up, and a little grin. The navigator smiled back and returned the thumbs.

*   *   *

Tuesday

'Hi, Lynne, how's it goin' there in Geneva?'

'Pretty good, Mr President. Tian Yi's playing hard to get, but I think we have them on the run. Art Patterson did a good job softening up their officials. I've taken a tough line, as we agreed, and it's beginning to pay dividends. They've cracked on the bootlegging and agreed to impose penalties with real teeth. We had to give way on some of the customs procedures. Nothing we can't cope with.'

'What about the army and their software company, the one that Bob Tyne rants about?'

'Sunrise. So far, they've refused to give ground on that. They won't comment to us even off the record, but the Brits tell us they're making some pretty emollient nosies to the Europeans about it. My instinct is there's a deal to be done there.'

'What'll it take, Lynne?'

'First, we have to keep up the pressure on the Europeans, so the feedback they give the Chinese is robust enough. We'll do what we can in Geneva, but we need you to call the German, the EU President, and for safety's sake the Brit.'

'I thought the Brits were onside, same team as us.'

'They *should* be okay. However, if the French get a big European thing going, they could try to steamroller them. The British Foreign Secretary is a spineless wimp. I want them stiffened, just in case.'

'I'll do it. What else?'

'To get the Sunrise thing, we may have to give way on some other things.'

'Like what?'

'Financial services, insurance. They want an extension of the transition arrangements.'

'How long?'

'They're asking for eight years. I guess they'll settle for five.'

'I can live with that. Banks and insurance don't carry many votes.'

'Thank you, Mr President. That's all for now. It'll play out over the next few days. The big one will be the Council meeting on Thursday. I'll meet privately with Tian Yi tomorrow and try to hammer out a deal. If we can get agreement there, the Council will be a formality.'

'Good luck, Lynne, keep me posted. We *need* this one.'

'What the hell are you doing here? You're supposed to be in Maui.'

Larry Abraham was always delighted to be visited by Marianna, especially with the minimalist approach she took to summer dressing. The gentle bounce beneath the lime green designer tee shirt was utterly *delicious*. Business was business, though, and he was getting concerned about how much she owed the firm for their work. It had taken the silly girl far too long to realise Brett would never go ahead without a pre-nuptial. Now she was trying to insist that the agreement include *outrageous* conditions. By the sound of it, Brett was losing patience with her. If Marianna didn't land this big fish, she would become a very doubtful receivable.

'We had a fight at the airport. I left him standing there at the check-in desk, looking *the* most total idiot.'

'*Why*, Marianna, *why*?'

'I told him I wanted him to say yes *before* we went on vacation. This'll teach him a lesson. Maui's the dullest place on earth if you're on your own. I *bet* he calls as soon as he lands and agrees to everything.'

'What if he doesn't? I think you're crazy to go out on a limb like this. You may be one hell of a good-looking woman, Marianna, but you're not the only girl in the world. If Brett gets lonely over there, he might find solace someplace else.'

'He wouldn't *dare* . . .'

*   *   *

'Calum, we are all pleased with your progress and your renewed commitment to the project.'

'Thank you, Colonel Bo.'

'Montgomery and I wanted to see you again to brief you on timing. We have been alerted by our superiors that there *may* be an operational need for your special services in the coming days. I hope that will please you, after all this training.'

'I am looking forward to playing my part.'

'My superiors have also asked me to inform you that if you are successful they will reward you with a sum equal to that which you won in England. They will also assist in creating a new identity, so that you can live anywhere in the world you wish, or, if you prefer, you can enjoy a luxurious, secure life in China.'

'Thank you. What about May? That's all I really care about.'

At the left side of Bo, Montgomery stared hard at the floor, his face iron, his fists clenching and unclenching under the table. Bo kept his calm smile.

'This is a free country, Calum, though it may not seem so to you. We cannot compel May to do what she does not wish. However, if she is willing to live with you, we will be more than happy to facilitate it.'

'Thank you.'

'Good. Now, as a precaution, we want to move you nearer to where you might be needed, to a base somewhere in the Taiwan Straits. I will travel there too, and Colonel Montgomery will accompany you to supervise your deployment.'

'May, what about May?'

'Calum, I have already told you. If she agrees . . .'

'No, that's not what I meant. I want her there at the naval

base. I can't stand to be without her now. If she's not there, I can't think, I can't function.'

'Calum, I hardly think this is necessary. She will be reunited with you as soon as the operation is over. It will be a matter of a few days.'

'I must have her there.'

Montgomery grunted intimidatingly. Bo kept to gentle persuasion.

'Calum, this may not be possible operationally. There could be a degree of physical danger. Surely you wouldn't want to expose Miss Chang to that?'

'I won't do it without her. Take it or leave it. I *mean* it, Colonel Bo.'

'Very well. Allow me to look into it again. Even if it *were* to prove feasible, it will *not* be possible for her to share your quarters on that base. Rooms there are very small and strictly for single occupation. She would only be able to visit you in daytime.'

'That's better than nothing.'

'In the meantime, you should prepare to leave. We will be flying you there this afternoon.'

'*If* May comes.'

'As I said, we will consider it.'

* * *

Wednesday

Liao took his early flight from Beidaihe to Seoul with definite misgivings. On the surface all was well. He'd called Tian Yi in

325

Geneva before he left. She came out of her talks with O'Neill to take the call. Everything seemed on track. She'd kept the Euros sweet and made the Americans sweat. Now it was time to talk turkey, as the other side would say. She would string O'Neill along until the very early hours of Wednesday, Geneva time, to heighten the sense of drama, then offer the juicy ransom of Sunrise, and take delivery of doubtless well-planned American concessions. In the absence of any surprises from other quarters, the Council meeting would be a friendly stroll through familiar territory. The communiqués would be written and agreed beforehand, ready to be released the moment the meeting ended. It looked straightforward.

This was what was worrying Liao. It was all *too* easy, too unopposed. At the two Standing Committee sessions since they all arrived at Beidaihe, Chen had not *once* raised Geneva. Why was he keeping so quiet?

* * *

Jack was worried about Morag's health, but wasn't sure what he could do about it. For all that she seemed in good spirits, she looked exhausted and at times seemed to have trouble breathing. As soon as they got to Okinawa, he suggested the medics give her the once-over. She refused point blank, and brusquely told him to concentrate on the job. He did his best not to heap more questions on her, especially after they transferred to the sub. Now it was mainly the other way round anyway; more her advising them what Calum was up to.

'He's arrived now, he's at the naval base.'

'What else is he saying, Morag?'

'Nothing. He's frightened. He thinks they will kill him afterwards.'

'I hate to say it, but he's probably right.'

'Jack, you must promise me faithfully that you will do everything in your power to save him. I have helped you to the best of my ability, and so has Calum. You owe this to him and to me.'

'Sure thing, Morag. We'll do what we can.'

'"What we can" is not good enough. Unless you give me your word as the gentleman I profoundly hope you are that you will do everything humanly possible, I will . . .'

'I've never seen you so agitated, Morag. Just *what* will you do?'

'I'll turn you into a newt. Don't forget my reputation in Sgurr nan Creag.'

'I wouldn't want that, Morag, newts don't get to eat cheeseburgers. You have my word that we'll try. I'm not sure how we can manage it, that's all. It may be hard to get *near* enough to have a go. Let me think about it . . . Now, are you comfortable in your cabin? Captain Farrell's vacated it specially.'

'I won't forget to thank him, Jack. I'd no idea submarines were this size.'

'The *Hammerhead*'s one of our newest. Five hundred and thirty feet long and over fourteen thousand tons of displacement when submerged. Now, Morag, you *are* sure you can stay in contact with Calum when we're underwater, aren't you?'

'So far it seems to make no difference at all.'

'Good. Anything else we can do for you?'

'Yes, Jack, I want to see *them*.'

'What's *them*?'

'The nukes.'

'Morag, it's a State secret whether any of our warships are carrying nuclear missiles.'

'Try telling that to the enlisted men. I asked one of them and he blurted it right out.'

Balletto sighed and shrugged his shoulders.

'Okay, Morag, you win. We'll ask Captain Farrell to give you a personal tour, including the control room, propulsion plant, torpedo tubes, and your precious nukes. Then we'll meet back at the wardroom for something to eat and another look at that map.'

* * *

'Thanks for calling back, Mr President. Excuse me for bothering you so early. We couldn't get through to you last night.'

'Yeah, Lynne, tricky day yesterday.'

More like Trixie than tricky, if she knew her Head of State.

'We have it, we have it all. She cratered.'

'How long did you two go on?'

'Eleven hours. Till three in the morning.'

'How did it play out?'

'She played hard to get for hour after hour, twisting this way and that, but in the end I nailed her. She's not half the negotiator she thinks she is.'

'She was up against a class act, don't forget.'

'Well, *thank* you . . . The main thing is we have Sunrise, with no strings attached. Full dissolution of their monopoly powers and sale of one hundred precent of the equity to the Chinese public and international investors.'

'Great stuff. What about our concessions?'

'I had to go out to six years on banks. Apart from that, it's as we agreed.'

'Excellent.'

'Mr President, I think it would be a good idea if you placed a call to Bob Tyne. Tell him the news.'

'Lynne, it's four o'clock in California.'

'So what? Let's wake the bastard up. *He* doesn't mind calling me at all hours . . . Seriously, there is a reason. The Council meeting starts in one hour at two, local time. Word will start leaking out and soon it'll be all over the wire services. He'll be mad as a wounded coyote if we don't tell him first. He'll want to be on to his friends, crowing like crazy.'

'I can call him if you want, but wouldn't it be better to wait till the deal's actually done? Imagine if I tell Tyne, and then there's a glitch . . .'

'It's a done deal, Mr President. There will be no glitches, believe me. She wouldn't *dare* renege on this.'

'Okay, if you're sure. Hey, well done, Lynne. Great job.'

*   *   *

Liao's day with the Korean President had been dull, and the dinner had dragged interminably, with toast after dreary toast. The warm summer air made the flight back bumpy. His rage was of Moses proportions when he was told, on touchdown just before midnight.

Chen's ambush had been exquisitely timed. If it had been at the formal Committee meeting in the afternoon, Liao's allies could have reached him in Seoul. He could then have spoken to Zhang and tried to avert the calamity. But Chen held his fire until late at the Committee members' banquet, when Liao was back airborne, and only minutes before the WTO Council meeting was due to begin. When Premier Chen telephoned her from the banquet room, Tian Yi's face turned ashen and she put her future in jeopardy by insisting on hearing the instruction from the President himself. Tian was horrified when that faint, familiar voice muttered his confirmation. Her lines of retreat were completely cut off by Chen's ban on any consultation with the Americans. If she could have called O'Neill and asked the Secretariat for an adjournment, something might have been salvaged. Now that was ruled out. Worse, Chen insisted that she let the Americans speak first. Tian Yi would have to dishonour herself, backing off from all they'd agreed. Who in the international community would ever trust her again?

*   *   *

Lynne O'Neill looked radiant, sleep or no sleep. Art Patterson's people had got a hairdresser round to his residence, and she had put on a snappy new dress. There would be lots of press afterwards, and lots of TV, too, and she wanted to look *good*. Art reckoned the Council meeting would last no more than an hour. One, maybe two hours with the press, a quick glass of champagne, and she should be in the air and Washington bound by six.

As she entered the new purpose-built chamber, she beamed right and left, radiating goodwill to all. Minister Tian was last to come in. As she sat down, surrounded by her entourage, O'Neill tried to catch her eye. It didn't work. God, she looked a fright! The lack of sleep had clearly got to her. So much for Chinese stamina. O'Neill tried again, but Tian Yi seemed obsessed with the floor in front of her. Funny woman, not to enjoy a moment like this.

The chamber was crowded with delegations and WTO staff. Although only Hirsch would speak for the Euros, all their ambassadors were there as observers. Lynne O'Neill gave a little wave to the German ambassador, Gunter Hoch, and Christopher Ransome, who had both dined with her earlier that week. The Director General began the proceedings, explaining in his Calabrian singsong the background that those present knew well. Then round the room, one by one, so all could speak and none would listen. They were all waiting for Lynne O'Neill. She selected her most considered, most statesmanlike voice.

'Director General, honourable delegates, ambassadors, it is always the profound wish of the government of the United States to resolve problems amicably and under the aegis of our great international institutions such as the World Trade Organisation. As you are all aware, the US played a major role in the development of the GATT and its evolution into the WTO. The WTO is still a very young organisation and organisations show their strength and their worth when they are tested. The matters we have been discussing recently here in Geneva represent the first major test to the fabric of the WTO. In our opinion, the discussions, though frank and direct at times, have been conducted positively and in a manner which demonstrates how much the international community needs to preserve and develop this framework.'

There was a mild murmur of assent from the chamber. Were they slightly less moved by her eloquence than she expected? No matter. She pressed on.

'That is why, despite myriad difficulties, the US has endeavoured to play *its* part in resolving these matters within the WTO framework and procedures. Moving on to substance, the US has certain proposals to table additional to those already agreed last week and earlier this week. I refer in particular to the transition arrangements for China in relation to banks and insurance. At the time of the WTO ratification by the Chinese government, they agreed that the transition arrangements should be three years in each case. It has since been their experience that this will cause severe problems in practice. On the assumption that a wider understanding can be reached . . .' She tried to smile at Tian Yi; again there was no eye contact. '. . . the US wishes to propose an extension to five and six years respectively for the arrangements for insurance and banking.'

There were nods and a positive groundswell around the chamber. Silence fell again and all eyes turned to the Chinese Minister, seated at the opposite end of the immense table. She took thirty or forty seconds to compose herself. Christopher Ransome was watching the body language of her entourage. He had seen Chinese be friendly, be tough, be frightening, be inscrutable. The way they were all staring downwards, looking hang-dog, was distinctly odd. What *was* going on? Tian Yi cleared her throat.

'Director General, honourable delegates, ambassadors. The government of the People's Republic of China wish to record that they strongly associate themselves with the sentiments of

Special Trade Representative O'Neill about the need to resolve issues of international trade under the rules and procedures set out in the World Trade Organisation agreement. We are grateful for the positive and amicable way in which WTO delegates have attempted to resolve these issues and it is our heartfelt wish that it is possible to reach final agreement.'

Uh-uh, thought Ransome, something's up. Can O'Neill's deal have unravelled?

'We are also pleased by Special Trade Representative O'Neill's proposal in relation to banks and insurance.' She paused. 'I will now come on to the proposals that were tabled last week in relation to the disposal of certain assets belonging to our armed forces . . .'

One of her officials buried his head in his hands. By God, thought Ransome, they *have* unravelled. He turned towards the other end of the chamber. He had a hunch that for the next few seconds the more interesting body language would come from Lynne O'Neill. Tian Yi continued.

'. . . We have considered this most carefully, and discussed it at great length with the respresentatives of the People's armed forces. The question of disposing of such assets is a new question which is not directly addressed by our Constitution. However, our legal advisers inform us that in their opinion, the armed forces cannot be compelled to make any such disposals. It would require their consent . . .'

O'Neill's face was a kaleidoscope of changing emotions. Confusion was the only constant as she listened.

'My government has earnestly and in good faith sought that consent . . .' You could hear a pin drop now. '. . . Unfortunately, it has not been forthcoming.'

O'Neill's head was swivelling wildly from left to right. Ransome could see that she hadn't *got* it yet. Elsewhere in

333

the chamber there was a sort of quiet pandemonium. Then O'Neill's stentorian voice rang out.

'Now, wait a minute, Minister Tian. Do I hear you right? Are you saying that the army will *not* dispose of its holding in Sunrise?'

'That is correct.'

'I don't *believe* this . . . and you've got the goddam *nerve* to claim that the army has to make up its own mind, and your precious Party has no control over that? That's what you're saying, right?'

'That is the position, according to our legal advisers.'

'Well, I can tell you *right now,* Minister, that the US government does not buy that for one moment, and nor should any other right-minded member state. Yours is *not* a free country, Minister, you have *no* real elections, and *no* democratic rights. And if there is *one* good thing about your reprehensible, barbaric system, it is that the Communist Party can order *anybody* to do *anything* they want.'

'We must beg to differ. Our government has been advised differently and we will follow that advice.'

'I just won't take this, I'm afraid. You're talking crap and you know it . . .'

There was a flash from Tian Yi's eyes. The temperature was soaring now, the tension in the chamber palpable. No-one paid the slightest attention to the Director General's call for calm. Now Ransome's eyes were back on Tian Yi's face to watch how she handled the continuing onslaught from O'Neill.

'. . . The Government, the Party, the army . . . you're all the same goddam thing, or at least you're all in one big bed together.'

Ransome saw Tian Yi turn to one of her officials. She half

whispered, half spat a comment. It was the first time one of their asides had been clearly audible. Then he saw her eyes swing through the chamber, as if searching for something. She stopped at *his* face, found *his* eyes, and held them for a second before the diatribe continued.

Ransome stayed long enough to hear Signor Fratelli announce a postponement of the final vote until the next Monday, then raced back to the UK Mission and placed a call straight through to the Permanent Under Secretary.

'You're sure, Christopher?'

'Absolutely sure, Tom, she knew I was there. I'm convinced she said it for me.'

'I'll tell the Foreign Secretary and Number Ten right away. You'd better repeat it slowly. I'll take it down phonetically.'

'Four characters. Tong Chuang Yi Meng. It's an old proverb.'

'And it means "Same bed, different dreams"?'

'Yes. It means two people or groups can be physically together but have hugely differing opinions. O'Neill had been banging on about them all being in one big bed together.'

'And you're sure of your interpretation?'

'In the circumstances, yes. I *think* she was trying to tell me there's a battle going on. God knows between which factions. It's the only thing that explains it. It would *never* be the Chinese way to agree a deal privately like they did with O'Neill, and then renege in public session. Their instructions must have been changed at the last moment.'

'Most interesting, Christopher. I wonder, then, what Tian Yi thought she might achieve by alerting you.'

'It could be that she wanted us to know they're at sixes and

335

sevens in Beijing, and simply changed their minds. As you and I know, governments can be capricious . . .'

'Can't they just!'

'. . . However, I think a much more likely explanation of Tian's proverb and whole demeanour is that whoever changed those instructions wanted to cause the maximum havoc.'

'Mmmmm. *And* the maximum embarrassment for the Americans, perhaps. But, Christopher, what would that achieve? Whoever's in charge in Beijing *can't* want the whole WTO against them, surely.'

'Certainly not. However, if they are not willing to force the army to dispose of those assets, and yet want to stop the WTO finding against them . . .'

'Then back out of the deal with Americans, goading them into immediate unilateral action and making *them* the bad guys? Perfect. Rather smart.'

'Tom, what if she was trying to warn us Europeans, trying to get us to *stop* the Americans reacting unilaterally. Hinting that we *should* take them on in the WTO, that we *should* be tough on them, *should* smoke out the baddies?'

'Christopher, even if what you term the "baddies" exist, we've no idea who they are, how strong they are, or whether it will make a difference. Don't get me wrong, I like your proverb and I don't doubt she *was* trying to say something. But how far do you think we should push this?'

'That's for you and Ministers to decide. The one thing that's certain is if we can't get the Europeans to back tough WTO action, it'll be impossible to keep the Americans onside. And, unless Tian Yi's leading me a merry dance, I'd say that unilateral US action may lead to some unknown calamity. Seems to me we need to see if the temperature in Washington can be brought down long enough for them to listen to reason and do some urgent lobbying in Europe before Monday.'

'Much food for thought, Christopher. I'd better get on with it.'

23

Thursday

Protocol required that President Zhang was never disturbed before eleven. Liao went at ten. Chen had anticipated this and was already there, waiting in an ante-room. Liao had a queasy feeling that he had been comprehensively outflanked, that he was losing the game of mah jong. They sat in silence, drinking tea, until they were ushered in by Zhang's principal private secretary.

More than ever, Zhang's ghostly pallor hinted that his lease on life had all but expired. His strands of white hair were gossamer thin. He sat tightly hunched in an attempt to conceal the stabs of pain that his cocktail of drugs could not control. Liao plunged right in.

'President, I wish to protest in the strongest possible terms about the substance and manner of the decision the Standing Committee took yesterday.'

'Is that so?' President Zhang had expected some comeback. However, even in his weakened state, he did not altogether care for the tone of Liao's voice.

'Those instructions have caused grave damage. We had engineered a highly satisfactory package of measures, far superior to those when we first became members of the WTO.'

'That may be true, Party Secretary Liao, but do not forget that at the time we joined, we expected some *latitude* in the way we implemented the measures. It has proved different in practice. We have been watched like hawks.'

'Even so, the package we had provisionally agreed this time is by any standards satisfactory.'

'Not to the army.' Chen's calm, slightly sneering voice, was in marked contrast to the passion and tension in Liao's. 'Comrade Liao, you need not fear any tricks. Your supporters on the Standing Committee spoke for you in your absence. Frankly, it would have made no difference if you had been here. The President shared my view that this was the right course.'

'And why was it brought before the Committee at all? It had been agreed at official level. The forces had been consulted . . .'

'Consulted yes, satisfied, no. Their supreme commander, Gao Xin Min—'

'Gao. Of *course* . . . your old crony.'

'I will ignore that remark . . . Gao Xin Min reported that the plan to deprive the army of Sunrise was causing grave concern among the younger officers, and making them question the degree of support the army could expect from the government. Yesterday he sent an urgent request to the Standing Committee to reconsider before it was too late. We would normally have waited for your return, but that option was not open. The WTO Council was about to meet in Geneva and we had to issue new instructions to our delegation in time. You were of course informed as soon as possible, when your plane from Seoul touched down.'

'You could have radioed the plane.'

'What difference would it have made? And this was too *sensitive* a matter to trust to radio.'

'In any case, President, I must insist that we reconsider. It is not too late to instruct Minister Tian to . . .'

'Party Secretary, we have decided.' Zhang's voice was tired.

'But consider the consequences. If the WTO now rules against us . . .'

Chen jumped back in.

'They will not. The French will see to it that the Europeans will not support any such move. Otherwise France will lose certain highly valuable harbour development contracts.'

His voice had become nasal in its dismissiveness. The game would soon be over and he would be rid of Liao . . . permanently.

'In that case, the Americans will take unilateral action against us. The cost to us will be enormous. Billions of dollars.'

'Which we can afford . . .' Chen had an answer for everything. '. . . And if we cannot, the Japanese will lend it to us. But do not be so sure the Americans will do this. They are not fools. If they go against us, in the end *they* will be forced to climb down. Their corporations with investments here will *demand* it.'

'You do not understand the American situation, Chen. Their President cannot take this lying down. If only for his electoral prospects, he must act.'

'Nonsense. You claim I do not understand America, yet you fail to show the most elementary grasp of it yourself. The American people care nothing for the outside world. As long as they have plentiful supplies of gasoline, Coca-Cola, and hamburgers, they care *nothing* for what goes on elsewhere. And if the President is nonetheless foolish enough to penalise us, he will be soon see our response.'

'You mean *Taiwan*?'

Chen went to answer, then stopped himself and deferred to the President. The old man pulled himself forward a few

341

inches from the padded backrest. The effort cost him considerably and he had to pause until his breathing lightened again.

'As you know, Party Secretary, we have waited very long for the day that Taiwan is restored to us. Many is the time we have come close to authorising direct action. We have always drawn back for fear of the international response. At the time that decision was right. Our armed forces' weapons were inferior, and over water sheer numbers might not have been enough. More important was our economic situation. We could all too easily have been strangled by the West when we were no more than a faint gleam in their business eyes. If they had cut off supplies of their money and technology, our economic development would have been stillborn. Now everything is different. The foreigners have committed so much here that they cannot draw back without inflicting enormous pain on themselves. They have no choice but to keep investing in China, *whatever* we do. The military situation has changed, too. Today our armed forces are equipped with modern tools of warfare. The Taiwanese may still fight, but they cannot prevail. Comrade Liao, I have waited long for this, and Premier Chen reports that the army wants to act soon, before the younger men are softened by prosperity and lose the stomach for killing.'

'President, was *this* also decided yesterday?'

'No. The final decision can only be taken when we see how Washington reacts to its final defeat in Geneva on Monday.'

Liao realised there was nothing to be gained from prolonging the debate now.

'Thank you, President. Naturally, I will be available at all hours of the day and night.'

*   *   *

342

'Hartmut?'

'Pierre Alain, it is good to hear from you. You are in Provence, I hear. How is the weather?'

'Too hot. I *hate* vacations. The press requires that I take them. Is it not ironic that one must try to convince them that the President of the Republic is on top of his job by *not* doing that job?'

'You are always droll, Pierre Alain. What can I do for you?'

'This China matter in Geneva . . .'

'Ah, yes, I have had our British friend on to me, and the American is scheduled to call in an hour. Everyone is becoming agitated on this subject. I fail to see why. It is the summer season. There is no real crisis, so they invent one.'

'Ab-*solument*. It is important that our two countries maintain a sense of proportion, that we keep our heads when all around are losing theirs, no?'

'Indeed.'

'So, Hartmut, may I presume that your opinion on the subject is as we discussed before?'

'Basically, yes. To be honest, Pierre Alain, I think the British have a point when they say the Chinese have behaved dishonourably and provocatively. They argue, not without conviction, that if we give in to the Chinese now there may be no end to their demands.'

'We can cope with that, I believe.'

'And the British are right when they say that unilateral action by the Americans would be very damaging for the WTO.'

'Yes, that may be so, which is why we believe that in the end the US will not take those steps.'

'Mmmm. Have you heard the British prognosis that some

343

power struggle has developed within the Chinese leadership?'

'It *could* be true. With Zhang's health failing, who knows what battles will go on for the succession? However, the British exaggerate for their own ends. For the moment, Zhang is still in control and they know that. The English are pawns of the Americans and wish to stir up this tale. They want to use it to press for a tough line in Geneva, that is all. We should pay no heed to it.'

'Perhaps, perhaps.'

'As you know, the final WTO vote will now be taken on Monday afternoon. The EU will decide its postion at a meeting of foreign ministers in Brussels that morning. I presume we can count on German support?'

'I see no reason why not, Pierre Alain, if nothing else changes.'

'Good. Well, I will go back to my wife and return you to . . . what?'

'Global warming. The price I pay for having the Greens in my coalition.'

'I'll trade you them for my wife.'

*   *   *

'Mr President, Bob Tyne is on the line.'

'Not *again*. Say I'll call next week and try to calm him down. Tell him I'm holding him to his promise to give us to the end of the month. Jesus, this is beginning to drive me *mad*. I've got Lynne O'Neill wanting me to nuke Beijing – it must be the wrong time of the month – the CIA saying Taiwan is about to be invaded and the Brits coming up with cockamany tales of power struggles in Beijing. And all based on what ? A crazed fortune teller and an ambassador who reads lips. If anyone heard how we make decisions in here, I wouldn't get a single vote. Come *on*, guys.'

'Mr President, it's not just our psychic. The satellites are showing massive air movements around Fuzhou. Everything points to this being a serious invasion force.'

'Sabre rattling. They've done it before. I bet it's all to pressurise us on the trade stuff.'

'With respect, sir, we don't think so. We see the link with Geneva – the timing can't be a coincidence – and no doubt the outcome there may influence it. However, both the Pentagon and ourselves think the buildup's for real.'

'Okay, Johnny. Over to you, Gerry, what's the State Department's take on the British theory?'

'No way of knowing for sure. There *could* be something in this proverb stuff. We're less concerned about that than the wider picture. If the CIA and the Pentagon are right, there must be a serious chance that if we impose unilateral penalties on the Chinese, they *will* invade. Our advice is not to announce any penalties, at least until we have exhausted all efforts to persuade the Europeans to back us up. That might require a trip on Air Force One to meet with the German. He holds the key.'

'Jesus, Gerry, have you seen my program over the next few days?'

'You could be there and back in fifteen hours. This may be the only way. Otherwise, as sure as dogs have fleas, they'll go with the French.'

'I still don't *get* the French. Seems they do a better job for the Chinese than the Chinese embassy. What's their pay-off?'

345

'That we don't know, Mr President. It could be something specific that Zhang or Chen promised de Murville, or it could be general opportunism. They probably figure that whatever happens now, our share of China trade will drop sharply. They want some of the leftovers. There is of course another explanation . . . They may genuinely disagree with our approach.'

'Bullshit. There's something in it for them, I *know* it. Johnny, how hard have the CIA tried to find out?'

'We've tried everything we can in Beijing, sir. If there is a deal, it's been kept to a very small circle.'

'How about Paris?'

'Nothing's turned up from our usual sources.'

'Try again. Leave no stone unturned. I don't care what it costs. Make some Frenchmen very rich if you have to. *Find out.*'

'We'll do our best, sir.'

'. . . Excuse me for interrupting, Mr President.'

'What is it, Carla?'

'Your call to the German Chancellor. We have him on the line.'

'Oh lordy, lordy, what do I say to him? Okay, put him on . . . *Hi*, Hartmut. How ya doin'?'

*   *   *

Friday

An overweight Frenchman of around fifty and a younger, fit-looking American lunched uninterestingly in a tightly

346

packed little bistro off the Boulevard St Michel and then walked back towards the Seine. In these dusty summer days it was hard to see the water for the squadrons of great glass dragonflies, the *bateaux mouches* that plied their trade by day and night. The two men took one of the inclines down to the old towpaths and walked on. The silence, unbroken without embarrassment from aperitif through coffee, ended.

'We need to ask you to think again, François. And with the greatest possible urgency.'

'Why so?'

'There are events happening in the wider world. The information we seek has soared in value. Yesterday it was the usual price . . .'

'So it was not worth much.'

'Today and tomorrow its value is stratospheric. By Sunday it will be falling fast, and by Monday afternoon it will be worthless.'

'How much is today's stock price?'

'More than you can possibly imagine. Why not have a guess?'

'Fifty thousand dollars? A hundred, maybe . . . More? Two hundred? . . . You must be joking. You are the most tight-fisted people in the world.'

'Five million.'

'Five *million*? . . . You are joking. What do you take me for?'

'I take you for someone who knows what money can buy. Including Claudine.'

'Ah, you know about my new . . . indulgence? How interesting.'

'Five million dollars, in numbered Swiss bank accounts. Not just one account, of course. We are well aware that you cannot supply this information yourself. The money is partly to reward you and partly to equip you to open the mind of some of your colleagues at the Elysée. We propose such a sum because we suspect anything less may not be sufficient to overcome your friends' . . . scruples. Are you willing to try?'

'Why not, for such an old friend.'

'Do you have ideas who might be . . . approachable?'

'An inkling.'

'Who are they? I need to know.'

'My friend, you confuse 'need' and 'like'. You would *like* to know. If I get this for you, it can only on the basis that you *never* know where it came from. I will *need* to give assurances accordingly.'

'Very well, but documentary, it has to be *documentary*. Hearsay's no good.'

'I understand. *Eh bien*, since time is so pressing, I should stop chattering and return to the Rue du Faubourg Saint Honoré.'

'You know where to reach me.'

The Frenchman left with a wave over his left shoulder without looking back, and walked up the next incline and over the bridge. The sun had gone in a little, allowing him to remove his sunglasses.

* * *

Saturday

'There . . . no . . . higher. Perfect. I *love* the way you touch me, May. It's the only thing that keeps me going.'

'I'm so proud of the way you've bounced back. I'll never be able to thank you enough, darling Calum. Are you apprehensive?'

'Apprehensive? More like shit scared. I'm determined not to foul up though. I've *gotta* do this right, not only for you and your people, but for another reason, too. If I don't deliver, they'll take you away from me, I *know* they will.'

'I'm worried about that, too. I'd hate to risk losing you, so it *is* vital that you make it. Let me massage you a bit longer than usual. You need to *relax*. Did they say when to expect something?'

'Jason said to take it easy today and tomorrow, but to be ready for action on Monday. They know I need the moon, so I guess that means Monday night. I'm so tense I squeak every breath I take.'

'That's what *I'm* here for, to help take your mind off it. Since you're going into action with Bo and Jason, it's good that you feel a bit more comfortable about them now.'

'Yeah, it took some time. I hated them for the way they used me, but I can see they were only doing their job. In fact, the other day I got to thinking it was pretty decent of Bo to take a chance on me after I'd run off like that. And kicking Jason out of the army on that girl's say-so was pretty harsh. As long as the US isn't being harmed, I guess it's okay for him to be doing this. How do *you* feel about him?'

'I'm glad he's on our side. You don't always get to see his strategic mind at work. It's quite something. And he's such a natural leader.'

'Hey, you don't have a thing about him, do you? I'd *die* if I thought you were sweet on someone else.'

'You silly boy. How could I have room in my heart for anyone but you?'

'Is that really true? Gee, that's good to hear. Come here.'

'No, darling, I *have* to leave now. Remember, they gave me a curfew of eight o'clock. I'll see you in the morning.'

Calum was glad he hadn't yet found the microphones at this new base. The natural temptation to turn and make his speeches directly into them might have been too great.

* * *

'Monday night. He is waiting for Monday night.'

'To do what, Morag?'

'No idea, Jack. I don't think he knows himself. He's really scared now. He doesn't need to try to communicate it, I can sense it all too clearly.'

* * *

'Seems fifteen hours was optimistic, sir. The State department have advised that seeing only the German Chancellor would be too *obvious*. We'll have to route you through London and Paris first.'

'Oh, *no*.'

'We know how much tomorrow's golf match with Tiger meant to you, Mr President.'

'I know, I know. Don't worry, I won't forget my motto. "Re-election, stupid." When do we leave?'

'Eight p.m. tonight. The British Prime Minister has agreed to come out to Brize Norton on Sunday morning for a brief discussion. Then on to Paris. The President insists on doing it at the Elysée. If it's any consolation, he's breaking a vacation in the South of France with his wife to come back.'

'Big deal! Remember his wife? He probably *loves* me for interrupting it . . . What am I supposed to say to him, anyway?'

'As little as possible. Go through the motions. You say "please", he says "non", and on we go to Berlin.'

'And you're sure it's okay to show the Chancellor this five million dollars worth of French Presidential memo? If I'm gonna take that chance, you better brief me what these harbour contracts will be worth to French companies.'

'Our people in Beijing reckon eight to ten billion dollars over six years.'

'And German companies will be screwed, too?'

'Absolutely. Two have already formally announced their intention to tender for the business. They don't know that they won't have a chance.'

'Okay, that'll do for now. If I *have* to go on this trip, I wanna take a little time out this afternoon. Could someone arrange *something* to keep my wife occupied?'

* * *

Sunday

Calum lay awake in the darkness, trembling. At the desert base May's physical presence at nights had comforted him hugely, though they could never risk one honest word and chose not to make love in front of the cameras. It didn't matter;

having her beside him was the important thing. She had spent the whole day with him again today, but now that she was back in her own room, he felt miserably alone, and monumentally scared. What made it ghastly was having so much time to think, always reaching the inescapable conclusion that once their need for him was over, they'd kill him. How would they do it? If they realised he'd double-crossed them, he hated to *think* what manner of execution they might select.

What would May be thinking? In the cave, before they went back to the base, they had agreed it was impossible to make any real plan; all they could was improvise. The one thing they settled on was if Calum succeeded in having May spend time in his quarters, they could use her massages as a code. If she skipped doing his feet, they were torturing or maltreating her. If she missed out his temples, they *knew*. Each night as he lay there, his nerves would rise as she got to those parts in the routine. Feet and temples were included every time, keeping his slender hopes alive.

Was he *mad* to hope? It wasn't very likely she'd keep her word. The chances were that she'd told them everything as soon as she got back to the base. Why not, she was a professional Chinese agent, wasn't she? What would be more natural? Was her head really going to be turned by enthusiastic but incompetent sex with a terminal American loser? Why should she have any feelings for him beyond sympathy or pity? They had told each other a hundred times how much they loved each other, but that was only for the microphones. The problem for Calum was that *his* protestations of love had come increasingly to reflect an uncomfortable reality. The vice-grip of his feelings for Marianna had mysteriously evaporated like a lifting migraine, displaced by a

352

new, very different strain of love: gritty, diamond-edged, industrial strength. He had to keep reminding himself that May had probably only slept with him to ensure her survival in the cave.

But what if she *really* hadn't meant to tell? Had they got it out of her, massage code and all, with threats of retribution against her family or through some ghastly torture that didn't leave marks? If so, they would know he was in contact. Had they worked that into some plan of their own, so he might be leading Morag's friends right into a trap? Oh God, it didn't bear thinking about.

Who *were* Morag's friends anyway? It could only be the UK or US government. It seemed they didn't want him to know too much, in case *he* was tortured. A few days before, a thought of pure horror had crept up on him and had haunted him ever since. Was *any* of this real? He'd been *so* blithely confident that Morag was hearing him. What if she wasn't there at all? Was dead, like May had said, or just weaving away in Sgurr nan Creag, oblivious to Calum's dramas. What if this was *all* his imagination? Minds were funny things: they played tricks. Why should Morag, whose trust he'd betrayed, go to such lengths to help *him*? He was sensing so *vividly* her telling him to do the right thing, not to disappoint her again. Could this all be some weird guilt trip? Did he want *so* badly to make everything right with her, to convince himself that she hadn't abandoned him, that he'd unconsciously woven a whole fantasy around it? Jesus, please *do* not let this be true.

What if it was? What could he do? Throw himself on the mercy of Bo, and own up to the whole charade? It would be a sort of sweet relief to stop struggling. If he told the truth before it was too late, and co-operated with them, they might spare him . . .

No. He knew he couldn't do that. Something strangely fundamental had changed within him that had finally sealed off his well-worn path along the line of least resistance. Morag's phrase floated into his mind. This time he would have to answer to *himself*. Though it was ninety-nine percent likely that May had betrayed him or been forced to, he was *not* going to take the one percent chance that she hadn't. He *loved* this woman. However much he might be betrayed, he couldn't do any more betraying himself. Whatever grisly fate he might face, for once in his life he had to do the decent thing. For Morag, too. The telepathic contact with her might all be his imagination and it might not: there was no way to find out. It was *he* that had begged for her help over the ether. Whether her response was real or not, he *had* to act as if it was. If he was to get through this, he would have to dig deeper than he'd ever dug before. Could he summon up the ghosts of his warrior ancestors and ask to borrow a little of their guts, fury, and implacable bloody-mindedness?

*   *   *

Air Force One made its last touchdown before heading back to Washington. For the Brit and the Frenchman, the President had taken a standard-sized retinue. The German he wanted to play differently. Of course, the soldier with the nuclear key had to come along. Other than that, he would keep it to one single aide. He was disappointed that the Chancellor was surrounded by a whole posse.

'Hartmut, how good to see you again. It must be . . .'

'Four months. G-Seven in Toronto.'

'Toronto, of course. That was a non-event if ever there was one.'

'One of the duller ones. I contented myself with some fine doodles.'

'Do *you* do that, too? I thought I was the only artistic one.'

'All the leaders should compare. Perhaps we should arrange an exhibition. The psychologists might find some correlation beteween the nature of our doodles and the substance of the discussion.'

'Now, there's a good idea . . . By the way, Pierre Alain asked me to pass on his warmest regards.'

'That is most civil of you, but quite unnecessary. He did it himself by telephone, five minutes after you left him. It does not sound as if you made much progress together.'

'Progress, no. I felt it was important to stay in touch with him on this, all the same. He thought your views would be closely aligned with his own.'

'I might prefer it if Pierre Alain left me to speak for myself, but in principle that is so. Unless, of course, you have brought important new insights with you from Washington.'

'Possibly some new perspectives. Hartmut, there is a strategic aspect to this whole business that is of vital importance.'

'Yes?'

'The CIA have gathered extremely persuasive evidence to suggest that China may be on the brink of launching a military attack on Taiwan. I have brought some satellite photographs to illustrate this point. Dan . . . thank you. These are pictures of the airbases near Fuzhou and Shantou. From this wider angle you can see their proximity to Taiwan. This sequence of shots shows the contrast between a normal level of activity six months ago and the buildup over the last few weeks.'

'I agree it looks significant. However, the Chinese regularly do these things, don't they? They have conducted exercises in that area before, surely?'

'Yes, but never on this scale.'

'There is one thing I do not understand, Bobby. If the Chinese *were* to be contemplating an all-out attack, wouldn't they try to conceal it? From these photographs, it looks as if they are doing it quite openly. There seems to be no attempt to camouflage the planes. Look, there they all are, sitting in neat rows, waiting for your spy satellites to picture them.'

'There could be a reason. What if they *wanted* the US to know? They might calculate it will either persuade us to back down in Geneva, or prompt us to send warships into the Taiwan area. In the first case, game, set and match to them. In the second, it's intolerable provocation from the Imperialist paper tigers, and Taiwan gets invaded as a response.'

'So where does this all lead you, Bobby? What's your point?'

'Hartmut, the first of these two cases isn't an option. You know as well as I how atrociously the Chinese have behaved in Geneva. The United States cannot be seen to back down in the face of this double-dealing and we *will* not. However, if we are not supported by other WTO member states and are forced to act alone, we believe the result will be Chinese military aggression and large-scale bloodshed. This *must* be averted. The US will do whatever we can to play our part, but we *need* the help of our major allies. This is one of those moments, Hartmut, where we all have to stand up and be counted. You know that the meeting in Geneva tomorrow is our last chance, and with everything balanced as it is, Germany holds the casting vote.'

'What do you want me to say? I have already given Pierre

Alain and my other European colleagues a clear indication of our likely position on this subject. We Germans do not like to be thought inconsistent. However, I will give urgent thought to what you have said and . . .'

'Hartmut, could I take a stroll with you in the garden for five minutes? Alone?'

'As you wish. We can go out this way . . . After you.'

'Thanks . . . I wanna take a look at your roses. While I'm doing that, I have a piece of paper I thought you might be interested to look at. I needed a translation, but I guess you read French.'

'Not without my glasses. One second while I find them . . . Hmmm . . . Most interesting. Can you can vouch for its authenticity?'

'Yes, I can.'

'May I keep it?'

'That would be difficult. If they ever found out, the French would close down our entire embassy in Paris.'

'I understand. You may be assured that this matter will not be far from my mind. I hope you have a good flight back. We meet next in Madrid, I think.'

'Let's compare doodles afterwards.'

24

The shock waves of Monday's Geneva result reached Beidaihe a little after midnight. Zhang's secretary relayed to Chen and Liao the President's refusal to bring forward the meeting scheduled for 11 a.m. on Tuesday. When the appointed hour came, tension and emotion rippled through the room. This was the most momentous Standing Committee meeting any of them had ever participated in.

Enfeebled as his body might be, the fury in Zhang's countenance was startlingly evident. Chen's two supporters looked extremely uneasy, but he himself looked unabashed, even when Zhang put him on the spot.

'Premier Chen, you *assured* me this would not happen.'

'President, my confidence in the French was misplaced. We will know better than to trust them again.'

'*You* trusted them. It was *your* judgement that was wrong.'

There's fire in the old man's grate yet, thought Liao. Chen looked surly, wounded but not fatally. The final battle, the mortal combat was yet to be joined. Zhang turned to Liao.

'Party Secretary, what is your view? How should we respond to this impudence?'

'President, it is hard to know what to do for the best. Premier Chen's game has been lost. The WTO cannot reverse their line against us now. They have given us a last twenty-four hours to reconsider before authorising implementation of their decision. Accepting that ultimatum would be painful, demeaning even . . .' Chen snorted furiously '. . . but not as humiliating as climbing down after months of intransigence. If we bite the bullet now, it will scarcely be noticed in the world media: a one-day wonder. The public both here and abroad understand little of trade talks and care even less. If we allow this small pimple to grow into a giant sore all the world will be watching and it is an encounter we *cannot* win. I say give way. The overall deal is a good one. It is a pity we played our hand badly, that is all.'

'We did *not* play it badly.' Chen's temper was lost now. If they had been younger, they would have been physically at each other's throats. 'This was no more than a prelude. We will *never* accept this humiliation. If these barbarians think they can mete out such treatment to us, let them see how we respond. Party Secretary Liao, *you* want the world's newspapers to be full of accounts of our defeat in Geneva. You will not get your way. They will be filled with other news. News of a glorious victory.'

'You are mad, Chen. You cannot still want to persist with this insanity.'

'Can I not? Speak, President, tell him your will.'

'It is not to be *my* will. It must be this Committee as a whole. And I tell each one of you before we vote that, whatever the result, I expect all of you to respect and support whatever the decision is. Do you accept that?'

They all nodded gravely.

'Very well. Give your views. I will speak last.'

Chen and Liao waited while their four colleagues made short speeches and voted. Two for action, two against, inevitably. Zhang turned to the leaders.

360

'That leaves the two of you. Do you vote as you have spoken?'

They looked at each other and nodded. They had all known from the beginning it was in Zhang's hands.

'My friends, there are moments in one's life when one feels the call of destiny. I do not have much longer for this office, perhaps for this earth. Ever since 1948, it has been my most earnest desire to see the reunification of our country. Hong Kong and Macau have returned to the fold. It is my greatest wish before I die to visit Taiwan as a Province of the People's Republic . . .' He paused to catch his breath. Liao looked down. '. . . However, such a personal desire I would gladly suppress if the timing was wrong. If I felt it was too soon, if the chances of recovering of the island would be greater in the future, I would counsel patience and abandon the dream of seeing this in my lifetime . . .' The breathing was getting more difficult, the speech more laboured. '. . . *However* . . . that is not the advice we have received. It is the view of our armed forces that this might be not only our best chance, but our last. I have reflected on whether they are right . . . and I have concluded they are. I vote in favour of the attack.'

'Tonight.' Chen was in back in charge. It was *his* now. It was clear that everything was prepared. Liao was reduced to asking questions.

'What are the battle plans?'

'The Supreme Commander has recommended a massive missile attack followed by parachute landings. When the main installations are secured or destroyed, sea landings can begin.'

'What about the sabotage plans?'

'He recommends against it.'

'And you support him?'

'Not necessarily. That is for the Committee to decide. An all-out attack will give certain success, but at a price. The Taiwanese have mobile rocket launchers which might bring down some of our airborne troop transports. If the fighting continues, they could have some success against our naval deployments. They might even attack the mainland. In the end, however, they are bound to surrender.'

'What is his assessment of the alternatives?'

'If our Special Forces can go undetected for five or six hours, their sabotage operation could do so much damage to the Taiwanese fighting capability that resistance would crumble. Their ability to attack the liberating forces would be much reduced. Bloodshed on both sides would be far less. However, if they are detected before they complete their tasks, the Taiwan regime will realise our intentions and may order pre-emptive missile strikes on the mainland.'

If they thought the President, slumped and breathing irregularly, was finished, they were wrong.

'I will not countenance failure. However, I do not want to go down in history as a butcher of our own people. It is I who will be blamed, not any of you. Premier Chen, unless our armed forces can guarantee to disable the key defences before hostilities start, I will never sanction the main attack. Do you understand?'

'Yes, President. As I said, I was not necessarily in agreement with General Gao's view. It will be done as you say.'

'Good. That is agreed then. Leave me now, I am tired. I wish to go down to the water and bathe. I love Beidaihe, and this may be my last summer here . . . Premier Chen, I want to be kept posted. I do not wish there to be any reason, whether my sleep or my indisposition, which deters you from

362

telling me *exactly* what is happening tonight. *Everything.* Do you understand?'

*   *   *

Calum was left cooling his heels in the briefing room for nearly two hours. It didn't surprise him when Montgomery came in alone. He would have *enjoyed* making Calum wait.

'Okay, Calum, the Chinese are too busy, so they've asked me to brief you. In one hour, at nine p.m., we will embark on a submarine and sail, submerged, to a point fifteen nautical miles due east of T'aitung. You know where that is, on the south-east of the island. We will be sailing in company with one other sub. Aboard the subs will be a hundred special forces. They will be landed on the island to pave the way for the main attack. They will target military and communications installations and airports, knock out TV and radio broadcast capabilities, and assassinate political leaders most likely to favour resistance. What we're looking to you for is one thing only, Calum. When our sub has reached that position, it will surface momentarily and put you, me, and some marines in an inflatable. We will then tell you the planned special forces landing site. Your job is to advise whether they can land there undetected. Yes or no, that's all. After that they will be fanning out over the island. That will be too complex and involve too long a time-span for your predictions to work. This is it, Calum, what you've trained so hard for, the biggest moment of your life. If this sabotage operation fails, the whole invasion might have to be aborted. Will you give it your best shot?'

'Sure will, Jason, as long as I can stay cool enough to strut my stuff.'

'Good man. The sky is clear, there's plenty of moonlight. The sea may be a little choppy, but nothing serious. Well, that's about it. If you have no questions, better go to your room and get ready.'

'Can we take May on the submarine with us?'

'Oh not *again*, Calum. This isn't an exercise, this is the real thing. We can't have distractions. That sub will be *so* crowded already.'

'Jason, believe me, I feel kinda dumb even *asking*. I'd like to be tough and calm like you. I'm not, though, and I need all the help I can get to do this work. You know if I ask Bo, he's bound to agree. Why don't we cut out the middleman and agree it between us Americans?'

Montgomery nodded and smiled. He knew Buchanan was right about Bo, and he didn't feel like being sent as a messenger boy by this inadequate little creep.

'Okay, Calum, I'll have a word.'

'Attaboy, Jason.'

Montgomery grimaced, then smiled. The jerk wasn't taking the piss, was he? Nah, he'd never have the nerve. Must be imitating him unconsciously, like a child.

* * *

'Jack, Jack, they're on their way.'

'Where?'

'East of T'aitung. He's trying to say how far off, but I'm not

364

sure. His tension is terrible. It gets in the way awfully. It took him ages to get that through.'

'Does he know the attack zone?'

'I'll keep trying, but I don't think he does.'

'Okay, Morag. Captain Farrell, how closely can we shadow them without them spotting us?'

'It's less about distance, and more about sound. Make any noise and we could be detected a hundred miles away. What we have to do is keep our speed down. Above a certain speed, our propellor develops what's called cavitation. Vacuum pockets form as the screw turns, making a signature that transmits easily through the water. Cavitation speed varies with the design of the sub and depth. For the *Hammerhead* it's only nine knots near the surface, much higher deeper down. Just like us, those Chinese subs will be trailing half a mile of cable packed with sensors listening out for that cavitation sound. However, thanks to Morag's help, we shouldn't have too much of a problem. Since we have some idea where they will head first, we should be able to get into the vicinity early and listen out for them as they arrive. If they're planning on landing troops, they won't want to start too far offshore from T'aitung. My guess is twenty miles, not more. To keep out of harm's way, we will need to be a further fifteen miles out to sea.'

* * *

The tension in the Oval Office was unbelievable. His staff had never seen the President quite like this. Sure it was important

365

for his re-election and all, but this went beyond that. For some reason he *cared* about this one and was obviously enjoying it. If the number of coffees he was getting through was any guide, his nerves were twitching as much as anyone's.

'Carla, you'll have to say no. I can't miss this. Tell them I'm rewriting a speech.'

'They'll *never* believe that, sir.'

'How about reviewing the new gasoline tax proposals?'

'You'll have to do better, Mr President.'

'Okay, say I'm in bed with my mistress.'

'*That* gives me something I can work with. The Pentagon will alert you the *moment* they have anything.'

'Everything's ready if they launch a full-blown attack?'

'Everything. The TV cameras will be here and your statement's ready. Madeleine Milne at the UN's all primed.'

'Good, no other calls, then.'

* * *

'Calum, we have arrived at the point where we will surface. Are you ready?'

'Ready as I'll ever be, Colonel Bo.'

'Then listen carefully. For security's sake, the submarine will have to submerge again very quickly. The moment we surface, you, Montgomery, and two armed marines will jump in an inflatable. We will dive again as fast as possible, leaving only our high frequency antenna above the water line. We will keep radio silence except for one moment. When you have your steer, yes or no, Colonel Montgomery will radio the answer down to us. If it's no, you will wait till we try an alternative location. If it's no again, we abort. If it's yes either time, we and the other submarine will make directly for the landing zone. Five hundred metres from the beach we will release the special forces, who will swim ashore with their weapons in waterproof containers. Only when the task force has been delivered will we come back and collect you. If all goes well, we'll be celebrating. Okay?'

'Yessir. Colonel Bo, can I take Miss Chang up there with me? I'm so tense, I can hardly operate. She's the only thing that can calm me enough to predict.'

'Colonel Montgomery, what d'you think?'

'Crazy. No way she should be put at risk. What if someone starts shooting at us or the boat capsizes?'

'He has a point, Calum, you'd be putting her at real risk. This isn't another stunt, is it? You're not going to run off again . . . ?'

'No, I was . . .'

'. . . Just a joke, Calum, there's nowhere to hide out there, and no engine on the inflatable . . . Should we ask Miss Chang . . . where is she? What do you say, Miss Chang, will you take your chances on the surface?'

'If those are my orders.'

Montgomery leapt back in.

'Colonel Bo, I must insist, can I have a word in private?'

'We don't have much time, Montgomery. Make it quick. Come over here.'

They walked a few yards out of earshot.

Montgomery hissed, 'I *don't* want May seeing me shoot him.'

'Chang is smarter and harder than you think, Montgomery. She asked me if we would kill him, and smiled when I told her. Not that she knows we will do it so soon. If her contempt for Buchanan is as great as I believe, she may *enjoy* watching. It may seal the bond between you . . . Let us get on now.'

They walked back to where Calum and May had stood, saying not a word, but looking intensely in each other's eyes.

'Okay, Chang, it is agreed. You'd better get a life vest on, too . . . Now, Calum, we need you to *concentrate*. The first choice landing zone is Shanyuan beach. Remember it from the map? Eight miles north of T'aitung. Do you need to see it again?'

'No sir, I got it.'

'Go for it, Calum, this is your big moment . . . Okay, tell the Captain to surface.'

Inside the sub had been comfortingly like a cocoon, insulated from the real world, like it was a game they were playing. The deadly reality of it gripped him again as they clambered out of the hatch, down the rope ladder and into the wildly bobbing black inflatable. Calum was last in and lost his footing. If one of the marines hadn't caught him, he would have fallen overboard.

They settled down into position. The marines were carrying stubby Uzi-style automatics. Montgomery kept the radio set in his hand, ready to pass on the vital word. Fifty or more yards away, the sub's antenna dipped in and out of their sightline.

Five minutes passed. Calum's eyes were screwed shut, his fists clenched tight in concentration. God, it was hard with the adrenalin coursing and his pulse racing. A real prediction would have been out of the question in this state. All he needed was to send a telepathic message, but even that was eluding him.

'Hurry up, Calum, what's takin' you so long?'

'Will you shut up and quit wrecking my focus?'

'Come on, Jason . . . give him a chance.'

May's intervention only held for two minutes. Montgomery was fretting. If they didn't get a move on, the timing of the entire operation would be thrown out. What if the sub had been picked up on Taiwanese radar?

'Calum, you *gotta* do this *now*, or you'll blow the whole thing.'

'Shaddup.'

His nerves were wrecking it all, throwing his brainwaves too far out of kilter. He was going to screw up *again*. One more try.

* * *

One hundred fathoms down, and thirty-five miles to the east of Taiwan, the USS *Hammerhead* glided silently, slowly through the black water. The circle round Morag in the control room had grown to fifteen, all waiting and worrying. They knew they mustn't distract her. All the same, it was hard for the CIA boys and the submariners to stay still, doing nothing, the way the tension was ratcheting up by the minute.

'No, he still can't do it. It's all in a mist.'

'Can you say something to calm him for one minute, anything at all? We desperately need the landing zone. Shadowing their subs there won't help at all unless we can warn the Taiwanese in advance. Otherwise, they'll be all over the island before we can intercept them.'

Morag thought of an old Highland tune and played it over and over in her head.

'I think it's clearing. He's coming through. Yes! Jack, Jack, it's Shanyuan beach!'

'The sneaky bastards, I *knew* they'd take it from the East. Captain Farrell, let's get right onto our friends on the island. Morag Buchanan, you're a superstar.'

* * *

Calum opened his eyes, unclenched his fists and called out.

'YES! . . . Tell them *yes*.'

Montgomery hit the button on the radio.

'Do you read me? Do you read me? It is "yes", repeat "yes". Good luck.'

They all watched as the antenna was dragged under and down. They were on their way.

Montgomery didn't waste time. He tapped on the shoulder of one the marines, who handed over his automatic. Now that the acting was over, Montgomery's face, quite clear in the moonlight, was contorted with contempt and hatred. With practised hands, he smoothly clicked the magazine into place, chambering the first round. No-one else moved.

'Okay, Buchanan, you did your job. Now you're gonna get what you've had comin' for a *very* long time . . . You men, move over. You too, May. Do it, NOW.'

They all shuffled sideways, leaving Calum alone at one end of the inflatable. His end rode up higher in the water. Montgomery was directly opposite, his gun pointing right between Calum's eyes.

'For weeks now, I've been rehearsing what I'd say to you

at this moment. Now that it's come, I've decided you're not worth the waste of my breath. I have only two things to say to you. One is that along with the smart-ass lawyer who fucked me over, I despise you more than any human I've met. The other is what I want to be on your mind as you draw your last breath. While *you* are rotting on the ocean floor, I'm gonna have my legs curled round this woman of yours, showing her how it feels to be with a *man . . .*'

He leered disgustingly. To Montgomery's irritation, Calum showed no visible reaction, not even fear, so he pressed on.

'. . . Okay, buddy boy, better start praying to any God you got . . .'

Without looking down, he flicked the lever for single round firing.

'. . . Bye bye, buddy.'

May Chang leapt from her seat.

'WAIT! No, not *yet*, Jason. I haven't had *my* say yet. It was my body he defiled. You were right, Jason, I should've been with you from the start. What did I get instead? This re-*volting*, re-*pulsive*, dis-*gusting*, *reptile*. Well, I can tell you, Buchanan, your very touch turned my stomach. Look at you, what are you? A failure . . . a loser . . . a *nothing*.'

Calum waved one hand dismissively. In the circumstances, his voice was extraordinarily calm.

'May, I hate to spoil your speech, but you were just to fill in the time. I only said all that shit about love to keep you happy. You were a . . . distraction. Better than MTV, most of the time. Your face is not bad, but when your clothes come off . . . *so* disappointing. You were never much of a lay. All the time we were doing it, I was fantasising about Marianna. Montgomery's welcome to you. He'll soon lose interest.'

'You . . . *little* . . . CREEP.'

She flung herself headlong across the inflatable, rocking it violently, scratching fiercely at Calum's eyes. Calum tried to pull her off. Montgomery half rose. The marines, mesmerised, bobbed up and down with the waves.

'*Let go of my hands, you scumball.*'

Calum let go and she fell back onto the floor of the inflatable. Unsteadily, she scrambled upright, took a step back towards him and spat revoltingly full in his face. Then she turned round.

'Jason, give me that thing. *Give* me it.'

'Siddown, you idiot, you'll have us all in the water.'

'GIVE ME THAT FUCKIN' GUN! . . .' You could have heard her in the Philippines. '. . . Or I'll never, *ever*, have *anything* to do with you. I *mean* it, Jason!'

'May, I don't think . . .'

'NOW!'

'You better know what you're doin', May . . .'

'NOW! NOW, NOW!!!'

'Okay . . .'

The Chinese marines looked relieved. If she kept leaping about like that, capsizing was a serious possibility. Montgomery held it out.

'. . . For Chrissakes aim for his head so you don't hit the boat.'

She grabbed the gun from Montgomery and surged back towards Calum.

'Okay, you little . . .'

She stumbled forward, half sprawling towards him, twisting round in her fall. As her back rammed against the inflatable's side, two feet from Calum, the gun was already trained directly at Montgomery's midriff.

'Oh, no. Oh, *NO*. You fuckin' BITCH.'

'Shut up, Jason.'

She turned to the second marine.

'You, gun over the side.'

Her Mandarin sounded harsh. The astonished marine meekly obeyed.

'Okay, Jason, now your pistol.'

'Fuck you, lady, you're not doin' this to me. I'm not bein' fucked over by a woman twice. You wouldn't have the balls to use that, and I'm gonna make sure that if you do, you'll put a big hole in the side of this thing.'

He let go of the radio, slid down low, reached to his side, and slowly and deliberately raised the flap off his waterproof holster.

'*No*, Jason, don't make me.'

Montgomery grinned and confidently began to slide out his handgun. May's finger tightened on the trigger. Montgomery kept on bringing out the pistol.

BANNGG!!!

The pistol flew off into the water and Montgomery lurched forward, dark blood spurting everywhere. Until they heard his rasping breath, they all thought he was dead. With an extravagant effort, he heaved himself back, then slumped against the side of the tiny craft. It looked like his shoulder was blown half away. Through the blinding pain and nausea, he somehow managed to speak.

'You . . . wait . . . till that . . . sub . . . arrives . . . oh *shit*, you stupid bitch.'

Montgomery had been right. She *had* hit the boat's sidewall, and water was slopping in. The inflatable was constructed in sections and wouldn't lose all of the air, but that weakened wall was too low to keep out the waves. The marines started desperately bailing with their helmets, but the water was already gaining on them. An inch, then two, and before they could do much, five inches of water. Calum joined in the bailing, and May did what she could too, with one hand still holding the gun. How long could they survive in the water with their life-jackets if it sank? One of the marines managed to nudge Montgomery up a touch, keeping his head clear of the rising water.

May put her mouth to Calum's ear and whispered something. He shook his head and kept bailing. They all worked on, ignoring the exhaustion. Montgomery fell silent, his breathing more ragged. If help didn't come soon, he would lose too much blood to survive. His shoulder was too smashed to attempt any improvised tourniquet, and in that sea, getting one on him would have been impossible anyway. How fast did that sub travel? How long would it take to drop off its deadly cargo and come back? They were losing the battle, they wouldn't be able to hold out much longer. Calum took off his life-jacket and forced it down over Montgomery's head to replace the punctured original, unintentionally making him yelp with pain.

* * *

They had practised the drill fifty times, and the special forces, clad in black diving suits over lightweight fatigues, were out of the two submarines in less than five minutes. The subs dived again and were gone, one heading straight back to base, and the other returning to pick up the group in the inflatable.

The hundred black figures swam towards the shore strongly, smoothly, slicing through the low waves, towing their heavy, black-wrapped, buoyed-up cargoes with supreme ease. Every one of them was a trained assassin and a demolition expert. They were all highly trained in martial arts, had a fabulous level of fitness, and could survive for weeks in hostile territory. They swam in a co-ordinated pattern, maintaining their stroke till their feet grounded two yards from the water's edge. Creeping soundlessly up the sand, they dragged the big bags clear of the water and towards the long grass where their arms could safely be decanted.

They were no more than ten yards from the grass when the lights came on, dazzling them with their brilliance. A crackling voice from a megaphone announced the presence of a battalion of Taiwanese soldiers and their batteries of machine guns encircling the beach. The swimmers were given ten seconds to surrender and the decision fell to their leader, one of the toughest and bravest soldiers in the entire Chinese army. He would have taken on any odds, any opponent, however small the chance of success. He was also a professional, and could see when the chances were zero. He raised his hands and barked an order at his men to do the same.

*   *   *

Their luck ran out. The next wave, bigger than all the others, swept in and capsized the boat. May let go of the gun as she went under. The air in her life-jacket soon had her back up to the surface, gasping for breath. For a moment she thought Calum was gone. Then his head bobbed into view and she swam over to him. The two marines were managing to keep Montgomery's head up so he could breathe. Huge ox of a man that he was, he was fighting back the black waves of pain, knowing that sleep now would spell death. He hung on grimly to consciousness, willing that sub to get back.

Calum and May clung together, her life-jacket giving enough buoyancy to keep both afloat. May tried to get out the words.

'*Why* didn't you let me kill myself . . . while I had . . . the chance? Whatever happens, I'm *not* going back on that submarine. Do you know what they'll do to us? I'll drown myself first.'

Another wave crashed over them, ripping them part, filling Calum's lungs with more sea water. He spat it out and fought his way back to her arms.

'Morag's begging me to wait . . . *watch out for this wave* . . . try to hold on a little longer.'

'Okay . . . *shit* . . .'

Another wave crested over them.

'. . . but if that sub gets here first, *promise* to hold my head under the water.'

'I promise. *Watch out, here comes the next one.*'

*   *   *

At 11 p.m. the Taiwanese President placed his call to Beidaihe. The number at Zhang's villa, a Chinese state secret, had been checked and re-checked by both the Taiwanese and their American allies. As soon the principal secretary heard the import, he did not hesitate to put it through to the old man's study. The conversation was short, sharp, heated, and decisive. Zhang was forced to agree to telephone Supreme Commander Gao personally.

The moment he heard, Chen demanded to see the President. He was refused.

*　　*　　*

'No, Jack, the answer is negative. I *can't* take a risk like that.'

They were standing close together in the control room on the upper deck, Farrell, his Executive Officer, plus Balletto, Radek, Orson and Morag. She looked tiny next to them all and now that the sparkle had gone from her eyes, incredibly old. The group's exhilaration was fading fast with this clash of wills.

'There's a man's life at stake, Farrell.'

'And I'm not going to take chances with the lives of the hundred and forty men in this submarine to save one life.'

'How can you say that after what he just did?'

'I'm sorry Jack, that's the way it is.'

'Tell me, Captain, the *Hammerhead*'s much bigger and faster than their sub, right? *If* we tried, would we beat them there?'

'Hard to say. Our top speed is twenty-nine knots. Their's is probably twenty-one or twenty-two, but they're slightly nearer. Right now they're doing twelve to fifteen knots. If we both went full out it would be a close run thing. I don't think they will. The moment either of us went that fast we'd both be running blind. When a sub makes so much noise itself, the sensors can't pick up anything quieter than the sound of a torpedo being discharged.'

'Would the Chinese have authority to fire at a US submarine?

'How the hell do I know? I'm not planning on finding out. You really think I'm crazy enough to head *straight* towards a hostile sub?'

'Even if they did loose off a torpedo, couldn't you defeat it with decoys?'

'Balletto, if they fired at us, we would have two options. Sure, one is to keep going and rely on our decoys working. They're stuffed full of electronics, cost a million bucks apiece, and, since they've never been used in anger, we've no idea if they actually *work*. If not, nuclear subs don't come with a one year no-quibble warranty. The other option is to turn and slow below cavitation speed to confuse the torpedo's acoustic homing system. What *you* need to understand is that neither of these options is foolproof. This is the ultimate game of Russian roulette. And I tell you, we're not playing it today. Unless you can get authorisation from the Pentagon or the President himself, the answer's no.'

The other officers looked away. Jack turned to Morag at his side. He'd given it his best shot, really done everything he could, *surely* she would see that. Morag's eyes were closed, her arms hung limply by her side. She was crying. Jack glanced across at Radek and Orson for some understanding. They were looking daggers at him. He tried to mouth an apology to Morag. Slowly she opened her eyes. The pleading in them burnt him up. Oh *fuck*, a tale like this would cost him his pension.

'Captain Farrell, I am carrying with me a special general authorisation from the President. It's in a pouch in my bunk.'

'I don't believe you. I need to see it.'

'We don't have *time*. I'll show it to you later. It's *real*, for Chrissakes.'

'Are you on the level, Balletto?'

Jack took a step forward and eyeballed him.

'You calling me a liar, Captain? You wanna call the White House?'

Farrell turned and went to his post.

'Okay, Exec, ahead full.'

'Ahead full, aye.'

'And have decoys readied.'

The USS *Hammerhead* surged smoothly forward. In the control room, the three CIA guys huddled together in silence. When she was sure Farrell wasn't looking, Morag looked across at Jack, thanking him mutely with the moist sparkle in her eyes. Then she went back to *willing* Calum to hold on.

For ten minutes now Balletto had kept a profoundly worried weather eye on the young men with the headsets looking so intently at their screens. He watched them jump as if electrocuted. One of them yelled out,

'*TORPEDO, TORPEDO, TORPEDO . . . Torpedo bearing red four zero.*'

Farrell screamed at the Exec: '*Starboard thirty.*'

'*Starboard thirty, aye.*'

'*Slow to five knots.*'

'*Five knots, aye.*'

'*And prepare to fire decoys.*'

'*Prepare decoys, aye.*'

'*Fire decoys one and two.*'

'*Fire decoys one and two, aye.*'

'*Dive to one hundred and fifty fathoms.*'

'*Dive to one hundred and fifty fathoms, aye.*'

Balletto had gone paler than the rest. For an instant he caught Farrell's eye, but got no sense what the Captain was planning to do next. Farrell walked over and stood behind the guys at the console. The senior one started calling out.

'Torpedo two thousand yards and closing . . . Fifteen hundred yards. Twelve hundred yards. One thousand yards.'

'Fire decoys three and four.'

'Fire decoys three and four, aye.'

Jack Balletto was praying to all the Italian saints his mother had ever taught him for the torpedo to go for one of the decoys.

'Eight hundred yards and closing. *It's not going for the decoys.* Six hundred yards.'

'Shit . . .' Farrell turned frantically back to the Exec. *'Release airstream.'*

'Release airstream, aye.'

Balletto had no time to guess what the hell an airstream was.

'Four hundred yards. Two hundred yards. Prepare for impact.

They clung to whatever came to hand. Jack saw Radek grab hold of Morag.

KERRRRBOOOOOOOOOOOMMMM.

Arms and legs went everywhere as they were thrown all over the place. The ship twisted violently and the lights went out, bodies tumbling onto the floor.

The lights came back on and the ship slowly began to right itself.

Farrell was back on his feet.

'Damage report.'

'Damage report, aye.'

Over the intercom the Exec spoke quickly to several men, then said, 'No damage reported, sir.'

Farrell wiped his forehead with the back of his right hand.

'It must have gone for the airstream.'

The remark lent Balletto enough courage to ask Farrell.

'The old tricks work best. Airstream is just one gi-normous bubble. Seems it still fools torpedoes better than the latest electronics. Now, clear out of my way, Jack. *Exec, at two hundred fathoms what's our cavitation speed go up to?*'

'Sixteen knots, sir.'

'*Okay, dive to two hundred and return to original course, fifteen knots.*'

'Two hundred fathoms and fifteen knots, aye.'

Morag and Radek came over to Jack, the question written all over their faces. Jack shrugged his shoulders. He had *no* idea what Farrell was doing. He left it five more minutes before plucking up courage to venture another enquiry. Farrell replied without taking his eye off the screens.

'They had to take evasive action in case we fired back. It pushed them three miles off course. From the moves they're making, I'd say they're not sure whether they hit us or not. At their current depth and speed of twelve knots they're cavitating like mad, so we have no problem hearing them. They are trying to pick up our trace, and can't go any faster without jamming their own sonar. If they keep looking for us long enough we may still have an outside chance of getting to the pick-up point without them detecting us. If they decide we're hit and go full out there's no way we can overtake them.'

*　　*　　*

The sudden foaming came to their left, then the hissing,

breaking, boiling of angry water. May began ripping at her life-jacket, determined not to be taken alive. Before she could yank it off, the vast prow burst majestically into the night air, like some giant whale.

Somehow Montgomery found the strength to cry out weakly in triumph. On and on, the whole sleek shape came into view, towering above them.

'What the . . . ?' Was it his wound? Was he hallucinating? To his wild, staring eyes, it looked much bigger than before.

25

Wednesday dawned brightly in Geneva, banishing the low cloud that for days had concealed the distant view of Mont Blanc. The Chinese delegation at the Hotel des Bergues had made little use of the deeply padded beds over the weekend. When they came to pay their bills, the room rates would be dwarfed by the cost of their phone calls to Beijing.

Tian Yi had no new suit to put on for the occasion. A little variation in her make-up substituted well, and she contrived to look in great shape. She wanted some fresh air before entering the chamber and told the driver she would prefer to walk, taking the lovely path past the Perle du Lac restaurant and through the lakeside gardens to the WTO building.

The atmosphere was electric and the chamber was thronged. Everyone was there, all but the French ambassador, who unaccountably was missing. Someone had spoken to the Secretariat and prevailed on Signor Fratelli to cut to the chase. It went against the grain for the Director General, who believed that the dignity of his organisation was best preserved by maintaining proper procedures at all times. However, he gave way gracefully and invited Tian Yi to speak first.

'Secretary General, honourable delegates, Ambassadors. On behalf of the Chinese government, I am pleased, indeed particularly pleased, to announce that following our further consideration of the proposals tabled some days ago in relation to intellectual property, we are now in favour of the proposals. The Chinese armed forces have, on more mature reflection, voluntarily agreed to surrender their ownership of Sunrise. The corporation will be privatised in its entirety as soon as possible. We will also announce measures to promote greater transparency in software services procurement by government controlled agencies . . .'

She went on, reading the prepared statement, the serenest look on her face. Christopher Ransome couldn't help smiling. He was looking forward to the evening enormously, and had already made a discreet call to his cook to request something special. He hadn't intended to make the invitation at all, in fact. It just sort of popped out when he passed Minister Tian on the way into the chamber. The immediacy of her acceptance, and the radiance of the smile that accompanied it, had quite gone to his head. As soon as he was sure no-one was looking, he executed the tiniest leap in the air.

* * *

The helicopter came low over the brow, scattering sheep, ruffling the heather. The pilot searched for a while till finding the right place and lowering it gingerly, masterfully, into the narrow street. Net curtains were swept back, so that frowning, curious faces could stare. A few of the more shameless adults stumbled outside. The blades swung on round and round, the massively lubricated bearings taking for ever to come to a halt.

Who was that going into Morag Buchanan's house, dressed

384

in a bright orange jacket, blue jeans and Nike trainers? No, it *couldn't* be. Not *herself*, looking like *that*. If that *was* her, what was she doing dressed like that, and coming back in a *helicopter*? They'd have to get the tweed man to visit her and find out as soon as the helicopter left.

The co-pilot kept watch on the craft. The pilot himself was soon regretting offering to carry the box for her and accepting that invitation for a cup of tea. Inside it smelt decidedly old-fashioned. He was very relieved when, a bare half hour later, she was ready. She took no clothes with her, only a few books, a few old letters and family photographs. They all fitted comfortably in the little flight bag they had given her. The box was a case of Jack Daniels. She left it there with a note for the tweed man to find.

If the population of Sgurr had been surprised to see her arrive like that, they were flabbergasted when she left the same way. The co-pilot helped her step back inside and fasten her seat belt, and in seconds the rotors began whirring again. The people stepped backwards, all wearing severely disapproving scowls. As the helicopter rose, swung on its axis, dipped its nose and picked up speed, Morag glanced back at her house, the burn and the peak of Ben Mhor; but not once at the bemused little assembly.

*   *   *

They slipped him in and out of the White House without anyone noticing. The fuss over his lottery antics was long forgotten and China's excursion to Taiwan had never leaked out. Carla gave him a quick guided tour round the place before ushering him into the Oval Office. The ceremony was performed swiftly and informally, but not without dignity. Then the man in the white jacket came in with a silver tray bearing champagne flutes.

'It's tough luck that you can never reveal why we gave you this medal.'

'That suits me just fine, Mr President. You have my word of honour I'll never mention it to a living soul.'

'Your word of honour's good enough for me. These gentlemen were planning on having you sign something, but in the circumstances, I don't think that will be necessary . . . Calum, I would like to add my personal thanks and appreciation for what you did. We may never know exactly how important it was, but my hunch is the welfare of a whole lot of Taiwanese could be looking different today if you hadn't been there.'

'Thank you very much, sir, I appreciate that. Mr President, about Miss Chang . . .'

'Oh yes, you heard that her parents asked for asylum? We helped her get a message through to them from our submarine and they hi-tailed it round to the nearest carabinieri. I understand we're going to help them settle in San Francisco.'

'I meant Miss Chang herself.'

'I know. That may be difficult for some time to come. She broke some heavy-duty Chinese laws, you know, and they are strenuously demanding her return. We are very anxious to re-establish good relations with the Chinese government. Party Secretary Liao will visit Washington next month. As you will be aware, President Zhang has annointed him as his successor and we must treat him with all possible courtesy. I'm afraid we will have to keep Miss Chang in custody and wait till then before determining her future.'

'I understand. What about Montgomery?'

'*That* we've resolved to our, and I imagine *your*, satisfaction. We thought of indicting him here. Montgomery is no longer in the US military, so it would have to be civil. Frankly we're not sure what to charge him with. And our legal system is notoriously undependable and inconveniently public. That would be unfortunate, as we have agreed with the Chinese that bygones should not only be bygones, but silent bygones. So we looked into it. It turns out that one year ago Montgomery renounced his American citizenship and was awarded Chinese nationality. So we've decided to send the good ol' boy back on home. He'll get a place there, like he always wanted. Should suit him fine, provided he likes Chinese food and doesn't enjoy travelling or indeed leaving home at all. He *will* have the consolation of having Miss Osborne with him. By the way, Calum, the CIA would like me to ask you if you would be willing to make yourself available for special assignments in future, *if* the need should arise.'

'I hate to disappoint you, sir. I think that was enough excitement for one lifetime. I plan to get my stimulation from painting from now on.'

'Well, I'm sure sorry to hear that. If I were in your shoes, I might decide the same. Will you pass two messages to Morag Buchanan from me?'

'It'd be a pleasure, sir.'

'First, tell her I've agreed to her plea not to have Jack Balletto dismissed from the CIA. He was lucky, because the navy are still pretty mad at him. Second, on election day, if she feels like turning the Republican candidate into a toad, that'd be dandy.'

*　　*　　*

It took some time to get the house sorted out. It was the view that had grabbed Calum, and indeed it was outstanding, the sparkling ocean perfectly framed by gnarled old pine trees. The house itself was a bit of mishmash of Japanese and Californian styles, and he restyled it so comprehensively it would have been easier to knock it down and start again. The cost was exorbitant, but the builders worked superfast, and now, with the perfume of new woods and the soft fall sunshine caressing the senses, it all seemed worthwhile. He could think of nowhere better to grow old.

Morag couldn't get over it. The room Calum built for her was entirely new. All the architect's attempts to make her express views on materials and fabrics failed. She smiled beatifically at him and shook her head, so Calum gave them a free hand. It was the right call. Free of client meddling, they came up with a style and a decor that worked superbly. The only thing Calum insisted on was a concealed cabinet, to be filled with every conceivable vintage of Bowmore whisky. He kept Morag away from it during the construction so it would all be more of a surprise. He got his reward when he took her through to inspect the finished product and saw for himself the tears in her eyes and the hands clasped to her mouth in astonished delight.

Her first night in it was less successful, however, when she found the luxurious bed just too soft. So the builders knocked up a little wooden cot like her one in Sgurr nan Creag, and in *that* she slept blissfully. During the day she would sit for hours on her little verandah, looking out over the gardens and the ocean, an enchanted smile never far from her lips.

As the visit of Liao neared, Calum was one big bundle of nerves, all too readily convinced that some dread wrinkle in the two countries' relations would despatch her back home and slam the door for ever on his dreams and prayers. Daily, he scoured the papers for China coverage, in feverish dread of reading of an ill-considered outburst or condemnation from some American politician or businessman. None appeared. Liao came and went on a magic carpet of smiling goodwill, and the press photos of the leaders' handshakes went straight in Calum's scrapbook.

The day after Liao flew back, Calum heard from Jack Balletto, who rang to hint obliquely that it was time for a small party, *provided* he was invited in person. He would bring a present with him, a veritable fistful of green cards for three Changs and one Buchanan. When, two days later, the car swung up the drive, bringing her home to him, Calum thought he would die of happiness.

* * *

The phone call from Marianna came early one idyllic morning, while the three of them were breakfasting out on the terrace. Calum answered it on the cordless phone. As soon as he realised who it was, he got up and walked off deeper into the garden.

'Is that you, Cal? Hi, it's *me*. Long time, no talk. How *are* you?'

'Oh, pretty good.'

'How long you been back?

'Two or three months.'

'Why didn't you call? I only heard yesterday. My lawyer, Larry Abraham, found out, completely by chance.'

'I've been busy. Haven't had much time to contact many old friends.'

'Well, I hope I'm more than an *old friend*. I hear you have a great new place in the hills above Santa Barbara.'

'A modest wooden shack.'

'Not what I heard. So what will you do with yourself now you're back?'

'Not broking, anyway.'

'I wondered if you'd have another try at painting. You're *so* talented at it. I always thought you could make it real big as an artist if you got the chance. Particularly now that you have the financial bases covered.'

'We'll see. How's Brett?'

'Tell the truth, Cal, I don't know, and I'm not sure I care. We didn't go through with the marriage thing. We may split up. In fact, we kinda have already. I've moved out.'

'Why?'

'It's sordid, Cal, really sordid. He has this thing to prove, you know, like at his age he's still attractive to all the women in the world. Well, I found out and I can tell you, he messed with the wrong chick.'

'You walked out on him?'

'Yeah, sort of. Now he's moved the goddam bimbo in . . . Anyway, I'd tired of him, outgrown him, if you know what I mean. Brett can appear very attractive on the surface, all that impressive razzle-dazzle. Deep down he's real shallow.'

'So, what happens to you?'

'Remember Laura from the telephone company? I've been staying with her for a while. Anyway, enough of me. Let's tune in to all *your* news. Where did you *go*? After England, I mean?'

'Asia.'

'I *thought* so. You sound much *calmer*, more together, know what I mean? They say spending time in Asia is good for finding the inner you.'

'It worked for me.'

'Cal, I've really missed you. I can't wait to catch up with you and see over that new home of yours. In fact, one of my reasons for calling is I plan to be your way this evening. Would it be okay if I dropped by? We could go for a walk at the beach and maybe catch dinner together. How does that sound?'

'Today's not ideal, Marianna. I'm still busy getting the house in order. Maybe another time, or if I'm down in LA.'

'Oh, don't be so *unspontaneous*.'

'I'll give you a call in a few days' time. How about that?'

'Nothing doing. I don't wanna let another day pass by without meeting . . .'

'Marianna, this is *not* a good idea. I need some more time before I see you.'

'I'll be there about seven. I found out your address.'

'There's something you should know . . .'

'If it's another woman, don't worry about it. I had my fling, so I won't blame you for yours. If she outstays her welcome, we'll just have to blow her out of the water, won't we?'

'Marianna, you don't understand . . .'

'Save it for later. Bye.'

He switched off the phone and walked back over. May's voice was bright, but there was a flicker of concern in her eyes when she asked.

'It was *her*, wasn't it? So . . . ? How did you feel?'

'I always knew that until we talked or met, I couldn't be *sure* how I would really feel. I thought that at a minimum I would want to be friends, if only for old times' sake. Now I find I feel *nothing*. I don't ever want to hear from her or see her again.'

'You don't *have* to, if you don't want to.'

'Not quite. She's coming here today.'

'*Today?* When?'

'Seven o'clock. I tried to put her off, but she wouldn't take no for an answer. She got the address somehow. I can't bear to see her. Why don't we all hide or go out?'

'Wouldn't she just come back another time? Don't be too hard on her, Calum. She's happily married, isn't she? As long as you aren't in love with her any more, what's the harm in being sociable?'

'Things have changed. They didn't get married, after all. She's moved out of Brett's house. I think she's on the hunt for alternative accommodation . . . like *here*.'

May's eyes opened wide in alarm.

'That's different. Calum, are you absolutely *sure* how you feel about this? If you need some time to sort yourself out, I'll understand. I could travel around for a while, give you time to think things through.'

Morag said nothing, but watched Calum very closely.

'No, May, I don't want you, or Morag for that matter, going *anywhere*. I'll have to think of a way to convince her it's over.'

'Surely if you say there's a new woman in your life she'll . . .'

'You don't know Marianna. She'll take that as a challenge.'

'Why not simply say "no", then?'

'Marianna's odd about the English language. There are some expressions like "thank you" that she understands but never uses, and others like "no" that she uses all the time, but can't understand.'

'Look, Calum, if it's only your money she's after, why not give her it and be done with it? As long as we have a little to live on, I don't care. I can get a job.'

'NO! . . .'

Calum and May were both startled with the ferocity with which Morag uttered the word. It was the first time she had made any comment concerning Marianna.

'. . . Over my dead body. That woman does not deserve *one* penny. I will be happy to say so to her face and tell her to leave you in peace.'

Calum smiled sympathetically.

'Thanks, Morag, but it would be water off a duck's back. Once she gets an idea in her head, it takes gelignite to dislodge it.'

Morag was unabashed. She had decided the time had come to make a stand. This Marianna might find that two could play at being difficult. Morag turned to May.

'Child, I've never said a word about it, but those were some *dreadful* tricks you played on my poor grandnephew . . .'

May hung her head. She hated the thought that Morag might disapprove of her.

'. . . However, I will be willing to forgive you on *one* condition.'

'What's that, Morag?'

'That you use some of that skulduggery of yours to persuade Marianna. Normally I wouldn't approve of deception. However this warrants an exception. In fact, if I can be of any help, I'll happily join in. So, get your thinking cap on. And you, lad . . .' Morag turned to Calum, '. . . will do *whatever* May instructs.'

Calum and May nodded like obedient schoolchildren. Seconds later a sparkle was already appearing in May's eyes.

* * *

'Oh, hello. Is this the Buchanan residence?'

'Yes. Welcome to the Temple of Beauty.'

May bowed deeply and ushered Marianna into the hallway where Morag stood. Both May and Morag were wearing flowing white robes hurriedly but skilfully fashioned from bed sheets.

'Excuse me, I don't understand, are you Mr Buchanan's domestic staff?'

'We are his slaves, his servants. This is Sister Andromeda. I am Sister Clytemnestra.'

'Hi, I'm Marianna. Can I have a word with Calum? Where *is* he?'

'He is worshipping at the Altar of Munificence. He asks you to wait until his prayers are over. Please, come and take a seat out on the terrace.'

She followed them out. May could see why men fell for her. What an amazing figure! It was clear she had dressed strategically for the encounter, with her highly toned honey-coloured legs and fine bosoms on unstinting display.

'Wow, this is *some* view. Forgive me, I'm being kinda slow here. I haven't quite figured out who you two are, and where you fit in. Did you run across Calum on his Asian travels, is that it?'

'We are part of his Sisterhood.'

'*His* Sisterhood? How many of you are there?'

'Twenty-five. The number is growing. We have initiation ceremonies almost every week now.'

'And what is it *exactly* that the Sisterhood does? I mean, do you have a God or something?'

'Calum is our deity.'

'You *are* joking, aren't you? Are you actresses he hired to play a joke on me? Surely he didn't think I'd fall for this. Tell him to quit being a jerk and come out here right away.'

May and Morag looked quizzically at each other, their faces a picture of total mystification. Marianna began to lose confidence that this *was* a joke, and she didn't care for the way the old hag was leaning forward, staring at her long blonde hair.

'Hey, what's going on? Why're you looking at my hair like that?'

'It's *so* beautiful. Such a pity it has to come off.'

'What the hell d'you mean, come *off*?'

May took over again.

'Calum told us you might join the Sisterhood. We will have the next initiation ceremony tomorrow. We must purify you by cutting your hair off and bathing you in asses' milk . . . You are allowed to grow it back later, as we have done.'

'This *definitely* isn't a joke, right? You *are* for real?'

'Of course. Initiation is the most sacred, the most holy rite in the world. The timing for yours is *perfect*. The day after tomorrow we are going to Beverly Hills to beg for alms. It will be wonderful if you can join us. I'm sure you have many generous friends whose homes we can call at.'

Marianna jumped to her feet.

'I wanna word with Calum right *now*.'

'You cannot interrupt his worship unless you are clad properly. Come, shed those worldly garments and put on the white robes of the Sisterhood. We will help you.'

'You keep your hands off me. Say, if this is all true, how come Calum didn't mention it on the phone?'

'He said he tried to, but you would not listen.'

Marianna recalled Calum *did* sound like he was trying to tell her something. No matter, she'd soon sort this out with him, have him back where she wanted. She couldn't let this religious garbage deflect her, not with the way things had gone with Brett. There were no obvious candidates around right now, and if she didn't act fast, the word would spread that she was getting past her sell-by date. She *needed* Calum like never before. Without another word, she raced off into the house, yelling 'CA-LUM' repeatedly at the top of her shrill voice. Morag and May let her go and stayed where they were on the terrace, making sure their chuckles didn't carry too far.

She found him in the fourth room she checked. Until earlier that afternoon it had been his studio. The paints, brushes and canvases had been well hidden. A trestle table with a red cloth on top formed the altar, complete with two of the biggest white candles Santa Barbara could offer. The air was thick with incense. His robes were of electric blue.

He was kneeling, with hands outstretched, incanting in the unfamiliar tones of some exotic foreign tongue.

'Calum?'

He appeared not to hear her.

'Hari Krishna, Hari Krishna.'

'Calum, sorry to interrupt your worship . . .'

'Hari Rama, Hari Rama.'

'Calum, Ca-*lum.*'

'Alleluia, Alleluia.'

He cursed himself for not remembering to think up a proper series of chants. Luckily at that moment Marianna crept up behind him and tapped him on the shoulder. He started, as if woken from a trance.

'Sister Harridana!'

'No, Calum, it's *me* . . . Marianna.'

'I know. I chose Harridana as your name for the Sisterhood. Don't you like it?'

'It's . . . very nice, but Calum, what *is* all this stuff? Why don't you and I slip out of the house away from your . . . Sisters, and go have a quiet talk?'

'I have made a vow never to leave the Temple of Beauty. You must come and join me here. You will be more fulfilled than you can imagine, spending your days close to my sacred presence, worshipping and serving me. Oh, Marianna, you cannot know how happy I am. I've found the inner me. For so many years, I was confused and unhappy trying to be a broker. Why didn't I think before of becoming a deity?'

'Calum, I'm absolutely sure if we spend some time together we can soon get things back to normal.'

'*Normal?* What a very dull idea. I never want to return to an earthly plane. Now, Sister Harridana, why not divest yourself of the heavy burden of those clothes and worship me with your body.'

'What? You are *sick*, do you know that? Wild horses wouldn't make me join your perverted Sisterhood. I came here to try a new start with you. I can see that's impossible. You don't need a wife, you need help, *badly*. I *pity* you.'

'You're *sure* you won't join us?'

'I don't *ever* want to hear from you again.'

'Too bad, Marianna. Have a good life, then. Is it all right if I stay kneeling while you see yourself out? I have to finish my worship.'

She hesitated for a moment, then without another word, turned on her heels and marched fiercely out of the room. On the long walk to the front door his strange foreign chanting rung on and on in her ears.

'Hara Kiri, Hara Kiri.'

He was panicking now. He *had* to keep the chants going in case she came back.

'Pee Knut Bah Tah, Pee Knut Bah Tah.'

She skidded to a halt right by the door. Hang on, that last chant almost sounded like . . . Could that little creep be . . . ? She swung around. The two strange sisters had magically reappeared behind her and now stood blocking the way back, arms folded, the Oriental one looking kind of formidable.

Marianna listened out again for the distant voice. It was back on Alleluias. No, it must have been her imagination. With a last defiant snarl at the two women, she stomped out, slamming the door mightily behind her.

Morag and May went and stood by the broad wooden door, listening carefully. The moment they heard the car screech angrily away down the drive, they swivelled slowly round, put their arms gently around each other, and squeezed very tight.

POCKET
BOOKS

BLACK CABS

JOHN McLAREN

Three London cabbies take on the might of
international investment and banking companies as
they attempt to make a killing on the stock market.
Using information that they overhear from indiscreet
clients they have already amassed a tidy sum, but
this could be the big one. . .

Unfortunately, it seems that things are getting out of
hand when a top financial executive is found
murdered in the back of a black cab.

Against their will the cabbies are drawn into
revealing the cover-up which is being perpetrated at
the very top of the banking world.

ISBN 0 7434 4946 0

PRICE £6.99

**POCKET
BOOKS**

PRESS SEND

JOHN McLAREN

Hilton Kask is a whizz-kid systems inventor on the
brink of a breakthrough with a highly sophisticated
Artificial Intelligence package. The great American
dream is finally within his grasp. Then the
unthinkable happens . . .

A team of venture capitalists unite to blow the dream
out of the water. Then the unthinkable happens . . .
Again.

Hilton dies. *Or does he?*

For his enemies, Hilton has some ambitious plans.
And revenge has never been sweeter than when it
reaches from beyond the grave.

ISBN 0 7434 1493 4

PRICE £6.99

**POCKET
BOOKS**

RUNNING RINGS

JOHN McLAREN

The Hills have hit hard times. Their latest drugs
operation has been beached, and the restaurants and
clubs the ring runs as fronts are haemorrhaging cash.
As head of the villainous dynasty, it's down to
Ronnie to turn things around.

Unlike her brothers, Ronnie's daughter Primrose
wants nothing to do with organised crime, but her
management-consultant boyfriend, Rupert, soon
develops other ideas.

Together they run rings round the police, but when
Rupert plays with fire in his love life, too, he reckons
without a woman's fury and a villain's very personal
style of justice.

ISBN 0 7434 1524 8

PRICE £6.99

**POCKET
BOOKS**

This book and other **Pocket** titles are available from your book shop or can be ordered direct from the publisher.

☐ 0 7434 4946 0 **Black Cabs**   £6.99

☐ 0 7434 1493 4 **Press Send**   £6.99

☐ 0 7434 1524 8 **Running Rings**   £6.99

☐ 0 7434 1494 2 **7th Sense**   £6.99

Please send cheque or postal order for the value of the book, free postage and packing within the UK; OVERSEAS including Republic of Ireland £1 per book.

OR: Please debit this amount from my:

VISA/ACCESS/MASTERCARD ....

CARD NO..

EXPIRY DATE..

AMOUNT £ ....

NAME..

ADDRESS...

....

SIGNATURE...

www.simonsays.co.uk

Send orders to: SIMON & SCHUSTER CASH SALES
PO Box 29, Douglas, Isle of Man, IM99 1BQ
Tel: 01624 83600, Fax 01624 670923
www.bookpost.co.uk
Please allow 14 days for delivery.
Prices and availability subject to change without notice.